S L O W
FUNERAL

Tor books by Rebecca Ore

Alien Bootlegger and Other Stories
Being Alien
Becoming Alien
Human to Human
The Illegal Rebirth of Billy the Kid
Slow Funeral

S L O W
FUNERAL

REBECCA ORE

A TOM DOHERTY ASSOCIATES BOOK
NEW YORK

SLOW FUNERAL

Copyright © 1994 by Rebecca Ore

This book is printed on acid-free paper.

A Tor Book
Published by Tom Doherty Associates, Inc.
175 Fifth Avenue
New York, N.Y. 10010

Tor ® is a registered trademark of Tom Doherty Associates, Inc.

Library of Congress Cataloging-in-Publication Data

Ore, Rebecca.
    Slow funeral / Rebecca Ore.
        p.   cm.
    "A Tom Doherty Associates book."
    ISBN 0-312-85201-0
    1. Witchcraft—Virginia—Fiction. 2. Women—Virginia
—Fiction. I. Title.
PS3565.R385S57   1994
813'.54—dc20   94-2976
                                                             CIP

First edition: July 1994

Printed in the United States of America

0 9 8 7 6 5 4 3 2 1

I'd like to thank Jim Beard and Laura Chiudioni, Theresa Croft, R. D. Howell, Margaret Prunty, William Sowers, and Ed Stone for information and signs. I'm especially grateful to my editor, Claire Eddy, for suggesting Bracken County had a novel in it.

Also, I'd like to thank the woman on Stuart's Main Street who said, "How can you get a god to work for you unless you can threaten to go to another god?"

I'm dedicating this book to the memory of my paternal grandmother—
NANNIE SUE ORE BROWN

S L O W
FUNERAL

1

RECALLED FROM BERKELEY

That morning, if Maude Fuller had been a horse, people would have said witches had been riding her, leaving her hair in brown knots, her body sweaty, her long nose puffed, her eyelids thick around her eyes. But, no, sex and a technical man left her that way. Ultimately, though, she would figure she had been witch-ridden.

Maude, who hated witches, lived in a Berkeley witch house where she was the only real witch. The morning after she met the man at the bar, Maude woke up in the house with a call in her brain. Her Bracken County kin wanted to nag her home. She looked to see if her new lover, the engineer who was curious about magic, lay beside her. Nope, just a sweat blotch on the linen.

Last night, Doug (wasn't that his name?) announced to the bar in general, "In the forties, one of the atomic scientists was a disciple of Crowley's. That's what a real witch would be like, a real twentieth-century god, not some poor hippie." He'd been blond, good broad mouth, snub-nosed, in his thirties. A few acne scars gave him character, but also hinted to Maude an adolescence spent with computer kits and shortwave radios, not girls. He looked like he ran and lifted weights, not excessively, just enough to broaden the shoulders and keep his hips trim.

Maude said, "You're sort of right, but you don't quite understand it."

Doug was a man who got hard-ons from intellectually stimulating conversations with women.

Perhaps the argument's energies attracted her kin's attention. *Don't want to go home.* Maude pulled on a robe. She'd never gotten used to Berkeley's casual nudity, as much as she slept with—fucked—strange men. From the basement room on cold concrete, Maude, smelling of her latest lover, went upstairs to the bathroom.

The bathroom door was open. Susan, the blonde wannabe witch from Ukiah, sat on the floor with one of Maude's Ferragamo shoes. Her pupils were so dilated she seemed black-eyed. LSD. The toilet gurgled as if trying to digest something large. "I'm debating the fate of your Ferragamos," Susan said. Maude looked in the toilet and saw her left shoe. Susan cuddled the other shoe in her arms.

Dumb cunt acidhead. That engineer had more idea what a real witch would be like, Maude thought as she pulled her left Ferragamo out of the toilet. She shook out the water and wondered if she should call on her own powers to dry it. The call in her brain intensified enough for her to recognize her grandmother. No, not even just a little magic.

In the past, on the fringe between Atlanta and deep magic, a truck smashed her parents.

"Ferragamos are amazing symbols," Susan said, handing Maude her other shoe. "Can you dry it with my hair-dryer?"

"I wish you'd asked me before you tried to drown one of my shoes and worship the other. Where did Douglas go?"

"Douglas?"

"Douglas, the guy I came in with last night." The engineer wanted desperately to have weird sixties weekends. He must have had long hair then, Maude thought.

"He had to go to work," the girl said. "You know, with the shoes we can bring in money."

If they were both dry and polished, if I had on a Leslie Fay on top of them, or a charcoal suit with a white silk blouse, if I told them I went to Barnard and faked the rest of the resumé. Maude felt her left foot squish in the wet shoe. "By putting one in the toilet?"

"My mother has them. My mother is rich. So how did you get them?"

"I inherited the shoes from my mother. My father bought them for her for her forty-fifth birthday. Daddy wanted to prove he could do better by her than her own people. The Ferragamos and a house in Atlanta were all he could do for her." Maude had fled Bracken County in the Ferragamos.

What had her mother meant, leaving her the shoes? To say, *honor your father's people, flee the witches.* Or to say, *here's the best he could do for me.*

Susan said, "Mom's stingy about what she sends me."

Maude shrugged and squished to her car with one wet foot. The fog might have hallucinated the ten-foot-tall agaves in the yard, rosemary and palm trees, a dream desert for a bitter city fog. Maude never got used to Berkeley weather.

She'd fled both her mother's possible messages and drifted, having magic slip through her from time to time, not wanting to concentrate on magic, but never committed to the other world. She came to Berkeley which was logic-shaped enough to fight will-shaping. But Berkeley had an undertone which made it seem more familiar than a purely logical city. Maude knew she hadn't completely rejected magic's temptation. *I'll be good now, but not forever,* she thought, spinning a twist on Saint Augustine's request that God should save him from sin, but not quite yet. Berkeley dabbled in magic.

Semiotic hash, that's what these Berkeley witches make. Fake magic repelled most real magicians. Karmachila, the psuedomagic collective, kept Maude safe from the fate threads spun out and cut by the Norn who lived in the abandoned spinning and weaving store in Bracken on the road to Kobold. The Norn's presence was just an example of the thousands of deals between entities and men, men not always winning, never winning forever. The Norn herself, who spun fate close and personal, came to the wishes of a woman who couldn't admit she'd left her child alone in a dangerous hunting time. The Norn spun death for the man who'd fired the gun, and for the woman who called her up.

People feared their passions in Bracken County. Passions called up old entities furious that their worship had been neglected.

She remembered her mother's burial in the cemetery by the old family house. The living needed to keep watch over the dead, but her mother married one of the powerless locals from tenant farm stock. He'd gone to Virginia Tech and majored in civil engineering. His people took his body back. One car crash, two funerals. *A funeral, I'm being called back for a funeral,* Maude realized. As far as she knew, her grandmother was still alive. Maude had called Grannie Partridge from a pay phone last week. So the witch kin knew she was in Berkeley. Her Grannie didn't follow the witches these days, but made mind patterns in quilting fabric and thread, logical interlockings. Maude wished all those geometric energies could have gone to building machines, computer programming, but her grandmother was born too early.

After she parked the car at Tilman Park, Maude changed into the hiking boots she always kept in the back of the Mini-Cooper and went out into the chaparral.

A hawk circled overhead. It didn't feel like a magical hawk, but rather a biological one waiting for her to flush game for it. One feather was missing, shot away, perhaps, an unlikely touch for a magic hawk.

The sage smelled like sage. Maude sat down under a tree near the top of the ridge and looked down over Berkeley and the bay. She opened her purse and looked at her fake ID, the medical card, the food stamps. No one looked closely at insane people's IDs. The social security number was real—a British guy who'd faked citizenship to work and get food stamps in America showed her how to get one from a dead child.

In Bracken, I'd have had to kill the child for it, Maude

thought. The brush suddenly smelled like end products: chemical tars, burnt ash, soap.

Bracken County was calling.

Maude told Bracken County that it was insane by twentieth-century intellectual standards.

The chemical smell intensified. The fog carried Bay Area traffic fumes and industrial gases. Maude's nose found them over the sharper natural smells which faded as her brain identified the industrial odors: electric ozone, burnt grease and rubber, sulfur.

Olfactory hallucinations are rare, Maude told herself. She picked a sage leaf and crumpled it under her nose. Sage, then mold. Maude sat breathing until her brain tired of all the odors.

I need to do something. Maude looked at her watch and saw 12:00, noon. The sun wasn't overhead, but noon wasn't invented in California. She picked herself up and brushed away the duff on her backside and legs, then walked back through oaks with leaves grown tiny and thick against drought.

When Maude first saw the Bay Area landscape, she thought it was scrub from overgrazing. No, it was scrub by its own nature.

Bracken County oaks had full juicy leaves. Bracken County dandelions grew tender leaves.

In Bracken County, the air smelled of whatever the majority wanted.

That's true of Berkeley, too, Maude thought, here the majority wants car and industrial smells. She broke into the magic pulling at her thoughts by looking at her watch again, time cut to bits logically. 12:20. *Did I really sit thinking so little for twenty minutes?* Minutes lost from a magic instant, Maude walked faster, got in the car, and drove to Alameda County Mental Health Clinic at Berkeley.

The clinic was dismal, a small redbrick building with a flat tar roof. Maude sat twice a week through a group therapy session for stabilized psychotics and got her welfare. It was easy to be declared insane. Maude just told them witches wanted her and suicide seemed more moral than becoming one.

"But I believe in the impersonal universe," Maude said aloud as she got out of the car, only she knew the other one was real, too, a personal universe with no accidents. She wondered some days if she was insane. Perhaps Bracken County magick was just small-town mass paranoia? Magick with a *k*.

Maude suddenly realized her life in Berkeley was grubby, a fool's game, without even insanity's romance. Whether that was part of the current Bracken County call to her or sheer reason, Maude wasn't sure. *I've always been ambivalent, my one true schizophrenic symptom.* She signed in at the clinic and sat on an imitation-leather couch until the social worker, Alice, called her group in. Even though two upholstered couches had spaces to sit, the black guy who suspected Maude faked insanity for welfare sat down in a hard chair. He was one of two blacks in the group. He always wore a suit, overpressed and stiff as though Salvation Army disinfectant or cheap dry cleaning had damaged the wool. He called himself the Reverend Julian Springer.

Maude wondered why he sat in uncomfortable chairs when he didn't have to. The group room had folding metal chairs; his ass would be pained enough in a minute or two.

When everyone who was coming had checked in, the social worker, who was impossibly fat, shepherded them into the group room, with its double doors and recorders whirring on the therapist's desk.

The others moved in tiny jerks and had face muscles sludged with disease and major tranquilizers. Maude tried to flatten her affect, felt even more stupid coming here than ever. *Why is it better to be a fake mad woman than a witch?* Did she ask herself that, she wondered, or did Bracken County?

"We need to go around the room and talk about what happened to us over the weekend," the social worker said, sitting down in a large fake-leather covered chair. Maude doubted the woman could get her hipbones, much less the rest of her butt, on a metal folding chair.

This weekend, the group seemed to have done the usual things people on welfare did: window-shopped, got thrown out of bookstores for excessive browsing, went to cheap movies, watched television, sat in the library watching sane people. Maude hated the banality of the insane. *In Bracken, even the madness . . .*

"I'm using a false ID," she said to them. "I'm not really crazy. I've been faking it."

The social worker controlled her face after seeming startled for a second. Her expression settled back into that of professional concern. She said, "What is your real name?"

"Maude. My social security number is . . ."

"Why are you telling us this now?"

"Don't I get arrested?"

The other black guy, whose ribs showed below his cutoff T-shirt, said, "You bullshitting again?"

"Why do you want to be arrested?" the social worker asked.

Bracken County's got me but I don't want to go back. Maude knew the explanation would sound crazy. She said, "I just wanted attention."

"You phony strumpet, cheating the poor." The Reverend Julian Springer said this, the one who'd always felt she wasn't insane. Maude thought he hated her because of her Southern accent.

The rest of the group, all certifiable, looked at Maude as though they all agreed, all hated her. They also looked at her as though she hogged the trick of escaping insanity, kept for herself knowledge that they craved.

The social worker looked at all of them, then said to the group, "We're all supportive of each other here."

A redheaded woman with greasy hair and the jerky movements of antipsychotic drug brain impairment said, "We always wondered why she wasn't on meds."

"She *is* on meds."

Maude felt more fear than she had when she confessed to faking her ID. "I am on meds." She didn't take them.

"Maude's doing fine," the social worker said, meaning *for someone with chronic paranoid schizophrenia.*

Maude realized everything she said was heard allegorically. She said, "I think I ought to transfer back to Virginia."

Even that meant something more to the social worker, who said, "I guess you don't feel wanted here."

The rest of the group imperceptibly nodded. "She makes a mock of being really insane," the young black guy said.

The social worker said, "Roger, I wonder if you're not being hostile because you can't reach the people who hurt you in Georgia."

"No, I'm hostile because the bitch's not walking like a robot from the drugs."

"We can give you more meds for that."

Maude felt guilty. She sat back and didn't comment on any of the other stories. The social worker finally said to her, "You may have more education than these people, but is it fair to sulk if you're not the center of attention?"

"Sorry."

The Reverend Springer asked, "Is she supposed to have a car?"

The social worker couldn't find an allegorical meaning for that one. "Do you have a car, Mary?" She was probably trying to figure out why this paranoid schizophrenic called herself Maude, what *Maude* meant.

"A fake ID doesn't bother you, but a car does?"

"You didn't tell us you had assets."

"Yeah, I've got a car. It's old."

"Austin Mini-Cooper," Springer said. "She whores in it."

The social worker wrote something down. Maude decided she'd drive back to Virginia that night, stay just outside of Bracken County and call in.

Just as she was leaving, the social worker called, "Maude?"

Maude turned. *So it is your name,* the social worker seemed to be thinking as they both stared at each other a moment. The social worker said, "Faking insanity is a sign of serious illness."

"I could just be crazy with a fake ID so I don't embarrass my family."

"Do you have other assets under your real name or another fake name?"

Yes, Maude thought, but didn't say. *I have powers. I can bespell time itself.* She said, "Can you keep my secret or do you have to report me?"

"You should have told me in private."

"You don't like to see us in private," Maude said.

"Most of the time, you guys just want extra attention, competitive with each other as though I was your mother. Individual attention just tempts you to act out or fake symptoms. The group focuses you on other people's responses."

"So, I'll see you next week," Maude said, faintly imitating the therapist, meaning the exact opposite.

"We can set up an appointment to contact your family. Perhaps they'll be more supportive than you think. Do you still hear voices?"

But will I be as supportive as they want? Maude thought. She said, "Only from real entities," and left.

I need to leave, I need not to leave. Maude knew the social worker would assume her ambivalence was a sign of illness, but Maude doubted a drug could make up her mind. She opened the door to her room in Karmachila, saw a note on top of the dried semen on her bottom sheet. *Doug called, he wants you to call him. Thanks, Susan.* He'd given both his work and home numbers.

Maude wondered if Susan thought she would work sympathetic magic putting the note over Douglas's come. She called Douglas's work number. At least, I know he's single because he gave me his home phone number, she thought as the secretary put her through. But then Maude remembered this was Berkeley.

"Hi, you asked me to call?" she said, putting the statement in question tones and feeling silly for doing so.

"Maude? You sound different."

"Not drunk," Maude said.

He laughed, then asked, "Do you want to meet me for dinner?"

"Sure," she said. Inertia could keep her in Berkeley. She was curious to see how the social worker would react to her confession. Inertia delays decisions in cases of real ambivalence. And Douglas had been eager and grateful.

"Have you been living in that commune long?"

"Karmachila? A year," Maude said, her good opinion of him evaporating. She hated being an exotic to men. A long, cool body like hers, with big eyes close to thyroid-deformed and a high-bridged Anglo nose ready to hook witchwise in old age, should have a vagina immune to chlamydia and yeast infections, should burst with secret passions to match the eyes and belie the small tits. *I don't like screwing when I'm bleeding,* she thought about telling him, but didn't, instead waiting for his next words.

"I could cook you dinner at my place," Doug said, meaning, perhaps, *I really want to get laid again but sober.*

"You don't know much about me," Maude said, meaning, *you don't know I've been declared psychotic.* She realized she listened to him the way the social worker listened to her, allegorically, antagonistically.

"I miss who I used to be, when I spent months on the road, had Beat dreams. You had the guts to stick with it."

"That's what I am," Maude said, "a person who was freeze-dried in 1973."

"The kids are bringing back the sixties," Douglas said.

"Where's your house?" Maude asked.

He gave her an address in the hills. Maude hoped her left Ferragamo would be okay by then.

* * *

Douglas's front door was a puzzle—not a literal one but an ornate bas-relief sculpture in wood and glass that at first looked technical rather than artistic. Maude looked at it and how it almost fought the 1940s brick house with the asymetrical entrance porch roof that swept to the ground on the outside. She rang Douglas's bell and heard something whir. *If he has a camera over the door, it's quite hidden.*

"I'm an engineer, hope you don't mind," Douglas said as he opened the door. The interior visible behind him made Maude wish for a technical education. The walls were real plaster, the doors were solid wood with brass hardware. But everything was slightly skewed to match the angled abstractions and crystal of the front door.

She felt a slight breeze as she crossed the threshold. Douglas said, "It's an air curtain. Keeps the bugs out."

"You're a technical wizard, then," Maude said, wondering if she could get him to follow her back to Bracken County. He could work technology against the magic.

"You don't hate engineers? I thought everyone in Berkeley who wasn't one hated us."

"I'm Southern," she said. "In the mountains, half of us are nostalgic for the future." She could see her father hadn't been this kind of engineer.

"Oh. What brought you to Berkeley?"

"I was fleeing the ones who are nostalgic for owning people." Magic, she added to herself, but she'd never admit that to him. She also wished she hadn't been so quick to screw him. "I hope you didn't get the wrong impression, the way we met. I'll say that I don't usually meet men that way if you'd feel better."

Douglas lowered his head and said, "You want to see my kitchen?"

"Sure."

As he led her, he said, "So, what should I say? You seemed so weird at the bar, claiming you really knew the difference between real magic and hippie wishful thinking.

Now you've come to dinner in a suit and scruffy Ferragamos, your hair in a twist that looks almost like a Klein bottle.''

"I inherited the shoes. And one of my crazier housemates tried to flush the left one down a toilet. I suppose she felt it symbolized decadence."

He laughed. They were in the kitchen, an engineer's dream of microwaves, power stirrers adapted from lab equipment, and ultrasonic cleaners. All the mundane kitchen equipment hung from hooks over the two stoves: pots, woks, forks, spatulas.

A man's kitchen, Maude thought. A woman would have put everything up in the black lacquered cabinets that ran in a U around the room. She opened one—empty.

"It's set up like a true workspace," Douglas said.

"I see." Maude opened another cabinet and saw cans and jars of staples. So he did hide mundane food. "So what do you want for dinner? Shall I cook for you?"

"You're so different tonight."

"I'm not drunk," Maude said. She sounded mean to herself and wondered if he'd take offense. He'd taken the two-days-younger Maude to bed. Perhaps he preferred her? "I'm sorry if you were expecting some New Ager who'd freak at your kitchen, think you were an ecological disaster before you left the house to design vast systems to mechanize away what little magic was left in the world."

"I do wonder about what I'm doing some days."

"So do I. I recycle, I'm on welfare which cuts into the defense budget and ecologically incorrect spending of the middle classes, I . . . Maybe we could trade?"

"And you live in a house that's into magic research. That's what your roommate told me." Douglas went to the glass-fronted refrigerator and took out some large shrimp. The shrimp were uncleaned, with the heads still on. They looked unspeakably expensive and very fresh. Maude's mouth exuded saliva.

"You're not allergic to iodine, are you?"

"Oh, no. I love shrimp."

"Prawns. I thought I'd grill them. I've got some great bread from this little bakery." He began cleaning the prawns.

Maude wondered if they'd been cultured in some high-tech filtered system, if they were freshwater prawns. She'd read about Hawaiian prawn culture. *An engineer's meat, if they are.* "I could make the salad."

"Sure."

She washed her hands and looked through the glass refrigerator doors. "Try the garden," he said. "In back."

He had raised beds with imported soil over Berkeley's black adobe. Maude pulled out radicchio and some red leaf lettuce, then some radishes and parsley. She came back and saw the salad spinner sitting on the counter.

"It's not battery operated?" she asked as she took the greens and salad spinner to the sink. Douglas shook his head and turned the prawns over a gas grill built into one of the stove tops.

Maude whirled the salad dry and found balsamic vinegar for the dressing.

"Oh, on welfare and you know what that is?" Douglas said.

"Remember, I inherited Ferragamos."

"Remittance woman?"

"Are you trying to hurt my feelings?"

"No. Why are you on welfare?"

"Because I'm crazy. I believe witches are trying to recruit me and technological cities keep me safe. I'm half attracted to the witches, only my father, who was a technical man, not a witch, wanted me to keep out of my mother's people's business."

"I hope I don't remind you of your father." He turned off the gas. Maude felt alienated, distanced from him as he slid the steel skewers from the prawns. "Why would Berkeley keep you safe?" he asked after he snipped dill over the prawns. "People hate engineers here."

"People hate what they depend on but can't control."

"I suppose I'm guilty of that. You really believe in witches?"

"That's what I said to get declared crazy."

"So, you're a thief, really. A scam artist."

Maude thought, *he's found a way to explain me away.* "Yes, I suppose I am. I confessed yesterday in group."

"Because of me?"

"Do you think you're that much of a psychological catalyst?" Maude smiled.

"I'm sorry I left before you woke up, but I had to get to work."

"I wish . . . never mind. I'm sorry." She found the virgin olive oil to go with the balsamic vinegar and mixed a dressing in a cruet.

"Couldn't your family help you?" They sat at the table. Maude could sense that he'd optioned the concept that she might be crazy, would buy if she couldn't come up with a better explanation. *Good liberal, he wants to help.*

"They want me to come home." Maude knew if he believed in magic, he'd defend it. People in Berkeley who believed in magic never hated it.

"Why don't you?"

Maude shrugged and ate one of the prawns. It was fabulous. She felt the magic pick at her. Douglas looked concerned.

"Want to come with me for a visit?" He leaned away from her as if she'd been too fast, vulgar. Maude knew she seemed a touch desperate. "Maybe after we get to know each other better."

"You need to get off welfare. You're not crazy."

"You're trained in psychology?"

"It's obvious when someone is mad enough for welfare. You'd make me very uncomfortable if you were that insane."

"Instead of just a little uncomfortable?"

"And if you were insane, you wouldn't be so able to gauge the impact of what you say on me."

"I'm an impact statement, all right."

"Don't *try* to sound nutty."

Maude ate her salad and finished off another prawn. "I'd be embarrassed to go back now with nothing. My father wanted to prove he could fight the powerful people, Bracken's ruling class, and win, make one of them an honest woman. My grandmother, she was active with the powers that be when she was younger, but . . ."

Douglas leaned back from the table and looked at her. "Perhaps we should forget about last night and make this the first date."

Maybe the next time should be the first date. Maude said, "I love your door. An engineer with esthetic sense, I'm impressed."

"I play the guitar, too."

"I used to play mandolin, but the strings bit my fingers." A metaphor, not a Bracken County reality, but Maude visualized strings with tiny mouths biting blood out of her fingertips after she said it. Would Bracken County mandolins make it real if she took up a mandolin again?

Douglas pulled out his guitar and began playing "Saray Allen." Maude felt the ballad shaping and taking a life, but not here in Berkeley protected by microchips.

"Do you know 'Lord Weary's Castle'?" she asked when he finished.

"I know of it," he said. "The professors tried to figure out who wrote the ballads. It's obvious that some of the ballad writers were social critics."

"Bards, after sundry punishments, could be hanged in sixteenth-century Scotland," Maude said. "That's the best reason I could think of for not putting your name on your work. I've seen people whose lives seemed modeled after ballads."

"Maybe the ballads were mimetic?"

"You don't hang mere journalists."

He looked at her as though he might decide that she was crazy. "You're obsessed by where you're from, half of you

redneck, half antebellum aristocrat. I've met other South-
erners who had the same problem."

"I have a hate-love relationship with the place," she
said, "but it's not precisely the South. Nor precisely the
mountains. It's the interzone." *Between magic and reality,* she
thought.

"And because you slept with your lover and someone
saw you leave the motel or his house at five A.M., that made
you the town slut."

Maude said, "No, it wasn't like that."

"A black friend?"

Maude shook her head. He seemed less interested after
she rejected his romantic story about her early sex life. "I
didn't want to get involved in a family quarrel. But now, I've
got to go back for a funeral." *Is this mundane enough?* "Why
are you, an engineer, so interested in magic?"

"I sense the gestalt of the problem, then work out in
terms I can transmit to others what I already know. I
thought perhaps magic used such a sense in an exaggerated
way. I kinda hoped it might be more real than that, but if all
I got was more intuition, I'd be pleased. It's mostly metaphors, your 'powers-that-be,' that sort of thing."

"But what really intrigues you is Aleister Crowley's sex
magic."

"I read up on that because someone like me was involved in it. I certainly can get laid without magic."

Maude didn't reply but began picking up the plates.
After she'd loaded the dishwasher, Douglas asked, "I'm
sorry. Do you do anything physical besides sex?"

Maude wondered if he wanted her to weed his garden,
perhaps. "Right, we need to share other interests besides
magical sex. I like to walk. Hike."

"Backpacking?"

"I just have a sleeping bag and pack. I can't afford the
rest of the equipment." Doug looked down at her Ferragamos. She said, "I didn't inherit a tent."

"You're obviously not happy with the way your life is

going. Maybe you need to get away from Berkeley to be able
to consider what you're going to do next. I'd like to take you
camping next weekend.''

She'd turned out too weird or too reasonably neurotic
for his cock tonight. Maude felt rejected, but considering
how stupid she'd been to want him to come with her back to
Virginia, she was lucky she'd see him again. She nodded.

He kissed her gently, and said, "I'll pick you up at your
house about nine. Can you get up that early?''

"Even welfare people have appointments and alarm
clocks."

"Don't categorize yourself."

She leaned against him at the door, but he didn't kiss
her again. She said, "Language is categories."

"Don't make the map smaller than the territory."

"Maps always are." Maude remembered a map in
Bracken County that a person entered as though it were a
world. That map was a malignant maze, larger than its surface. She could visualize it now, a brown thing that looked
like it could have been drawn with squid ink on a split
sheepskin, framed in a holly and ebony frame, a map of
Bracken County perhaps, nothing quite right, every feature
somewhat familiar. The witches donated it to Kobold
School. The nonwitches hung it so high only the boldest
children got trapped. The witches didn't mind. Witch children could escape.

One summer, when she was back visiting, she heard a
child crying from the map. "It only traps fools who won't
listen to warnings," her grandmother told her.

Maude, at eight, couldn't verbalize why she thought it
was unfair to hang such a map in the grade school.

She came back from her memories to Doug's voice saying, "Okay, we're being rabidly metaphorical. Don't limit
yourself to a diagnostic category."

"I know I'm not schizophrenic. Except maybe my ambivalence. I guess I'd better get going. Thanks for dinner."

Douglas watched by his sculpture door until she got in

the car. He went back in his house when she turned on her headlights.

Maybe I'm wrong and the Bracken County rich fake their magic to keep other people from challenging them. I wish.

2

GAME PLAYED WITH
GREEN STONES

Maude sold plasma on Thursdays. The regular clients at the plasma center tended to be street Maoists, people waiting for New York State to transfer their unemployment benefits, or kids sent over by the big cult house just off campus. This Thursday, Maude walked in and used the toilet. Under a revolutionary message, a cynic had written: IF WE CAN'T GET IT TOGETHER FOR CIGARETTES WITHOUT SELLING PLASMA, HOW CAN WE GET IT TOGETHER FOR A REVOLUTION?

My sentiments precisely, Maude thought. She sometimes wondered if the plasma sales drained vitality from her, but the money lifted her millimeters from the very economic bottom. The money kept her emergency fund intact. It was beer money. Meeting strange men in bars money.

The technician found Maude's file and sat her down in the chair. "Left arm," Maude said. The manager of the plasma center sat in a chair across the room, selling himself his own plasma. Maude had quit wondering if he did this to reassure the donors or if he was weird about needles.

The plasma center's feel was something of a beauty shop, a conspiracy of denial. No poverty, we're all students here, the technician's finger seemed to imply as it moved the counterweight over so the bag would take a pint and no more. The technician watched her finger as though it was a familiar foreign thing that knew what it was doing better than she did.

Maude lay back and closed her eyes. She planned to buy

something to take camping with this money. Her eyes opened briefly when the technician took away the plastic bag filled with plasma and blood cells, then again when the woman returned with her red and white blood corpuscles in sterile saline.

While the chilly fluid dripped back into Maude's arm, she felt as though she'd surrendered to a machine vampire. What had seemed tolerable last week seemed utterly degrading today.

For a couple of dollars more, would I rent my cunt? But then, didn't she rent it for dinner already? Maude felt like a reanimated corpse as she walked on Telegraph Avenue, past panhandlers who claimed to be too medicated to sell their own plasma. *What does Douglas want?* She took a bus down to Mental Health.

The other patients were hostile; the social worker didn't refer at all to her confession on Monday, but rather said, as the session was breaking up, "Mary, I'd like to talk to you."

Maude stopped. The woman was looking at the needle hole in her arm. After the others had left, the social worker said, "You're doing drugs."

"No."

"What's that needle hole in your arm?"

"One of my roommates is trying acupuncture."

"You're lying."

"I'm doing saline. It makes me feel like a corpse, cold saline infusions." Maude hoped her lie was bizarre enough to seem a likely symptom.

On the table behind the social worker's chair, a *Physician's Desk Reference* lay open to the entry on Prolixin, an injectable antipsychotic. The social worker said, "I'd like you to come to Inpatient for an evaluation. We'd like to try a new medication."

"I've met a man and we're going camping this weekend."

The social worker looked like she wanted to call in huge orderlies but simply nodded and said, "Remember how exploitative men can be of someone as sick as you are. Monday, then.''

Prolixin, what a technological alternative to being powerful, the voice from Bracken County said inside her brain. The social worker would call the voice *thought insertion,* a symptom that her illness wasn't being properly controlled.

"A friend says the American Psychiatric Association is redefining schizophrenia," Douglas said Friday at 5:30, as Maude helped him load the car with the two backpacks and a large umbrella tent they'd use if they stayed in a car camping site. "Too many psychiatrists out in the boonies overdiagnose it. He suspects for insurance purposes."

Maude was annoyed that Douglas had talked about her to a friend, but then he was concerned. "One can pass as schiz even in cities."

"Don't you think you ought to stop this? I'd rather you ran some magic scam with your wack housemates than be on welfare. If you deny you're sick, they'll wear you down until you think you really are sick and then you'll really be fucked. You ought to see my friend. You have MediCal."

And tell him about the voice calling me home?

Douglas checked over the equipment, the extra oil, and the bottle of antifreeze. She asked, "Where are we going?"

"I've got maps for the Sierras, for Mount Tamalpais, for Santa Cruz redwood territory. What's your pleasure?"

"Something different. I'd like to see the ocean." *In case I have to leave the Pacific behind soon.*

"We could go to Point Reyes. I don't have maps for that, but it's pretty hard to get lost with the ocean on both sides."

"Point Reyes, then."

"The Sierras are wilder."

"I haven't carried such a large pack before."

Douglas drove through San Francisco so they could pick up some cannoli and fresh basil and then they crossed the Golden Gate Bridge with the sun setting into the Pacific fog. Maude stared at the landscape, the bridge across it.

"To me, it's just another city," Douglas said. "I grew up in Albany, just up from Berkeley. It's always interesting seeing it through the eyes of an Easterner."

"That's kinda why I wanted you to come back with me to Virginia." She felt him stiffen and was sorry for her insistence.

"Would they think you were crazy back home? Do they know?"

"They might, to both questions."

"Were you diagnosed there?"

"No. But I'm scared to go back."

"Maybe you shouldn't go back."

Maude sighed and they were silent for the duration of the sunset. Doug said, "We don't have enough light to hike anywhere. We could stop at an inn, a motel."

"I'd rather not spend your money like that."

He looked at her and smiled. "But I'd have to spend my money to go with you to Virginia?"

"We could drive." *He has a job, fool.*

"What's the nearest airport?"

"Roanoke."

"Tonight, we'll stop at a hotel."

Maude remembered the Eagles' song about California hotels where one could never leave. Magic seemed to bring them to a Victorian hotel surrounded by dark bush and whistling fog. A slice of Bracken County right here, Maude thought as Douglas got out of the car and checked in. Probably as Mr. and Mrs. Douglas. . . .

He came back to the car, followed by a small wiry man who could have been an Aztec. Douglas picked up his pack and the man picked up hers. Maude followed them into the lobby, which was done in holly inlays on a dark wood and red plush. The place seemed ritualistic. Maude saw what was either a Chac Mool or a metate standing on stone legs by the fireplace, its slightly dished top patched where the stone oval had been cracked in half between the legs. Would a woman have a metate that fragile to grind corn on every day?

"Strange place," she said to Douglas.

"I love these little inns up in the hills," he said. "Just right for getaways."

The man walked behind them as silently as if he stalked them. For a moment Maude had forgotten he was there, but when she turned her head to look at Douglas, the man popped up in her peripheral vision. *Maybe I am paranoid*, Maude thought, *or maybe he makes you forget him to seem a more discrete host?*

The room had its own fireplace and a huge double canopied bed. A stained sink with two taps marred the room, no, jolted Maude out of the Victorian seductions of the rest of the room. "The toilet is in the hall," the small man said. He sounded like the owner, not a bellhop. Douglas fished in his trouser pocket, but the man frowned slightly and left.

"It's beautiful, isn't it?" Douglas said. Maude almost asked if he'd brought women here often, but she realized he hadn't seen this particular inn before, much less the room. She nodded. He went on to say, "But the sink is an anachronism."

"Better than a well and wood stove."

"When I was in college, I used to piss in sinks. I outgrew that." He went to the door and looked both ways, another sign that he hadn't been here before. Maude feared how the Aztec would treat her if he knew they weren't married. Douglas spotted the toilet sign and went down the hall.

Maude looked around the room. It seemed to look back. "You're very pretty," Maude said to it, "but what do you do?"

Seductions. The room didn't mind Douglas's engineering. Here wasn't logical. Maude knew there were other magics on the continent, but this place felt like Bracken County.

Bring us the head of an engineer.

Douglas came back and said, "The toilet is an old water closet. The chain is brass and the pull is wood."

"And no steel at all," Maude said. She looked around the room and noticed that the room was plastered, the sink faucets also brass. Magic didn't like iron because what humans did with it cut magic's power.

But then Maude saw that the floor was nailed and she relaxed, even though she knew magic and steel weren't utter enemies. She opened her bags and found her bathrobe and towels and went to the bathroom herself.

The shower was completely tiled with shower heads not just overhead but along the wall, three of them at shoulder, waist, and knee heights. The water control device was contemporary—pull out and turn the pointer to the mix of hot and cold—but the brass shower heads themselves seemed older. *Did the Cretans at Knossos have showers along with their running water?* Maude wondered as she soaped her body with the hotel soap.

She rinsed and turned off the spray, knowing she'd have to leave Berkeley now. The identity she borrowed from the dead Ohio baby was compromised. Maude looked in the mirror, almost afraid she'd see something other than herself looking back at her.

The mirror was fogged. Maude didn't wipe it off but went back to her room.

Douglas's eyes were huge, the pupils dilated as though belladonna worked on them. He said, "The bed has real linen sheets."

Maude felt her cunt grow heavy. Seductions. She told herself that she needed an outsider to come back with her to Bracken County. The soap, the sheets. Rosemary branches as large as Maude's forearm burned in the fireplace.

Douglas rolled a condom over his cock. Good, Maude thought. She then wondered why; the first night he hadn't. Or had he? "Why?" she asked.

"Sorry, but I'm not drunk now."

Oh, yes, you are.

Her cunt pulled his condom off. He rolled off her and stared at the ceiling, breathing very hard.

Maude shuddered and pulled the condom out.

"I'll trust you," he said.

Don't, she almost said as she fell asleep. They both woke up in the dark and screwed again, fiercely. Maude felt her magic stirring.

In the morning, they were almost shy with each other. He turned his back to her as he pulled on a robe and went to shower. When he came back, he said, "If you don't mind, let's just do a day hike and come back here tonight." As they packed rucksacks, Maude sensed that he was almost afraid of her body, glancing at her hips when she wasn't looking. They left the heavy packs and tents behind in the room.

"I really like this hotel," Douglas said on the stairs. "I hope you aren't disappointed that we're not going camping."

Whatever, Maude thought, *we're out beyond America now.* She wondered if the hotel was built directly over the fault, electric effects from rock against rock responsible for the feel of the place. Or was it geomancy, rock with powers of its own?

The Aztec was sweeping when they came down the stairs. He smiled when Douglas said they'd be back that night.

They got in Douglas's car and drove onto Point Reyes's ancient granite. Douglas said, "It's old granite, like the Farallons, that won't erode away like most sedimentary rocks." The road crossed a cow barrier and Maude saw holsteins watching them through the fog.

"Like the Blue Ridge," Maude said. The mountains could almost be this foggy.

They parked the car at Drake's Beach. Maude saw seals swimming parallel to the shore. "After the sun's been up longer, we'll come back and look for jadeite," Douglas said.

They found a trail and began walking. After a while, Maude heard sea mammals hooting and moaning down below. They were at the cliff face. Douglas said, "Sometimes you see sea elephants, when there's no fog."

The cliff could be undercut, Maude thought, a fear at

her spine; the land could move. She moved back and said, "What if we're here when the earthquake comes?"

"What 'the earthquake'? We'll always have earthquakes here. It's your first big one that you Easterners think of as 'the earthquake.' We Californians . . ." He stopped as though he just realized she might think he was being rude or bragging. Or perhaps he was thinking about following her to Virginia. *Me or my vacuum cleaner cunt.*

He backed away from the cliff as though he felt something. Maude wondered if she was sensitive enough to the earth's electricity to pick up tension rising between the two plates. He said, "I just realized the cliff face could be undercut and we haven't had a quake in a while."

Maude said, "That's what I was afraid of."

The land seemed unsteady as they walked through it. Shortly after noon, they were back at the beach. Douglas showed Maude a piece of jadeite, a small green lump that looked as though it had been tumbled in a jewelry drum, but not with the final polishing rouge. She bent over the sea wrack and found her own stones. "What are the red ones?" she asked.

"Jasper."

So she picked them all up—jasper, jadeite, and the occasional black stone. Some of them looked like small animal brains.

"Are you tired?" he asked, meaning, *do you want to go back to the hotel and fuck?*

"Maybe there's a concert somewhere or some musicians who'll be practicing tonight that we could drop in on," Maude said, meaning, *we can't spend all the time in bed.* She tried to brush the sand off her legs—tiny fragments of jadeite and more common silicates.

They headed back to the hotel without discussing further what to do next and passed the Aztec who was working in the front flowers. The sand seemed to have left a jadeite grit trail between the beach and the hotel.

"Jade was a sky stone," Maude said. "The Chinese made it into flat rings."

"This is jadeite and the Mayans liked it," Douglas said. He laid her back on the bed, swept her shirt open, and dropped pebbles on her belly, watching them bounce.

"Do you really believe in magic?" she asked, feeling around her for the stones. *I don't want a stone bruise.*

He said, "I haven't met anyone truly sane and competent who really believed in magic. I wish there was magic, though."

Oh, well. "You'd like to bury me in jadeite?"

"I like to watch them bounce." He dropped another one. "I'd like to make love to you surrounded by stones."

"The reality is they bruise."

He stopped and found all the stones, then began to kiss and undress her. Maude felt like the stones were watching, as the seals had watched them looking for stones.

"The seals," she said.

"What?"

She couldn't talk right then, and forgot about the seals. "What about the seals?" he asked after they'd slept for a moment.

"I wonder why they watched us so intently."

"Probably wondered what we were finding to eat. We probably looked like we were foraging for food."

The stones gleamed on the nightstand. The sky beyond the window was clear with half the moon visible.

Maude wanted to leave the hotel, take Douglas back to his engineering and meticulous kitchen, and go somewhere completely flat, the Midwest, a city like Omaha, with logic and no magic stones, no jadeite, no staurolite stone crosses and Xs.

"So you don't really believe in magic?" she said. "What if I said someone put a sex charm on us?"

"I'd say it was a great metaphor," he said, stretching his body. "But I have been thinking that maybe I could take a few days off and go with you back to Virginia."

Maude sat up on the bed and looked at the stones. One, the size of her first thumb joint, seemed the king stone. She picked it up and said, "Let's think it over in Berkeley. I've got to . . ." What would he think if he knew she had a safety deposit box with $3000 in cash in it? "I'll be driving in the Mini-Cooper."

"You could pick me up at your airport later. I'll just be staying a few days. I could come down for Thanksgiving."

Soap, stones, nakedness, and linen—a trap to catch a man in. "Yes, you could come later after I figure out what's going on."

3

CROSSING THE REAL

Sunday night in the Karmachila house, Maude and Douglas sat around a table with all the magic groupies while Susan threw coins for an I Ching reading. Douglas smiled as the coins gave Maude's journey all solid black lines. Susan looked up the hexagram in the paperback manual and said, "First hexagram, powerful but with a minor reservation."

Doug didn't have to look it up, Maude realized. She wondered what divination the jadeite and jasper pebbles would make for Douglas.

The housemates assumed Maude would be back, would get into farming, would come back with fabulous stories. "A friend of mine lives near there," one of the boys said.

Above the quartz vein that kept his kind out of Bracken County, Maude thought. "Give me his address and I'll look him up." She handed him her address book.

"I don't know if he's there or on Vashon Island up in Washington," the boy said, scribbling.

Doug seemed fascinated by the crystals hung in the windows, the tarot deck by the telephone. Maude asked, "So what are they great metaphors for?"

"Humans need ritual," Douglas said.

"Yeah," Susan said, hugging him. Maude wondered if he would see Susan after he came back to Berkeley. Maybe he won't leave Bracken County.

Douglas stayed the night. The next morning, as Maude went out with him to his car, she saw the older black psychotic, the Reverend Julian Springer, watching her. He looked like a part-time Bracken County preacher in his shabby suit, one of those working-class men called to holiness, fighting the witches with magic almost equally as malignant. Led by possessed ministers, each little church's ten or so parishioners locked themselves into ideosyncratic views of the divine, convinced they, not the church next door, had the true vision.

Maude nodded at him. He looked from her to Douglas and back. Maude felt nervous, as though the man would inform on her. So what? Whoring, he'd said. She kissed Doug good-bye for now, his phone number safely in several places.

The black man's legs worked in tiny jerks as though he were a robot. He walked one step toward them as Douglas got in his car, then away. Maude looked back but the black man had disappeared in a mass of suits commuting to work.

After Douglas pulled away, Maude took the stones they'd gathered and threw them, stared patterns into them, reading her own mind. She was deeply ambivalent. One way, Douglas linked in with the technological insurgents; the other way, he died. But Maude felt relieved that she couldn't see him coming back to California. She swept the stones up and gave them to Susan, not wanting a link between Point Reyes and Bracken County.

As Maude packed the car, she looked for the black man, but couldn't see him. *About now,* Maude realized as she looked at a clock, *they're waiting for me to come to group.* She looked around at the agaves and rosemary plants, and remembered mountain laurel and rhododendrons. *So much for here.* She drove to her safety deposit box in Walnut Creek.

Everything worked so well for her—the sky was sunny, the views from the hills beautiful, the bank clerk who took her back to the safety deposit boxes utterly unsuspicious, no paranoid vibes. The clerk left Maude in a privacy booth. Maude opened the box and saw her money. She counted it, all $3000.

"I won't be needing the box any more," she told the clerk, handing her the key.

Clear skies and a drive over the Sierras. Maude wondered if the high passes could be snow-blocked this early in October. No, just cold.

The Mini-Cooper was crammed. Maude sat down beside her backpack and looked east for a second, then turned the key in the ignition. *We're off to see the wizard. . . .*

Going back into the old world. The superhighway ran up the Sierras by Lake Tahoe, through the forest into scrub. A hundred and fifty years earlier, the crossing killed people. Only freak weather could kill now.

The Sierras dropped off rapidly to the east, a scarp face from archaic earthquakes off the Richter scale. The air became drier. Nevada and Utah, two human reactions to the vacant lands—grab pleasure or worship an afterlife that promised a franchise in divinity and one's own planet. At each Nevada gas station, Maude saw a slot machine and a woman who could have been a whore. She stopped at Elko for the night. The slot machines churned in broken randomness, the house odds set. Maude wandered around the hotel's casino for a while, looking at the big men with holstered guns. She put a quarter in a slot machine and five more quarters dribbled out. Enough, she said to herself, and she went to bed.

The next day, Maude was in Nebraska, a country like an old chronic simple schizophrenic, all flattened affect, corn along I-80 through the entire state. Maude drove into the night rather than stop there. The heartland bothered her worse than Berkeley's hectic social and botanical landscape, exotics transplanted out of their homelands to make bold stands. Midwesterners either rebelled or acquiesced under that huge blank sky whose only clouds threatened tornados.

Maude stopped in Iowa near Davenport. The car needed oil. As she arranged with the gas station to change the oil and check the fluids, she felt dislocated, compelled to get back in the car and drive forever. *Road grip.*

After Maude walked down to the river and up by Sears,

the road grip eased. Back at the gas station, she watched the mechanic pull the Mini-Cooper out of the service bay. He looked at her oddly as he handed her the keys. Going home seemed stupid now, crazy. "Where's a good motel?" she asked him.

"Howard Johnson, up near the highway. You going camping?"

"No, home."

"We used to get lots more road people through here," he said. "It's the main point to cross west."

Maude remembered Douglas's comments about the kids reviving the sixties. No, only the kids of the communards, and she'd seen one short-haired child at a hippie wedding look at the older people as though he planned to execute his parents and all their friends when he became president. She paid the gas station attendant and said, "Well, I'm not searching for America, myself." She looked down at her jeans with Susan's rainbow embroidery and sighed. *Forgot what I was wearing.* She paid the man out of the fifty she kept in the visible part of her wallet.

By now, Social Services would have called her at Karmachila. *Gone? Oh, hope she lands in a jurisdiction that won't just give her carfare and send her on to the next county.* Some crazies got organized about their camping equipment even if otherwise completely disorganized. They had tents and sleeping bags and little cookstoves, and camped in people's yards. Maude noticed that the insane had no special word for the sane, not like drug users and criminals and straights. She thought this lacking word was the pitiful thing about the insane—that they accepted the others as normal, themselves as deviant.

Maude remembered how the younger black guy told the group how Social Services in various jurisdictions gave him bus fare to leave. He'd seen Yosemite before the rangers sent him out for illegal camping, had seen Washington before the cops drove him into Virginia, had actually spent time in Phoenix House in New York taking job training in sales clerking before he left there on his own. "That was my most difficult move," he'd told the group. "But I really wanted to come back to Berkeley. I had family here."

So, too, Maude thought, I must go home. She felt like a drifter even in the motel, watching the pay movie so she wouldn't feel too broke, wouldn't seem so much like another fool on the road a decade too late. California seemed as remote as Cockaigne, a particularly vivid dream.

In the morning, Maude walked down to the water again and saw the sun rise over the Mississippi. She loaded herself back in the car and drove to the bridge. The West was behind her. She'd meant to shower and wash her hair in Davenport, but forgot. Her eyes were bloodshot. *Maybe I am crazy.*

Her car seemed stronger, as though the Davenport mechanic had done more than change the oil. Home to a universe that works on personal deals—so much like a paranoid's fantasy. Maude covered her eyes with dark glasses.

Then there was Zanesville, Ohio, in rolling country, not like the industrial cities to the north. Maude thought the southern Ohio farmland looked like an innocent version of southside Virginia. She imagined a Quaker family on the Underground Railroad feeding a mulatto woman running from the father who owned her. For the first time since leaving Berkeley, Maude felt sane, focused. *I'm going to help my grandmother. We're going to fight the magic. Doug will see magic is cruel.*

She passed through West Virginia with its place names like War, Route 460 going east, the East River Tunnel. Maude stopped in Blacksburg and drove by the logic-binding Virginia Tech campus. Anyone with a Virginia driver's license could access Tech's discourse universe. Maude went to the visitor's office and got a parking permit. Blacksburg had always been reason's outpost, the country child's exit to the outer world. Maude had $2750 left. She went to a bank on Main Street and opened an account under her real name, with her real social security number. *Here I am.* She kept $250 for the drive home, her new driver's license under her true name, and a couple of days to reconnoiter.

Maude sat in a bar, listening to Bob Dylan. *And what will I do now?* Her grandmother needed her. Her grandmother's rich kin wanted her. Bob Dylan converted to Christianity. Maude could convert to magic, let the entities speak though her, perhaps stay alive centuries on other people's energies. Trap children in maps.

Run, Maude thought. *Do no evil.* Maude saw herself ten years from now, rolling across the country in buses paid for by various social services, her pack and tent tattered, the Ferragamos moldy leather shreds to prove she'd had rich kin once. *Is this a real fear or is this Bracken County's vision of me?* She found a pay phone and called her grandmother.

"Hello?" her grandmother, Partridge, said. She sounded more tentative than ever. Perhaps Partridge should have left Bracken County when her daughter died. Perhaps she should have just relaxed and become the witch she was supposed to be.

"Grandmother, it's Maude. Would it be okay if I came home?"

Her grandmother didn't speak for a while. Maude felt rejected, crazy to cross the country before she knew whether she was welcome or not.

"Aunt Lula's helping. I don't know if I need you, too, or not. Maybe you ought to stay out of it."

Lula was a homeless woman who tended her sick relatives. *So I'm reduced to that,* Maude thought. "If there's room."

"Maude, Aunt Betty was asking about you just last week. You still in school?"

"No, Grandma, I was in Berkeley but I wasn't in school."

"Where are you now?"

"Blacksburg."

"Oh, you are just about home. Your momma went to

school there, knew a woman majored in mining engineering. We couldn't talk your momma into Sweet Briar.''

"Grandma, do you need me to help?''

"Lula's doing fine. My mouth hurts, though. Can't wear my teeth, can't eat.''

Shit. "I'll be down in a couple hours.''

"Lula's sleeping in the bed with me, so you can have the guest bedroom.''

"And I bet you're . . .'' Maude couldn't finish with *using pee rags not toilet paper.* Old women went back to their childhoods, using outhouse customs and saving jars just to look at.

"You did finish college. Betty can get you a teaching job.''

"I'll see you in a bit,'' Maude said. She hung up the phone and went back to her car. *Well, all the way, little Cooper.*

Mud Pike to Route 8. *Magic begins here, with churches full of people admiring God for the earthquakes he uses to punish the Californicators.*

Maude saw a computer consulting firm just outside Christiansburg. The landscape seemed ruptured between the building and the cow pasture behind it.

A slice of alien geology, a microplate, the whole Blue Ridge province came from elsewhere. And, below the Blue Ridge, the Bracken County allochthon, an even smaller microplate, started moving 600 million years ago. About 500 million to 400 million years ago, it slithered over the Sauratown Mountains. Trapped in place by normal faults in a 300-million-year-old downdrop, the allochthon screamed in iron-alumina-silicate crystals, a billion stone X's, cursing as it ground against the Blue Ridge, trapped in place, its reverse overriding done. The Blue Ridge formed quartz crystals on its parallel edge, but the staurolite crystals were opaque.

Maude remembered how impressed she'd been when Aunt Betty told her Bracken County wasn't rooted in America, but instead floated, stalled, between an ocean that didn't happen and very ancient earthquakes. *What is human life to a thing embedded in deep time?*

Old, senile rock. Maude found out in Berkeley's geology library that what Betty told her was essentially true, not that geologists attributed personality and intentions to even the strangest rocks. Maude knew better, but wished her version of the allochthon's history had been a fable.

Bracken County developed over the allochthon, fought its battle to stay still and different, both the county and the squeezed rock. The ocean formed anyway from a different spreading rift.

But the old rock holds its people and its one endemic fish, Maude thought as she looked down from the parkway. *What happens down there happens because something or someone intended it to happen.* She remembered how snappish her parents got with each other when they drove up for family vacations. Each time, Bracken County separated them, her mother to her witch kin, her father to his Christian people.

Maude had preferred her mother's people until she heard the child crying from the map.

Driving back to Atlanta after those summer visits, neither parent looked at the other until they'd passed Greensboro. Then her mother would always say, "I always forget what it's like," and her father would laugh and say something about superstitions on both sides being excuses for Marxist class war.

I'm doomed to it. Maude got in the car and drove. Small logic-bound spaces pocked the landscape—machine design shops, small factories—then Maude passed Annie's Laundrette and Family Nautilus, a juxtaposition bred of poverty and a craving for pleasures advertised in magazines. A collage economy, nothing quite able to pay the rent on its own. Strange semiotic combinations—grocery and sporting good store, deli and tax service. *I'm almost back.*

Then, at the ancient fracture line between the Blue Ridge and Bracken County, she hit fog and couldn't see much beyond her. *I'm not supposed to see.* Maude wondered if she could accommodate herself to the county, at least until she decided where to go next, but not focus on the magic interconnections, much less get involved with them. The fog lifted just before the Taylorsville boundary.

The car seemed to have gained two additional cylinders and a new carburetor. Maude slowed it down to pass through Taylorsville. The town could have looked like San Francisco with its hills and wooden houses, but didn't. The little wooden houses up steep stairs overlooked a trailer court.

Maude turned through Shuff Spring to go the back way to Kobold. She passed the Shuff Pool Hall, which wavered in its magic between the actual wreck—the one intact room set up with a soft drink machine, wood stove, and pool table—and the virtual pool hall, with chrome, asphalt parking lot, and players coming in with $1000 custom pool cues. *Shim's magic must be getting weak.*

Maude was amazed at how quickly the magic seemed normal here while the telling of it got her declared insane in Berkeley. Wart Mountain behind her, she went over Little Dragon's lowest ridge and then across Gold Pan Creek, full of rusty-sided suckers, Bracken's endemic fish.

The trees wavered between green and autumn's red and gold. Sourwood was already purple. Maude felt the real car stutter, as though being made magic stressed it.

Maude drove down to the store to buy some gas before she went to her grandmother's house. The car was knocking now.

Aunt Betty pulled up in an old Essex. Betty was older than the Essex, had been old as long as Maude could remember. Her hair was grizzled gray, not one shade but many, and Aunt Betty fastened it back in a bun secured with a turquoise clip. Her eyelids lay hooded over her grey eyes, the flesh standing off from the eyeballs, not adhering to it. Betty's eyes always scared Maude when she was a child. The irises were solid grey, no darker rim, and stared out like steel punches with the pupils as black central pits. *Your soul*

goes down there. "Maude, I'll see you down at your grandmother's. You need some additive for your car, and don't
let the boys fool with it."

"I'll see you there," Maude said. Betty seemed to have
been expecting her.

"Afraid of me, still? You've always been so imaginative,
Maude," Aunt Betty said.

"Are you chastising me or praising me?"

"It depends on what you use it for." The Essex moved
away from Maude's car. Maude knew she'd be distracted by
waiting for Betty if Betty didn't come soon to her grandmother's. Betty held Maude's time until Betty chose to arrive.

The house was almost in the road, just a small hedge and
yard in front. Other than mowing, no one had worked outside in years and the plants had grown together in a tangle.
Maude parked to the side of the house by a blue and white
Buick.

A woman Maude hadn't seen before came out. She was
scrawny, slightly bent, with a narrow face all wrinkles over
bone. "Lula?" She looked like she needed care herself, not
like someone who should be taking care of Maude's grandmother.

"You're Maude. You didn't need to come."

"I wanted to see about my grandmother."

"I'm taking care of her."

"Well, let me come in and visit." Maude picked up one
of her suitcases.

Lula looked suspicious, but unlocked the door for
Maude.

"Grandma?"

The room Maude remembered as a dining room in back
of the house had a double bed in it. Her grandmother, thinner than ever, looked up at her from the bed. Maude saw
blood around a crack on her grandmother's lip. She turned
to find Lula, but Lula was right behind her.

"What has she been eating?"

"I can't eat," her grandmother said.

"I fix her potato water and milk. I'm really economical."

Maude knew that wasn't enough. "Has a doctor seen her lately?"

"No," Lula said. "Doctor would just waste her money."

So I came back for a battle with this hag. "Are you comfortable, Grandmother?"

"I don't expect to be at my age. Maude, I've been very good, but I'm so tempted."

Vitamin C. Her grandmother wasn't getting enough vitamin C, so her gums hurt, her lips cracked. Maude realized she wasn't waiting for Betty, but as soon as she realized it, she wondered who sent Lula to her grandmother.

"I think if we had a blender, you could eat more comfortably."

"She doesn't need a blender," Lula said. "And I ain't gonna use one."

"Oh, I'll take care of it."

"Who sent for you?"

Her grandmother said, "I didn't know whether I should have or not."

Lula looked down at Maude's grandmother. "Pa'tridge, you owe your cousin Betty." Lula pronounced her grandmother's name, Partridge, in the Southern way, without the *r* after the first *a*.

"Aunt Betty seemed to have been expecting me, too," Maude said.

"Betty wants you one way," Lula said. "Pa'tridge doesn't know what she wants. She's always been a bit crazy, haven't you, Pa'tridge?"

Maude remembered hearing about her grandmother's depressions, both medicine and magic proof. She'd wondered if they'd actually happened or if Partridge simply hated, for good reason, the world she was trapped in. "Looks to me like you need help yourself," Maude said to Lula.

Lula said, "I'm what she needs."

Maude waited for Aunt Betty to arrive. She sat down in a chair beside her grandmother's bed. Lula went into the kitchen and came back with cold cornpone that she gnawed on with plastic teeth. The message was *we eat leftovers and I'm not feeding you.*

Then, without knocking, Betty came in, smiling at Lula, nodding at Maude and her grandmother.

"Partridge, isn't it good we have Maude home again? I'm sure I can help her get a teaching job."

"Grannie Partridge isn't getting enough to eat. We need a blender."

"You've never understood dying, Maude," Betty said.

"She isn't going to become a spirit. She doesn't believe in that, so it won't happen."

"I'm not sure," her grandmother said.

"No," Maude said as her head ducked reflexively. But then, if her grandmother called her, she'd made *some* accommodation to the magic. "And we don't know if the spirits are the people they claim to be. I've heard enough about spirits to have my doubts about them."

"The alternative is believing in your own final oblivion," Betty said. "Perhaps the afterlife we imagine says more about us than it does about any final reality."

"There are so many things to believe in," Maude said.

"History, central planning," Betty said. She looked at Lula and smiled. "Your daddy thought we lived in a political democracy, but an economic dictatorship. He was always full of little sayings like that."

Maude said, "All I'm concerned about now is that my grandmother, your cousin, isn't getting enough to eat. I've heard the spirit is made from the person's last moments, what mood they're in when they die."

"A nice compromise," Betty said.

"Too much fuss," Lula said. "Where is this person going to stay?"

"Here," her grandmother said. "She's my granddaughter."

"Oh, I was thinking she'll rent one of my houses," Betty said. "After she starts teaching."

"I don't want to teach," Maude said. "I barely finished college."

"What do you want to do?" Betty asked. "Stay on welfare? Embarrass the family?"

Maude didn't wonder how Betty knew about the welfare. Instead, she hoped Douglas would come visit, bring her technology to counter the magic deals. "I don't want to charm children into accepting their witch-determined fates."

"Oh, you're very silly to think that's all teaching is," Betty said as though she were one of Maude's Berkeley social workers. "We believe in an afterlife. We offer hope. If that did no more than ease dying, I'd say it was useful. You want us to be bad, maybe you should ask yourself what's so bad about yourself that you anticipate oblivion."

"I don't look forward to it."

"Perhaps you took our local myths too seriously."

Maude felt the world she'd believed in turn insignificant. Betty's steel gray eyes held hers. Maude said, "Are you telling me there isn't real magic here after all? It's all metaphor?"

Betty smiled.

Her grandmother said, "But . . ." The word was tentative, but it opened room for doubt. Maude looked at her. Grannie Partridge was almost in tears.

Betty said, "Why would anyone imagine an impersonal universe? Even the computer wizards want to find personality in microchips, or put it there."

Partridge found her voice, and spoke strongly, "The rain falls on the just and the unjust. The race is not to the swift."

Betty said, "That's the cruelest God anyone could imagine." Maude realized the biblical promise dismayed her, too.

4

THE BALLAD CHAINS

That night, Maude stood in the guest bedroom listening to Lula talking to her grandmother, sounds not distinct enough to resolve into words. If Maude closed her bedroom door, they'd be inaudible.

I need a beer. Maude wondered what legal place sold beer in Taylorsville, and how late. She put on her coat and found the skeleton key that locked the front door. *I've got to see who's still here.*

The only place open for on-premises drinking was the Mayo River Boogie Parlor, with the live caged dancer over the small dance floor. Maude remembered hearing about knife fights there when she was a girl, but now, after having been a welfare crazy, she doubted much would faze her.

As she stood in the Boogey Parlor drinking her one beer for the night, a man with a fake hand—hooks with blunt ends, really—came up and worked the hand in her face, the springs going *ying, ying, ying* as he not quite clicked the hooks together. He stopped playing with them and asked, "Don't you remember me?"

Maude recognized him by voice—a trouble-bitten version of Jake Hughes, who she hadn't seen since she left for college. "Jake?"

"You back?"

"For a while, at least."

He twitched his hooks and said, "Bracken County eats its young. Move back, Maude, and you're doomed."

"So what happened?"

The bartender answered, "Tripped out on LSD and ran his hand into a feed auger."

Jake's face muscles seemed to wobble. Maude knew what the bartender said was true. Jake always claimed a man needed drugs or an awesomely tough automobile to deal with mean Bracken County.

"It was like magic," Jake said, "not that anyone seemed to have gained an extra hand."

Maude knew, or thought she'd known, that magic too often slants off in its own direction after a witch sets it to a task. "If it were magic, the witch might have been careless. She or he might not have been aiming to take your hand." She drained the rest of her can.

Jake began babbling about silicone and soluble crystals. Maude left and went back to her car.

The car started, but died in the bar drive. It wouldn't start again. Maude suspected the car was vapor locked and wouldn't start until the engine totally cooled down. She'd only been in the bar fifteen minutes, enough to half cool. From an earlier bout of vapor lock, Maude knew she'd have to wait until the engine cooled completely. Meanwhile, all the bar guys tried to get her to let them fuss with her engine. *Teach me to stop for beer at that place,* she thought. *I can't let the boys work on it. Someone might spell it so the car'd roll me only into his driveway.*

An older man said, "Looks witch-drained. You got plenty of witches in Kobold to take care of it."

Maude learned as a child that mention of witches called them near. She said, "It's vapor locked. I'll have to wait until it cools."

When Maude finally got home, Lula came out walking on bare feet with yellow calluses and fiberous toenails. "It ain't your house," Lula said, curling her toes, one foot wiping the other, the calluses like polished horn, the nails like splintered wood.

"Not yours, either. It's my grandmother's." Maude slipped by the woman, holding her away with one hand.

"Smell the liquor on you. Gonna tell Betty and your grannie."

Maude started to explain that she'd just had one beer, at the Boogey Parlor. But then she had been at the Boogey Parlor, and everyone knew what that was. "I'll get some at the store to keep around so I don't have to go out for it when I want it."

"Berkeley," Lula said. "California. Californicators."

Mornings, the old women gossiped in the Kobold Post Office while the postmistress put up the mail. Two days after Maude's car stalled at the bar, Maude came in and saw Aunt Betty. Betty leaned forward as though about to pounce, her face looking pre-Colonial.

"Hi, Aunt Betty, how things going?" Maude asked, switching to her country accent. She wondered what plans Betty had for her, but this day seemed to have space enough for mutual courtesy and several erratic world views.

"How are your adjusting to Bracken?"

"I heard that the secret was to get to a city once a week."

"I haven't left in years. Last trip was to visit a spot in up-state New York. So far away, yet so much like home, only colder. You'll get to that stage eventually. Come over and visit. Lula can take care of Partridge."

"I need help with my car."

"What kind of help?"

Maude said, "The compression's down. In Berkeley, one guy told me it needed a new carburetor, but that seemed okay driving cross-country. I think it's vapor locking when the motor's half hot."

"Of course, you want me to put a protect hex on the physical work."

Damn Betty. "No."

Betty smiled. "But you came back. You could have stayed in Berkeley, got more drugs to smother the call in your head."

The overhead lights flickered in their gas tubes and

chrome boxes. One man—all Kobold men seem like leather-covered sticks—came in, looked around, and saw Betty looking at Maude. All the other women were quiet. He didn't go right to his mailbox, but leaned against the wall and flipped through the wanted posters, listening.

Betty said, "You worry that if you give in to magic, your mind will mush up? Magic hasn't hurt my mind and I'm of an age where outside . . ." Betty broke off and shuddered slightly.

Magic toys with us now.

"Afraid?" Betty asked. "Don't want to learn the magic?"

"I know some of it." Halfway across the county, Maude found out later, a man was gored by a jersey bull. The man knew the bull. The goring came from the legend in which the familiar turns vicious. And as the human dies, he finds out he's been worshipping a black god all his life.

A trooper shot the bull. The bull collapsed, knees in human blood. This happened when the post office clock hands shivered, then clicked to 11:18. Maude asked, "How do I know you're the good guys?"

Betty shook Maude's chin. "Maudie, we're the good guys because we've got great taste. And because we have power."

Maude wandered around Bracken County most of the afternoon, trying to get out. But Bracken was trapped in a magic Möbius and all the roads led back to Kobold.

The Mini-Cooper rapidly lost compression, backfiring, tread rubber left black and smoking behind. Ghost blight.

At the Kobold Grocery, Aunt Betty stood by the gas pumps with a bottle of STP Gas Treatment in one hand. She held a ratchet wrench out in the other, and moved it as though blessing Maude's car.

The car engine stopped knocking.

"Why?" Maude asked.

"If you go out, you might find ways to hate us. Your atti-

tude matters," Betty answered, putting the STP on top of
the leaded-gas pump.

"I want to have my body here, helping my grandmother,
and my mind elsewhere. I need to get away some."

"If you're here, you can choose whether to be on top of
magic or under it, not magic or no magic." Betty waved the
wrench around at Kobold Grocery, the abandoned brick
bank building, the modern chrome-trimmed grade school.

Maude heard children shrieking, the *tamp, tamp* of bas-
ketballs in the schoolyard. "I don't think magic is necessary."

Betty stood with the wrench up between her breasts.
Suddenly, Maude visualized Betty as a young woman, but
Betty had never been young even when Maude was a baby.
Betty said, "Magic matters. And we're family. We love you."

"A funny love," Maude said. Betty looked infinitely pa-
tient, attached behind the eyes to something limitless.
Maude added, "Family love is for the relation, not the person."

"All of us have a place in a larger pattern here. Not a
logical pattern, perhaps, but a personal one." Betty's
wrench hand sank and she pulled off the socket and put it
in her dress pocket. "Do you really prefer to be a unit in a
mob?"

"I like being just a person." Maude got back in her car
and tried to start it. The Mini-Cooper sounded like a Model
T Ford. Maude asked, "What's wrong now?"

"It absorbs the time it saves you," Betty said. She
climbed back into her Essex, whose paint seemed finely
wrinkled, like crepe.

All Maude wanted was a universe that worked the same
for everyone. No deals. But now her car wouldn't feed gas
into the engine. She saw the STP bottle sitting on top of the
gas pump, but left the car at the store and walked home.

When Maude came back for the car, someone had put
the STP in her tank and left her a note saying he'd done it
as a favor.

* * *

Maude found a blender in Taylorsville and brought it and some vitamins home to feed her grandmother. Rain began falling on the drive back. *I'm not going to stay here forever. I wish Douglas would call.*

The house seemed small against the clouds and trees whose fall leaf color faded. Maude carried in the blender. Lula said, "I'm not going to use it."

"It's all right. I'm going to use it."

"I'm not gonna clean it."

"I'll do that, too."

"You ain't gonna get rid of me."

"I'm here to take care of my grandmother."

"Maude?" she heard her grandmother call.

"Go in and see her," Lula said, as if speaking before Maude could act would make Lula someone who gave orders in the house.

"I answer to her," Maude said. She put the blender on the counter and went back to see her grandmother.

Partridge looked frailer than ever, sweat soaked. "I fell. I hurt my arm."

Lula came in. "Ain't nothing but a strain. She got herself back to bed."

"It hurts real bad, Maude."

Lula sat down on the bed beside Partridge and smoothed away some of the sweat. "The undertaker has a woman who dresses out the female corpses," Lula said. "She washes them and puts on makeup, and their prettiest clothes."

"Stop that, Lula. I need to take her to the doctor."

Partridge looked at Lula, then at Maude. Maude knew she didn't want Lula to stay anymore, not with her morbid fantasies of women corpses dressed and powdered by other women. Partridge said, "I'm hurting."

Maude pulled the covers away. Her grandmother's arm was visibly broken. As she called for an ambulance, she wondered if Lula had broken it.

The hospital seemed like a battleground between paradigms—magic versus science, healing versus the medicine of explanations that tied bacteria to a greater design. *Oh, please,* Maude thought and wondered to what god she could pray.

An intern came out from a city for rotation and he brought in reason, X rays, and surgical plaster. A local nurse took Maude out while the intern set Partridge's wrist. Then the doctor came out and said, "Do you take care of her?"

"I just found out she hadn't been eating. I got a blender today."

"She needs food, care for her bedsores. Whoever's been taking care of her . . ."

"An old kinswoman has been taking care of her. I knew something was going on and came to help. I just got here."

"I'd like to have a social worker talk to you. Maybe make some visits."

Maude said, "I've been living in Berkeley for a couple years." She wanted him to stop accusing her of failing to take care of her grandmother.

"Her arm's been broken for hours."

"I was out."

"You can't leave her alone."

"Lula was with her. I've got to get rid of Lula. Do you know an agency, someone who could help?"

"That's why we need to have a social worker talk to you."

Maude said, "Call social services. I need to get rid of Lula." When Maude started to walk, she shook. The doctor's face softened.

Back at the house, Maude found that Lula had opened the blender box. The box was empty. Maude first looked through the trash while Lula watched. "I took it apart," Lula said.

"Did you break anything?"

"I'm not bad," Lula said. She turned as though she'd been insulted and went to the bedroom. Maude followed and saw her stretch out over the whole double bed.

By midnight, Maude had found the cutter blades with

the knives, the rubber gasket with the canning jar lids, the motor with the power tools, and the blender jar with the vases. So Lula believed herself to be good? She could leave an arm unset for hours, but wouldn't, perhaps, actually kill.

Maude thought about trying out the blender but dreaded Lula's anger at the noise. Maybe someone else could take Lula in? She took the blender to her room and put it in her closet.

In the morning, as the two women ate oatmeal, Lula said, "You had someone call while you took Partridge to the hospital."

"Who?"

"A man. I told him you weren't home."

"Was his name Doug?"

"Don't remember." Lula squinted at Maude over a spoonful of oatmeal. "Maybe."

"I'll call him," Maude said.

"You meet him in the bar the other night?"

"No, he's someone I knew in California, an engineer."

"It's your grannie's phone. She won't like you running up calls to California. You say you met this guy in a bar?"

"No, I didn't say." Maude felt her face getting red. *I hate feeling like a teenager.*

Lula ate her spoonful of oatmeal. Her narrow face looked relaxed, even dreamy. "So you're not going to call him on your grannie's phone."

While visiting her grandmother at the hospital, Maude heard about a garage off in the country that she hadn't considered—Burton's Speed Shop. The physical therapist who came in to talk to Partridge about rehabilitating her arm was from outside Bracken. She told Maude about Burton and said, "He's really good with the bills, too."

So Maude called him from a pay phone and took the car in. The shop felt rational, a clutter of radiators, crankshafts, wrenches, and other mind-shaped metal. The man was taciturn in the way of good mechanical people, asking questions and listening to both Maude and the car.

"I can drive you home if you can leave the car."

Maude wondered how long it would take. She'd be trapped in Kobold until the car was fixed. He nodded at her when she said, "I need to get up to Blacksburg."

When he dropped her off, he said, "Sometime soon, you've got to get the engine rebuilt or buy a new car. If you buy a new car, don't buy it here. You'll pay $1000 more for it." *And it could be hexed,* he seemed to be thinking.

"And it could be hexed," she said.

"I keep to my tools," he said. "I don't let anyone else touch them, either."

When she got the car back the next day, it ran as well as it ever had and she drove it very fast toward Blacksburg, over the faultline and up the Blue Ridge and over, to her money on Main Street in Blacksburg, and took out another $250. She then walked around Blacksburg, by the university, by the tattered posters for poetry readings and political rallies. History was between times, after the sixties, idling slack, something coming, but all the good radicals who'd mocked the Mr. Joneses had no idea.

Early fall, historically as well as seasonally, Maude thought. She noticed that outside Bracken the scope of her concern expanded.

And what winter comes? Would that be historically, or just personally?

Maude went in a bookstore that felt like home, and stood reading in various sections until a thin boy clerk came to within four feet of her and watched. So she bought a copy of the *Village Voice* and a *Roadside Geology of Virginia* and a hiking guide for the area.

The clerk at the counter checked her out on a computer, impersonally, without comment. Maude wondered why she felt relieved, then realized she'd have to hide the *Voice* from Lula.

Maude found a restaurant with ferns in the window and a music system which played preconversion Bob Dylan. She bought a falafel sandwich and ate it while remembering all the similar restaurants and bars she'd been in, in New York,

Berkeley, and San Francisco. She could sit here all night, until closing, and know the people who came in would know something about the general theory of relativity, about the subconscious, about DNA. At least one person any time of the day or night would know about Noam Chomsky's claim that all languages were the same in their deep structure and that language was innate.

The universe didn't change its responses here to comply with particular human will. Maude finished her sandwich and left a tip. She found a ticket on her car, which she'd parked in the visitor's parking lot. For a second, she felt punished and paranoid, but read the back of the ticket and realized that all she had to do was tell them she was neither a student nor a faculty member. So, slightly uneasy, she wrote down her address and social security number and put the ticket in one of the campus mailboxes.

Back home, Lula said, "Betty wants to introduce you to her niece. She said maybe you're lonely for people your age. And they had to keep your grannie another day at the hospital, so I think you should pay for it. And Betty brought a little package from the post office. It's on the dining room table. It rattles."

"Betty's not supposed to pick up my mail."

Lula shrugged. "She was doing you a favor."

"I'll talk to the postmistress."

"If Betty asks her for your mail, the postmistress will give it to her."

"Arrgh, I'll get a box in Taylorsville."

"You planning to bring drug or smut into the county?"

Maude picked up the box and knew from the outside return address, Karmachila, that, at the least, Douglas had come back to talk to Susan, and that inside were the stones from the magical beach at Point Reyes. *I don't want to open the box.* She rattled the box, wondering if she could shake the truth into the stones.

"Stones we gathered from a beach," she said to Lula.

"You haven't opened them."

"But I know these stones," Maude said. "I don't need to open them right away."

"Geomancy," Lula said. "It's the first magic anyone learns." She unfolded Maude's *Village Voice* and scowled at the headlines, then, with just her fingernails, picked open the first page. Maude felt trivially rebellious. "You've got to pick up your grannie before ten in the morning."

Supper was cold cornbread and pinto beans. Lula said, "I don't waste electricity."

When Maude took her books to her room, she noticed that all the bulbs had been changed to 25 watts. But the blender was still where she left it. She looked through the walnut side cabinet and found a 60 for the reading light and two 100-watt bulbs for the overhead fixture.

Lula caught her changing the bulbs and said, "Electricity burns the eyes."

Lula woke Maude up. The windows were mostly dark. "Sun'll be up soon, if you want more light."

Maude felt disoriented. "I read late. I don't have to get my grandmother until ten, right?"

"If you woke up now, you could read by natural light and not waste money."

"I think the estate has enough for me to live reasonably."

"You came to leech off her."

By now, Maude couldn't possibly go back to sleep. She got up and took her books to the dining room, where some light was coming in through the east windows. "Who hired you?" she asked.

"I needed a place. Your grannie needed a helper and all her closest kin left her here."

"Where were you before?"

"With other kin."

"Don't they need you anymore?"

"Sent me out. Cruel man." Lula disappeared into the kitchen. Maude felt guilty for asking, but could understand

why the man asked Lula to leave. She knew Lula's abrasive-
ness stemmed from insecurity. No, from anger at her de-
pendency. Lula wanted the authority and power she felt
around her.

Maude could grow up to be Lula.

At the hospital, when Maude asked about her grandmother,
a nurse came out and said, "We need to talk about her dis-
charge plans."

Maude followed the nurse into a closed office. The
nurse, an RN, looked over a chart and then said, "She's
malnourished. I know it's common among you people . . ."

"I bought her a blender. I just got here. I went to college."

"Sorry. Her regular doctor says she won't last out the
winter. The hospital resident is quite upset."

"I was upset when I saw her."

"The other woman there, Lula?" When Maude nodded,
the nurse went on, "Lula says you weren't there when your
grandmother fell."

"I wasn't. Lula could have called the ambulance herself."

"You should have someone reliable there at all times."

"Grandmother wants Lula."

"Your grandmother isn't able to make the best decisions. You might want to hire a practical nurse." The nurse
stood up.

Maude nodded and followed the nurse to her grandmother's room. Partridge was sitting on her bed, dressed
neatly, wearing gloves and a hat even, a sling holding her
broken arm. An orderly with a wheelchair came in just after
Maude and the nurse.

Partridge said, "Why can't I stay here longer?"

"Because you're not really sick anymore," the nurse
said.

"I am so sick."

"We're going to give your granddaughter instructions
on how to feed you."

Partridge shook her head slightly. "I'm such a burden."

Maude said, "No, you're not."

Partridge said, "I've got Lula to take care of me. You can get away."

"She's too old to be responsible for another old person," Maude said. "I wasn't doing anything important with my life."

Partridge stood up, her good arm pushing her off the bed. The orderly steadied her and helped her into the wheelchair.

When the Mini-Cooper crossed what Maude felt was the hospital's rational boundary, her grandmother moaned.

"So you feel it, too?"

"Magic. I've been bad to magic."

"You want to go away? Leave here and live with me somewhere else."

"Betty says you were on welfare in California. For being crazy."

"I faked being crazy for the welfare. I didn't want anyone to know where I was."

"Just take care of me best you can. I don't want to be a witch anymore. I want to just die."

"You've got to start eating better."

"Lula was doing best she could."

"She refused to consider using the blender to make your meals. She sleeps in the bed with you. It's disgusting."

"We used to all share beds."

"Grandmom, we've got to hire someone reliable."

"I need Lula. I might need her real bad."

Betty's Essex was parked beside Partridge's house. Maude felt sticky, as though spiders had been spinning webs over her while she slept. She helped Partridge out of the car and held her up for the walk to the house. Betty was sitting in the living room, visible in the window, but she made no move to help Maude with the door or her grandmother. Maude got the door open and her grandmother inside it.

Betty and a woman Maude's age sat in the living room

with Lula. The woman wore a brocaded silk dress and had kohled eyes. She had the other family body plan, a body that looked chunked out of oak, dug up from a bog and bleached. Her nose was snub, her cheekbones broad and boxy, her hair black, eyes grey, but not so perfectly grey as Betty's. Betty said, "Maude, this is Terry. She's my favorite niece. Her husband's going to be buried in the family cemetery along with Partridge."

"Partridge isn't dead yet."

"Neither is her husband, but sometimes the men who marry our women aren't agreeable to being buried in their wives' plots. Your daddy wasn't. He wanted to be cremated in an electric fire and spread out over Atlanta. But John's different."

"Is her husband old?"

"No, he's young. And he's kin. I reckon they could get an annulment for consanguinity, if this were the Middle Ages and we were Catholic." Betty smiled.

Terry said, "I'm not expecting to lose John soon, but it's an eventuality."

Maude nodded and took Partridge back to her room. Lula followed, but Maude said, "Hadn't you better go back and mind the guests?"

"You do that. I'll take care of Partridge."

From the living room, Betty called, "Maude, come back here and talk to us. Lula can put your grannie to bed."

Terry watched Maude come back and sit down. Betty said, "Partridge will be buried in our cemetery. You two should get to know each other. Terry's moving back here while her husband works in Richmond. Terry is a potter."

Terry nodded. Maude wondered how much of the surrounding magic Terry felt, whether she worked with it or not. "It's a strange county," Maude said. "It has no roots in the continent." Maude remembered her stones then. Was this woman a counter or a player?

Betty said, "Miss Allen at the post office gave me your mail." She handed Maude a postcard from Douglas. He'd mailed it over a week ago.

"I'll get my own mail, thanks," Maude said.

Betty didn't bother to argue. She just smiled and looked at Terry as if pointing out that Maude, after all, had been declared paranoid. Betty stood up and said, "I'll leave you to talk. Maude can take you home."

The two women didn't say anything as they listened to Betty's car drive away. Then Terry said, "Amazing how she keeps that old car running."

Maude said, "You'd swear it was magic. So your husband works in Richmond?"

"He's a computer tech."

"The postcard Betty gave me is from a man in Berkeley who's an engineer. And you're a potter. Could I see some of your work?"

"Sure. I make memorial urns. I also moved here to hunt my hawk. Betty's letting me live on the old farm."

Maude was a sucker for falconry. "Where did you go to school?" she asked, almost as much to distract herself as out of genuine curiosity.

"Swarthmore."

"I went to NYU, but I spent time around Columbia. I was in the Strike of 1968. Do you remember who Mark Rudd was?"

"The student radical?"

"I remember him going around a radical meeting getting cuddles from the women. It reminded me of alpha ape behavior," Maude said. Maude hoped she'd found someone local who didn't think Marx was a demon.

"Why don't you come over and stay a while. I'm sure Lula has things under control."

"I really shouldn't leave Partridge alone with her long. She deconstructed our blender."

"What?"

"She put the cutters in with the knives, the motor, I suspect, where power tools had been kept, the blender jar with the measuring cups, the rubber gasket with the canning jar gaskets—the really old style gaskets for the shouldered jars."

Terry said, "How many gaskets did you try before you found the right one?"

"It wasn't that bad. All of the old canning gaskets were cracked. But you can see why I'm nervous about leaving Partridge with Lula."

"Remember, Betty said you were to take me home. I didn't bring my car," Terry said, as though she'd expected Maude to be polite, not merely useful.

Maude said, "I can't stay long." They went outside and drove off in Maude's Mini-Cooper.

"Turn here," Terry said. They went to a place at the base of Wart Mountain where the family founder, a man with eidetic memory, made his fortune, not a large fortune by national standards, but sufficient for western Virginia.

"Roare's place," Maude said. "I'd wondered where you'd find open enough land to hunt falcons." She guessed almost a thousand acres were in pasture.

"Betty owns it now. I think it looks like Scotland. John and I were in Scotland for our honeymoon. The Highlands have a wonderful feel to them, the lords and the crofters."

"Is the old house still standing?" Maude asked. She saw it then, a vernacular classic, two stories in front and a wing off the back, porches on all sides, and three chimneys on the outside walls. There'd be a loft over the kitchen and dining wing, two large rooms downstairs off a main hall, two upstairs to match, with a window at the top of the stairwell, opening west. "Same house."

"We're going to build something modern. The old house seems too creaky."

"Haunted?"

"Powderpost and clicking beetles."

"Haunted by insects." Maude knew that another name for the second species was deathwatch beetle.

"Oh, do you believe in hauntings? I'm planning to do an oral history of the family myths." Terry started to take Maude's coat. "Look, while you're here, why not see the hawks and some of my pottery."

"I really need to go." Maude wondered why Terry insisted.

"I was so afraid I'd only have old kin here. And you like hawks. I could tell by your expression when I mentioned them."

Maude said, "Show me, then."

"I just have one now, out on her block, her perch. Here's something I made." Terry picked up a shallow dish from the entryway table and showed it to Maude.

The pot was thin-walled with a slight asymmetry at the lip. Maude asked, "Is it a lamp?"

Terry said, "It's a ritual lamp." She looked at Maude as if confused for a moment about whether the ritual could be real.

Maude sensed Terry was embedded in magic whether she believed in it or not. "I like it. I'd like to buy something from you if I could afford it. Now, the hawk?"

They went through the house, which was paneled in beaded sealing. When Maude was a child, she'd wondered why people put *ceiling* wood down their walls, but later saw the name in print. She touched the raw pine, polished by generations of hands touching it. Terry said, "We're thinking about taking the paneling out and using it in the new house."

Maude said, "You'd have to fumigate it."

They went through the front hall and out the door to the side of the stairs. It opened up onto a porch. Just beyond the steps, Maude saw a redtail. Terry said, "Meet Belle."

Maude had seen prairie falcons in California that seemed tainted by magic. But this redtail hated both her jesses and any attempt to make her a hawk icon. Terry put on a gauntlet on the porch and went out to the bird. "What I really want is a gyrfalcon, but that would be illegal."

"You could get away with keeping a gyrfalcon if you just hunted on your own land."

"Belle, want a rat?" Terry pushed the gauntlet under the redtail's breast. The hawk stepped onto the glove. She looked at Terry's hands, then swiveled her head to look at Maude, then swiveled the other direction to stare at a small outbuilding. Terry, hawk balancing on her glove, walked over to the building.

"Need help?" Maude asked as Terry began opening the shed's door one-handed, the hawk flaring its wings.

"Could you pick up two mice? There're other gauntlets on the porch."

Maude saw the box of hawk gear and two gauntlets. One looked like a medieval relic, its leather quilted and studded, a gold ring at the bottom of the wrist. The other looked like an all-leather welder's glove. Maude felt more comfortable putting that one on.

She caught the mice, though, in her bare hand, as Belle the hawk watched, head forward, cocked. When a mouse squeaked, Terry said, "Lay the mouse on the gauntlet, hold its tail. Belle'll jump over."

Belle jumped onto Maude's glove and grabbed the mouse. Her talons were blunt, not pointed, and she seemed more like a constrictor than anything else as she throttled the mouse with her feet and then swallowed it headfirst. Dinosaur kin. Maude touched the hawk gently with her other hand. The hawk seemed utterly indifferent to being touched and that indifference isolated Maude in her primate's tactile curiosity. The bird seemed to say, *You touch. I eat.* But Maude knew the bird had no words in its head, perhaps visual maps like dreams. How did a hawk organize her mind?

The hawk stared back at the outbuilding where the mice were caged. "Can she have another mouse?"

Terry said, "Belle's very predaceous."

Maude touched Belle's breast again. This bird did seem quite realistic.

"Terry, do you ever feel as though you'd stepped into history. Or myth?"

Terry asked, "What do you mean? I'll take Belle now." As Terry came toward them, the hawk tried to fly and fell below Maude's glove in a tangle of hawk leashes, jesses, and wings. Terry steadied the hawk with a hand to its back and helped it onto her gauntlet. The hawk flared her feathers, then settled them in discrete jerks.

"Did you ever hear about Bracken County magic?"

"Sure. The locals all think Grandpa Roare cut a deal with the devil for his success. He was successful way before he came here. All the poor locals, they're just jealous. We can put the hawk up now and I'll show you my horse and the dogs."

As they walked to the stables out from the house, Terry said, "Betty gave me the dogs." They were penned near the stable. Maude had never seen a breed like them before, tall-legged hounds with rough coats spotted brown on white, almost like a liver setter. They bayed.

Inside the stable, a small grey horse moved around a stall. "She's a Connemara-Arab cross," Terry said. "Excellent for following hounds."

Excellent for the Wild Hunt, Maude thought. "Do you also like to either hike or fish? There's a good tailwater fishery around here for brown trout, and the Appalachian Trail isn't far."

"It's odd to make artificial places for trout."

"They don't seem to mind that their water's being oxygenated by turbines."

"I wish sometimes that we didn't have powerlines and cars, that we rode horses and hunted with bows and arrows, nets, and hawks. 'The fowlery I defy and all his craft.' "

"That's from Chaucer, a few years after the Black Death brought on the Renaissance by shifting power from the killer lords to the merchants."

"You're too cynical, Maude." Terry seemed dream-drugged. "Paranoid, maybe."

"Most people throw that word around without knowing in the least what they're talking about."

"You don't trust Aunt Betty. She's a marvelous character

in her old car, with her jewels and gloves, her art collection, maintaining a presence in the county.''

"A presence?''

"Style, taste. Courage. But I am glad you're here so I can have someone from the family my age. In the country, you can only trust family.''

Maude realized Betty brought this woman here, just as her grandmother brought her back. *I am tempted by magic. I hadn't realized that before. I feel so cheap and cynical when I attack it.* "Well, let me know when you want to get together again.'' She realized she'd stayed longer than she'd wanted. Had Terry charmed her?

Terry said, "John's coming down for the weekend. We should have dinner.''

5

YOUR GRANNIE HITS ME
WITH HER CAST

Lula sat in the narrow kitchen that used to be a porch and said, "Your grannie hits me with her cast."

Maude put stewed apples and some vitamin C powder in the blender, then said, "You can sleep in the other bedroom. Grandmom needs to be able to get to the bathroom easily."

"You're not used to our ways."

Maude turned on the blender and Lula twisted away and covered her eyes as if the thing had shrieked. Maude said, "If Grandmom wanted scurvy, she wouldn't be eating what I've been making for her since she got back from the hospital."

"I'm going to take that cast off. It hurts me."

"You maybe should be thinking about who else you know that needs a nurse."

"You didn't hire me. You're just a leech."

"I'm her granddaughter."

"And where were you when she broke her arm, anyhow?"

"I was out."

"You go out all the time. It's not what a woman taking care of her kin should do."

Maude went in to feed her grandmother, who was sitting up by her sewing machine. Partridge said, "Someone's took off the treadle belt."

From the kitchen, Lula called, "You don't need to be piecing quilts now."

Maude said quietly to Partridge, "Does it bother you that she sleeps in the bed with you?"

"She's right. It's the way we grew up." Partridge fed herself, wincing as the food touched her sore gums, but still eating.

"To sleep with someone . . . ," Maude couldn't say *with someone who's dying*, so she finished, ". . . with someone who's sick. She's got no concern for you, didn't want to use the blender to make your food, wants your cast off so it doesn't bother her when you're sleeping."

"Do I hit her with it?" Partridge asked.

"You need it on."

"She's right. I can't sew with my arm in a cast."

"Grandmom, she shouldn't hide the treadle belt."

"I hear you all arguing. You're closer kin, but Betty likes Lula better. She says Lula would be good for me."

"Grandmother, you've had such a hard life. I want to . . ."

"Everyone wants to do something for my last moments, Maude. Hire a black Christian."

What? Maude knew her kin thought the Christians were silly. "Why black?"

"Because I heard they died with smiles on their faces and didn't come back talking to their kin."

"Perhaps that's oblivion, not going to heaven."

"They're pretty confused about whether you wake up in the arms of Jesus or sleep in the grave until resurrection, but I won't be made a mock of. I'm not going to use witch ways to keep on going, either. I'm sick of all of it."

"We wouldn't see you anymore."

"I want to be buried in a churchyard. I don't think it's really our people we see slipping from the graves at the old place."

"What do you think we see?"

"Spirit mockers. Now, drop talking about that. I want to piece a quilt. I cut it out."

Maude searched through the various compartments in her grandfather's oak desk. She found the treadle belt, but she also found a revolver. Partridge nodded. "Your grand-daddy had a cousin who was a deputy. He took it off a murderer."

Maude moved a short lever on the gun and swung open the cylinder. It was unloaded. She said, "A killing gun."

"And willful. It needs to be well kept, considering the county."

Maude closed the cylinder and said, "Does Lula know it's here?" Of course, she did, she went through everything in the house.

Partridge said, "You should get rid of it, if you're afraid of it. If you're afraid of it, you'll empower it."

"I better keep in mind that it's nineteenth-century technology," Maude said as she closed the revolver up in the desk and turned to fit the leather treadle belt to the Singer. "Guns and sewing machines both, machines from when it changed."

"My Singer's not nineteenth century. Got it in 1954. It's got all sorts of attachments."

Meaning that to Partridge this treadle machine was as modern as she could imagine. Maude found an ice pick and punched a hole in the leather to put the staple through, then found the instruction booklet and oiled the machine as the diagrams suggested. She felt calmer, as though both the gun and the sewing machine were machines against magic. "I could sew together your patches."

"You sew?"

Maude wanted to ask how hard it could be if all the little old ladies did it. "I could learn."

"It's a courting device. Shows a man you know how his mind works, all geometric. Like he courts you with intricate language when even plain talking's hard for a man, and you court him with something hard for a woman, piecing spaces. Piecing this quilt will see me out. It's my last quilt."

"Don't say that." Maude realized that perhaps to keep Partridge alive beyond this last quilt could be cruel. "Well, Grandmother, as you wish."

"I'll live to see you piece it."

"How long will that take?"

"It's a log cabin. Not too terribly long. The best one for getting a man is windmills. You might start cutting you a windmill."

"I always thought piecing a quilt was tedious."

"It is tedious. That's valuable. Shows a man you've got patience."

Maude opened the piecing bags and saw rectangles of cloth strung on thread, various colors and various sizes each strung separately. She felt intimidated and motivated.

"You begin by sewing the red strip to the print," Partridge said. "Use the thin masking tape as a seam guide. Lay it straight, right on the edge."

Lula came in and said, "My momma didn't use no masking tape. She handpieced them, wrapped them up after midnight so they wouldn't get witch-tangled."

"Maude's learning," Partridge said. "And there's no point in handpiecing since the machine came in. Machine piecing's tedious enough."

Maude thought that the machine and cloth going under it revived Partridge. She was passing an honest skill to a new generation. The women quieted as the machine whirred. Maude handed what she'd joined to Partridge, who said, "You need to redo here. There's a seam ripper in there somewhere."

Seam ripping was the most tedious part of it, but Maude got the seam right and felt accomplished.

"She's gonna die from your making it," Lula said.

"I'd have died sooner," Partridge said.

Maude took her grannie's good hand and squeezed it gently. The skin felt like old dressmaking patterns.

Maude called Douglas. "Hi," he said, meaning, *what is this about?*

"I'm piecing a quilt."

"Back to the land and all that."

"No. It's more like geometry in cloth, though this pattern isn't so complex."

"I've been thinking about you, Maude."

"Can you get some time off?"

"I may have more time off than I'd been expecting. The company I'm working for is talking about layoffs. You need any engineers in rural Virginia?"

"Probably not. I don't know. What's your specialty?"

"I've worked in optics, in film processing, computer images. World's a bit behind me at this point."

"Can you call me back? I promised I wouldn't talk more than three minutes."

He did, and Maude realized she was terribly relieved. That embarrassed her.

"I could come see you for Thanksgiving, if you're not having family visits."

"That's next month." If Partridge died before then, it would be in another era.

"I'd like to see how things shake out here."

"So I have to face Halloween alone?"

"I've been thinking about you, Maude."

"I'm happy to hear that. I got the stones."

"The stones?"

"The stones we collected at Point Reyes. Someone at Karmachila sent them to me."

"Oh. I gave them to Susan. I . . . ."

Fucked her. Thought so. "I'd love to see you at Thanksgiving, then, and thanks for calling back."

"Are things working out for you? You're not too unhappy?"

"I'm getting to know my grandmother better. I've still got my car, and I've got a cousin here. She's got a falconry license and an Connemara-Arab hunter."

"Sounds neat. I'll call before then."

"I'll send you some photos of my grannie's quilts."

Mid-October was the season of the last overflights of National Guardsmen and the sheriff's deputies looking for drug patches. Most older Bracken County people hated having the helicopters overhead because that much unadapted machinery in the air spread logic all over the place and killed magic. Even people who didn't rely on entities allied themselves to people who did, made secondary use of the magic. But the children looked around when the machines flew. Freed of a compulsion to stay in the county and fetch and carry for someone powerful, some local kids from the powerless classes joined the military under the protection of its vast machines—the helicopters, the jets from Norfolk that flew practice bombing runs against the high school, afterburner booms canceling a teacher's drone forever. And left, got educated, and never came back.

Maude heard the helicopter motor behind Taylorsville, almost as though the helicopter was larger than the town. The magic whipped away, leaving a hundred scuffling merchants with mortgages. As though they'd never seen it before, one or two stared at stock they could never sell in Taylorsville without magic: Guatemalan handicrafts, Orvis fly rods. The witch women's beauty faded. The witch men's faces became vapid or looked cruel. The other locals looked at their patrons and shuddered.

The Mini-Cooper, which had been running well after the favor-doing stranger put Betty's gas treatment in it, seemed to be an elderly car again. *I need to take it to a real mechanic,* Maude thought, then remembered she'd been planning to do this since she came here. Maude wondered if Betty could get out at all on a day with helicopters flying.

At the grocery, all the bok choy looked like it had come from California by truck on a hot day. Maude wished she'd planted a fall garden, but it was too late now. She bought some frozen pita bread and a couple of cans of garbanzos and peanut butter to make poor hippie *hummos bi tahani. I hate the food here. They've spent their whole lives eating what the Cherokee used for field rations: cornbread, beans, and some greens.* Maude felt more aggravated than usual, no magic seduction laying a glamour over the difficult lives, the deep loyalties given by the powerless to those who never planned to honor their workers' faith. The helicopter felt like it was directly overhead.

Back home, she unloaded the groceries while Lula fussed at her for buying garlic and parsley. "Frills, don't need 'em. Tongue shouldn't be catered to."

"Lula, I miss the food I'm used to."

"You didn't grow up here, that's a fact."

"My dad and mom were from here, but they developed a taste for better food, more interesting food."

"We can't afford to feed you like a foreigner."

"Garbanzos are cheap enough."

"Chick peas. What's wrong with pintos?"

In the afternoon, while the helicopters flew over the ridges behind the house, Lula sat in the room with Maude and Partridge. Maude sewed quilt squares, very carefully and very slowly. Lula said, "I don't have nobody. No home. You understand that, don't you?"

"Yes," Maude said. She looked over and saw how gnarled Lula's hands were. One side of Lula's face seemed drawn. *Stroke?*

"My blood pressure's bad. Hearing them helicopters doesn't help. Montgomery County sheriff said he didn't want them bothering people."

Partridge said, "Montgomery County's different. It's got Virginia Tech."

Lula said, "Betty was such a help to me. I'm not much on my own."

Maude, wanting to goad Lula while she was under the machines, said, "I haven't seen Betty or her car today." *Remember, old woman, your patroness can't stay up to logic.*

Partridge said, "You know you won't see Betty today."

"While you were out, we decided that I've got to stay," Lula said.

"She hasn't got anyone," Partridge said.

"Not much power, either," Maude said. "Not cross-cousin bred or outcrossed to other entity-ridden families." Maude felt petty, but Lula so tempted her to be mean.

The helicopter flew away and Lula's face straightened and her hands seemed somewhat less gnarled. Lula said, "Pure *t* life is mean without something to believe in," as though she stole Maude's thoughts. She got up to fix more cornbread and pinto beans. When she was done, Maude would use the blender to make something Partridge could eat. Then, after Lula did the other dishes, Maude would clean the blender.

Two days later, Maude finished piecing her first square. Because working on the quilt seemed like conjuring death, Maude stopped sewing. Partridge noticed that Maude just sat in front of the machine, not treadling, and said, "You don't understand. I could die sooner if I didn't have the quilt to wait for."

"I could be finished piecing in two, three months. I feel weird about it."

"I want to be buried in that quilt. I like seeing you at the machine, by my bedside. I'm sorry I didn't teach you earlier."

Maude found the pieces for the next square. Partridge seemed satisfied.

Terry called Maude on Friday and said, "Why don't you have dinner with us. You've got someone who can take care of your grandmother, don't you?"

"She doesn't do blenders," Maude said.

"Partridge wasn't starving before . . ."

"She was. I could blend up a soup and let Lula reheat it, I guess."

"John's going to be here. I've been telling him about the helicopters that have been flying over this week. He says they're probably doing war games."

"No, they're looking for marijuana growers waiting for the last minute before frost."

"War games would have been more romantic. Well, can you come for dinner?"

"Sure."

She went to her grandmother and said, "Would you mind if I went to Terry's for dinner?"

"Supper or dinner?"

Maude remembered the local usage. "Supper."

"Don't stay too late."

"I'll fix something for you before I go."

"You resent being here, trapped with old people? When I was your age, I took care of my children and my old people."

Maude said, "I didn't expect to have to do this. I'd like to get out more. It's not that I resent you, please understand that."

"I would go out more, too, but it's too late. You shouldn't leave me with Lula."

"I need to get to know my other kin."

"Yes, gad about with the living." Partridge drew her covers up to her chin and looked away from Maude. "Go, then. Leave me to be tempted. You're such a self-centered bitch, gadding about, striding broad to open your legs."

Maude remembered another time when Partridge was difficult, arguing with her father's people over the disposition of his body, telling them their God put them in a subservient position, saying that she mocked the Christians behind their backs, saying they were the Sunday Morning Church of the Saturday Night Sinners, thieves and backstabbers who did as they pleased because Jesus would forgive them even if the people they wronged or stole from wouldn't. Even though her father hadn't gone to church since he fled Bracken County with his bride, Maude's father's people took her father's corpse anyway and buried it sanctified. "I'll be back by midnight."

"Close up the sewing machine now, so the threads don't get spirit-tangled if you're late."

Maude put away everything connected to the quilt and drove to Terry's house.

Terry drove a midsized sedan in dark blue. Her husband's car was a Bronco, which Maude thought was an odd car for a computer technician. The Bronco had gunracks. Maybe this man wasn't meant to live in Richmond.

Terry came to the door with her husband. "Hi, Maude, this is John."

"Your truck?"

"Yes, makes quite a splash in Richmond." John seemed to be peering at the world from behind two sets of glasses, one the real glasses he wore, the other some metaphysical distorters. A man ripe for bad magic, Maude thought.

Terry said, "John likes the country. He's spent time in Idaho, at Hayden Lake, wasn't it, honey? His father's family is old Richmond stock, tidewater plantations and all. His mother's kin to us." Maude followed her cousins into the living room where a semiautomatic pistol lay in parts on newspaper.

"A semiauto . . . Colt?" Maude said, trying to be polite.

"Like guns?" John asked. "I can get you a great deal on an Uzi clone. I've got a dealer's license."

"We've got a revolver at the house."

"If I get laid off, I'm going to move here and get a concealed weapons permit. Terry says everyone here has one."

"Lots of people do." Maude felt that the difference was that local people grew up with guns. Even though the locals understood how to handle guns better than most, guns still fired by alleged accident during family arguments, refused to make clean suicides, and whispered constantly about the power of 140-grain bullets and smokeless powder. They evoked killer entities.

"I wonder if I could bring down a helicopter," John said, putting the gun back together and aiming at the ceiling.

Terry said, "I told him about the helicopters flying over looking for dope." She didn't seem to find John's gun talk at all disturbing.

Maude wondered if he was teasing what he assumed to be her peacenik sensibilities. Or did Terry magic him into this? "You ought to introduce yourself to your neighbors, telling them you're going to be target shooting, and reassure them that you're not careless with guns."

He didn't answer her, just lowered the gun with his trigger finger stretched out along the frame, not curled against the trigger. Maude hoped that meant he'd had some training. Terry smiled at him. Then Maude wondered why she was invited to their first dinner together after a week apart.

John put the gun in a belt holster, then asked, "So, what do you do?"

"I take care of my grandmother and sew on a quilt."

"What did you do in Berkeley?"

"Stole from the system and sold plasma."

He smiled at Maude as if seeing her as a social bandit straight out of his fantasies. She felt tugs pulling her into that posture, her mood swinging to tough, sexy, and cynical, a shoplifter, a woman who played badger games without a partner, busting middle-class balls. She tried to push his image of her away and found it entangled in her own self-image. Concentrating, she separated the images, pushed his away. He said, "You must be bored here after being a thief in Berkeley. I'll take you shooting."

"I'd rather see the hawk hunt."

Terry said, "She didn't really steal like those black kids you play with in Richmond. Betty said she was on welfare under a fake name. Dinner's ready."

"That's still stealing from the system," John said.

"I'm certainly hungry," Maude said, slam-changing the subject.

Maude thought she'd never seen food like Terry's dinner in Bracken County. A duck lay glazed on a platter, its skin spiced with ginger and Szechwan peppers. Beside the duck, Terry put steamed Chinese rolls and cut scallions, saying, "It's not precisely authentic, but I like steamed buns better than the pancakes."

Without asking, John put a Guinness Stout at each place. Maude sat down as Terry brought over a tureen of hot-and-sour soup. "As good as a salad," Terry said, ladling soup into Chinese bowls.

Maude could forgive much weirdness for a meal like

this. She said to John, "So you're a computer tech. I've thought about learning how to program."

"Not needed these days. Unless you're an ace. More and more companies are using packaged programs. Soon, a clerk will be able to do most computer work."

Maude wondered if he was an ace.

Terry said, "Luke and Betty are stopping by later."

Maude tried to remember when she'd last seen Luke, Betty's husband. He'd been a looming terror figure when she visited as a child. "I hardly saw him even though we visited here most summers."

"Luke never cared much for children," Terry said. "But he and Betty were great friends of your grandmother's."

"I don't know when they got together," Maude said.

"In church," Terry said.

Maude felt weird about the sort of Christianity the locals professed. Their God sent poverty and earthquakes to the Nicaraguans and set the local believers in a place where their wishes could make their God come true. The catch was that *all* the gods came true in Bracken County. Still, she couldn't imagine Betty at the local church. She asked, "The Baptist Church?"

"Yes, but they're not Fundamentalists, you know," Terry said. "They go socially, to support the community." She turned to John. "Maude knows all sorts of folkloric things about the county."

Maude said, "The local NAACP has a ghost secretary who was described as the widow of a white man when she was arrested for murder in 1910. Progress both pleases her and pisses her off." She wondered if they were too liberal or too conservative to hear the rest of it. But John had black street contacts, so Maude continued, "Her daddy offered $100 to any of his daughters as could marry a white man."

"What did a black man do in the late nineteenth century that he could afford to make such an offer?"

"He made liquor," Maude said. "His daughter did, too. That's why she had to kill a man. He wouldn't pay her for her liquor."

"If the magic was real," Terry said, "she could have gotten money magically."

"Conjuring isn't always in human interests," Maude said. "What you deal with has a will of its own. It's the personalized universe of the ancients. So sometimes, you don't call, you just do. You use your own will, not an entity working through you with its own purposes."

"Just do," John said. He pulled his pistol and dry-fired it as a punctuation to what Maude had said, then asked, "But how do people know they're using their own will? Maybe they're just tricked into thinking they have free will?"

His question threw Maude back to her terror after her parents died. Accident, design, accident, design. At her mother's grave, Maude had begged for an answer. Her emotions drew five deal-making entities, old gods, the embodiments of discarded philosophies, the spirit of alchemy, each more seductive than the one before, offering power. But none of them answered her question, not even with a lie.

At her father's grave, the universe emptied itself into a blank. She went back to graduate from NYU without parents in the audience.

College proved to be another magic station charming children into believing the world would consider them special if they finished its programs, Maude realized when she went for job interviews and was asked to take typing tests.

Perhaps she'd gone truly paranoid then, desperate to know where magic ended, where the universe she'd dearly wished to believe in began, that dream universe of level playing fields and meritocracy and rules that worked the same for everyone.

"Maude, you've taken a long time to think," Terry said.

Maude blinked. "Sometimes, you have to trust you're doing the right thing, know you aren't overwhelmed by emotion. People here used to be so much more dramatic, more emotional. Times have changed, but the black woman widow of a white man wishes they'd change even more."

Terry said, "And thoroughly modern people, modern enough to have an NAACP chapter, believe this?"

"In this county, it's not belief," Maude said. "To not work with the spirit personalities or be used by them, you have to willfully not work with them. You've got to force logic on the situations."

"It's an interesting world view," Terry said. "That you can force logic on a situation."

"So maybe this gun has a spirit?" John said.

Maude nodded, not sure what John wanted to hear.

Terry said, "But do you believe this?"

Maude felt the magic around them, but they seemed unconscious of it. "I don't believe in it," Maude said, deciding to seem sane at the expense of all the local truth.

They heard the old Essex coming now, making the even more archaic sound of the fierce, noisy, hill-climbing motor of the World War I era Essex. The car pulled up and two people got out.

Maude thought she would have remembered Luke more clearly since they'd met before, but realized she'd never dared look directly at him when she was a child. He was huge, like a bull through the shoulders, and had shaggy grey hair, but wasn't as wrinkled as Betty. Beside him, Betty fussed with her purse. He made her feminine, not the matriarch she was around the women.

"Our uncle's pure male essence," Terry said. Maude wondered if Terry spoke metaphorically or magically.

"Luke and I are going hunting tomorrow," John said.

Terry opened the door before the old couple could knock. "Maude said she hardly remembers you, Uncle Luke."

"No, I don't suppose so," Luke said. He looked at her as if he knew all about the men she'd picked up in Berkeley bars. "I didn't meet much of Partridge's children when they visited."

Maude realized Luke would have aggravated any self-possessed man around him. John could like Luke because

John had an entity behind him, was in the magic so unself-consciously he was oblivious to it.

Luke sat down, his huge hands curled slightly on his thighs, his legs spread. "John, I hope you move here permanently," he said.

Maude looked at Betty. The tensions between Betty and Luke were complex: sexual, reproductive, competitive. Betty seemed smoother, less wrinkled, sitting beside Luke. She said, "Maude, I hope to come down to see Partridge soon."

"Maybe you can help me with Lula. I've got to do something about her," Maude said. "She wants to take off Partridge's cast so she can sleep better with her."

"Partridge still alive?" Luke asked. He seemed more like the farmer then, less like the magic male.

"She said she'd live until I finished piecing her quilt," Maude said.

"Women can do that," Luke said. "Men would rather die than face an anniversary without their powers."

"I'd better get back to her," Maude said. She looked at a clock and realized she couldn't get home before midnight.

"We'll call you," Terry said. John nodded over his pistol.

When Maude got home, Lula sat treadling the sewing machine in a pool of light. Partridge's white cast showed against the shadowed bed. Partridge looked from the sewing to Maude. Her pupils seemed enormous, almost as though she was in shock.

Maude touched her grandmother's hands. They felt clammy. "Lula, it's late. I think my grannie needs to get some sleep."

"Thought I'd help you," Lula said. She looked at Maude and smiled.

"You might need to sleep in the other bedroom tonight. Partridge is sweating."

Lula treadled and flipped the lever that threw the belt

off the pulley. She closed the machine and then said, "Just tonight."

Maude sat down on the bed after Lula went to the other room. "I saw Luke," she said to Partridge. "And I met Terry's husband, John."

"Luke is a power of a man, isn't he?"

"He makes Betty look feminine, not matriarchal."

"It's a spell she had to have to catch him."

"Who's the winner?"

"She thinks she bespelled him, but she had to use the spell to get him, so I think he has her."

Maude smoothed down her grandmother's hair, still not completely grey. "I can't tell whether Terry or John believe any of it or not."

"Maybe you just hallucinated that child screaming from the old school map. Maybe we're just crazy ladies. Maude, I don't mind if Lula helps with the quilt."

Maude wondered how much Partridge was suffering. "You in any pain?"

"If I talk about it, it will get worse." Partridge settled down in the bed and pulled up the covers with her good hand. "Maude, you wonder much about that truck killing your momma and daddy?"

"All the time. It's the riddle of my existence. Was it an accident? What does that imply about the universe? Was it a spirit killing? Who did it? What happens to me? Did—"

"I'd rather die to oblivion than think about it anymore."

6

WORKING THROUGH
TIME-BOUND MEN

Sunday morning, Sister Marie prayed over the local radio to a Jesus who made her moan as though he were a fertility god from Dahomey. Maude listened and treadled out squares. Lula was at the Baptist Church, probably praying hurricanes down on sinners, begging God to send sexual plagues to the deviants.

"That's not the right kind of black Christian," Partridge said. "That one's African. She just calls her god Jesus."

"I thought so."

Partridge said, "The form of Man coming through time-bound men, oh, Jesus, sweet Je-e-sus. I'm too old for that, now."

"Did you worship him earlier?"

"Too afraid when I was younger. People lost respect for you unless you bound with one man."

Sister Marie called for a hymn and the piano that had been playing jazz behind her preaching segued into the European notes.

"She seems very powerful," Maude said. "I've always liked listening to her."

"Funny she does it on the radio," Partridge said.

"Terry and John and Luke and Betty are coming over after dinner," Maude said. "Luke thought you were dead already."

"I wouldn't do that to you."

Maude thought a corpse staying animated to see its grandchild again seemed romantic. Romantic, she realized, because it was, in the great world, unreal. "I'd be glad we got a chance to talk even if you had died before I came back from Berkeley and I had to talk to your ghost. I'll keep you living on in my mind after you die."

"Don't do that here."

"I'll remember you."

"That's different. I don't want my soul eaten. I don't want a semblance of me walking among the living. I don't want to be trapped inside your mind. I want to go to heaven to see my folks. All the people I cared most about are dead."

Maude tried not to resent that, but did. She pulled out the quilt pieces and began sewing.

"I don't know you enough to care as much about you," Partridge said after Maude sewed two hems. "And your youth makes me old."

Maude almost said, *I need to do something besides wait for you to die.* The radio brought them a white preacher, who hysterically breathed on *'ah*'s at the end of every word in a diatribe against the witches and feminists. And evolutionary socialists, too, Maude thought as she cut the radio off.

Partridge began saying, almost in singsong, "When I was young, I wanted to be a teacher. The men wouldn't let me. When I was young, I miscarried a baby girl and had all men-folk. When I was young, I wanted to ride sidesaddle, but my daddy didn't let me. When I was young, my mother hit me with her eyes, mean eyes worse than a blow." She sat up in the bed. "Maude, I'm still just eighteen inside."

"I know, Grandmother."

"What do you know? You don't take care of children. You don't do a job of work."

"I'm going to take care of you." Maude tried not to be resentful.

"But there's nobody coming after, so who takes care of you?"

Maude finished another seam and tied off the threads in a tailor's knot, guiding the knot down the two threads with a pin. She wondered how the old women who'd sacrificed years of their youth to take care of their aged felt now. *Hi,*

Grandma, we've come to take you to the nursing home. Perhaps, Maude thought, she was morally superior because she would do this without expecting anything. *Other than for whatever estate was left, the house.* She finally said, "I'm going to look into things I could do here, start a small business."

"You mean that? I think you should become a teacher." Partridge sat up in the bed and glared at Maude. "Satisfy my dream."

"I don't like children that much."

"I took you in every summer. You brought me an outsider's view of things, Maude. And you just think you don't like children. You're still a child yourself."

So neither spoke for a while until the company walked in through the door, Luke and Betty, Terry and John, and Lula coming in behind and stopping to fuss in the kitchen. Maude wondered if she'd cleaned the blender and put it up, or if Lula would come out fussing.

"Dishes in the sink," Lula said.

"We took Lula to dinner," Betty said. "We thought she needed a break and you are here now, Maude."

Meaning, *clean up your mess.* Maude got up and washed the dishes, listening through the open door while Betty and Lula fussed over Partridge as though she were a baby, not someone eighteen trapped in an eighty-six-year-old body.

John came to the door and said, "We did good shooting yesterday. We got a deer."

"It's not hunting season yet."

"Luke said I could do anything I wanted on my own property. You even said we could keep a gyrfalcon."

Maude noticed that John still had his Colt auto holstered on his hip. "So, how did you kill the deer?"

"I strangled it and bit out his throat."

Maude flinched. John laughed. Lula said, "Oh, I heard you shot it with your handgun. Did Maude tell you she found a revolver here?"

Luke said, "Partridge's kin-in-law took it off a killer. He died three years later after a still raid."

"Was he shot?" Maude asked.

"No, he died of pneumonia," Luke said.

"He wouldn't have died these days," Maude said. She wondered if magic aided the pneumonia. "How old was he?"

"Thirty-eight."

"The caliber of the gun?" John asked.

"No, the gun is a 32.06 Colt," Maude said.

"I want to see it," John said.

Maude felt like this was a bad idea, but Lula went to the desk and pulled it out. John took it in his hands and said, "A real murder weapon."

Terry flushed as though he'd said something sexual. Luke put his arm around Betty and nodded down at her. Partridge squeezed her eyes closed.

"Aren't you supposed to check to see if a gun is loaded when you pick it up?" Maude asked.

"With a revolver, you can see the bullets in the cylinder, in back of the charge holes," John said, but he swung open the cylinder, spun it, pushed the ejection rod, then snapped the cylinder closed again. "Can you get ammunition for it anymore?"

Lula opened a small drawer above the writing surface and pulled out a change purse with a cross embossed on it. "Here," she said, squeezing the purse to open the spring closure.

"Did you go through everything?" Maude asked.

"I'm kin," Lula said.

John opened the cylinder again and put the bullets in the charge holes. "Doesn't do to have an unloaded gun."

Maude said, "You can put the gun up now." She'd unload it later.

Betty said, "Maude, let's go up to your room for a moment."

Maude stood up before she realized it. Magic, force of personality, whatever, she walked with Betty to the room on the far side of the house.

"You can't fire Lula," Betty said.

"She would have let Partridge starve to death."

"Partridge is dying. You can only slow her down."

Maude looked at Betty's grey eyes and wrinkled skin, wondering why Betty needed Lula in at the death. "I want her to be comfortable. She wants to have some sense of an afterlife."

Betty laughed. "Now?"

"She doesn't want to be made mock of."

"We're going to put her in our family cemetery so she can be comfortable around her people."

"She wants to be buried in the Baptist Church grave-yard."

"I think not. She isn't even a church member. Besides, we've got her daughter buried with our people. But I'm not here to argue that. I'm saying you can't fire Lula."

"Lula is sleeping in the bed with her. She says the cast makes her uncomfortable and she's threatened to take it off. Lula is also putting together quilt squares on a quilt Partridge wants to be buried in. She's planning to live until it's finished."

"If Partridge is clinging to life until we get this quilt made, I think you ought to let me have some of the pieces."

"I want to make the quilt for her."

"She must be in pain."

Maude wondered if she was keeping Partridge alive for her own needs, but saw Betty lean forward, wrinkles deepening on her lips, smiling. Maude said, "I'll take care of the quilt."

"Lula will call me when Partridge is finally dying. We'll be with her."

Maude felt that was ominous. "She'll die in the hospital. It's more comfortable."

"I wonder if California would want you on welfare fraud charges."

Maude didn't speak, but she didn't make any promises, either. She picked up the postcard from Douglas and rubbed it between her index finger and thumb. Betty said, "Luke likes John."

"I think he's a bit nuts. And what is this hunting out of

season? I thought you had to have damage control permits
to take deer that were destroying crops."

"Not on the old farm," Betty said. "It's enough on Wart
Mountain that game wardens would get lost on it."

"He's a computer programmer. Logic circuits should
keep him safe."

"He can imagine living forever as a program. I'd say that
was as magic a thought as any in Bracken County. What's a
logic circuit compared to silicone immortality?"

"So death doesn't bother him. Is that why he can play
with guns and killing?"

"It bothers him that the interfacing and transfer meth-
ods might not be invented in time. But he thinks magic into
machines. He may even be able to do something with the
helicopters."

"But even if a computer thought it was him, he'd be
dead."

"That's why he has to work in Bracken County."

And die here, too. "And then Terry can access him forever."

"Even join him."

Maude wondered what Doug would say to this. "I wonder what would happen if the computer program realized it
was deluded into thinking it was an engineer."

"The county can deal with a computer if it's not aware
of its internal logic. Who among us knows how our brains
process information? Thinking is magic."

Maude said, "What about the logic pools around technical equipment even here?"

"Perhaps people choose world operating systems. I find
the machine one cruel, so I erase it and boot up magic."
Betty smiled, as though pleased that even she could use
computer jargon. "Some people depersonalize the universe into something generated by vibrating strings and
quantum averages. Others say God doesn't play dice with
the universe. Machines don't kill magic. People do."

"You're quite pleased to be on top of the magic."

"Maude, we're offering our system to you. Partridge rejected us. Now you can join us, maybe even change Partridge's mind. You and your father's people weakened her in the first place."

A professor told Maude once that the numbers and laws men found in the universe were the numbers and laws inside their own heads. If that's true, then logic is a smaller projection of the human into the universe than magic. "I'm tempted," Maude said before she realized that she was truly tempted.

"Come by tomorrow and I'll begin teaching you."

"And leave Grandmom alone with Lula?"

"I told Lula not to touch the cast. She listens to me."

When they went back to rejoin the group, John said, "Lula, if your daddy said black snakes were poisonous, then they must be." Maude noticed that Partridge was asleep, or listened with her eyes closed.

Lula pointed at Maude. "She tried to argue with me otherwise and my daddy said it."

"Perhaps in this county, the black snakes are deadly," Maude said.

Lula said, "If I'd had magic . . ." She didn't finish. Maude wondered what Lula would have wished for: a house of her own, a castle, great clothes, youth, a husband, a job that paid money, not food, a bed, and cast-off clothes.

Youth didn't seem possible for Lula. Youth didn't seem to be possible even for Betty. Or maybe Betty preferred age's self-containment to beauty's impersonal lure. Luke pulled out a flask. "It won't make you young, but it will make you feel pretty good."

Lula stared at John. "If I can't help around here, will you take me in? I don't think Maude would take care of me."

"Sure, we'll take you in," John said. Terry looked at him, her eyelids opening and half closing, lips pulled back. Not quite her idea. "Terry may have to take me in, too. If I get tired of being alone in Richmond."

"I think we'd better go now," Terry said. "We don't want to tire Partridge."

Lula stayed in the room with Maude as the others left. The old woman said, "Did Aunt Betty tell you to mind your manners?"

Maude said, "No, she said you wouldn't touch Grannie's cast. I'm glad someone can take you in if this becomes too much for you." She waited by Partridge's bed until Lula went off into the middle bedroom, then she went around through the kitchen to the front of the house and her own bedroom.

As Maude undressed for bed, she wondered if she was being too mean about Lula. As she put on her nightdress, she thought her life in Berkeley seemed like another incarnation, connected to this life only by a car. Tomorrow, I'll go walking, Maude thought as her body jerked around sleep.

When the conjurors become hereditary, Maude's dream told her, then they are a problem. They become cruel people, rapists, think they're a different species and that most folk are their dogs and cattle. Other people killed the conjurors while a woman beside her explained.

The two dream figures, one Maude, the other not-Maude, walked in the dream to see a stone man with Luke's face dying, telling his killers, the real human beings, about tunneling electrons in silicon.

And a woman led her aside to a small house in the country, 750 square feet, built in ovals, room enough for one. Maude wrote down the information on how to get the plans for this house, then went outside to see Lula young again. She felt guilty, not sure why.

When Maude woke up, she realized she'd told Betty she'd come for her first magic lesson, but instead planned to go hiking. A woman in Maude's Berkeley other life once said, "Hey, get into your people's magical systems, learn more about them. Magical systems are metaphors for underlying social truths."

Maude wondered if she preferred her parents accidentally killed or murdered? If they were murdered and she chose the universe of accidents, she couldn't get justice. If they died by accident. . . . The magic universe could trap a child in a map, but Maude felt the universe of physics and engineering principles made a void where questions about morality and the value and meaning of a particular life could hardly be asked, much less answered with any authority.

Maude put on a dress to show respect for Betty.

"I sent the maid out so we won't be interrupted. Here are the cards," Betty told Maude, fanning the tarot on the kitchen table at the old stone house in Taylorsville. "We stole them from the hippies, but they work as well as witch stones."

A circular fluorescent tube lit the table. Maude wondered if that tube was full of foxfire. No, probably even Betty used real electricity. If helicopter rotors could whip magic away, below had to be a metaphysic more real than what Betty could teach her. Suddenly, magic seemed nonsense. "Tarot cards," she said to Betty, "are a structured Rorschach test using Western cultural archetypes."

Betty's fingers, nails glazed with clear polish, laid down the Major Arcana and tapped each one. "Call them archetypes if it helps you."

"They're just cultural impressions of mental patterning systems."

"Perhaps," she said, "you'd rather be walking on Wart Mountain."

Maude saw the Juggler and didn't know if the character was male or female. Trickster archetype. Betty tapped that card twice. *Pay attention.* The card was a surface over something more real.

Then Maude watched as Betty shuffled the cards and laid three down for a quick reading—House of God, the Moon, and the Wheel of Fortune. Maude winced.

"You recognize these . . . archetypes?" Betty asked, drawling out the word *archetypes*.

Maude knew she was the watery thing between God and the Wheel of Fortune. Betty said, "I didn't need cards to tell me you were indecisive."

"I didn't either. If you were really powerful, couldn't you just sweep away my wavering?"

"Even when you reject your entities, magic makes you strong. You're born to it. Focusing techniques make you stronger." Betty got up and turned on a gas burner under a teakettle. "If not for magic and my entities, I'd have been dead years ago. I'm Time's repository."

Feeling irreverent, wanting to break the spell, Maude said, "And your car, too. So you coerce the universe to keep you healthy."

"Coax the universe or bend metal around its rules, subvert it or pollute it—ultimately, what is the difference? The universe of regular rules is doofus sometimes . . . sometimes." Betty stared at the teakettle as if she'd speed the boiling that way. "Oh, Maude, why do you want to throw away being special?"

The water boiled, a shrill whistle in the kettle spout. As Betty poured, Maude got a sudden image of Jake with his claw hand, clicking his hook.

"You think we exploit people like Jake," Betty asked. Maude felt a presence behind Betty, who now seemed an entity's flesh puppet. "What's inhuman doesn't have to be bad," the thing behind Aunt Betty said.

"What's inhuman isn't my kind."

"But you're family," Aunt Betty said.

Maude didnt' want to look at *Le Chariot* or *Le Diable*, felt pulled to *La Roue de Fortune*, like car wheels turning, bearings colliding in their races. There's no God qua God in the tarot deck. Tarot signified a universe of deals. "Magic made

Jake run his hand into a feed auger, tripping on acid,"
Maude said.

"What did Jake need a hand for?" Betty asked. "To inject drugs? He's saved from much grief by not having a dexterous hand."

Maude fled. The Mini-Cooper sputtered and knocked, strained from the elevation and denser magic at the Bracken County fault zone. Over the mountains, Maude went to the Tech library, looking at the hierarchy of information on a computer screen. In Bracken, she thought, the right hemisphere, conscious, perceives gods and deals and timeless patterns. The left half of the human mind, Bracken's unconscious, dreams logic and an end to everything.

A truck, driven by a drunk, alcohol doing medically understood things to his neurons, crashes into no one in particular. An accident. The universe of quantum physics doesn't take life personally.

Maude shuddered and blanked the screen full of neurological references. She closed her eyes and saw Jake's hook reaching from the old school map. Her father's voice from memory said, "My people trust in Jesus but Jesus doesn't pay out in this lifetime, so I went for engineering."

Her mother spoke from another time. "Life, basically, is a nightmare until you learn to control the dream."

7

STONE PATH

Maude went walking on Wart Mountain carrying the old revolver—loaded, unlicensed, no handgun carry permit. She felt like she was tempting evil, up by a creek filled with fish who stared at her and ran through the water. Trout or the endemic rusty-sided sucker or generic scared fish, she didn't know what.

She put a paper plate against the mountain, in a road cut, and fired at it, the gun bouncing in her hand. *I am dangerous.*

Back in Taylorsville, she felt everyone smelled the gunpowder and lead on her hands. She went into the Clerk of Court's office and got the form for a handgun carry permit and then just stared at it.

The black man from Berkeley who wore suits to his group therapy and psychiatric drugging stood across the street. Maude thought she finally had gone crazy, but it was him.

"See you went home," he said. "They missed you out of group, but hippies drift."

"Why did you come here?"

"I'm here to block the way."

"What way?" Maude asked. She realized she'd completely forgotten about the gun for a moment.

"The crazy way. The welfare way. Maybe more than one way I'll be blocking."

"So you're going to tell them I used a fake name in

Berkeley.'' Maude felt Betty brought this man here, or the jadeite pebbles, though thinking that was crazy.

"I followed the stones," he said. "I fight the stones."

Meaning he followed the stones, or he read the address when Susan mailed the package and asked her what she was mailing.

For a crazy minute, Maude thought about gunning him down and removing the evidence, but Betty already knew about her welfare fraud. "Man, your paranoia will be *real* here."

He looked at her, the whites of his eyes yellow and lumpy. "Better attacked by real demons than being crazy," he said. "I am the Reverend Julian Springer." He moved in the fine jerks of the permanently drug-damaged as he turned and walked into the art store at the head of Main Street.

Maude went back to the Austin Mini-Cooper and sat in it with her heels on the dash. The unmagical reality was the man was here, a witness, however insane, to what she was in Berkeley. Her family wouldn't talk about it unless she defied them, but he could. She thought about the implications: no welfare here, no sliding around the system feeling martyred. But then Maude remembered how the insane also drifted. Perhaps this man wouldn't be here long.

He's my conscience. As soon as Maude thought that, she laughed, but stopped very quickly. *Live a long time, Grandma, 'cause after you die, I don't know what I'll do.*

Her legs began to quiver so she pulled them down. So, Maude thought, what's next? She remembered she had to buy groceries. Then she wondered whether the stones from Point Reyes did lead the Reverend Springer to her and what magic would be like to a dignified psychotic in Salvation Army suits.

When Maude brought the groceries home, Lula said, "John has been arrested in Richmond. You've got to go over to see Terry right now."

As Lula put up the groceries, Maude pulled the revolver

out of her purse and cleaned it using the cleaning kit she'd bought before she went shooting. She really wanted to leave it dirty, with spent brass in the charge holes, let the thing corrode. Partridge watched from her bed. Maude asked, "What was he arrested for?"

"He was working at home and some black boys tried to rob him. Justifiable homicide. They were after his guns."

Maude didn't want to know if this happened exactly when she fired the old revolver, then was sure of the connection. Did she make it happen or did its happening draw her to the revolver? She looked over at Partridge and saw that her grandmother looked worse. "Grannie, you worried about John?"

"You're going to go to Richmond, bring him back?"

Lula said from the kitchen, "Your Aunt Betty says you ought to go."

"Why is he coming here? He's got a job in Richmond."

Lula said, "He's got death threats in Richmond."

Partridge said, "Maude, come back quickly."

"You have to wait until after Thanksgiving, Grandma. I want you to meet Douglas."

"A man you picked up in a bar," Lula said.

"Bars in California are different," Maude said. *The Reverend Springer has a big mouth.*

"Where's he gonna sleep?" Lula asked.

Maude almost said, *with me,* but thought she ought not to shock her grandmother. "On the couch in the living room."

The telephone rang, her cousin Terry on the line. Terry said, "I'm sure that John just wanted to frighten the boy."

Maude said, "He shouldn't talk about his guns so much."

"You're not saying he tempted those boys into breaking into our house, are you? I'd like you to bring him back. I can't leave the animals."

"Why can't he drive himself?"

"He's afraid the black boy's family will try to kill him."

"I'm not a bodyguard. I could take care of your animals while you go."

"They'd recognize my car, but they might not know the truck. They know me, but not you. I'll take Lula off your hands if you do this for me," Terry said.

"What is the catch?" Maude asked.

"You've got to get his guns out of the house before they're stolen or the police confiscate them."

"Oh." Nothing magical, just illegal. "I'll need you to pay for my gas and expenses."

"Thanks a lot. I'll drive the truck over and give you directions to the house. It's near the Fan, the old part of Richmond."

Maude looked at Lula and wondered if getting rid of her would be worth bringing John back from Richmond.

By the time Maude got to Richmond in Terry's pickup, John was back in the house, freed, a justifiable mankiller. He came to the door with a gun in his hand and said, "I've got seven death threats on my answering machine."

"When do you have to go to court?"

"I told the police where I'd be. They'll let me know." He went into the house and dragged out a footlocker. Maude knew it contained guns. "They've suspended my federal firearms dealer license until the case is officially cleared, but the assistant commonwealth's attorney said he doubted they'd press charges. I didn't even have to post bail."

"Are we leaving right now?"

"Why stay around here and wait for them to shoot me?"

Six hours in, six hours back. "I'll have been on the road all day."

"We can't stay here. Maybe you'd like to stop at a motel after we're sure we're not followed?"

Maude wondered whether he was so justified to kill. "Let's get on the way then."

She helped him load the footlocker onto the truck bed,

then carried out his boxed clothes and a few pieces of furniture. "What are you doing with the rest of the furniture?"

"I've arranged for it to go into storage. I've sent the computers on ahead. They'll show up at your house tomorrow."

"My house?"

"So we have some advance warning if the boy's family is looking for me."

Maude wanted to leave John on the street and drive away, leave Terry's truck off the road somewhere and hitch to a place she'd never been before. "Don't you have a car here?"

"Yes," he said. "You'll drive it. I'll drive the truck."

Maude was grateful she wouldn't have to share a car with him. She'd seen enough of his type of crazy in Berkeley. Generally, they stayed away from the clinics, but bored you with theories. But then, he had shot a boy who was breaking into his house.

John handed her the keys and a cap, smiled at her, and said, "Can you tuck your hair under this cap? Good luck." He probably had a disguise in his luggage, a wig, a woman's coat.

"The boy's family will forget after a while," Maude said. "According to psych researchers, people only stay angry for about ten years."

"I'd called in sick. That's why I was home. I'm quitting my job. All I really need is the computers."

You did lure the kid in. "Well, let's go then," she said. She put the key in the ignition of his car and noticed that he seemed relieved when it started and didn't blow up. She wondered if the kid he'd shot had been one of his street buddies, the black thieves he knew.

Maude pulled away from the house and found the road across the James that would take her home through the country, with possible variations if she did feel she was followed. She opened the glove compartment to see what maps he might have. A 9-mm Beretta fell out. When Maude pushed it under the seat, she felt another holstered gun there. She was ferrying his handguns. Immediately, she slowed down to 55 and debated whether she should stop and lock the guns in the trunk or leave them where they were and hope she wasn't stopped for anything.

If she pulled over, someone passing might see her with the guns and call the police wondering what was going on. *Guns could make me paranoid.* She decided to simply drive through the rest of the hours, go straight home, call Terry to come pick up this rolling arsenal, and drive away in her Mini-Cooper.

At Amelia Courthouse, she stopped at a gas station and bought three caffeinated sodas. Amelia Courthouse was far enough away from Richmond to be more like the country than northern Virginia. Historical markers told her about the Confederate Cabinet's retreat, about mines. A couple million years earlier, it was a lake with extinct fish, Newark series Triassic rocks.

The continuum punctuated. Maude knew the sodas would make her need to urinate, but she needed the stimulation. As she threw away the bottle she'd drunk by the car, she looked around to see if anyone with a Richmond sticker had followed her here, then told herself not to buy his paranoia.

The next bottle she finished on the ridge road between Halifax and Danville. She dropped the bottle in the back and found a gas station where she refueled the car and used the bathroom. *If the guns get stolen while I'm in here, I don't care,* she said to her mirrored face over the sink.

But no, the guns were still in the car when she drove on to Danville. She tried to turn on the radio and got a PBS station at the end of the dial, faintly playing Gregorian chants. No problems, over the Danville extinct series of lakes and onto the volcanic side of the Bracken allochthon.

Factories replaced the volcanoes. Most of the people were misshaped by potatoes and cornbread; a few dressed better on an average day than any millionaire New Yorker, since money here came harder, so its owners displayed it more aggressively. In a mirror factory, a man went mad and threw blank glass across the floor, then fled weeping. He did this once a year, was fired, then rehired, a cycle in his own particular hell.

Dead, gassy volcanoes ripped from their roots. Whatever the rest of the allochthon was, this side was most evil. Maude felt almost comforted by the guns.

The guns seemed to stretch under the magic, iron swirling around the barrels, reorienting the magnetic direction of each piece. She remembered the smoking muzzle of her own gun.

At her house, she saw the old Essex alongside Terry and John's truck and her Mini-Cooper and thought about driving off into the night. But what was there to go to? She pulled in beside the Essex and went inside.

"Were you followed?" John asked. Terry, Lula, and John sat with Betty and Luke on the formal living room chairs, an interrupted discussion visible in their postures.

"No."

"We can go home now," John said.

Betty asked, "Luke, what do you feel?"

"They didn't follow me," Maude said again. "I was alone on some of the road coming down to Danville."

"Luke?" Betty asked.

Luke said, "She's right. Nobody followed her. Nobody is at the house now. It's our county. He's safe now."

Maude went to the rear bedroom to see Partridge. Her grandmother lay in the center of the bed with her eyes closed. Maude smoothed back Partridge's hair and returned to the living room, where everyone except Lula was standing up, the interrupted conversation completed.

"Thank you, Maude, for driving John's guns," Betty said as though thanking a servant, isolating Maude from the group.

"Anything for kin," she replied.

"Almost anything," Betty said. Luke helped Betty with

her coat. She smoothed her beige gloves and straightened her hat while Luke got into his own coat. John looked at Luke and helped Terry with her coat.

"Gonna be a hard winter," Lula said. Maude noticed she also stood with the others.

"Partridge won't live through it unless she's extraordinarily lucky," Luke said.

Terry said, "I suppose not."

"Partridge won't leave much of an estate," Betty said. "Maude will have to find work."

"She won't die tonight," Luke said, pulling out the Essex's keys. The four of them murmured good-byes and left Maude and Lula standing in the room.

Maude knew some people sat nights with their sick kin to keep away excessively old people like Aunt Betty and Uncle Luke. The sitters never explained why they drove away wrinkled old people who'd never been, in living memory, young, but the feeling was that those old people sucked souls. Lula muttered and went to Partridge's room, Maude following. Lula, like a spoiled dog, climbed into the bed with Partridge.

"You have your own bed," Maude said.

Lula said, "What are you going to do, drag me out?"

"If you hurt her, I will."

Partridge said, "Oh, please don't fuss. Country people are used to sleeping together."

Maude wondered. She felt a hatred for Lula that scared her. It seemed to have a personality of its own. "Don't hurt her arm, Lula." Could she learn magic from Betty and turn it against Betty's creature? The hate stirred around her spine.

Maude closed her eyes. She tried to pity the homeless woman who went from dying cousins to childbearing nieces to sick distant kin, always locked in a mind that had to numb itself or recognize how wretched her life was. In America an old woman could rot alone, her flesh putrefying, joining her shit while she was still alive. Tending the old was difficult, but a challenge to character rather than intellect.

The hate found a reason in Maude's attempt to kill it. Maude knew why Lula wanted to get rid of her—job competition.

On Saturday, Maude drove to Terry's house and saw the jack-o'-lantern grinning from the porch. In the yard, Terry wore whipcord pants, a pouch on a belt, and a heavy linen shirt. She held Belle, the redtail, on her gauntlet. John came out, dressed in camouflage, with an assault rifle and backpack over his shoulder.

Belle looked indifferent, moving slightly on the glove. Maude saw the long cord with the small swivel at one end in Terry's other hand. Terry said, "We're going to work her on the line."

"You're going to scare the hawk if you shoot that gun," Maude said to John.

"She needs to get accustomed to gunfire," Terry said.

Maude didn't say anything, but followed them through the field on Wart Mountain's shoulder. The hawk spread her wings slightly and crouched to keep her balance. John went ahead of them and set up a target at the end of the field. Maude saw that he'd at least put it against a hill.

He fired the gun in two bursts. The hawk flew up against the leash, then fluttered down, wings spread like a chicken about to be killed.

"I've rigged it to almost fire auto," John said, smiling at Maude.

Behind the hill, another gun fired, then further away, yet another gun. Guns talk to guns.

"Why don't you practice down at Betty's so your neighbors won't know you've got such guns?" Maude said.

"We want our neighbors to know," John said.

Maude wanted to say *wasn't that what got a boy killed in Richmond,* but didn't. Terry went to the hawk and wound the leash in her hand. The hawk climbed back on the gauntlet and began smoothing her feathers.

"Do you want to shoot?" John asked. He pulled another clip out of the backpack.

Maude was tempted. As she took the gun, she felt a magic jolt come from him. Whether he believed in magic or not, it was in him. Maude looked at Terry and saw an aura around her that excluded the hawk. Whatever their conscious selves believed, their underselves were deep in magic. Maude turned away from them both and looked at the target. John came up and pulled off the safety, then said, "Fire."

She shot the gun a bullet at a time, then listened for the people talking gun back at her with their own weapons.

"It's like dogs barking," Terry said, soothing the hawk, which had stayed on her glove this time.

"Guns to mark territories," Maude said. She returned the assault rifle to John. They walked back through the field, following Terry, to a mowed place with a couple of cages containing small domestic rabbits. The hawk looked at the animals while John ran parachute cord through a ring on top of the cage, then down to the bottom of the door. He tied the cord to the door, then picked up the other end and walked backward until the cord tightened.

The redtail bounced on Terry's glove. John pulled the cage door open and chucked a rock at the rabbit inside. The hawk pounced on the rabbit and squeezed. Terry ran up and covered the rabbit's body with her glove. The hawk spread its wings and ate the rabbit's brain, then stepped back on the glove to eat the chicken neck Terry pulled out of her game pouch. The rabbit disappeared.

"So you trick them," Maude said.

"Hawks aren't good at object consistency," Terry answered. The pouch at her waist was swollen, full of rabbit, and she had blood on the linen tunic. Maude wondered why linen, why white.

They walked back to the house. Terry fed Belle another mouse and reattached her to the block while she was distracted. She coiled the leash in her hand. Maude saw that it was made of extremely fine leather cords braided round and oiled to a dark brown.

"Where did you get the hawk gear?"

"Some of it in Japan. They hunt goshawks, not falcons, and I figured redtails were a more predaceous bird than most Eurasian buteos, more like a gos, though really a Cooper's hawk is even more like a gos, being an accipiter, but Coos are a bit crazy."

Maude felt outclassed. She'd never traveled beyond a day into Canada. "Oh."

"I was a kid, then, just buying stuff I didn't know I'd ever be able to use. We taught English there. Some old samurai lady showed us her household relics. Not all Japanese like high tech and Sony."

Maude felt money behind her cousin, an upbringing in a place where her mind was nourished. Terry was as predaceous and as innocent as her hawk, taking privileges without questioning them, being a witch without acknowledging magic. *Maybe*, Maude reminded herself, *my envy finds excuses.*

Terry served a cassoulet, with real goose and white beans, and they drank red wine until Maude dropped her edginess.

Then she wondered if they felt sorry for her. "I've got to get back. Lula won't use the blender."

"I expect she didn't like having you come in and criticize her. After all, she'd been taking care of Partridge for over a year."

"But she was starving Partridge," Maude said.

"Do you really know that? Did you take your grandmother to a doctor?"

"They told me when I took her in to have her arm set."

"Oh, Betty didn't tell me," Terry said. Maude wondered if Terry believed her. John was cleaning his rifle and seemed oblivious. Women's talk, not something he'd hear.

"It's true enough."

"Betty trusts Lula."

Maude wondered if she should say she didn't trust Betty, but then these people, as much as magic enhanced them, didn't confess to believe in witches, spells, or soul suckers, but instead talked about quaint folklore. "I think Lula sucks up to Betty."

"If Partridge wants, she could fire Lula."

"I don't think Partridge wants to be cruel. Lula doesn't have any other sick kin now, except the people who asked her to leave." Maude remembered living with friends in California, before she got welfare. She wondered if she'd seemed as strident, as defensively opinionated.

"Betty likes her," Terry said, as though that was enough.

While shopping, Maude saw the Reverend Springer again. He smiled at her and said, "An angel made a face in my pointing finger and told me to paint."

"You look happy." *Do I think he's a witch, too?*

"I fit here," he said.

8

DIFFERENT EYES, DIFFERENT IMPROBABILITIES

Doug broke Maude's isolation. When his plane landed, she felt as though she'd gained an ally, an engineer like her father. She'd forgotten how much magic enchanted him.

He came out of the gate with a carry-on bag and a light coat. Maude also had forgotten exactly how tall he was. He'd gotten puffy around the waist since she'd seen him last, as though he'd been too busy to run and lift weights. "Hi," he said, kissing her with a gin-flavored mouth. He spoke more like a Yankee than she'd remembered, too.

"I've got my car."

"The Mini-Cooper? Amazing that you've kept it going so long. I've brought my backpack and a winter tent."

"You may have to sleep out in the yard. Lula won't approve of you being in bed with me."

"You said you had a couch."

"Actually, we've got a spare bedroom. Lula's sleeping with my grandmother." The cast was off, but the arm was still tender. Maude wondered if Partridge would die with a crippled arm.

"You look worried. I could rent a room. You do have motels in your county, don't you?" He looked around and found the stairs to Baggage Claim. The carousel eventually brought around a large canvas sack. Douglas pulled the sack off the conveyor and unzipped it, checking to see if the backpack had come through without damage.

"You've braced between the frame," Maude said, seeing wood pieces at right angles to the aluminum frame.

"I'd like to get a hardshell shipping box, but . . ." Doug folded the canvas and tied it on to the backpack, then swung the pack onto his back.

Maude realized a backpacking engineer was going to be weird for Bracken County.

"If you don't have a campstove, we ought to stop at an outing shop and buy one."

Maude almost said she didn't. Going by Blacksburg would delay getting back to Bracken County. Douglas as theory seemed great. Douglas among the real witches began to seem awkward. "I've always had one. Sometimes, when I was in Berkeley, I needed to get away."

"I've been thinking about getting away from Berkeley."

"You're very away from Berkeley now."

"I've heard about Floyd County."

"The counterculture back to the landers, yeah."

"So, let's spend a few days with backpacks on. Your sleeping bag zippered into mine, and all that."

Maude wondered if she'd dare leave Partridge alone with Lula. For a few days, Partridge could live off milk and potato water. "I'll have to see if I can leave my grandmother."

"We can hire someone to take care of her."

"I can't ask you to do that. Besides, there is a woman helping now, only she's set in her ways. My grandmother can't eat solid food, but Lula won't use the blender." Maude wondered if she'd sound like a crank if she complained more. Let him meet Lula.

"You could blend the food, freeze it, and have Lula heat it up in a microwave."

"We don't have a microwave," Maude said.

They drove back to Bracken County by the Blue Ridge Parkway. Douglas pointed out all the trail heads and crossings. Maude wondered if he'd feel anything when they crossed into the Blue Ridge magic fringe.

When they crossed it, he said, "I can't believe I'm here."
Then he was quiet for several miles.

"Do you want to stop at Lover's Leap?"

"Overlook? Sure."

"You tired?"

"Some. I've always wanted to see the East."

"Hard to do from here. It's bigger than California."

"And older," he said as they pulled into the overlook.
He got out and stared for almost a minute, his legs strad-
dled, both hands on the overlook wall. Maude liked the
mountains better in winter when the rocks showed. She
wondered if he did also.

"All the leaves are gone," he said. "I know that's the way
it's supposed to be, but it feels wrong."

"California greening up in the winter always felt wrong
to me," Maude said. She wondered if his sense of wrong-
ness came simply from the bare trees.

"There are some pines, hemlocks. And rhododendron.
We've got rhododendron out west."

"Not like here," Maude said.

"And it's all a grey brown, not a yellow brown."

"Cold got it, not drought. When I saw so many grassy
hills in California, I thought they'd been overgrazed,"
Maude said.

Douglas didn't answer, but returned to the car. Maude
got back in the driver's seat and looked over at him. He
looked cold.

She said, "I've always wanted to see this place through
alien eyes. A Californian will do."

"Even the air is different."

"Sometimes, I think even the physics could be different."

He looked over at her and said, "Do you really believe
that."

"Why not?"

"The same laws work everywhere."

"And the universe doesn't cut deals."

He laughed, but then said, "Perhaps we don't understand all the connections."

Maude said, "How would you prove magic?"

"Science is a negative cutout of the universe, a compendium of what we know it isn't and some theories we haven't disproved about what it is. And engineering uses things that consistently work for nerds and anyone who punches the right buttons. Sometimes, I'd prefer a system that forced people to make personal deals."

"Oh," Maude said. "They said different things about science in high school. And from what you were saying in the bar when we met, I thought you believed in magic."

"I bet your school taught you to think science was an absolute system. Science types want lay people to know enough to appreciate science, and appreciate enough to give money. Magic? I'd like to believe, that's all."

"I'd like not to believe," Maude said.

"So, what is this magic you believe in? Is it consistent? Does it follow rules? Can the technique be taught?"

"It's personal relationships with the universe. Everyone is a puppet of an entity, maybe more than one entity, and they think they're at least making deals, at best, commanding the entities."

"You'd have to prove to me that this car, say, works for you, but wouldn't work for me."

"A horse might."

"But a horse does have a personality."

"And a car doesn't?" She looked at him.

He said, "Pull over and let me drive. You're looking over at me too much."

She found a place to pull over and let him have the wheel. He turned the key in the ignition and nothing happened.

"Shit," he said.

"Maybe I should drive."

"So, what's the trick? Or did it coincidentally break a timing belt while we were talking about it?"

"You want to believe in magic, don't you?" Maude said. "Let me try." They traded places and the car started just fine.

He said, "This isn't magic, it's coincidence. What happens is that people hate believing in an arbitrary universe. They take a coincidence like that and imagine the car intended to run for you and not for me."

"Want to try again?" Maude asked.

He laughed. "You know your car better than I do."

She said, "I'm glad you're here. I was beginning to think the universe could cut deals with people."

"But that would make it even more random, statistically."

"Huh?"

"Yeah, an observer who didn't know about the deals would find the universe to be quite chaotic."

Maude thought about that and said, "But if you knew the people, what happened would be obvious?"

"In a magic universe, would everyone have magic powers?" he asked.

"Of course not," Maude said. "If magic worked for everyone, it would just be physics."

He said, "I've got to think about that for a bit."

"Remember, magic has intentions of its own. Lots of different powers, some in conflict with others."

"Can you let me try the car again?"

"No, I know the road better than you do."

He asked, "Do you really believe what you've been telling me? We're beyond flirting in a Berkeley bar now."

She said, "Can you disprove it?"

"Let me try to drive the car again."

Maude pulled over and traded places with him again. The car engine started. The car ran for about a hundred yards and died. Douglas coasted off to a convenient shoulder. The ignition worked, but the car engine wouldn't feed gas.

"If it had done that on the mountain, we couldn't have pulled off so easily," Maude said.

"But we might have coasted farther," Douglas said. "What happened now?"

"Vapor lock is the engineering explanation," Maude said, "but if the car starts again without cooling off completely, I'd say the witches were trying to get your attention."

"Vapor lock. You ought to use higher octane gas."

"I use Aunt Betty's gas treatment."

"Like STP? Added octane."

"Let me try it," Maude said. But this time, the car didn't start. "It is vapor locked. You say a higher octane gas will help?"

"In an old car, I'd say so."

Maude got out and raised the hood so the car would cool faster. Doug stayed in the car for a while, then got out himself and began pottering around the roadside cut. He found a fairystone, one of the perfect crosses that was so rare.

"We're right on the faultline," Maude said when he showed it to her. "Bracken County has its own microplate. It wasn't originally part of North America."

"Geology affects people," he said.

"Does geology have a personality?"

"Different rocks grow different plants. Elevation affects climate, drainage. Those things affect people."

"Nothing personal about it," Maude said, smiling.

He said, "I reserved judgment on magic, myself, but the concept does fascinate me. But do you believe in magic?"

"When I was in California, you thought I shouldn't be getting crazy welfare. Are you beginning to wonder?"

"No. If you learned these stories as a child and haven't had real training in science and technology, you could believe them without being crazy. Consider religions. They're intellectually nutty, but no one gets committed for believing in Jesus."

"You found a perfect fairystone in a roadside cut where

hundreds of people have been looking for fairystones. The normal crystal formation is an X."

"High odds don't imply intervention."

"You want to play with magic, though. That's what intrigued you about me. That's what took you to Susan after I left."

He closed his hand on the fairystone. "I'm not your husband."

"She sent me the jadeite stones. She's just a wannabe witch. The stones have more personality than she does."

"Look, you didn't have to leave California."

"I did too. Nobody was taking decent care of my grandmother." Maude got back in the car. The engine started; the gas kept feeding. Douglas sat down in the passenger side, his hand still gripping the fairystone.

"I'm sorry," he said. He looked down at his fist and said, "The stone seems to be squirming."

"It wasn't really a cross, but rather another X," Maude said. By the time they got to the house in Kobold, the two staurolite crystals making the cross weren't at right angles to each other.

"I remember when it was a perfect cross," Douglas said.

"Perhaps the magic wants your attention," Maude said.

"We just saw what we wanted to see."

"How do scientists and engineers guard against that?" Maude asked.

"The results have to be the same regardless of who does the experiment. And bridges have to stay up regardless of the engineer's personal charms."

Neither of them said anything more until Maude pulled into the driveway at her grandmother's house. Doug opened his hand and showed Maude the fairystone. It still wasn't perfect. Lula opened the door and said, "You didn't come straight back."

"We had car problems," Maude said.

"And you stopped to look for fairystones," Lula said, seeing the one in Douglas's hand.

"This is Douglas's vacation," Maude replied.

"You've got a grandmother to think about," Lula said.

Douglas picked up his backpack and his carry-on bag, saying, "I asked her to let me drive."

"And the car vapor-locked," Maude added.

Lula looked at them. Doug smiled at Lula and said, "I didn't know the car didn't like men."

"I don't like men myself, but if you're polite, I won't mind having you around."

Maude said, "He can sleep in the middle bedroom."

"You must have known each other a while in California."

"I met her in a bar. She said she lived in a wannabe magicians' commune and I was intrigued."

"Let's pretend magic isn't real," Maude said.

Lula started, "Maude's a don't-wannabe witch. If I had her chances . . ."

"The magic's real. But the magic's mean," Maude said.

"She's afraid of it."

"Something happened to the fairystone," Doug said. "As I don't think *I'm* crazy, I'll consider that this might be a pocket universe. Maybe the iron ore and quartz focuses mental energies."

"How'd you know about the quartz?" Lula asked.

"I read about it in a Virginia trail guide. I plan to take Maude camping with me while I'm visiting."

Maude realized if she and Doug wanted a sex life, they would have to have it in the woods. "How's Partridge?" she asked.

"Holding up," Lula said.

Doug held the door for both of them. Lula nodded at Maude as if her man was better than expected for a Californian. "Here's your room," Maude said in the middle bedroom. Doug stopped to lay down his bags while the two women went through to Partridge's room.

Partridge sat up in the bed. She looked at Doug silently for a moment, then said, "Turn around, but to the right."

He did. Maude wondered if he was as embarrassed displaying himself as she was watching. He came around posed like a sculpture, one hip cocked.

Partridge said, "You're a fine figure of a man." Maude wondered if Partridge heard too much praise as a young woman and revenged herself on dead men by ogling young males.

Douglas said, "If you need, I'd be glad to hire additional help. Maude said Lula alone is a trifle burdened by all your care."

Maude wondered where he picked up his Southern phraseology.

Lula said, "If you buy us a microwave, I can heat up what Maude fixes before she goes off with you." Lula seemed sly.

Douglas and Partridge laughed. Douglas said, "If you can't work a blender, why a microwave?"

"Don't have to clean it," Maude said.

"Don't cut when you clean it," Lula said. "Blenders are mean, all those blades and pieces to lose."

Maude almost warned Douglas that Lula was trying to see what she could get out of him. Instead, she said, "We can't take long trips because I'm not in shape, so we'll see how it goes." She didn't want to leave Partridge with Lula for very long.

"Where can I get a microwave oven in this county?" Douglas asked.

"Not here," Lula said. "You have to bring it in from the outside."

"You can just heat my food on the stove," Partridge said. "Such a fuss, you make me feel guilty for being old."

Lula, her eyes half closed and lips pulled back, turned toward Partridge.

Douglas said, "Let me get settled in." He walked away and shut the door between the two rooms.

Lula told Partridge, "Maude's brought in an engineer who's fascinated with magic."

Partridge said, "I don't know what's worse, people who

use magic without admitting it or people who are sentimental about magic without understanding it.''

Maude thought Douglas would understand magic better if he met some of its victims, so she took him to the Boogey Parlor. The most light was over the pool table where three men, one in bib overalls, shot pool. Jake stood at the bar, clicking his hook to "Faster Horses, Younger Women, and More Money" playing on the jukebox. He looked around when Maude said "Hi, Jake," and frowned when he saw she was with another man.

"Oh, Maude. Imported or local?" Jake asked.

Doug said, "What?"

"Must be imported, because I don't remember him."

"Hi, I'm Douglas Sanderheim. I'm here from Berkeley on vacation."

"Strange place for a vacation," Jake said. "You're here because of Maude."

"She told me about the place. Some."

Jake clicked his hook once, sharply, as if the noise would make both of them go away. Maude put her hand on Doug's arm and said to Jake, "He's fascinated by magic."

All the men at the bar went silent, heads tilted toward Jake. Their hands holding beer and fried foods slowed, then they drank or chewed as quietly as they could, listening. Jake said, "Yeah, magic does fascinate, doesn't it? You get all fascinated into thinking you can walk on air, Douglas, my man. And crazy people like it here too, because boogeys really are after them."

Doug looked around the bar and said, "I'm just curious."

"So was my kid," a man murmured from the end of the bar.

"A fairystone bent for him," Maude said. "Maybe. Doug thinks maybe he just saw what he wanted to see."

"Oh, if only I could see what I want to see." Jake looked at his hooks. "So the stone piqued your curiosity?" He whis-

tled, then said, "Here, boy." He whistled again, waving his
arms. "Have we got your attention now, Mr. Douglas from
Berkeley?"

Maude didn't explain that she'd been better in bed with
Doug than she suspected was naturally possible. Doug said,
"Maude wanted me to see this bar. Why?"

"We're the magic victims," Jake said. "We lost kids to
unseemly curiosity, hands to feed augers we were sure were
off, eyes to exploding receivers in brand-new rifles. We get
carpel tunnel syndrome after working in a factory for half a
day. Our wives sew tiny stitches into the web between the
thumb and pointing finger when they try to mend our
clothes." He spread his good hand and pointed to the web
with his hooks. "Unlucky bastards, us."

"Perhaps you just blame the magic for natural enough
failings," Doug said. "Maude, I'd just as soon have pizza.
Isn't there a place in town?"

Back in the car, Maude said, "Why is an engineer so fascinated with magic? My father became an engineer because
he hated it." She'd been reluctant to talk about her father's
profession before. Men resented being like their women's
fathers.

"I like the idea of a personal relationship with the universe. The principles I work with work even for people who
don't understand them. I hate empowering the weak."

Maude almost said her dad loved making water safe. *No
daddy comparisons wanted, thanks.* She said, "But you didn't
make that stone realign itself."

"If there's magic, perhaps it was trying to prove it really
existed. *You* weren't going to enlighten me."

"You'd have thought I was crazy if I told you how much I
did believe in it. And fear it."

"Can't you work some magic?"

"I suspect I can slow time. My great aunt wants me to
learn more." Maude wondered if her fears of the magic
were irrational. She drove to the pizza place, and when they
went in, she felt the safety of an ordered place without

magic. The Italians took their orders for a small pizza. Two kids played Donkey Kong.

"I've seen engineers become flat personalities, stereotypes," Doug said. "I wondered if working in fields that were so rule-dominated made people less interesting characters."

"I've wondered if character didn't come from the evil in people. If life is better, people aren't so competitive."

"That machine is too noisy."

"More peaceful," Maude said. "No jangling entities."

The waiter brought their pizza. Doug said, "It looks like real Italian pizza."

"It should be. They're real Italians."

Doug lifted a slice and tasted it. He pulled away a bite, opened his lips, and breathed in heavily. "Hot," he said. "It *is* real pizza."

The waiter said, "American style, actually."

Doug asked, "Do you have magic in Italy?"

"I wouldn't know," the waiter said as he started back to the stainless steel pizza oven. "My father got me out of Palermo before I could talk."

The Donkey Kong machine bonged steadily. One of the boys playing it came over to their table and said, "My daddy is so happy about machines, he restored an old 1951 third-generation McCormick combine."

Doug didn't say anything.

"So, with the combines we lose some beauty," Maude said.

"No reapers singing as they scythe the grain," Doug mused. "No harvest home celebrations."

"My daddy used to scythe the grain and he didn't say nothing about no singing," the boy said. He went to the counter for more quarters and returned to the Donkey Kong game.

"Some computer programmer invented that. The programming took more work than most business programs. What a waste, to steal quarters from kids," Doug said. "Do you think a man could be happier restoring combines than he'd be working with his body in unpolluted countryside?''

"Yes," Maude said.

Doug ate the pizza and then got up to pay for it. Maude decided she'd call Terry and see about getting them all together. She was curious how Terry would react to Doug's talk about magic.

John came to the door carrying a semiautomatic pistol in his left hand. The porch light bouncing off his glasses made him seem blind. His lower lip looked glossy. Terry came up behind him and said, "We saw a Cadillac with a Richmond sticker yesterday. John's worried."

Maude asked, "Have you heard from the court?" Doug looked at the gun and then at John. The gun reflected a distortion of their faces in its stainless steel as John holstered it. John's face looked both babyish and waxy.

"Come in," John said.

Doug asked, "Why are you so afraid of people from Richmond?"

"I shot someone in Richmond."

"He broke into our house there," Terry added.

"Trying to steal this," John said, touching the holstered gun with his fingertips. "A responsible gun owner cannot allow thieves to put his guns in the criminal system."

Doug didn't say anything and didn't move. Terry said, "Do come on in."

Doug stepped through the door, saying, "So you're Maude's kinswoman?"

"Distantly," Terry said. They all followed her to the kitchen, where she pulled a casserole dish out of the oven. Crayfish, whole three- and four-inch-long trouts curled tail to nose, and scallops lay half submersed, half browned, in a cream sauce. Terry said, "The scallops we bought. The crayfish and trout are local."

"Who fishes?" Doug asked.

"We've got our own wild trout stream," Terry said. "We

netted everything this afternoon so they'd be fresh." She put rice from another pot into bowls, then ladled at least a trout and a couple of crayfish into each bowl.

Maude knew the game warden would cite them for the trout if the stream wasn't protected by the Wart Mountain magic. Doug seemed uneasy about the trout. He said thanks when Terry handed him his bowl and then sat down by Maude on the opposite side of the table from John.

"Doug, would you want to come shooting with me?" John asked. "If you're not one of those California nuts who think all guns should be banned." He smiled.

"Isn't it too dark tonight?" Doug asked.

"This weekend," John said.

"We need another deer," Terry added.

"I'll think about it. Could you tell me where you keep your plates? I'd like something for the trout bones."

Terry went to the cupboard and brought Doug a plate. He pulled the trout out onto it and began separating the tiny bits of meat from threadlike bones.

John repeated, "We need another deer. Two guns are better than one."

"I'm not much of one for hunting."

"Well, if you get a deer in front of you driving home, hit it for us," John said. "Call me and I'll come finish it off."

Doug didn't reply. Maude looked at Terry and saw she was beaming at John. *Let's change the subject,* Maude thought, then she asked Terry, "How's your hawk?" Maude realized she could have changed the subject further yet, but better to veer off rather than jump.

John answered, "She's just a buteo, not very glamorous."

"We think we're going to get a gyrfalcon."

Doug said, "You can't get a gyrfalcon. They're a protected species."

Maude almost told him, *so are five-inch brook trout.* She wondered if Doug was going to turn her into the village explainer. He didn't seem all that willing to take her word for things.

John said, "Hunting and guns are a way of life here, Doug. Get Maude to show you her gun when you get back to the house."

"Do you have a gun?"

"We inherited one," Maude told him.

"I've never been comfortable around them."

"Mine saved who knows how many people from being robbed or raped at gunpoint," John said.

After finishing dinner and loading the dishwasher, they all went walking in the dark up to the mews. The redtail sat on her block asleep until the dogs barked. She opened her eyes and stared at them as though thoroughly disgusted, then hunched her head down again and raised her lower eyelid over her yellow irises.

John said, "They don't close the upper lid down; they raise the lower lid." He unsnapped the hawk's leash.

Doug said, "She was asleep until we disturbed her. Let's leave her alone." John snapped the leash back to the perch as a car pulled up to the house. They walked back and saw Aunt Betty's Essex parked beside Maude's Mini-Cooper.

Doug said, "An Essex? And still running. I'm impressed."

In the living room, Aunt Betty stood with her back to the door, wearing a long dark grey silk dress with tiny buttons running down the back. When she turned, Maude saw Betty's bead purse, beads on cord knitted into rose patterns. Her silk dress had cartridge pleats across the bodice. Betty looked at Doug and said, "So you found a fairystone that wouldn't hold its shape?"

Doug didn't ask how Betty knew. "I thought so, but Maude wonders if I was just seeing what I expected to see." Doug stayed on his feet even after John and Terry sat down. John's face looked blank. Terry's looked like a photograph, the strong cheekbones tilted slightly, her head cocked as though she was listening to something. Betty looked at John and frowned slightly. John sucked his lower lip and stood up, took off his holster and gun, then put them in a closet, locked the closet, and came to sit back down again. He seemed to be sleepwalking. Betty looked over at him and smiled.

Maude almost sat down herself, but didn't.

Aunt Betty said, "Doug, I'd appreciate it if you took Maude away for a few days. I'd recommend the Appalachian Trail above Roanoke. I'll make sure to look in on Partridge and Lula."

Maude wanted to protest, but couldn't speak. Terry and John seemed frozen. Betty said, "I've got to talk to them. John is a very dear boy, but a trifle overly trusting of guns. I'm afraid he's going to have trouble for his shooting."

Doug said, "Perhaps he deserves it."

Maude touched his arm and said, "Let's go. She wants to talk to them."

"But I also wanted to meet your Douglas," Betty said. She inclined her head. "So you're an engineer who likes sophistication, the arts. I must show you my prints some-day."

"Yes, ma'am," Doug said. "And you did say the fairy-stone changed its shape for me?"

"Yes, Doug, I said that, but then perhaps I'm a supersti-tious old woman."

"And perhaps not. Well, good-bye then," Doug said, nodding his head. As he and Maude passed the Essex out-side, he stopped and touched the car's hood. His hand lay spread and moving slightly on the Essex for a moment. "Ex-cept for the paint, it's in beautiful shape."

"Paint?"

"It's wrinkled. Maybe a bad restoration job."

"Or maybe it's wrinkled because it's so old," Maude said.

"It didn't feel like the original paint," Doug said. "Your Aunt Betty's some old lady."

"She's some witch." Maude wondered if her car would start or if the Essex had drained it. The battery seemed a trifle weak, but after a few tries, she got steady firing.

"I'd want my witches to be like her," Doug said. "Ordering people with her eyeballs. Did you see how John put the gun away? Who buttons her up?''

"What?" Maude said.

"The dress buttoned up the back with about a hundred buttons. Also, she had button-top shoes.''

"She has a maid she and Luke got out of an insane asylum in the tidewater.''

"And a humanitarian, too.''

"Only a desperate woman would be willing to fool with that many buttons. Aunt Betty's offered to teach me magic. If I thought it was just superstition, I might take her up on it so I could satisfy your curiosity by telling you what I learn.''

"If magic is real, you must take her up on it.''

Maude wondered what he'd think if she told him that one of the calls was for her to bring Bracken County the head of an engineer. "Unfortunately, I know magic is real.''

"Maybe, maybe not. But your cousin's husband is truly scary.''

"We agree on that, Doug, for sure.''

9

OTHER PEOPLE'S DEATHS

On the winter trail, only other people's boot tracks and litter broke into the experience. Maude said to Doug, "In the summer, the trail is one long party, gossiping about record-breaking through-hikers."

"The Pacific Crest Trail isn't much different," he said.

Through-hikers walk months between Georgia and Maine. Culture shocks hit the trail. Women from northern cities where there's no stigma against drinking in a bar find redneck bars in Georgia, then get followed back to their campsites and raped. People too poor to walk weeks on end rob hikers carrying $90 worth of freeze-dried food but only enough money to gas a car left a hundred miles uptrail. The Great Smokey black bears hop up and down in the trail to bluff hikers into dropping their packs. Lesbian activists run into backwood macho recluses. Men who don't like women hiking with dogs expose their bear knives in the shelters and the women come back hiking with .38 Specials like a third of the trail hikers, illegal in some of the trail states, but . . .

Maude said, "There's a mystique about the trail. Wilderness as cottage industry."

Maude had never hiked the trail in the summer, since the first time. She categorized it with the same set of memories as urban parties where she didn't know anyone—not a natural experience at all. "We won't need the tent," she told Doug as they packed.

"I'll pack it," he said, meaning, *it's for private sex.* "So what about Shenandoah National Park?"

Maude said, "It's a bit far. I know a place where the shelter's only two miles away from the parking lot. And in the other direction, we've got four-thousand-foot peaks."

"Foothills."

"Two-thousand to three-thousand-foot climbs."

"So, tell me which way to go," he said. Maude gave him the keys and hoped that the car would work for him. They drove at her direction up the mountain. Doug didn't speak much, then said as they turned onto the Blue Ridge Parkway, "It's different here."

"On-the-mountain people aren't so trusting of charisma and charm," Maude said. "Only magic left is the Sight, and that's more a problem than not."

"The land's been groomed," he said.

"For the tourists."

He didn't say anything for another twenty miles. Maude felt the relationship ebb as though it was a downhill curve on the parkway. "We're headed for the Religious Range, the Priest, the Cardinal."

He looked over at her. "Why Catholic?"

"I dunno." She felt that the names she'd never speculated about before were intrusions now. Ironic names, not sincere. "Are you bored here?"

He said, "Not at all bored, studying a new place, new realities."

Bored with me, though, Maude thought. Her reservations about magic probably seemed, if not paranoid, rigid and disspirited. A fairystone waving its crystal arms at him was charming. Her suspicions weren't. He thought he knew what magic was. His world was metal and silicon, bent to man's imagination. He thought charms would work the same way. She asked, "Did you and John get a chance to talk tech?"

"I'm not interested in guns," he said.

"Computers?"

"He's either an operator or a programmer. I'm an engineer. And he's nuts."

Maude said, "We've agreed on that already."

"If you lived where magic did work, you'd be silly not to learn how to work it."

"Would you like magic to bind you? Would you like to have something talking through you the way the guns talk through John?"

"Be nice if someone could magically keep his guns from shooting." Doug seemed to think magic was a tool, not a relationship.

"His guns found him. People aren't the only personalities in a magical system."

"What about your gun?"

The Colt inserted its image into her mind then. She tried to imagine anything else, but could smell the iron of it. "I should get rid of it when we get back."

"Isn't it a collector's item, though?"

"Maybe," she said, wondering how many of those Colts had been made. *Be Southern, don't argue, change the subject,* she thought. "What do you want to do when we get to the trail?"

"If it looks like rain, let's go to the closest shelter, then hike the other direction tomorrow."

"Okay." They returned to silence.

Several hours down the road, they parked the car at the parking lot where the Appalachian Trail crossed the road. Doug got out and looked in both directions. "Strange to think that little path goes from Georgia to Maine."

Maude got both packs out and said, "You want to leave the tent here? I don't think we're going to have to worry about privacy."

"Let's go uphill," he said.

"I haven't carried a pack since California," she said. He turned around and looked at her. Maude hoisted her pack and hunched her shoulders to raise it. She tightened the hipband, lowered her shoulders, and tightened the shoulder straps. He came over and put on his own pack, standing close enough to radiate body heat. Maude wondered if he wished he hadn't come here. The tent was still with him.

"Okay, so we take it easy this trip," he said.

They went down the trail to the closest shelter. People had deserted this valley but left their signs—cabin foundations, rock walls. Doug finally said, "Did they abandon this place or were they evicted?"

"People were evicted from the Shenandoah National Park, but I don't know about here."

"Agonal walls," he said.

"What?"

"Dying cul-de-sacs of pioneer enthusiasm," he said.

"Agonal?"

"Death agonies."

"Maybe their magic ate them," she said.

"Or they got caught between the old ways and technology," he said.

"Probably these people were bought out," Maude said.

"No, I feel something."

Maude didn't want to feel something. Humans lost here. She said, "I wonder if they took their graves with them." She let herself contact a bitterness worn vague by the years and hikers. So Doug could feel something. Maybe he could develop direct connections with entities and wouldn't be forced to serve a witch or adopt a world view rigid enough to hobble magic.

The path kept crossing and recrossing a small creek. Doug didn't say anything further, just walked ahead of her, the tent strapped to the bottom of his pack. The big silence went on, the silence that had continued even when they'd spoken to each other. From the angle of his neck, Maude expected an argument over something trivial. Why had she come to the woods with a 170-pound animal loaded with testosterone?

The sign pointed them to the shelter. "Hello, the shelter," Doug sang out.

It was empty. "In California, we'd be sharing it," he said. "I guess not so many Easterners walk." He slung off his pack and put it on the shelter floor.

"Not so many in cold weather," Maude said. "And not on a week day."

"So, how are you doing?"

"Fine." Maude put her pack beside Doug's and unstrapped her sleeping bag and pads. After laying down a plastic sheet, she unrolled her three-quarter-length pad sealed in rubberized nylon and the full-length piece of closed-cell foam she used under it. Then she pulled out her sleeping bag and fluffed it out on top of the pads. "Want me to do yours?"

"We could have gone to the Religious Range, then. Go ahead."

"I did fine for two miles," Maude said. She found his pad and sleeping bag and spread them by hers.

Doug grunted and began checking the spring, the woodpile, and the outhouse on the hill above the shelter. When he returned, he said, "You know modern backpacking wouldn't be possible without engineers. Nylon, delrin, and dural."

Maude said, "I'm opposed to magic, not engineering."

"For most people, they're the same. Engineered products you can use with minimal understanding and no commitment. Think about all the woowoo backpackers with their little Svea stoves and Goretex raingear pretending they've stepped back into the archaic."

"I can't. I'm just some dumb girl."

"I didn't mean you personally. But most people wouldn't know the difference between a car propelled by magic and a car propelled by gasoline. And it doesn't matter to them."

"For whatever I don't know about technology, I do know about magic."

"Your aunt isn't just another woowoo cultist. She's competent."

Now Maude understood what attracted him to Betty. Betty's charms were as polished and case-hardened as any lock, any set of valves and pistons. "She's very sure of her position in the magic. You're responding to her sense of authority."

"She knows both worlds. She can afford a personal maid to button her dresses and shoes," Doug said. "She collects prints. In California, all the occult people were marginal."

Like me, Maude thought. "She says she's cultured. I don't know if she's got more taste than you have. But if it's true, does that give her the right to take what she needs?" Maude felt chills run from back to front through the left side furrows of her brain.

"I don't like making things for people who use them without understanding them."

"That's not an answer, Doug," Maude said.

"If she takes from people who don't use or understand what they have, then . . ."

"Let me explain things to you, Doug. The magic keeps them from understanding. Witches charm them into accepting their positions in life, from the poor quality of their schools to the jobs that wreck their health. They don't have magic, they get used. Even some of the witches get used by the entities. Look at John." Maude knew she did have magic even though she'd tried to ignore it. On welfare in Berkeley, she could always cheat up an additional couple of bucks to go wandering. She rode time like a bicycle, hitting just the right moments at the bars, finding the perfect suckers to drive her to Marin for dinner.

"Maybe that's the losers' excuse," Doug said.

"Did we come here to argue?" Maude asked. She felt she'd tried to remind him that she knew more about magic than he did, that she'd been seeing and feeling it all her life.

Doug began to build a fire. Maude thought he'd gone back into the silence. But, after the match caught the kindling, he said, "I'm always curious about new phenomena. I

need to know about it. That's why I became an engineer.''
He squatted by the fire and looked at it.

Maude wasn't going to talk more about magic now.
Doug wasn't listening, but other things were. She was angry
that he wanted a magic that was just another engineering
tool. Because he was smarter than most people, he expected
to be able to use magic better. But the entities snuffled
around her, not him.

Be angry with him, good, something sang in her mind.

Get a grip, Maude told herself. *You don't go off to the woods
and pick fights with 170-pound mammals.* Trees and the valley
walls blurred the sunset. Maude pulled out her campstove
and lit it, then went to the spring for water. She knew the
trail guide advised treating it, but country people would
drink without qualms from a boxed spring, so she drank
before filling her water bottles. Doug added more sticks to
the fire. The quarrel they might have had faded. She
couldn't argue against certainty loaded with a lack of experience. His quarrel was with his technological world, the
dumb people who used his things without a relationship,
without even understanding how his tools worked. She
found she somewhat sympathized with that quarrel.

"So here we are," she said to him.

He turned his eyes up from the fire to look at her.
"Yes." She could almost see a grown-out beard in the stubble pattern. *Female diverts male hostility with a sexual display,*
she thought as her hips rotated. She blushed.

He got up and came to her, then sat her down with himself beside her, holding her firmly. His fingers felt half hostile. She waited to see what he did next.

"You're trembling," he said.

She ducked her chin and brought it up fast, feeling that
words might bring back the quarrel.

As he pushed her back and took off her clothes, she felt
lust grab her and deliver her to him. In the middle of the
sex act, he asked her, "Too tired?"

She was too aroused to answer, but aware enough to

know how he watched her while she squirmed on his cock.
Like an engineer, she thought, humiliated that he could be
so calculating while she was lost in their bodies.

In the morning, he seemed even more remote, as
though she'd embarrassed him. She said, "Do you want to
hike back the other direction?"

"What happened in California? It didn't happen last
night."

"I was used, then, I suspect, to lure you here."

"But you obviously enjoyed it last night. I felt so remote
I could have been using someone else's cock."

Maude almost said, *You felt like a sexual engineer,* but
didn't. "I'm sorry."

"We ought to go back."

Maude felt a call. She began loading her pack again.

Doug said, "I kept wondering if someone was watching."

Maude shook her head, then said, "Only by magic." She
wondered now why Betty had sent them away.

"After you fell asleep," Doug said, "I felt as though
you'd abandoned me in the dark."

Maude felt more irritated than sympathetic. She jerked
the compression straps on her pack and said, "Magic sent
us here. Magic's calling us back."

Doug said, "Someone died."

"Who?"

"I don't know."

Maude was furious that the witches told him, not her.
"If it's my grandmother . . ." What could she threaten to
do? The Colt revolver came to mind. Maude tried to fight
the image.

Doug said, "I don't think it's your grandmother."

John? Lula? Those possibilities were cheery. Maude said,
"Well, then we've got to get back." She remembered the
chill in her brain last night.

They retraced their steps by the cabin foundations. "I'm
sorry," Maude said. Doug didn't say anything.

* * *

They drove down to the interstate and to Roanoke, then got on the double-lane highway back to Bracken County, passing through the rough industrial edges. Maude said, "I always think of Blake when I go through here. People's lives spent in windowless factories."

"Better for cooling them," Doug said. "And we now have full-spectrum fluorescent lights."

"An engineer's solution to unnatural conditions."

He sighed. Maude hated the stretch of ugliness, the utter lack of design, of beauty. Then she wondered if beauty was a magic of its own. "I don't understand why it has to be so ugly."

"There's no *it* here. The factories aren't connected. No relationship between them," Doug said. "If I loved the purely functional, I'd defend it more, but you saw my house. Yet, I've met Japanese who would think this beautiful."

Maude felt like her quarrel with magic should ally her with something industrial, but the blank walls depressed her. "I wish you engineers would come up with more beautiful factories."

"My Japanese friends would say you need a new culture to see the beauty here."

"Doug, what do you think?"

"I think it's ugly, except for that old redbrick factory there with the smokestack. That's beautiful and probably polluting."

Maude felt a funeral on her brain, hearse tires rolling a vibration through her to match the real vibrations of the road. Then an old Essex drove into her mind, following the hearse like a predator following lame prey.

At the house in Kobold, no one was home. A neighbor in a trailer across the street came out and said, "Lula had a stroke. They're all at the hospital."

"Do you want to unload first or go right away?" Doug asked.

"Let's get the packs inside, then go," Maude said. She wanted to add, *it's only Lula. Lula, good riddance,* then Maude felt guilty.

Standing by Aunt Betty at the hospital, Partridge looked more alert than ever. Maude realized how alike they looked. "Grandmother, Aunt Betty."

They nodded. Betty said, "She's dead. Do you want to see her?"

"Not particularly."

Partridge said, "Now Maude can find someone for me. Maude, I'm sorry."

"Perhaps it won't be necessary," Betty said. "Maude could take care of you all by herself."

Doug put his hand on Maude's waist as though she were a dancer who needed steadying for a tricky move. Maude wondered why her grandmother seemed embarrassed. Then she saw Betty look sideways at Partridge. Partridge smiled, then pulled her shoulders up slightly. Betty's lips twitched and her eyelids tightened.

"I think I will go in and see her," Maude said.

Lula lay on a gurney by the emergency room doors. Maude looked through them and saw the hearse pull up. The nurse who'd led the way pulled the sheet back from Lula's corpse. The eyes looked like they'd been closed by force, the eyelid skin rippled downward from finger pressure. The mouth was slack, asymmetrical. The body looked flaccid.

Maude asked, "Did she die here?"

"No, she was DOA."

"A stroke?"

"Painless."

"We weren't home. Partridge . . ."

"Enough of a shock to get your grannie out of bed."

"Meaning what?"

"She exaggerates. Not that her arm wasn't broken that time, right, but she could be out of bed more. Obviously, she was able to handle this. Does she look better?"

"Did she call Betty first?"

"No, she called the rescue squad. Betty must have been listening to a scanner when the ambulance call went out."

Maude watched the nurse cover Lula again. The hearse driver and his helper came in and looked at Maude as if wondering if it would be indelicate to haul the old woman out now. Maude stepped back and said thank you to the nurse.

When Maude came back to the waiting room, Partridge was still on her feet, talking to Doug. Betty was slumped in a chair across the room. She looked both greyer and younger, as if she'd lost some wrinkles. The end of the black cane she held across her knees twitched. Her eyes came up and stared at Maude. "Your grannie could teach you almost as much as I could," she said. "I thought Lula would be good for her."

"I thought she liked Lula," Maude said, understanding something she didn't want to put into words about Partridge, Lula's death, why Betty sent such a worthless woman to take care of her grandmother.

Betty said, "I *thought* Partridge was too good."

"Maybe Lula just died naturally."

"Here, she might have," Betty said, meaning the rational hospital, "not at Kobold." She looked across the room at Partridge, who giggled at something Doug said. "But Lula's things . . ." Betty didn't finish the statement. Maude wondered if Lula's things could speak, get revenge. Old buttonhooks and the tatters and splinters of a slat bonnet chased Partridge in Maude's mind.

"You'd be silly to be the only innocent woman in your family," Betty said. "Especially considering you're a slut."

"Maybe Partridge did it to defend herself," Maude said.

Betty smiled, her eyelids half closed on her steel-colored eyes. "Partridge shouldn't be left alone."

Then, like a calculated distraction, Terry and John came in, dressed as though they'd been going to church, bringing in noise, cold air, and a small country woman between them. The woman blinked and said, "Where's Lula?"

"The hearse took her away," Maude said.

"She was going to take care of me now that Maude was here."

"Were you kin?" Maude asked.

"Enough," the woman said. She looked like a smaller, plumper version of Lula and Maude had no use for her.

Terry said, "We'll stop by tonight when you're back home." John nodded.

Maude felt Doug's hand on her waist again. She wondered when she'd be driving him back to the airport. Surely, he'd flee. These demands and people weren't his responsibility. Maude wished they weren't hers. Surrounded by suits, dresses, and nurses uniforms, she felt shabby and dirty in second-day hiking clothes. "Let's go home."

"There's no room for Partridge in your car," Betty said.

"We'll bring her," John said quickly. He sounded as though the death made an occasion for a party. Doug stepped away from Maude.

Betty said, "I think that would be fine."

In the car, Doug asked, "Do you want me to go?"

"I imagine you'd rather."

"Some incredible tensions there at the hospital."

"Partridge said she'd never work magic." Maude wondered if Betty could lie about it. "Maybe she didn't."

"You thought Lula was singularly useless."

"I'd have fired her, not killed her."

"Maybe firing her would have killed her."

"She had kin waiting to be taken care of."

"Partridge does look unusually well," Doug said.

"Maybe she's just relieved," Maude replied. From the stones up, almost all the county laughed at her. The technological pockets were indifferent.

10

BURIED BY MACHINE

They buried Lula in driving rain. The relatives she might have gone to take care of stared at the open hole as the undertaker's assistants pulled the straps out from the grave. The coffin was almost invisible at the bottom in the gloom under the canvas tent. Maude had wondered if Doug would stay long enough for this. He had. He stood back, talking to Aunt Betty.

Partridge came forward and dropped a handful of earth on the coffin. The other kin also dropped in a flower or two and more of the sticky red clay subsoil from the pile the gravediggers stood beside. From the tool marks in the clay, Maude knew the grave had been dug with a backhoe. Machines settled the dead. The backhoe wasn't visible now, but when the mourners had gone, the grave crew would bring it back and pull the clay over Lula's body in the undertaker's second-cheapest casket.

Some of the people moved off to the little frame Primitive Baptist church; others ran to their cars. Maude watched the grave crew pack up the straps, then walked through the graveyard to the shelter. She heard a motor start near the graveyard, probably the backhoe, hidden from the mourners. Lula would stay fixed in her grave. For an instant Maude felt guilty. *Poor bitch, all her life working for other people and couldn't roam as she willed as a ghost.*

Doug came up and said, "We've got dinner waiting at Luke and Betty's. Need an umbrella?" He popped one open.

Maude nodded and followed him to her car. The keys to the Mini-Cooper were in his pocket. He knew the roads and drove now.

Luke and Betty's stone house was in Taylorsville, just beyond where Main Street ended right-angled to the federal highway. Doug parked beside the green Essex with its cream tire covers. A wrinkled mulatto woman came to the front door, saying, "Come on in." She helped them take off their coats.

Maude remembered that the woman came from an insane asylum near Richmond, but she'd never seen any signs that the woman was psychotic. Perhaps she'd been a small-scale agitator in the tidewater. Whatever, she'd belonged to Uncle Luke and Aunt Betty for fifteen years. Maude asked, "Sue, how are you doing?"

"What now, Maude, you bringing folks from Berkeley, California?" To Doug, she said, "I remember Maudie when she was being a difficult girl." *Fifteen years and they put you on the day shift,* Maude thought.

"Folks? Just this one," Maude said, then she remembered the Reverend Julian Springer.

"There's another man followed you. He's really crazy, but here that don't matter. But faking mad, that catches up to you."

Maude wondered how much the Reverend Julian Springer had talked about her, that white woman faking madness when the witches wanted her. Then she locked eyes with Sue and connected to the woman who wanted out, out of Bracken County, out of being black in Virginia at a time when some blacks were lawyers and others did field work or stole to supplement welfare, out of being half-white and having nobody trust you.

Doug asked, "Who is the other man?"

"The Reverend Julian Springer," Maude answered. "He was in my group in Berkeley."

"When she was faking being crazy," Sue said. She turned and shuffled as though chained. Maude and Doug followed her to the dining room where Partridge sat bright-eyed between Luke and Betty. Terry and John weren't in yet. Sue went on past them into the kitchen and brought back a plate of shelled hardboiled eggs. The eggs rolled on the platter. Doug and Maude waited until Luke picked one up, then Betty. The eggs were cold and slippery. Terry and John came in the front door without ringing the bell. Sue shuffled to help them with their coats.

Maude said, "Sue's awfully old now, isn't she?"

"Arthritis," Luke said. "We wonder if she ought to go back to her people."

"Have you been paying social security for her?" Maude asked. Sue came back through. John and Terry sat down at the table and took eggs off the platter.

When Sue'd gone into the kitchen, Betty answered, "We give her room and board and a little spending money."

Luke said, "Her people could take care of her."

Maude wanted to say, *but she hasn't seen them in fifteen years.*

"Where was she from?" Doug asked.

"East of Richmond. One of those counties where they closed the schools over integration," Luke said.

Maude wondered if the woman had been a black teacher. She remembered when Sue had come but not much about her. Maude had been a self-centered child then, locked in bitter battles over proper duties and staying up to listen to Radio Moscow on a six-tube Hallicrafter shortwave radio. And setting her watch by the Naval Observatory, not on local time at all. Sue had come in once when Maude was listening to some Eastern European radio station telling her about Patrice Lumumba's murder by the CIA. Sue had said, "It's good to get both sides of the news."

Doug said, "What brought her here?"

"We looked through two state asylums for someone just right," Luke said.

"We could have gotten someone out of prison," Betty said. "But Sue's better behaved and more docile."

As Sue brought in a ham and cornbread, Luke said, "Asylum people are more grateful." He beamed at Sue as though she'd have no complaints about what he'd said.

Maude asked, "Could Sue help me with Partridge?" She noticed that the ham was a country-cured ham, flattened and dark skinned. It would be salty.

"I'm getting too old," Sue said. "But I have a friend."

Please, Maude thought, *let her be someone I'd want in the car when I take Partridge to the hospital for the last time.*

"Perhaps . . . ," Betty began.

"I'd like to interview her friend myself," Maude said.

"I should have some say in this," Partridge said.

"We've just buried Lula," Luke said. "Let's finish dinner first." He sliced the ham. As Maude expected, the meat was chewy and salty.

Doug said, "I love this ham."

Luke asked, "How much longer are you staying, Douglas?"

"I don't know. I feel like there's so much more here than I expected."

Maude saw Sue looking down at Doug, her eyes hooded. A corner of her mouth twitched. John and Terry tore their ham slices apart with forks, then ate the shreds. Maude asked, "What's happening with your court case, John?"

"What are you talking about?" Luke said. He looked over at Sue quickly, meaning, *we don't talk about our problems in front of the help.*

"John's always had a thing about guns," Sue said, meaning, *I know more than you want me to know.* Maude wondered if Sue had enough power to know but not enough to do, half-white, half-witch. Luke put his fork down. Sue's right eyelid began twitching and she backed out of the room.

Aunt Betty said, "He shot robbers. They understand that even in Richmond."

Doug put a piece of ham in between halves of a cornpone. Sue came back with gravy. Her eyelid still twitched. She looked at Luke and bowed her head. He smiled at her and the eyelid stopped twitching. Maude wondered if Doug had noticed Luke's petty meanness. He'd probably either side with Luke or say that the woman felt guilty or nervous about her attitude. When she felt contrite, Luke smiled and her eyelid relaxed.

That was the normal explanation. Maude didn't believe it.

"So, Doug, you and I could go into business here," John said. "You're a computer engineer and I'm a programmer."

"I'm an engineer. I didn't specialize in computers."

"It's the image that counts," John said.

Doug rolled his uneaten egg on his plate and didn't answer. Maude felt Doug's only hope was his dislike of John. Doug said, "I could stay until Christmas. Maybe later."

He's been laid off, Maude realized. *Something's wrong in California.*

Luke said, "Good, we need you here."

Doug looked at John, then back at Luke. "I have to leave by the first of the year."

Aunt Betty said, "That will be time enough."

They ate without conversation. Sue brought out a sheet cake and sherry at the end of the meal. Maude sipped the sherry and realized Partridge couldn't fit in the Mini-Cooper if she and Doug were going to leave together. "Perhaps I should take Partridge home, then one of you can bring Doug."

Partridge said, "I'll ride home with you, Maude. They want to talk further to Douglas."

Doug dipped his right shoulder and turned to look at Maude as though he hadn't heard about this before. Maude realized that the magic in the county had been unobtrusive recently, other than the fairystone waving its stone arms at Doug. A charming thing, a fairystone.

"Okay," Maude said. She wanted Partridge to tell her whether Lula's death had been natural or not. From the time she and Doug got back, she hadn't been alone with Partridge.

"We'll bring him home later," John said. Doug straight-

ened up and sipped his sherry. Sue stood waiting to clear off
the last of the dishes.

When Partridge got in the car, she said, "Sue got away
and read the Richmond paper."

"Got away?"

"She walks down to the library when Betty and Luke
aren't there."

"You don't approve?"

Partridge didn't answer. She looked more like Betty
than she had before, and Maude hoped this wasn't magically significant. When they drove by the abandoned weaving and spinning shop, Partridge said, "I'm going to fight
the bitch in there."

The Norn. The old Norse goddess who'd come to live
among us when she found a woman mad enough to conjure
her up, Maude realized. "There are worse gods." The Norn
at least spun as well as cut.

"You're against me. Sewing on my death quilt. Betty's
against me. Wants me fat to eat. The Norn bitch wants to
weave me off into one of her patterns. The old Colt revolver
whispers to me at night. I crave soul meat."

"Like Lula?"

"What about Lula? She died."

"Was she crippling you?"

"Old woman with hardly any powers like that?"

"And you have them?"

"Maude, don't you understand?"

Maude nodded. "Yeah, I understand. I guess I should
ask, what have I gotten from fighting the magic?"

"Precisely. Except that the magic pits its people against
each other sometimes."

"If Betty gets Doug, will she leave you alone?"

"Betty? Luke's the one who gets Doug."

Maude didn't quite know what Partridge meant by that,
whether Luke was the power behind Betty, which she'd always sensed, or whether Luke was the one concerned with
Doug. Maude said, "If I take lessons from Betty, can I help
you?"

In a suddenly frail voice, Partridge said, " 'Deliver me from temptation.' I surrendered to temptation, Maude. I promised your mother. Maude, when you screamed with that child lost in the map, I began to doubt. But now I'm old."

"Should I take you to Duke Hospital? They might have a gerontology department."

"I can't leave now," Partridge said. "Lula would give me my death back. I panicked."

"Oh, Partridge."

"You want me dead?"

"I didn't like Lula, but . . ."

"She gave me scurvy. She was the sorriest woman."

One had control of the food; the other of magic. "Did you use my dislike of her?"

"I balled up any emotion I could." *Saving hate like string.* Partridge seemed to age as she talked. "I panicked when I realized my guts were rotting. Peritonitis. Old people pick up words like that."

"Lula died of a stroke." *Please, grandmother, lie to me and say you didn't steal Lula's life.*

"But I'm not hurting in the guts now."

Maybe we're all nuts here, Maude hoped. A small insane county that draws others like it: the Reverend Springer, Sue, Doug, John. "I don't want to believe you're a witch."

Partridge said, "I think you'll have to. And you've got to admit what you can do, too."

"It's evil."

"What? Living on so long like Betty?"

"Grandmother, how old is she? She was old in photographs taken before I was born."

"I panicked." Partridge pulled her lips into a thin line and didn't say any more. Maude helped her out of the car. She'd lost whatever vitality she'd gotten from Lula's death.

When Maude got her grandmother through the house to the back room, she saw the bed and then saw back in time. Before she had her stroke, Lula lay down beside Partridge. Partridge rose up on an elbow and bent over Lula,

sucking her soul with a kiss. Old ladies in a death em-
brace—the image was so obscene Maude flinched back into
the present. Maude felt Partridge's intestines, like snakes,
squirm as though in her own body. She sat Partridge down
in a rocking chair and stripped the sheets off the bed.
Under the bed was a plastic bag. Maude pulled it out from
under the bed and looked in. The quilt top Maude had
been piecing was in the bag. Maude put it on the sewing
machine and got fresh sheets and quilts for the bed.

"You're not going to work on that," Partridge said.

Maude didn't answer, but remade the bed. She helped
Partridge back into it and covered her with the sheets and
another quilt from the closet.

"Does it have to be a quilt to die for?" Maude asked.

"It's committed," Partridge said.

Maude opened the bag and pulled out pieces of a
square that had been unstitched. "Maybe if we cut a new
square out of uncommitted cloth."

"I sometimes hated quilting. Whole women stitched
away in cloth."

"Tell me what they plan to do to Doug."

Partridge said, "Enslave the engineer part, kill the body,
the soul. Use the engineer part to ward off the wrong sorts
of development. It's homeopathic magic."

"If I warned him, would he believe me?"

Partridge said, "You could try. But if he doesn't listen,
will you still try to save him?"

Maude didn't know. "We need to talk about you, now. I
can't take care of you all by myself," Maude said.

"I'd be okay enough now if you weren't so disapprov-
ing," Partridge said.

Maude fingered the unstitched pieces of the quilt
square, the edge of the cloth distorted too much for an even
seam. "What do we do now?"

"I sure don't want to be food for Betty. Betty's a formi-
dable opponent, but you've got talent."

"How can we work magic? It's always hurting someone
else."

"If they had something worth saving, they'd have power, too," Partridge said.

"John showed his guns to the kids who broke into his house, didn't he?"

"Tempted them to steal? So what?"

"You were ready to die before. Resigned to it."

"Dying's pretty abstract until it's right on you."

Maude remembered watching vampire films when she was a child. Of course, the vampire would bite. Who would volunteer to die if they didn't have to? "I understand."

"You may understand, but you don't know yet," Partridge said. She seemed stronger, as if Maude's understanding gave her back the energy she'd stolen from Lula.

They heard a car pulling in the driveway and Maude went to the door. Doug came in alone, and the car, not Betty's Essex but Terry and John's car, pulled out again.

"John's crazy," he said.

"A lot of crazy people end up here," Maude said.

"Sue isn't really crazy. You aren't, either. But John . . ."

Maude said. "I suspect he showed his gun to the neighborhood kids."

"He took them shooting. Including the one he killed."

"Magic can be bad," Maude said. *If you were the magician eating power, then magic was good, at least for you. If you were eaten, however, not so good.* Doug looked at her, his face muscles tense.

Partridge said, "John reinterprets what he does."

"The Reverend Julian Springer really *is* crazy," Maude said. She felt a connection building between Springer and some power. Hers? Some black conjuror? The murderess's ghost who worked with her descendants in the NAACP?

"You drew the Reverend Springer here," Partridge told her.

Doug said, "Tomorrow, I'd like to see what technical work might be available." He seemed to shy away from the magic building in the room. Maude wondered how long it would take him to discover he couldn't work magic himself. She almost told him then.

"Did Betty say more about me?" Partridge asked Doug. "She told Sue not to give you her friend's name."

Partridge closed her eyes and pulled the covers up over her shoulders. "Did they bury Lula with a machine?"

Maude knew Sue's church, a Black Primitive Baptist one that had built a school for its children back before the Commonwealth of Virginia had schools for the children of ex-slaves. Predestination—the Presbyterians may have given it up, but here it saved the Primitive Baptists, because if man or woman was saved, they were born to be saved and nothing in time could change that. Predestination defended against magic, denied its powers. What was was willed by one power, decided before birth. God's mercy didn't grant exemptions from his physics and biology. Rain fell on the just and the unjust. The rich could not go to heaven any more than a camel can pass through the eye of a needle. Blessed are the meek. People who live off suffering are damned. There is no male or female in heaven. All pocket universes are delusions that collapse into hell. But nothing in this life could be changed without God's willing it to change.

But God willed the blacks a brush arbor church in 1870, then a building in 1889, and a school in 1904.

The black minister knew which woman was Sue's friend who needed the work. "You need someone truly saved in that house," he said. "This woman is good, but not quite one of us."

"I didn't ask Sue about the woman. You tell my aunt that if she comes asking."

"Pray to the Lord your grannie doesn't get where she can't afford to die," the minister said.

The whole county's crazy, Maude thought. She wondered why she left California.

When she got back to the car, Doug asked, "Did you find someone to help?"

"Yes."

"What's the point of having a Christian? Do you believe?"

"Here, what you believe is real. If that doesn't sound crazy."

"I didn't believe in magic fairystones until I saw one move."

"You didn't believe in what you were doing." Maude thought Doug's disbelief in his work's value had hollowed him out and left him available for other people's dreams.

"Luke told me about a cockfight," Doug said. "He wants me to go with him."

Maude said, "I'll go, too."

"He said it was for men."

"And rough women. I can stand the gossip." *You don't need to get excited over cockfights,* Maude thought.

"Is it as much a ritual as a sport?" Doug asked.

"Yes," Maude said. "Will John be there?"

"Luke didn't mention that."

Maude said, "I haven't seen a chicken fight in years."

11

CHICKEN FIGHTING

Luke sat in a crewel upholstered wing chair, resting his back on hours of painstaking stitches, wool tulips on cream linen. "You didn't understand me," Luke said to Doug. "I'm sending you to a chicken fight. I won't be going myself."

Maude asked, "But you don't mind me going?"

"I guess it wouldn't hurt your reputation, Maudie," Luke said. He pulled a drawer out in a small table sitting beside the chair and handed Doug a piece of paper. "Here's how to get there."

"Why aren't you going?" Doug asked Luke.

"I've seen chicken fights," Luke said.

"The birds don't understand they've got razor sharp steel strapped to their spurs," Maude said.

Doug pocketed the paper and asked, "What are the chances we'd be busted on site?"

"None at all," Luke said. "Deputies keep order."

They drove east following Luke's instructions into choppy country filled with second-growth forest, scrub fields grown up in red cedar. "They're black," Doug said, seeing men sitting on plywood porches attached to house trailers. "Is this arena in a black neighborhood?"

"It's all right. They hate the law too much to inform even on white people," Maude said.

"Will they be at the cockfight, too?"

"No," Maude said. "The industry has two audiences here."

"I want to learn about magic. Why is Luke sending me to a cockfight?"

"If Luke wants you to go to this, there's magic in it," Maude said. She wondered if the fight would be in a barn, the pit marked off with plywood and oil drums, the cocks brought to the fight in wood-barred coops, perhaps.

"I think we've come to a school," Doug said.

The building looked like a small coliseum. *For gladiator chickens.* Maude looked at Luke's map. "No, we're here."

"I thought cockfighting was illegal in Virginia," Doug said. "This place is obvious."

"Fighting chickens is a misdemeanor," Maude said. "Betting is the felony. And don't call it cockfighting. Locals don't say 'cock' in public."

A chainlink fence surrounded the place. Doug pulled up to the gate, where a man wearing a sweater over an orange jumpsuit checked first to see if anyone knew Doug then took their admission money. The man was shackled at the ankles.

"Prisoner," Maude said. "That's how tight the local laws are with this thing."

The man nodded at Doug and pushed a button to open the gate. A man wearing a rescue squad jacket waved them to a parking place. The man asked, "You need anything special?"

"What can you get me?" Doug asked.

"Luke knows you?"

"Luke sent us," Maude said. "I'm his niece, some times removed."

"The one who got followed back from California by the mad black preacher, right?" the man said. "Come on in. *Grit*'s covering us tonight." He handed them mimeographed programs.

"Grit?" Doug asked.

"Chicken fighting magazine," Maude said.

"Hispanics fight cocks in the Bay Area," Doug said. "I know something about it." He sounded dazed, trying hard to pretend he wasn't culture-shocked.

"I've heard when the folks from *Grit* cover fights that you get a lot of interesting sales booths," Maude said. "Come on."

"But this is wide open," Doug said.

"Just a misdemeanor," Maude said. Men pushed hand-trucks loaded with cat carriers. She and Doug went in the arena and saw bleachers surrounding a large central pit dug into the clay and lined around with cinderblocks. To each side of the main pit were smaller arenas with wire sides.

"Literally a pit," Doug said.

Maude explained, "They call them arenas. But the arenas need walls. Chickens would fall off a platform."

"I can't believe this." Doug looked up at the ceiling overhead—fiberglass panels on steel beams with stadium lights hanging from them.

Maude saw that the arena was filling up with men from every social spectrum in the county. Men who normally wore Italian suits came dressed in jeans with shirts no mill hand could afford, mill hands came dressed in polyester riverboat, cancer farmers wore overalls and the grim patience of their profession. One man came dressed like an Australian wrangler, his mustaches waxed, his overcoat almost to his ankles. He looked like he should be the pit boss, but Maude knew he was a dentist. Pseudo–Doc Holliday.

Doug was sweating. *Bodies heat the place,* Maude thought. She saw a man dressed in a suit moving through the crowd, his suit jacket slung back over his shoulder. He looked familiar, photographically so. She felt nervous about even recognizing him here. The only other man wearing a suit seemed to be taking and holding bets.

Doug looked down at his program and said to Maude, "I wouldn't begin to know how to bet."

Maude wanted to see the equipment dealers. She saw some of the men leave piles of the cat crates and walk toward the back of the building. She said, "Perhaps we could go this way."

Doug followed her as though he'd been drugged, stumbling over electrical conduit laid across the ground. There was a concession area behind the south-facing bleachers—a couple of men selling spurs and sparring mits.

Maude always loved well-made things. She picked up one of the spurs carefully by the socket. The socket fitted over the bird's natural spur. The metal spur was over two inches long, like a miniature saber perhaps, not as thin proportionately as a sword would have been, thicker so as not to break if it hit bone, sharpened like a sword, though, from the tip down to the socket. The handlers wedged the steel on the nonlethal spur halfway up a cock's leg.

Maude asked, "How much?"

"Seventy-five dollars the pair," the man said.

"I've got some forty-five," the man at the other counter said.

Maude shook her head and said, "Just looking. He don't have any chickens yet." She wondered how they'd react to Doug's California voice.

Doug said nothing. He looked at Maude and they went back to the bleachers. "What a cross section," he said.

"You're the only foreigner," she told him. The man beside her took off his windbreaker. He had on a T-shirt with the sleeves ripped off and had fat arms. On the arm next to Maude, the man had tatooed BORN TO LOSE. He didn't look defiant about it. He must have put that label on himself so nobody would bother to hit him.

On the other side of Doug was a cancer farmer, with fields and drying houses full of lethal fun, fun a man couldn't have if he farmed cancer and couldn't afford to miss one of the steps needed to keep the cancer from getting him during the growing. Cancer always brought a premium on the market.

The Doc Holliday imitator seemed posed in his clothes. He finally went up to one of the piles of crates and helped strap razors on one of the chickens, a black and red cock.

One man held the cock while the dentist pulled its legs back and strapped on the spurs.

"Who is he?" Doug asked, looking at the program.

"A dentist."

"He looks like a character. Is there time between bouts to bet? I'd like to bet on his birds."

"I've just heard about them," Maude said. She noticed a tough old woman taking photographs. The *Grit* editor was a woman.

The cock kicked convulsively when the dentist let go of his legs. The handler swung the armed bird in front of his body. Maude saw another man across the pit holding another chicken, multicolored and glistening under the lights. A man stepped down into the pit with the two men and their birds. The handlers stepped to the center of the ring and moved the birds at each other, then stepped back and dropped the birds.

The cocks crowed and jumped for each other, neck hackles flared. One spurred foot hung for a second, the spur stabbed into a wing bone. The cocks thrashed free of each other, then the black and red bird's spurs pierced the other cock's head. Blood spewed out. The multicolored cock shrieked and fell. The black and red bird crowed and tried to spur his handler, sidling around the pit with one wing down. The handler grabbed his neck, then picked the bird up, hands over his wings. The other handler slung the dead bird out.

Maude looked over at Doug. His eyes glittered, his pupils dilated. The men around them seemed to be yelling, but during the fight, Maude had not heard a thing.

Doug said, "Over so fast?"

Maude felt her pulse hammering, sweat dripping down her sides. "They're not pit bulls, but some fights do last longer."

The man tatooed BORN TO LOSE said "Dogs . . ." as though that word, breathed out on lots of air, explained something profound.

More bouts. Screaming. Crowing. Bleacher seats

boomed underfoot. Two birds, both viciously wounded, stalked each other on crippled feet. Their handlers swung them out of the main arena. One handler sucked blood from his bird's throat and then both handlers dropped the birds in the smaller ring on the left of the main pit.

Doug said, "It's pretty intense."

"It's the secret real America, the cockfight world."

During the break, Maude and Doug wandered between parked pickups and travel vans. They heard someone behind them say, "And Luke sent you?"

The man wore the suit and the vaguely familiar face. Maude knew she would recognize him if she saw his photograph in a news article. He said, "So, do you think you'll become an afficionado?"

Doug didn't say anything. Then he answered, "Yes, Luke sent me."

"You might be interested in this," the man said. He led them over to a new four-wheel-drive pickup with a camper back. His fighters, Maude thought, but then he switched on a light and opened the doors in the back of the camper. Inside were two small modern buildings set among trees and grass. Over them, as large as the bigger building, was a video monitor.

"What's it the model of?" Doug asked.

The man—the name Follette came to Maude's mind as if inserted—picked up a remote control and flashed different scenes on the monitor. Most were of empty rooms, but in one room, people were arguing with each other. Follette turned up the sound. "We have an obligation to our patrons," one man said. "You pure science people make them nervous." He wore a tiny vested suit as if suits were a disguise. Maude realized these were people inside the buildings. Real people who didn't know they worked in miniature.

Follette said, "It's not a model. It's my research institute. State and federal money I got for Bracken."

Doug said, "They're too tiny. I mean, so tiny." He wiped

his face. "It's magic, real magic, isn't it?" He smiled with a twitching mouth.

Maude said, "They don't have funding enough to expand."

"Lot of big fish in a small pond here," the miniature man who'd spoken earlier said. "You've got to respect them, not speculate about how stupid millionaires must be to stay in Bracken County."

Doug reached his hand out and touched the building. "I can't move it," he said. "Like it's as heavy as the real thing. How can your truck . . ."

"What are they researching?" Maude said.

"Tax write-offs," Follette said. "Doug, since you're not a witch, the buildings will be heavy to you. Maude's told you about magic, hasn't she?"

"But I didn't think you could do things like this to scientists," Doug said.

"You can trap anyone who doesn't understand what his principles should be," Follette said. "But I'm right proud of my little researchers. We're the smallest county in Virginia that has a fully staffed research institute and an art museum." *Follette's trophies,* Maude thought.

The little researchers came out of the little building and got in their miniature cars. The cars drove out of the parking lot and disappeared back into a city where they and their drivers were life-sized in private.

Doug said, "All I do with engineering is give aid and comfort to people stupider than I am. And you've got people like me on the back of your truck."

Maude said, "You weren't born to magic."

Follette asked, "Do you bet on chickens, Doug? Some of us bet on people. The entities bet on us." He came back to their seats with them. The two men on either side of them didn't protest.

Doug said, "Luke told me he'd explain more about how this county worked after I went to the cockfight."

"Perhaps you'd like to be one of my researchers," Follette said to Doug before the next two birds tried to kill each other. "I speculate you don't like the idea of working on the back of my pickup, but as long as I'm alive, you'd be safe."

Everyone stood up screaming at the birds. *Most exciting thing that happens for these people,* Maude thought, *and it's illegal. A message from your local establishment: the laws are there to be evaded.* She sweated and stared at Follette. He was as excited as any of them, his face turning pale when his bird died ten minutes later.

Doug looked like he felt betrayed. Follette said, "Well, that's chickens. What about my offer, Doug?"

"I'd like to see what Luke says."

"You can see the place without making a commitment."

In the third pit, another pair of cocks crept at each other. In the second pit, a handler wrung a bird's neck and tossed him out.

When the last cockfight was over around three A.M., Follette walked out with them. The dentist in Australian rig came up to him and said, "Ever thought of running for national office, George?"

Follette looked sick. "If I left Virginia, I'd lose my power."

He means that literally, Maude thought.

The night seemed filled with feathers, soft tatters of wind bumping against them. Blood scented the air. Follette walked off toward friends teasing him about his cock's poor performance. Maude thought she heard him reply he had to sacrifice a cock to Aescapulus, but wasn't sure she hadn't found words in sounds.

Doug said, "Everybody goes to chicken fights, don't they?"

"All the guys and some of the women," Maude said.

"I'd like to go again. I'm beginning to see the fascination in blood sports."

Maude wondered how miniaturization would affect Doug. "I think you ought to go back to Berkeley and design better artificial limbs."

"Don't you want me to stay?"

"I'd rather go back to Berkeley myself," Maude said.

"You have a tribe here. Family."

Maude shrugged. "A duty to my grandmother, but I'm not sure she couldn't take care of herself better without me. I remind her of her daughter."

They got in Maude's car. Everyone was leaving quickly, not staying to chat. As they went by the gatehouse, Maude saw a deputy and the pit manager standing beside the prisoner, counting money.

Doug said, "I wasn't sure what I thought of Follette. He's got a certain weakness to him, yet . . . I don't know."

"Uncle Luke doesn't like him much."

"A miniature research institute in the back of his truck—that really puts science and technology in perspective."

A coffin is already made for someone kin. Another coffin's coming. Doug's in the pit with John, Luke and Follette betting. Maude would remember Doug as the sexual engineer. They drove out onto the highway and turned west under the dark starry sky.

"I think I should warn you. Luke wants to use you against other engineers, against technological development in this county."

"If I worked for Follette, would I help bring in technological development?"

"His research institute is more for show, but with the right people, you could bring it around."

"I like the idea of a place where magic really works. Boy, did you see those people? Amazing."

"But you don't understand. Luke is a witch."

"Maude, I'm a good judge of people."

"Luke is a witch. You're not."

"Was he born human?"

"Yes, but he was also born witch." *There, I've warned him,* Maude thought. Doug hunched his shoulders and didn't reply. She wondered if she should have said Luke would kill all of him except the engineer bit, but she doubted Doug would believe her. His arrogance ticked her off just enough that she omitted the lethal detail.

When they came into the house, Partridge was sitting up watching late night television. "I'm hurting," she said to them. "I don't understand why I'm not doing something about it." In her lap were quilt squares.

"I've got someone coming to interview," Maude said. She picked up the cloth pieces from Partridge's lap. One square had been picked apart, then resewn partially by hand.

Doug asked, "Did you ever go to a chicken fight, Partridge?"

Partridge reared back to look at him. "I don't believe we had much in that line when I was younger. I remember fox hunting, the men riding to hounds."

"Blood sports," Maude said. "I'm sure there was cockfighting. Maybe the women didn't get told?"

"I don't remember it," Partridge said. She stabbed a threaded needle into the chair arm. "Help me to bed, Maude. I'll try to be good."

12

PREDESTINATION CONJURIES

One of Maude's father's people brought the new care-taker, Esther, to Partridge's house. Esther said, "I've got a car, but it's in the shop. If you could carry me back, I can start work today." She had a broad face, a flat, slightly turned-up nose, small traces of white blood. Maude recognized the man who drove her as Elehu, a distant uncle. He was thin and had white mustaches that drooped over his lip, white hair under a fedora. More dressed than usual for that side of the family, Maude thought. He stayed in his pickup truck. Doug came out and put his arm around Maude.

"Sure, we can drive you home," Maude said. "How many days till the car is fixed?"

"I can bring her here," the man told them. "I could even pick her up of an evening."

"That's all right," Maude said. "Thanks for offering."

"I'm kin," the man said.

"I recognized you from the family reunions."

"Kin on your daddy's side."

Maude remembered more. "You're a preacher."

"Right. We're sister churches, Esther's and mine."

"Segregated?" Doug asked.

"We don't worship quite alike," Elehu said, "but we believe in one God. Not crystals. Not lying entities."

"And what's your party line on evolution?"

The man ignored him. He said, "Maude, your daddy's people would like to see more of you."

Maude remembered them as she'd not in years: factory

workers, cancer farmers, one snapped spine, a couple dozen broken bones and lost fingers between them. They'd always been those people who lived lives out of country music lyrics, on the run from dangerous women, the women abandoned or brutalized by their men, the good marriages rigid, the children faithless. Elehu said, "I understand you've been hiding from your mother's people. The Reverend Springer said you were on welfare in Berkeley."

"We were both crazy there."

"He doesn't seem crazy to us."

Esther said, "I'd better go see who it is I'm tending." She opened the door as though she belonged there and disappeared inside.

Elehu said, "Don't treat her like a maid. She's got some nurse training."

Maude asked, "Isn't everything already worked out down to how I treat her? Predestined."

"Not so's you'd see it," Elehu said. "Only God knows what you'll do next."

As Elehu drove off, Doug said, "Seems poorer than the other side of the family."

"They don't work with the magic. What if they're right?"

"What does he say about the fairystones?"

"They're reminders of the Crucifixion." Maude remembered how cheated she'd felt when she learned in California that staurolites didn't just come from Bracken County.

In the rear bedroom, Partridge was sitting up in bed, looking somewhat drained. As Maude and Doug came in, Esther treadled the Singer and guided two quilt pieces through. She was saying, "Even people like Aunt Betty don't live forever. Eternity makes even a thousand years on earth look petty."

Partridge said, "You can go to heaven. I'd like to stay here a while."

"Same with me," Doug said.

Maude asked, "Can you get along with Esther, Partridge?"

"I'll corrupt her," Partridge said.

"I won't give you scurvy and I can work your joints through a full range of motion," Esther said. "I've had training."

"Nurse's aide, community college," Partridge said. Partridge was feistier than she'd been when Maude first got back from Berkeley. Maude wondered if Lula's gobbled soul informed Partridge's personality, proving the hippie maxim that you are what you eat. "But she won't have me malnourished. And she can bend my wrists."

"Don't work on that quilt," Maude said.

"Ain't you gonna need it?"

Partridge said, "Maude, let's talk this evening when Douglas takes Esther home."

"Can we leave you now?"

The two women looked at each other. Partridge said, "I'll be okay."

"Where do you want to go?" Doug asked.

"A city."

"I promised I'd have lunch with Luke, to tell him about the cockfight."

Esther got up and went into the kitchen. Maude looked at the desk where the old Colt revolver muttered about death. "Okay, we'll be back after lunch."

"Let's see if Terry and John want to go, too," Doug said. "We could visit Follette's research institute."

"Let's just go."

"Okay," Doug said, collapsing all the arguments Maude was going to make.

The Mini-Cooper looked dwarfed in the driveway. As they drove off, Maude thought about working on Follette's pickup truck bed. Driving up the hill where the research institute was, on Martinsville's outskirts, Maude saw the sky glitter, a huge lens looking down. "I'm not so sure I would want to work there," Doug said, "my brain all shrunken."

"Haldane's Law doesn't apply in a pocket universe. Your neurons are beyond physics. You won't get stupid."

"Little science pixies," Doug said. "But that's all we ever are to the general public anyway. Most laymen are too lazy to learn real science. They figure we've got a weird knack that makes us geniuses with microchips and steel, but we're supposed to be social and artistic idiots. Pisses me off."

They parked and Doug stepped out onto the asphalt. He scuffed it with his boot heel and said, "It doesn't feel like the back of a pickup. The whole concept is rather cute, actually." He began walking toward the entrance.

Inside, a receptionist stopped him. "I met Senator Follette last night and he told me I ought to bring you my résumé. I'm in fiber optics in Berkeley. We were looking at optical digital processing also."

"I can take your application," the receptionist began as Follette came out. "Sir, I thought you went back to Richmond this morning."

"I didn't," Follette said. Maude wondered if he really was on the road to Richmond, watching all this by shortwave television or sheer conjuring. He could have had a small version of himself waiting in a men's room closet, a puppet for dealing with his little science people. "Come, I'll show you around," he said to Doug, taking his arm and circling with his left hand, a motion for Maude to follow.

The building they were in was light inside, stripped down, floors tiled in synthetics, ceilings lowered with lights glowing through in high-tech fixtures. One office door was opened. Maude saw it had no windows. Follette took them all the way through to a greenhouse attached to the rear of the building. Two women were setting up tables and rummaging through a commercial refrigerator on the solid wall. Through the other walls, they saw the other building at right angles to the one they were in.

"Wasn't this a factory once?" Maude asked.

"Long time ago," Follette answered. "So, Doug, what do you think?"

"I'm a bit nervous about the greenhouse."

"Why?" Follette asked. He smiled slightly as though he knew the answer.

"Reminds me of the dipshit ecologists in Berkeley."

Follette said, "It's a nice place to eat. We're thinking about putting in some catfish tanks. Just for fun."

"Okay, as long as you don't think indoor catfish farming is the wave of the future," Doug said.

"We don't have any windows in the offices," Follette said, "so we've got this to bring people out, get them together for lunch. I thought you might be going into something with Luke."

"We're supposed to talk at lunch," Doug said.

Follette went to the glass wall and pulled a lever. Maude hadn't noticed two layers of glass until styrofoam beads poured into the hollow space between the inner glass and the outer. Follette pulled the lever the other way and the beads went whirling back to storage. "We've been working on some environmental stuff here, but it's all so expensive," Follette said after most of the beads disappeared. A few were stuck to the glass. Follette went up and flicked his fingers against the glass at one bead, then called on an intercom for Dr. Fisher.

The man they'd seen on the video came in. "Senator," he said, bowing his head slightly.

"Georgie, this is Douglas Sanderheim, from Berkeley. He's interested in talking to you."

"Berkeley? Lawrence Lab?"

"Corporate research."

"Oh." Dr. Fisher seemed disappointed.

"Communications technology."

"We're actually more interested in energy problems and agricultural problems here. I'm not actually one of the researchers, but since the patrons felt education would be part of the program, I came on board to help the researchers make better presentations."

Follette said, "Dr. Fisher has an education doctorate."

Maude wondered if anything they developed could go

operational for less than $20,000. Doug said, "Perhaps I could get interested in agricultural problems."

Fisher told him, "Even though I don't have a science PhD, I've studied at the Farallones Institute and New Alchemy before here. And I've worked with Ivan Illich."

Doug smiled a *now I know what you are* smile and looked at Follette who was checking the bead wall for clinging styrofoam. Follette looked over his shoulder at Doug and shrugged, then looked back at the bead wall. Doug said, "Georgie, have you studied chicken fighting?"

Follette turned around. Fisher said, "I've been suggesting to Senator Follette that he might consider making chicken fighting a felony in this state, not just the gambling. And we need better gun control laws, too."

"If all my people thought like you, I'd be pretty well pleased to make some changes," Follette said with a wink to Maude.

"If you ban handguns, you'd stop old people and women from committing most of the justifiable homicides," Maude said.

"Precisely," Doug said. "Guns empower people too weak to make good use of swords and knives."

Follette smiled, his lips stretching farther on the side Fisher couldn't see. Georgie Fisher looked at them as though they were mocking him. "It shouldn't be that way."

Follette said, "Now if we could just invent a soybean that would make people stop killing deer and deer stop eating crops, we'd all be so happy."

"Science isn't magic," Georgie said.

"How well I know," Follette said. "Could you take Doug around? I want to talk to Maude about her people."

After the two men went out, Maude asked Follette, "My father's people or my mother's people?"

"Does he know Luke could kill him? Can't you get him to leave?"

Maude didn't answer. She felt around her for magic, then said, "Doug's pretty arrogant about how important he is, what he can do. Luke charms him by pumping his ego."

Follette sat down at one of the tables in the greenhouse and nodded to the women at the food counter. Maude sat down across from him. "You're not really here, are you?"

"You didn't feel any magic, did you?"

"I don't always look for it."

"I felt you looking for it. You got some narrow-band powers but they could be intense."

"Maybe, but I don't want to develop them."

"Some of your father's people also had some power."

"And besides, magic's cruel," Maude said.

Follette sighed. "You're right on that, partly. Magic can be cruel. Why doesn't all this bother Doug? He's an engineer."

"He's always dreamed of magic. He thinks it's something like a science."

"Atoms don't have personality, despite quark charm. What we deal with has minds." One of the women from the food counter set a cup of coffee in front of Follette. He pulled a pill bottle out of his suit jacket pocket and took one. "And they get bored with their clients, sometimes."

"Are you and Luke fighting at that level?"

"We have. But I decided a few years back that human life meant more than entertaining archaic gods gone mad from lack of mass worship. I got earnest. I got boring. So, the personalities threw a little something at me."

"Would you be able to save Doug if Luke decides to sacrifice him?"

Follette sipped his coffee, then shrugged. "I'm a powerful man in my own way."

Maude filled in, *but a dying man*. "So what happens to Doug isn't that important."

"I was just a servant, public servant."

"You're not dead, yet."

"I got Bracken this research institute. But you saw Georgie. Had to hire someone who could keep the science people from exciting the mill hands with technological dreams. I'm disappointed that you haven't warned Doug that he can't learn magic."

"He's sure he can master anything. He wants me to master it too."

"And you tried to explain to him what magic is?"

"All but told him Luke would kill him. Couldn't quite say that because it sounded crazy. And Doug's so cocksure. His hero is an atomic scientist who was a disciple of Aleister Crowley."

"Fighting chickens are also cocksure. However, an occasional bird looks at the other rooster and goes, *oops.*"

"What part does Terry's husband John play in this?"

"He's amorphous bad news. Lured a kid he took shooting into his bullets."

Follette knows that? Maude nodded. She felt Follette reach out with magic toward the west. He sat quietly for a while, then shook his head. "Maybe the black kid's people will get him, but he's pretty heavily armored."

"Why do or did you and Luke do these things?"

"Besides the promise of living on so long? Magic's exciting, like a chicken fight." Follette smiled at Maude. She wondered if even his human-centered dreams came tainted by adrenaline addictions. He said, "You ought to be wondering what you're getting out of sleeping with a doomed man."

"We're all doomed, so I've heard."

"If the Christians are right, but I haven't seen Jesus visiting as much as I've felt that crazy Norn in the abandoned weaving shop petting the crab gnawing on my life threads. And cutting at your grannie's thread with that flint knife of hers."

"Nobody's seen the Norn in a while."

"Unless you're crazy vindictive, you don't go looking for a Norn. So, you plan to warn your lover about how lethal Luke's planning to be to him or you getting something out of Luke?"

"It's not one or the other."

"It always is something."

Doug and Georgie came in then. Doug said, "It's fascinating, but I can't stay longer. We've got to get back to Taylorsville to have lunch with Maude's uncle.''

"Luke. We've been talking about him," Follette said. He stood up. Maude wondered if he'd warn Doug himself, but Follette nodded at her.

In the car, Maude said, "He told me to warn you that Uncle Luke is going to pit you against John. I mean that in cockfighting terms.''

"Luke told me cancer turned Follette mean. You can't take him seriously.''

"You're sure?" Maude felt around Doug and found a magic cord feeding down through the sutures of his skull bones. The cord slithered out and away faster than she could trace it.

"Why would your Uncle Luke want to hurt me?''

"Because you're not a warlock.''

"I'm willing to learn.''

I'll try again. "You can't learn magic. You're born to it.''

"I'll ask Luke about that.''

"You trust my uncle more than me?''

"Well, Maude . . .'' Doug didn't finish but Maude reached out and found a vision of herself in a straightjacket in his mind. *Bastard.* She yanked the vision out of his head and felt the fabric of the universe around them tremble. The entities were watching. Doug said, "You were a welfare cheat. You picked up men in bars. Wasted your life. And you expect me to believe you more than Luke?''

"Shit, Doug, I'm not crazy. *You* picked me up, for crying out loud.''

"That's not what I remember. I remember you coming on to me because I said something magic.''

"You're the kind of man who gets a hard-on whether a woman excites him physically or intellectually.''

"Except for this hysteria from you, I've been having a marvelous time here," Doug said. "The mountains are beautiful. The people are friendly. The magic seems harmless to anyone who wasn't a doper.''

"And the land is cheap. Am I invited to this lunch with Uncle Luke?"

"He said he needed to talk to me man to man."

An entity whispered promises, *live forever, forget this dying man.* She tried to make herself small, an ordinary mortal. "I'll just bop off to the library, then." She wanted to tell Doug to ask Luke what magic could be learned, what magic came with the blood. With that reminder from her, an entity uncurled a helix of Maude's DNA, cooing, *shaped by us, bred from us.*

Jesus sacrificed himself, Maude thought, *a god to mankind, not mankind to the gods. Even if Jesus was only a philosophical concept. . . .*

"What are you thinking?"

"About what religions are," Maude said.

"What your uncle believes seems to work."

"Like voodoo," Maude said. "The real God is remote."

They didn't say anything more to each other until Doug stopped in front of the restaurant. Maude saw Luke's car, not the Essex but a younger but still old black Studebaker sedan circa 1947 or so. She said, "I'll walk to the library."

"No, it's your car. Take it."

"The library's not that far. Pick me up when you've finished talking to Luke."

Doug shrugged and pocketed the keys. Maude began walking toward the library. She looked at Betty and Luke's house when she came to the head of Main Street. Their maid, Sue, stood on the porch and nodded at Maude.

The Reverend Springer joined her on the sidewalk and said, "We need to talk to you." *We* didn't sound like paranoid expansiveness.

"I've got to be at the library when Doug finishes lunch with Uncle Luke."

He nodded, so Maude followed him to a neighborhood of small frame houses behind Main Street where the townspeople's black servants lived. Reverend Springer nodded at the houses and said, "It will all be torn away in a few years."

He turned up a bare dirt walk and led Maude into a board and batten house.

Paintings of Jesus, Mary, Saint Sebastian, angels, and great speckled birds covered the walls. *Why should I talk to this man*, Maude thought, *his paintings are crazy.*

"Don't you like my paintings?" Reverend Springer asked. He went to a refrigerator standing in the main room and pulled out four cans of soft drinks.

Two old black women came out from a bedroom. Maude knew that they were the grandmothers of the boy John killed. One was white haired and tiny. The other was huge, almost six feet tall and fat. Her hair had only a bit of grey in it.

"So the family knows where John is now."

"Only us," the big woman said. "We want Martin's soul back. We don't tell his father and the brothers if Martin's soul comes to rest. He ought not be a slave to the man who killed him."

"Martin fell to temptation," the little grandmother said. "John always be egging him on with gun talk."

Maude knew that Doug would have said that the boy didn't have to break into John's house. "How old was he?" she asked.

"Ten years old," the little grandmother said.

"Where's his mother?"

"She'd come shooting," the big grandmother said. "Same as my son."

"I don't know what I can do for you."

Reverend Springer gave each of them a canned soda. Maude opened hers and drank. The two grandmothers did the same. Reverend Springer said, "But do you want to help?"

"I've always hated the magic."

"I've always had a power to fight magic, but without magic around, the power's just craziness," Reverend Springer said. He opened his own soda and drank.

"Do you need the magic, too, then? If it makes you sane,

don't you really need it as bad as any witch?'' Maude asked. The two grandmothers huddled together.

"What's your lover doing in this?" Reverend Springer asked, not answering her.

"He's thinking he's going to be an apprentice when he's more like a sacrifice. Or a hold on me," Maude said, not realizing until she spoke that the latter could be another of Luke's objectives.

"I think I'd be happy to fade back into being a chronic hebephrenic if I worked God's will." He finally answered Maude's question.

Maude said, "Maybe the drug companies will find the right drug for you."

He said, "Do you understand how awful my life was, Miss Maude who pretended to be one of us to cheat herself a living?"

"I think so."

"If having magic to fight makes me sane, you can see I'm a tempted man."

Maude knew that he wanted someone to understand his sacrifice, if he made it. And if he didn't, he wanted her to forgive him. She said, "You can't kill all the magic."

"If you get us back Martin's soul, then we'd have no fight," the little grandmother told her.

Reverend Springer said, "Witches don't just give."

Maude asked, "Why have you brought me in on this?"

The Reverend Springer said, "We need someone who can walk into her cousin's house and feel for a boy's trapped soul. You take it and bring it to us."

"Why should I do this?"

"Because you will feel less guilty for being a thief from innocent people," the Reverend Springer said.

"Considering what I could have worked with magic, I am innocent." Maude looked at the paintings covering the walls and said, "Maybe we're all mad."

"Please," said the little grandmother.

"I'll think about it." Maude left the house and walked

back to the library alone. In the library, she picked up a copy of *Scientific American* and turned to the math section, trying to tear herself away from all magic. If she felt for the boy's soul, the entities would feel her. Perhaps she could find the boy's soul without magic. Neither John nor Terry seemed to know what precisely they were doing.

Doug came in and said, "I had a great talk with your uncle." He swung his arms around Maude and hugged her. "He reminded me to be nice to his niece."

"Did he say anything about Follette?"

"Nothing much, just told me to get back to him if Follette offered me a job. I brought you a sandwich and a Dr Pepper. Let's go up the mountain."

Outside the magic? Maude said, "Sure."

"Luke said Edgar Cayce is responsible for the hippies up in Floyd County. Cayce claimed to find geomantic energies up near Copper Hill."

"Power from old mining machines," Maude said. "Magic babble unites you with others who share your belief system. Has nothing to do with reality."

They drove up to the Blue Ridge Parkway. The magic faded after the fairystone belt, but Maude felt tendrils of it. The sky was blue. Around them, rock spines showed through the leafless trees. Pines and, then higher, hemlock accented the hills with green dots and patches. The car swerved up and around a logging truck at the one place they could pass. "Like magic," Doug said.

They drove into Floyd and walked around. "Like Bolinas," Maude said, "only colder."

"It's not that cold today," Doug said. "We could go fishing. I could trout fish all year round, Luke said."

"Did you ask him if you could be a magician, too?"

"He said you're a bit paranoid. Maude, I'm no fool. I could tell real magic from hippie enthusiasms."

"Am I better in bed than Susan, my witch wannabe roommate?"

"You're more real."

"Thanks."

"I've been looking for something that would get depth to my life, more complexities."

"Study biology."

"It simplifies us."

"Check out a major world religion."

"Polytheism is more complex."

"Master of complexities, that's what you want to be?"

"I want to master real complexities. Not fake complexities. All the hippie astrologies and magic systems do is test your memory."

Maude said, "When I've read science fiction, the stuff in magazines such as *Analog,* say, it seems like the characters are really thin. I wondered if that was an artifact of a technological society as much as bad writing. But if suffering like crazy makes great characters, then I'm not so sure the aesthetic pleasure is worth it."

Doug said, as if he didn't hear all she was saying, "Yes, in Bracken, even the victims, like Jake, are interesting."

"You want other people's lives to be aesthetic objects? I remember reading a Japanese poet's account of seeing an abandoned child. He felt intense pity for the boy, who was about a year old and fated to die of neglect. The poet also found his pity aesthetically pleasurable. Rescuing the boy would have been messy and unaesthetic. I thought when I read the poet's account that nowadays we mostly only do that with characters in books. But there's the cockfight culture. Men admire and love the birds they send to their deaths. Follette told us the entities and witches see normal mortals the way cockfight enthusiasts see fighting cocks. You don't understand that Luke could be perfectly friendly with you and still hand your soul over to a demon, eat it, feed it to John, whatever. Luke's lived too long to take short lives seriously."

"I want that, too," Doug said. "To live on."

"Better look to Jesus," Maude said. "Or science. Look what's happening to Follette—warlock's don't live forever."

"Follette lost his nerve. Luke says he can teach me magic. You don't understand man's magic, he says."

"So Luke says." Maude couldn't say more. She took his hand in hers and decided to help whatever dying ones she could. Get the black child's soul back. Find out, if she could, why Follette's entities threw him to the Cancer Crab.

Doug said, "I've seen that life's more than DNA complicating itself to propagate itself to complicate itself."

"There are better religions."

"This one works."

13

LIES AND GUNS

Maude wrangled an invitation to visit John and Terry by asking about Belle the hawk.

"She's flying well," Terry said.

"I'd like to see her."

"Perhaps you could come over Thursday afternoon and stay for dinnner."

"Is it hunting season?"

"Bring Doug, too. John needs to talk computers. He's designing a job monitoring system for a local company."

"Okay. Doug's been talking to the people at Follette's research institute."

"The funding will disappear when Follette dies."

Maude didn't feel the institute really mattered anyway. She said, "I'll see you Thursday, then."

"We can kill anything we want on our own property," Terry said, finally answering Maude's question. "Out of season, we claim the deer were damaging crops."

"I'll have to see if Esther can stay late. Otherwise, can we make it lunch?"

"Bring Partridge."

"She's not feeling up to traveling," Maude said. Partridge and Esther played Two-Handed Rook as Maude spoke.

"She'll be fine for a few hours by herself, I'm sure. Or Betty could visit for a while."

Maude didn't want Betty around. "Maybe we'd better make it lunch."

"You worry too much," Terry said.

Partridge and Esther seemed to accommodate each other well, Esther cooking the old food—cornbread, beans with fatback, greens with vinegar—and listening attentively without taking Partridge's growing testiness seriously.

"Why shouldn't I listen?" Esther said when Maude drove her home. "She's the one who's dying."

Maude wouldn't want to be bullied by that premise. Young people died, too. The old just knew to expect it. Maude wondered if Follette in his dying was occasionally as spiteful as Partridge could be to Esther. She asked Esther, "Could you stay on later Thursday night?"

Esther said, "If you could get me to pick up my car on Friday."

Maude wondered if she'd survive trying to steal the black boy's soul back from John and his guns. "Sure."

Esther directed her to a dirt road. A red and chrome trailer sat on cement blocks beside a half frost-killed garden. Only the turnip greens and collards still showed life. "Nice patch of greens you've got there."

"I can bring some for your grannie."

Maude didn't know whether she was supposed to say, *that's all right, we can get them from our kin,* or *I'm sure she'd appreciate them.*

Esther said, "Might as well take some. They'll be all died out by Christmas."

Maude halfway thought Esther was also talking about people. "Let me get them, then. You've been busy all day."

"I'll bring you a knife and a sack." Esther went into the trailer and brought out a paring knife and a brown paper grocery bag. She said, "If you just cut the outer leaves, the plants will continue to make."

Maude took the knife and cut greens for about fifteen minutes, enough to fill the sack completely full. She went to the trailer door and said, "Do you want me to cut some for you?"

"No, you need to be getting back to your grannie." Esther took back the knife. "I'll be bringing more from time to time. I love feeding people."

Maude asked, "What does it mean that a black woman would want me to look for a lost soul?"

"Sometimes, the soul is stole to work for a man. Christians don't believe this."

"Who would believe this?"

"Voodoo people."

"What would I look for if I had to look for a lost soul?"

"Maybe a little pot, a gourd. I'm sure sorry if someone believed a soul into such a trap."

Maude halfway wanted to kneel and ask Esther's blessing. She said, "We really appreciate the work you're doing with Partridge."

Esther didn't say anything, but nodded once and backed away from the trailer door. Maude took the bag of greens and went home.

When Doug saw what Maude brought in, he said, "You could grow bok choy here. It's a mustard, too. Esther wanted me to teach her how to cook Chinese."

The two of them washed the greens and cooked them. The whole bag boiled down to three small servings.

Partridge tasted hers and said, "Esther does them with some fat meat."

Maude said, "I thought that was beans."

"Grease improves everything. Here, Doug, you finish 'um."

"I'll see if you like them stir-fried next," Doug said, taking the greens off Partridge's plate.

When Esther came Thursday morning, she said, "I can stay over if Maude can get me to my car tomorrow morning."

Doug nodded. Maude went shopping for the weekend's supplies while Doug stayed home. She thought about stop-

ping by the Reverend Springer's to get more information,
but felt herself watched. *I can do this without attracting attention,* she thought.

Doug and Maude drove to her cousin's after three. John answered the door wearing camouflage and a Chinese clone
of the AK-47. He said, "Let's go out target shooting."

"Where's Terry?" Maude asked.

"Out with the hawk and the dogs."

Doug said, "I'd like to see the hawk."

"It won't cooperate with the dogs," John said. He had
an olive drab canvas bag hanging low on his hip. "Sure you
don't want to go shooting? The gun's almost automatic."

"Maybe later," Maude said. John walked them through
the house to the back. Maude put out a tiny feeler, but it hit
something solid. John looked back at her, grinning. Was he
even human, Maude wondered. She asked, "Have you
heard anymore about the shooting in Richmond?"

"They dropped charges."

"But you took the boy shooting?" Maude said.

"How did you know that?"

"I heard from some people," Maude said.

"They know where I am, then?"

"Who?" Doug said.

"The family."

"Did you play at voodoo with the boy?" Maude asked.
She felt like she was moving through cement.

The hawk cried out in the backyard and the cement
shattered. Terry, surrounded by the small liver-and-white
hounds, came walking up to them with the hawk on her
wrist. The cement built up again in jagged blocks, then
John walked away from them. "I'll shoot by myself if I have
to," he said over his shoulder.

"Why does he carry the gun so much?" Doug asked.

"The dogs barked all last night," Terry said. The hawk
peered at the dogs as though she wanted someone to make
them small enough to eat. Then she looked straight at

Maude, a natural bird burdened by symbolism staring down a woman who'd lay more symbolism on her. The hawk cried again and the pressure against Maude dropped.

Doug said, "Maude asked him if he played voodoo with the black boy he shot."

Terry said, "They were only playing."

Maude felt her body jangle as if she'd touched a 110-volt socket. "Playing with voodoo?"

"It's called voudoun," Terry said. "Belle's being uncooperative today." She walked over to the bow perch and tied the hawk's leash to it, then pressed the perch against the hawk's breast. The hawk stumbled onto the perch and turned to glare at the dogs.

"Maybe she's just being a natural hawk," Maude said. "She wasn't bred for falconry the way game chickens are bred to fight."

Doug said, "I thought you and John didn't believe in magic."

Maude wished he'd dropped it. Terry said, "John was just humoring the boy. We never thought he'd try to steal from us."

From the pasture above them, the Chinese gun rattled off a clip. None of the three spoke for a second, then Terry turned and walked toward the back door. Doug and Maude followed her.

"He's weird with that gun," Maude said.

"Sounds like he was firing on automatic."

"He's on our property," Terry said. "We can do anything we want on our property."

Maude wondered if Terry would tell her about a strange gourd or pot that John hadn't had before he came back from Richmond that last time. Doug and Terry began talking about country life as they walked into the dining room. One wall was covered above the sideboard with glassed cabinets. Maude wanted to extend her senses and test each container for trapped souls, but she feared attracting attention to her powers. Entities crowded the house.

Then Maude saw a dried gourd birdhouse, one shaped like a lopsided dumbbell, with green plastic clay blocking the entrance. A cord went around the neck between the large bottom section and the smaller upper swelling, tied once. *I'll just steal it,* Maude decided, *say I thought it was the boy's soul. At least I can say I tried.*

All this seemed so stupid. Did she want to save the boy's soul? She opened the cabinet and picked up the gourd. Was she wanting herself to save the boy's soul or was an entity guiding her thoughts?

John, smelling of gunpowder, reached around her and took the gourd. Maude asked, "Why is there clay stopping it up?"

"It's full of black powder," John said. He tied the two free ends of the cord together and slung the gourd around his neck.

Doug said, "Can I see it? I used to make black powder when I was a kid. We'd pour it across a road and set it on fire."

John said, "The black thief thought I was trapping his soul in here." He smiled at Maude.

"Did you?"

"Petit bon ange," Terry said. "If I remember my voudoun correctly. What you want working for you is *le corps cadaver."*

"Maude, why are you so curious?" John asked. "Here, open your hands." He took the gourd off his neck and began to pull the clay out of the hole.

Maude opened her hands. What John poured on them smelled of charcoal and sulfur. John put his lips to the gourd and sucked. "Maude," he said, his lips rimmed with grey powder, "did you tell the niggers where I am?"

"No."

"Then it was that crazy bitch Sue," John said. "Maybe we can drive her to suicide." He opened his mouth. Between his teeth, Maude saw a tiny black homunculus. "Petit bon ange," John said. His tongue went thin and long and wrapped around the tiny figure. His lips closed.

"What did you say?" Doug asked.

John swallowed. "Sue told friends of hers in Richmond where I was," John said. Maude realized only she could have seen the tiny figure in his mouth.

"Maybe you ought to go somewhere else," Doug said.

"I can't," John said. He smiled. "I win here. Maude, tell the niggers I ate their baby."

Terry said, "Are you staying for dinner? John, you need to wash the lead off your hands."

John opened his mouth impossibly wide. Maude heard the black child calling for help. None of the others seemed to have noticed anything. Maude said, "And he should wash the powder off his face."

"What powder?" John said. The grey powder Maude saw earlier around his mouth had disappeared. She saw the gourd in his hand, the plastic still in the hole.

"Can I see that?"

"We found it in the attic," Terry said, as though no one had spoken since John took it out of Maude's hands.

"It's very fragile," John said. "I put the clay in it to keep mice from eating it from the inside out."

"It looks like something you'd keep black powder in," Maude said. Had she and John been talking earlier in a separate time? She tried to feel for time whirls, but her senses seemed smothered.

"Black powder's kept in horns," John said.

"We used to make black powder when I was a kid," Doug said. Was he repeating himself, or was this the first time he spoke? Maude couldn't tell.

John smiled and put the gourd back in the cupboard. Maude decided to steal it.

Terry said, "The stew should be done by now. I'll put some cornbread in and we can eat in fifteen minutes."

Maude locked eyes with John, then looked away. *Don't look at the gourd again—no, it doesn't matter, he knows you want to steal it.* John, or the entity animating John during the lost time, seemed to be mocking her. Maude thought she could match anyone who wasn't consciously in touch with the entities, could probably match most witches if she allied with an entity. *Hi, John's entity, I can deal.*

John said, "I've got to clean my guns." He slung the Chinese semiauto over his shoulder. The bayonet was mounted.

After John had gone down to the basement, Doug asked, "Terry, doesn't the gun stuff bother you?"

"We have different attitudes about guns than Yankees do," Terry said. Doug and Maude watched her mix the cornbread and put it in the oven, then they went out to watch the mountains.

Wart Mountain trailed a cloud. Maude remembered going on top of a hill in San Francisco one foggy night and seeing stars through a void the hill and wind pushed through the clouds, a banner of clear air waving over and behind the hill. Now, she saw a cloud banner in clear sky.

"It's almost magical," Terry said. Then she looked at her watch and added, "The cornbread's done."

John came up from the basement smelling of gun-cleaning solvent and gun oil. He washed his hands at the kitchen sink while Terry took the cornbread out of the oven. Maude saw bowls, plates, and silverware already set out.

"It's venison stew," Terry said. "John killed the deer. I hope you're not a vegetarian, Doug."

"No."

"So many Californians who move here are," Terry said.

John said, "We're thinking about inviting this hippie couple over and serving them boar's head or suckling pig."

Maude said, "What's the point of gratuitously offending people?"

Doug said, "I wouldn't be offended." The others didn't respond to Maude at all. She felt shoved away from the others at the table, a welfare cheat who hadn't done much with her life.

John dried his hands and looked at Doug. "But my guns do offend you."

"Guns themselves don't offend me."

Terry said, "Let's talk about guns after dinner. John's got a federal firearms dealer's license and lots of catalogues."

Doug either flinched or shrugged, a body movement too tight to be interpreted, and asked, "Do we serve ourselves?"

"Yes, and you can pick out the meat if you don't want it," Terry said as though she didn't really believe a Northern Californian would eat dead deer.

Doug ladled himself a full bowl, trying not to avoid anything. Maude tried to eat only the vegetables, not wanting to eat illegal deer. Terry and John took the cornbread first, then served themselves the stew.

The stew was excellent, venison in a wine sauce, stewed for almost a day to turn the cartilage to jelly. Muscle fibers detached from the meat lumps and wrapped themselves around the vegetables. Terry added the vegetables late enough in the cooking for them to hold their texture.

Maude was impressed. The food relaxed her. "What can you hunt with a redtail hawk?" she asked Terry.

"She's figured out that we'll feed her, so I'm having trouble getting her to fly at rabbits," John said. "I'm thinking of sending her off downwind to prey at fortune, so to speak. Terry has hope for her."

"Shakespeare," Doug said. " 'If I prove her haggard, though her jesses be my dear heart strings, I'd loose her down wind to prey at fortune.' More or less."

Maude remembered *Othello* and felt criticized even though Doug would have been absurd to expect virgins at pick-up bars. She looked at him and said, "Othello thought he knew what Venetians were like. And he was dead wrong."

John said, "Blacks always can be fooled. Voudoun's a prime example."

Maude remembered the gourd. She felt a slight jolt, as though a magic line tightened. Be invisible, she thought, remembering how her father's people made themselves small.

Terry said, "I married John because few computer programmers read literature. So, Doug, you're also more than an engineer."

Doug nodded. Maude wondered if he would show enough interest in guns, however feigned and polite, to distract John while she went for the gourd.

While the women loaded the dishwasher with the dirty dishes, John went back downstairs for his gun catalogues and books on Mausers and Brownings. He brought them up and spread them over the kitchen table, saying to Doug, "See, I could get you a used Colt automatic pistol for $250."

Doug said, "I know someone who collects these." He flipped through the Mauser book.

"Mausers. I have one," John said. "Would you want to fire it?"

Maude thought as hard as she could without being magical, *do it, take him out.* But Doug must have shaken his head. John half-sighed, half-groaned, and flipped through his catalogues looking for something.

"I don't like guns, compared to you," Doug told him.

Terry said, "I didn't like them before I met John. Go shoot with him."

"Well, let me try the Mauser, then," Doug said. The two men went out the back door. Maude knew she could get the gourd if Terry went to the bathroom. She herself needed to urinate.

"Betty needs to get rid of Sue," Terry said. "Sue informed on us."

"I guess, but right now I've got to go to the bathroom," Maude said.

"There's one behind here," Terry said.

The toilet shared the waterpipes and drains with the kitchen. Maude wished she'd worn a skirt to hide the gourd, but no, she had on skintight jeans. The dishwasher began running. Maude used the toilet, washed her hands, then went out to see Terry mopping the counters. They heard gunshots. Terry said, "I'll be back in a moment."

Maude picked up her coat and went into the parlor and opened the glass cabinet, trying not to seem furtive. If Terry came back in the second before she wrapped the gourd in her coat, Maude planned to say she just wanted to see the gourd again.

Another gunshot, and a cry. Maude dropped the gourd. The clay stopper held. The gourd bounced. *Doug's been shot.* She put the gourd in the coat anyway. *He's not dead.*

Terry turned off the dishwasher and ran out the back door. Doug, supported by John, came limping back. His face was white and sweaty. He said, "I stumbled. The gun went off."

"It's just the side of his foot," John said. "I forgot to tell him not to put his finger on the trigger until he was ready to shoot."

I'm going to succeed at stealing this, Maude thought. She said, "Call an ambulance."

John maneuvered Doug into a chair and Terry bent to take off his shoe. Maude said again, "Call an ambulance." Doug cried out as the shoe slid off his foot.

"We don't know if he needs an ambulance. He may not have damaged any bones," Terry said.

Maude picked up the phone and called the rescue squad. "We need an ambulance on Route 666, the old Roare place near the fire road up Wart Mountain."

The woman who answered the phone asked, "What's the problem?"

"A friend stumbled with a gun and shot his foot."

"Oh, a shooting. The ambulance can't come until the police have checked the scene. And who are you?"

"Maude Fuller. My friend is visiting from California."

"Okay, we'll have someone right out. But they can't come in until a deputy says it's okay. I'll call the police, too."

"Thanks." Maude hung up and said, "They've got to send in police, too, since it's a gun shot."

Terry said, "I told you we'd be better off without an ambulance."

Doug gripped the armchair and looked blankly ahead. Terry seemed to have bent his foot to get the shoe off. The sock was soggy with blood. Terry got a dishpan, lifted Doug's leg, and set the wounded foot in it.

Maude said, "You stumbled?" Doug didn't appear to hear her. Terry peeled the sock off.

John said, "He's lucky he wasn't holding a full auto."

Doug said, "Ought to go home."

"You'll be fine here," Terry said.

"How long will it take for the ambulance to arrive?" Maude asked.

"I'll wash out the wound and bind it," Terry said.

"But I called for an ambulance. How long will it take someone to get here?"

"Depends on who's listening. The ambulance crews are all volunteers," John said. "But the cops are pros." He looked around the kitchen, then took the guns down to the basement. *Cleaning them,* Maude thought, *or rewarding them or getting them away before the cops arrived.* She hoped John was trading Doug's foot for the black teenager's soul.

Maude heard a siren. The car that pulled up was an ordinary car with a flasher so Maude hoped that it was a rescue squad medic, but a man in a deputy's uniform got out. He looked at the house and shifted his gun belt. Maude went to the door and said, "In here."

"Where's the victim?"

"Inside. He shot himself in the foot."

"Are you sure about that?"

"Yes. He's from California." Maude realized she was still holding the gourd inside her coat and went to put it in her car. The deputy watched her, then followed her inside the house.

Terry said, "Hi, Lewis," when the deputy came in.

"It's not your husband did this, is it?"

"John, no. He's in the basement cleaning the guns."

"I tripped," Doug said.

The deputy asked, "Was John near you? You having any problems with John?"

"No."

Maude said, "Can't you ask these questions after you get him to a hospital?"

The deputy squatted by Doug and looked in the dishpan. "Bone's broken. Not bleeding too bad. Man, you're lucky. Terry, you got a blanket?"

Terry went down the hall to the bedrooms and came back with a shabby woolen blanket. The deputy said, "The medics gonna need it when they get here. I'd better talk to John, I guess. Where's the basement?"

John came up then and said, "He was carrying a 9-mm semiautomatic Mauser when he stumbled."

"Where's the gun?"

"Downstairs, I'll get it for you."

"Let me go with you," the deputy said. They went downstairs and came back up, the deputy carrying both the Mauser and the Chinese AK clone in his hands. He held his trigger finger outside both trigger guards, alongside the receiver. "John, you need to teach people better."

The ambulance pulled up, but no one got out. The deputy went outside, talked with the people in the ambulance, walked by Maude's car and peered in, then got back in his car and drove off.

Two women and a man pulled a stretcher, an oxygen bottle, and what looked like a fishing tackle box out of the ambulance. They came inside and set the stretcher beside Doug's chair.

Doug announced, "I've got insurance."

"We've got a blanket," Terry said. One of the two women took it from her, looked at it and sniffed it, then folded it in half and began rolling it up tightly. The other woman lifted Doug's foot out of the dishpan, one hand holding the heel and the other the ball of the foot. Blood dripped into the dishpan.

The man took Doug's shoulders and nodded to the woman. The other woman finished rolling up the blanket and came over to help them get Doug onto the stretcher. Then she brought the blanket roll over. The man bandaged Doug's foot, then the woman who'd rolled the blanket used the roll as a soft splint for Doug's foot. She taped the U of blanket firmly, then nodded. The three of them lifted the stretcher. The first woman asked, "Does anyone want to ride with him?"

Maude thought about the gourd hidden in her coat. She answered, "I'll follow in my car."

"It's not that bad," Doug said. "It's just broken."

Terry told Maude, "We'll drop by later. Lewis said John could have the guns back after he writes his report."

Maude nodded and said, "Doug, I need my car keys."

"They're in the right pants pocket." The first woman medic pulled them out and handed them to Maude.

Terry restarted the dishwasher as though dismissing them. The medics carried Doug to the ambulance and Maude walked out behind them, got in her car, and followed the ambulance to the hospital emergency entrance. Maude parked her car out of the way. The deputy who'd been at the house came over and leaned on the car enough to push it down on its shocks. "What you got in the coat?"

Maude trembled.

"Could ya'll have been smoking dope?"

"No. It's not dope."

"They have to report it stolen for it to be stolen, but I can check for dope 'cause you sure are acting furtive and you were at a shooting. Let me see your coat, please." His hand slid to his gun butt.

Maude pulled the gourd from the folds of the coat. "A gourd that used to belong to the boy John shot in Richmond. His people wanted me to get it back. I know you're a friend of Terry's and John's."

"I know them," the deputy said. "I also know even when

you can't prove anything there are no accidents in Bracken County. And he's put his Chinese gun on full auto, but I suspect it will be back to how it's legal to be by the time I drive it to ATF people."

"Maybe John traded Doug's foot for the gourd."

"They can do anything they want on their property. We go in, we get lost," the deputy said. "Well, I got to talk to your friend."

Maude wrapped the gourd back in the coat and followed the deputy into the hospital. She felt the machines wipe out the magic and slumped into a chair. The deputy asked a nurse where the gunshot case was. The nurse pointed at the door of one of the three examining rooms. He went in. Maude wondered if the Reverend Julian Springer had a phone, but suspected he didn't. She went back out to see if she'd locked the car, then decided to drive down to the Reverend Springer's house and give him the gourd before John and Terry realized she'd stolen it.

But first she had to call Esther and tell her what had happened. A nurse gave her a hospital phone. Maude dialed. After two rings, she heard Terry's voice, "Hello?"

"You went to my house?"

"We wondered if you'd remember to call here. I'm taking care of Partridge while John drives Esther home."

Maude said, "Thanks a million. I'll be here a bit longer." She looked up and saw the deputy going toward the exit.

"They'll probably treat him and release him."

"Perhaps. I'll be home as soon as I know." Maude hung up and asked one of the white uniformed women in the hall, "Do you know what's happening to Doug, the guy with the shot foot?"

"They've taken him to X ray."

"I need to run an errand. Think he's going to be released tonight?"

"I seriously doubt it. He's got to have a couple of crushed metatarsals."

"Will he be crippled?" Maude felt a spasm in her own right foot.

"We haven't seen the X rays yet," the woman said. "Go run your errand."

Maude went out to her car and checked to see if the deputy might have taken the gourd. The doors were still locked. The gourd was still wrapped in the coat. Maude unwrapped it and put the coat on before driving off. The Reverend Springer's house was less than two miles away, no stoplights, only one stop sign. Maude looked at the gourd with the plastic clay stopper and got ready to drive.

A thought inserted words into her brain, *it's all for nothing.* Maude realized it was too easy, but then decided this could be John's magic fighting to paralyze her until he could retrieve the gourd. She turned the key and started the motor, then backed out carefully and turned around before entering the street. One right turn and she was on the highway.

And the deputy didn't ask her to take the stopper out of the gourd, didn't care what was in it. Maude checked behind her to see if she recognized the deputy's car. Deputies drove their own cars, not county cars, in Bracken County. At night, deputies were anonymous, almost invisible, until the lights and siren came on.

No lights. No siren. Maude turned down the road that led to Reverend Springer's. She went beyond the house to see if anyone had followed her. When passing the house, she noticed all the lights were on. Not seeing any other cars, she turned back and parked at his house. The house was very brightly lit.

The Reverend Springer came out on the porch, wearing dark pants and a white shirt. He seemed to be barefooted, but the glare of light coming through the door behind him made him hard to see. "Come in," he said.

"Doug, the man from California, had a shooting accident. Is this what you're looking for?" Maude held the gourd out.

He took it and said, "I hope so. Come in." Maude followed him into a room stinking of paint and garbage, lit with home movie floodlights. Reverend Springer had tacked canvases to his wall and most of them were wet. Maude recognized the local NAACP's presiding ghost, the 1910 bootlegging woman who'd killed the white customer who'd tried to cheat her. Reverend Springer had painted a series of the live woman in the various stages of the killing, beginning with the knife, then the pistol, then the shotgun, and ending with the pitchfork. Over the woman was her ghost in attitudes of horror.

"I keep the light so high to keep her from criticizing," Reverend Springer said, nodding at the paintings. He looked at the gourd, pulled out the stopper, then looked back at Maude and said, "They cheated you. Now they know you looking."

"You're sure."

"No little soul or body inside here. Did they catch you looking?"

"Yes. I went back and took it later." Maude remembered then the strange vision, out of time or a hallucination, of John eating the homunculus. "I had almost like a hallucination of the man who shot the boy eating his soul out of the gourd. Nobody else seemed to be aware of John doing this and the stopper didn't seem to be really removed."

"If John the Killer ate the boy's soul, then we got to cut it out of him," Reverend Springer said. "Or get him to throw it up."

Maude wondered how crazy they both were in reality.

Even though Maude hadn't verbalized her thought, the Reverend Springer said, "But this isn't reality. You best get back to the hospital."

"I can try again."

"I felt you was a witch. But you aren't nowhere near powerful enough."

"I didn't use my powers."

"Against them, you didn't use your powers?" He made it sound as though she'd been a fool.

When Maude got back to the hospital, she went to the nurse's desk and asked, "Where's Doug Sanderheim?"

"Taking him off to Baptist Hospital. He wants to make sure they put his foot together right with an orthopedic surgeon. He wanted a helicopter, but we told him his foot wouldn't go black before an ambulance could drive him."

Baptist Hospital was sixty miles away. "Can I see him before he leaves?"

A nurse pointed to the same examining room where Doug had been when the deputy went in to talk to him. Maude pushed through the door and saw Doug lying in a bed. His injured foot was outside the covers, bandaged in a steel splint. Maude said, "I heard they're taking you to Baptist."

"I don't want to be lame. I want a real orthopedic surgeon to work on it."

"I understand, but be careful the local doctors don't feel insulted."

"I told the deputy I felt like I was pushed, but John wasn't anywhere near me."

"You were pushed. Do you like magic as much now?"

"I need to master it myself."

Maude had already told him he couldn't. He didn't believe welfare cheats. "I can take care of you while you recover."

"Esther and Maude's nursing home."

"I've got to get back. I'll come down to Winston tomorrow."

"This is all so stupid."

I know, Maude thought, *and I didn't save anyone's body or soul.*

When Maude got home, Terry left quickly. Maude looked at Partridge and Partridge looked back, nothing spoken, but much said.

14

NO DIRECTION, NO RETURN

Maude's dreams tried to work Partridge's choking coughs into a cougar in the Sierras. But the cougar fell into a swimming pool and was drowning. Maude became confused, aware that something was wrong outside sleep. The coughs finally woke her. Feeling guilty for trying to stay asleep, Maude put her feet on the cold floor and went to check on Partridge. Her grandmother sat up in her bed, back against the headboard, coughing into her fist.

"Are you okay?"

"Why do you tamper with things?"

"Should I call the doctor?"

"I don't know why I wanted you back, anyway. You're so useless."

"I'm sorry." Maude didn't know how to react, to be pissed at the woman for being so critical, to be sympathetic because she was dying. "Are you okay? I'm supposed to get Esther and take her by to pick up her car."

"You should tend me yourself."

"I'd really go crazy."

"If faking being crazy didn't drive you insane, I sure doubt working like a responsible woman would do you any damage."

"Doug's going to be here, too."

"You fooling around with that killed boy's people got Doug shot." Partridge hawked up something into her fist and stared at it before wiping it away with a tissue.

"I thought I could save the boy's soul."

"Yeah, like Esther thinks I can be saved, only she's not arrogant enough to think she can do me personally."

"If I'd gotten the boy's soul back to them, they promised to leave John alone."

"John'll just kill more of them." Partridge coughed again, but not so harshly. "He gets excited by danger."

"Nobody else seemed to have noticed John eating the boy's soul. But the plastic plug on the gourd wasn't touched."

"Didn't seem touched. John's a bit young to get into soul eating."

"I know you ate Lula."

"Bit of bitter nothing. She was hellbound anyway. Saved her considerable torment." Partridge reared up in her bed. "You think I ate her for a few more months. You bitch."

"I know why Betty thought she'd be good for you. Good to tempt you into witchwork again. If you're okay, I've got to get Esther."

"Go then."

"After that, I'm driving down to North Carolina to see Doug."

"The sexual engineer." Partridge, her eyes sly, slid down into the bed. Her hips wiggled at Maude. Maude felt naked. Partridge said, "If you have any feeling other than lust for him, tell him to go back to Berkeley. He ought to get away while he can."

"I've told him he can't become a witch, but he doesn't believe me. He wants to learn magic. Luke told him men could learn, but women had to be born to it."

"Maybe you could put him away in that research institute old Follette carries around in the back of his truck. He'd be safe there."

"As Follette's pet? Follette's dying."

"Yeah, Follette's entity doesn't want him anymore," Partridge said. "He's not the worst of them, old Follette."

"You sound better."

"You want to hear me sounding better so you won't feel guilty sneaking off to see your lover."

Maude realized then that Partridge could live for many years, each one getting more difficult. Partridge looked up and said, "Maude, don't wish me dead. I don't know where I'd go."

Maude had always hoped that the dead just dissolved, though posthumous justice intrigued her when she wasn't feeling particularly guilty herself. "I'll be back."

Outside, the little Mini-Cooper looked battered. Maude opened the hood—*bonnet for this car,* she thought—and checked the oil, rubbing it between her fingers. It felt faintly gritty. She decided to ask Esther's mechanic to change it, then shut the hood and got in the car. Since Doug came, she hadn't driven her car often. She turned the key in the ignition. The motor sounded vaguely different, she thought, but perhaps the mechanic could check that, too.

Esther's trailer looked better. She'd just had a prefab redwood porch attached to the whole front of the trailer. Maude suspected she was seeing in this new addition the money Esther earned from her family. Empty flower pots of all sizes sat around the edge of the porch. In summer, plants would hang from the porch eaves and grow up from the floor—green stalactites and stalagmites. Esther came out and said, "I'll half about have my own brush arbor in the summer."

"It'd look like a green cave."

"I'd always wanted a good porch. You want to come in?"

"I'm rather in a hurry to get down to North Carolina. And I'd like to get your mechanic to change my oil if he has time."

"Yeah, you need to see about Douglas."

"I tried to save the soul of the boy John shot."

"He was either saved or not, way before you came along."

"His people wanted me to try."

"It's a trick, the business of souls captured by humans."

Maude bowed her head, not wanting to argue with her

grandmother's nurse. Esther added, "Well, let me get my coat then, and we can go pick up my car."

Maude wondered if Esther could fit in the Mini-Cooper, but she did, barely. As Esther pointed out the roads, Maude turned four turns off the highway to a cinderblock building surrounded by wrecks and junkers. Despite the ugliness, the garage felt as safe as the hospital, no magic jangling the air. She followed Esther into the building. A black man and a white man cranked on a winch to lift an engine out of a 1967 Corvette. *Which one's boss?* Maude wondered.

"Turner and Roach met in 'Nam fixing jeeps," Esther said. "Turner's daddy had some property here."

"Which one's Turner?" Maude asked, not sure whether Turner and Roach were first names, last names, or nicknames.

"Turner's the black man," Esther said. "Roach comes from Ireland somewhere on his granddad's side."

Maude looked around and saw a small Apple computer glowing in one corner of the shop, screen filled with figures. She wondered how these two country mechanics came to keep their accounts on a computer. When she looked back at the Corvette, the men were still busy. The two women waited until the men had the engine at a convenient stopping place, then the black man turned and said, "We had to work on you car valves, Esther. Something been burning them."

Maude said, "Would you have enough time to change the oil in my car? I've got to go down to North Carolina today to see a friend in the hospital."

The two men looked at each other, then Roach nodded. He came out with her and popped the hood of the Cooper, then checked the oil, feeling it with his fingers. "Had the compression checked lately?"

"No."

Roach didn't say anything, but closed the hood and opened the garage door over one of the grease pits. He came back and said, "Key?"

Maude handed him the key and he drove the car over the grease pit. As Roach began working beneath the car, Esther came from paying Turner and said, "I best get to your grannie."

"Sure. Thanks for staying last night."

Esther said, "What happens happens." She went to her car, a late model small Plymouth. Maude watched Esther drive off and thought about how fragile cars were.

After the oil change, Roach tested the compression. "You plan to junk it when the engine gets worse?"

"I'd like to keep it."

"We could rebuild it for you."

Maude wondered if Partridge would give her the money for the rebuild. "How much would it cost me?"

"Say $500, thereabouts."

"Soon," Maude said.

The mechanic poured borax over his hands and went to the sink to wash them. He said to Turner, "Check the computer."

Turner walked over to the screen. "It's okay."

Roach said, "We maybe could rebuild for less. You need to think about it."

"What's on the computer screen?"

The black mechanic smiled and nodded to his white partner. Roach said, "Witch alarm, among other things."

"I don't practice."

Turner said, "Don't think you'd have Miz Gilliculty for a nurse if you did."

Maude felt embarrassed that she didn't know Esther's last name. "Witchcraft takes from reality."

"That it does," Roach said. "And sometimes it's just a delusion."

Maude took the highway out toward the North Carolina line. She found herself in fog and turned around going toward Taylorsville. She got back on the road to the North Carolina line and found herself headed into Kobold.

Maude got back on the highway and her joints began to ache. The best way, she decided, is to sneak out.

Maude drove to the edge of the allochthon, her car skipping. Her head began to ache. She turned back, thinking to leave by a side road. She found herself stopped, off to the side, the North Carolina road sign visible ten feet away. She stepped out of the car, feeling nauseous.

Why? Why not? She thought she'd stopped the car pointed south, but when she looked at it, the windshield reflected the mountains to the northwest. *Can I even walk across?* She began to walk to the line. Zeno's paradox attacked her, each step increasing the half distances to infinity.

Then something beat her. She whirled, circled by invisible blows. The black grandmothers hunted John. John hunted Doug. She'd gotten in the way. Each blow hit realizations into her.

You can't leave until it's resolved. The thought inserted itself like a knife. The brain has no nerves, Maude tried to tell it. *But the mind can hurt,* the next thought told her.

Maude stumbled to the WELCOME TO NORTH CAROLINA sign and leaned her back against it, crying. *I don't want this to be real.* She imagined herself working for the two mechanics in their logic-ordered shop, the witch telltale on the computer. She didn't even know how the program worked.

Her car was waiting for her. She couldn't remember how she'd parked it. The mountains shone in her windscreen. They looked like Wales. They looked like Africa. They were the Blue Ridge Mountains.

Her nerves burned. She said, "Stop. I give up."

When she passed a creek, she stopped the car on the other side of the bridge and looked down into the water. She saw a school of rusty-sided suckers, but they weren't rusty now in late fall, out of breeding season. Trapped here, she thought, like an endemic fish.

"I couldn't get out," Maude told Doug after Esther had brought him back from North Carolina.

"Why not?" He walked in on crutches with Esther behind him.

"Magic."

"And you wouldn't fight it with your own magic." Doug lowered himself into a chair and swung his crutches to the side. "It's awfully lonely in a hospital without visitors."

Esther went in to Partridge. Maude said, "I tried to get away, but I won't become a witch just to keep you from being lonely."

"You're so superciliously scrupulous. You'd lie to welfare, fuck men you picked up in bars, but you won't work magic. I don't understand. It's like you want to be a loser."

Maude said, "Magic damages the world."

"I may be permanently crippled because you won't work magic or tell me how to work it myself."

"You can't work it. You must put yourself under the protection of someone who can fight it."

"I must?"

"Or go back to Berkeley. I'll go with you."

Doug sat in the chair for a while, then said, "You could protect me, couldn't you?"

"I don't want to be a witch."

"Not even for me?"

Maude wondered if some of her kin became witches because of the weak people who needed someone strong to protect them. A pickup and car crashed on the outskirts of Atlanta. A child cried by a black pond inside a map. Doug with his lame foot stared at her. "Doug, if you work in engineering, computers, create a common order . . ."

"I could work for Follette."

"Yes, you'd be safe for a while. But it's only temporary. Follette's entity set cancer in him because it was bored."

"Luke said men could learn magic."

And I'm just a woman he met in a Berkeley singles bar. "You believe Luke?" *I'm a woman who fucked and fucked up in Berkeley.* But Maude realized after she spoke that Doug's tone had been questioning. Her question drove him toward Luke.

"Do you know for a fact Luke's lying? If you hadn't tried to steal back the black kid's soul, I wouldn't have been shot. Yes, I believe Luke. You're not helping me."

"John's playing with your fear of guns."

"So what happens next?"

Maude realized her witch kin were also playing with Doug's curiosity. "Magic beatings, magic battles. I can't escape them, but you could." Perhaps he wasn't so sure of what Luke promised. "But I . . . magic unravels the real world." *Perhaps he's right and I am too scrupulous.*

Doug sat silently in the chair, swaying slightly as his heart beat. Maude felt the air darken, something trying to cloud her mind. Doug went slack-jawed. Maude saw the skull under his flesh—the hallucination of a moment, or real, she didn't know. He had steel bones in his foot.

Then, in her mind's eye, a bull charged, dilemma's horns gleaming. *If I work magic, he lives. Without my magic, he dies to make magic—Luke's magic—stronger.*

15

DOOMED TO IT

As the earth turned to winter, Partridge began dying in earnest. Her heart and arteries went flabby while she watched from her bed as Esther guided quilt pieces through the Singer. "Maude, I'm too cold," Partridge said. She turned in the bed. Her fingers plucked at the covers. She stared at them and jerked them up.

"Soon, you have a nice quilt to keep you warm," Esther said.

"It's my death quilt, bitch."

"I'm not superstitious."

Partridge said, "I wasn't plucking the covers the way people do before they die. I was trying to get warm."

Maude wondered if keeping faith with general reality paid off enough to justify old age.

As December ended, Doug began looking for work. He spent a lot of time talking to people at Follette's research institute. Maude felt doomed to wait.

Follette was dying, too, as he went between Bracken County, Charlottesville, and Richmond. He looked thinner and thinner, a man thrown to the Crab by his gods.

Doug said of Follette, "He's gotten some amazing things for this county. I'm just not sure the county knows what to do with them." He still limped, but was sure he'd be back to normal soon. If not, he'd have more surgery.

"I hate waiting," Maude said. She wasn't sure she'd been honest when she said that. She hated waiting for the conclusion. But if she could push the conclusion off into the indefinite future, perhaps that was better than getting to Partridge's death.

While Maude wondered what she really wanted, time went so slowly she could watch a snowflake descending for hours. As she watched one bunch of ice fibers whirling slowly down, Maude wonder how much of a witch she could be.

Esther touched her on the shoulder and the snowflake's crystals broke on the walk. Maude thought, *I'm a witch already, but not getting through time isn't the right solution.* Esther said, "Your grannie's asking for you."

Maude went in to her grandmother's room. The quilt top lay by the sewing machine. Maude picked it up and saw that it was almost completely pieced, just lacking the row of squares along the side. Partridge said, "I'm as ready as I'll ever be. If you won't wash my body, then you can at least sit to that work."

"I feel like all my life I've been waiting for something, holding time."

"Don't say that."

Maude felt the moment hold around them.

Partridge said, "Stones live in different time than we do. But I don't consider becoming a stone."

Maude felt the allochthon under her, helpless under centuries of rain, chunks and grains headed for the Atlantic, the allochthon itself unable to keep the ocean from opening. Allochthon trapped by normal faults, by normalcy. "The stone under us is conscious in its own way."

"Oh, Maude, can't you do something better? Delaying, always delaying what you're going to do with your life." Partridge meant something better than being on welfare or pulling them all to stone time.

Maude said, "You could live forever."

"Ain't nobody that amusing to the entities."

Maude remembered the cocks, the ones who fought on slowly, crippled but game, but lacking the flash to hold the main arena, left in the side pits to fight to the end. She remembered Follette's face after his bird lost.

"I'm linked with time," Maude said.

"Chronos always eats his children."

"Or maybe I'm not linked with time, someone else is, and I'm deluded into thinking it's me," Maude said.

"You want to keep your innocence?" Partridge asked. "Strange goal for a welfare cheat and fornicatrix."

"I wasn't responsible for anything."

Partridge said, "Finish my quilt. You might ought do some work."

Maude said, hating her flipness as she spoke, "After temp typing, waitressing, shoplifting, and a short gig sewing for a traveling minor rock band, getting on welfare in California seemed like a solid career move."

"Don't give me that shit," Partridge said. "I know witches from the inside."

Maude remembered herself drifting across the country, a drink bottle abandoned half-full in Davenport, Iowa, going west on the Grey Rabbit with pregnant runaway dental technicians, semipro whores, hippie mothers traveling cheap, and a business major whose hair seemed to get shorter and clothes more pressed from ride start to ride end. Maude remembered the semiwhore's marijuana, the feeling of total helplessness of being stoned incoherent in Buford, Wyoming, at three in the afternoon watching the local losers play endless pool. Had that been dope time or witch time running three P.M. in Buford for hours and hours?

"So you sift your memories, trying to see where you might have undone the chain that led your life to this moment," Partridge said. "You can do that forever. But it doesn't lead to the next moment at all."

"I . . . I don't want you to die."

"You don't want to deal with doing something new after my dying."

Maude tried to say *that's not true,* but realized that being here for her grandmother had given her a role she hadn't realized she'd missed until now. She wondered how much money Partridge would leave her, then felt guilty. "John's really safe from those black people," Maude said, almost asking.

"Depends on who they bring against him. Could be quite a witch fight. Why are you just sitting there? I don't need to be watched every second."

Maude turned to the sewing machine and began piecing the quilt. "Partridge?"

"You good enough to talk while you work?"

"Are you in pain?"

"Don't try to break my nerve. Lula broke it once."

"I'm not."

"I don't know whether it hurts worse later or not. If it eases, then I'm going in the right direction."

Maude said, "I guess after you die, I'll begin planning." The Singer treadled smoothly, the needle a blur, the feed-dog teeth pulling the cloth in steps too tiny and fast to feel as individual motions.

Partridge said, "You're not doing much. You could start planning now. Since we've got Esther here, you could go for your teaching certificate or try a trade."

"Don't you like Esther?"

"If I've got to have strange Christians around, then you need to do something more with yourself. Order seeds and trees and start a garden and an orchard. You best be planning now."

"I don't have any land. And it's winter."

"You'll have two acres around the house when I'm dead."

And that's all, Maude realized. "I don't know anything about gardening."

"You might ought learn. Hate to think I died for the integrity of a world you refuse to fit into."

"I thought I was doing good enough not to be a witch."

"Are you sure you're not practicing already?"

Maude remembered the slow snowflake just minutes before Esther touched her shoulder.

* * *

Aunt Betty invited Maude to lunch at a restaurant in Taylorsville after the roads were plowed. When Maude came in, Betty was sitting at a window table overlooking the courthouse. The little yard in front of the courthouse was covered with snow, a blanket of white on the memorial stones and the statues.

Maude felt rather allegorical and said, "Each whole flake is completely different than any other flake."

"Most snow doesn't come down whole but in clumps. And the individuality is as meaningless as human individuality normally is." Betty began to pull off her calfskin gloves.

Maude remembered the clump of snow needles that took so long to hit the sidewalk. "And you have to look under a microscope to see the crystal shape."

"There you have it, individuality isn't a normal human concern," Betty said. "Fitting in, however, is. Maude, you can't leave the county until you undo what you've done."

"What have I done?"

"You brought people against John. By the way, Sue's dead. Killed herself. Delusions of equality. I always knew the diagnosis was accurate."

"But you can't get rid of the rest of them because I helped them," Maude said.

"And you said you'd never practice witchcraft."

"I failed."

"You aren't much of a witch, Maude. Innate ability isn't everything."

"But I've got lots . . ."

". . . of innate ability. No, Maude, you don't."

"You're just saying this."

"We'll leave Doug alone if you help us."

"Then I do have some powers you could use."

"No, Maude, all I've ever wanted from you is a phone call when Partridge is dying."

"She wants to die into general reality."

Betty signaled for the waiter and said, "We want two specials and iced tea."

Maude hadn't seen a menu. She wondered if the special was human flesh.

Betty said, "You failed to make a place for yourself in general reality."

"How do I know I could make it in a pocket universe?"

"I'll help you."

"And you won't kill Doug."

"I won't kill Doug."

Maude almost asked *what about John and Luke,* but she realized that Betty could lie to her, that even if Betty the human decided to be generous, whatever was behind her might not. *And I can lie, too,* Maude decided.

"You're so transparent," Betty said. "I can't help you if you don't cooperate willingly."

"What about Terry and John?"

"They're so immersed in the life, they don't think what they have is unusual," Betty said. "Magic is so good when it's like that."

"I noticed they seemed oblivious," Maude said. She wondered if Betty was nostalgic for a time when she was like Terry and magic was normal and no one thought badly of a woman for using a lethal map to snare poor white trash and black children with unseemly curiosity.

"You're observant, but without skills to use those observations. Your mother did you a disservice in teaching you to observe."

The waiter brought two plates, each with a quiche slice, a macaroni and pea salad, and slaw. Betty smiled at the waiter and asked him, "How's your brother?"

"Maybe he'll quit drugs now."

"What happened?" Maude asked.

"Failed at suicide. There was a lot of it going around a couple nights ago."

"When Sue died?" Maude asked.

"When Sue realized what a waste her life had been and was going to continue to be. So she ended it, quite fitting."

Maude wondered how Sue's soul tasted. Betty said, "You

need to remember who I am, Maude. Why don't you come on home with me now?''

Maude almost asked, *What happened to Reverend Springer?* but caught herself in time, then wondered if she'd betrayed him anyway. She'd stop by his house later. "Are you going to show me more about the cards you stole from the hippies?''

"No, this time I'm going to show you my engravings." Betty smiled. After lunch, she put on her gloves before handling money.

"Drop by now?''

"Yes.''

"I'll leave my car here and walk over.''

"My Essex won't eat your little car.''

Maude felt foolish, but determined to leave her car parked on Main Street. Her aunt smoothed her gloves and said, "Ride in the Essex, then.''

Unless leather had been a factory option, the Essex didn't have its original upholstery. The hides seemed slightly unmatched. Maude wondered if these were man-killer bull hides. Betty put her finger to the throttle and turned the key in the ignition. She used both hands to shift into first, but the other gears came easier.

The car went its hundred yards or so and slid in behind the house. Maude followed her aunt into the stone base-ment. She saw one of the Reverend Springer's paintings hanging on the rock wall, a purple and green portrait of someone floating, off to Jesus perhaps.

"A Baconesque primitive," Betty said. "I'd have prefer-red a 'Screaming Pope,' but they're hard to come by lo-cally.''

Maude didn't ask how Betty got the painting, what she knew about the Reverend Springer. Betty showed Maude up a back staircase—narrow treads, completely boxed in— until they were three stories up under the eaves in Betty's library. In the center of the room was a big table covered with leather worn through to the wood, dusty. Without

Betty's asking, Maude found a feather duster and a rag and cleaned it off.

"Perhaps after Partridge dies, I could hire Esther."

"No," Maude said.

"I'll ask her myself. Maude, let me show you my Jasper Johns and my Minotauromachy."

"How could you afford a Picasso?"

"I bought it when it was new," Betty said. "The Johns I bought in New York from his printer out on Long Island." Betty went to a closet and brought back a large leather portfolio. She spread it on the table. "And the Oldenburg drawing."

"Doug likes art, too," Maude said.

"Does he?" Betty pulled out a drawing of a limp pen and lay it aside, then looked back in the portfolio. "Are you haunted by this?" She pulled out the Picasso etching.

In the image, a woman held up a candle against a rampaging minotaur. Disemboweled horses and another woman, mangled with one exposed breast, surrounded the woman with the candle and the minotaur. The fragile mortal against the unnatural.

"I've always liked the print," Maude said. She hated that she identified with the woman holding the candle.

"There's also his painting of the bombing of Guernica. The outside world has its own terrors," Betty said.

Woman against monster, man against machine, Maude thought. "Why do you have Reverend Springer's painting in the basement?"

"It doesn't fit in with our other things. It's a very aggressive painting." Betty smiled and continued, "It's been a long time since someone worked art against us, but we'll tame the painting and the painter eventually. Or break them both. After all, Picasso was a Communist once."

Maude pulled the Minotauromachy closer and almost touched the candle the woman held.

"Don't sweat on my Picasso," Betty said. "I love art, music. I'm worth more than those stupid drug boys. I'm a repository of historical information, centuries under my skin. You could take your own sweet time through my history. Aren't you curious?"

"Are we still going to die someday?" Maude asked.

"Magic wants . . . to be boss. Humans are the ultimate sacrifice. A little sack of packed humans like me . . ." Betty said her phrases as if she feared the words coming from her throat, wondered how they'd escaped. Then she threw her head back to show a pulse beating beside her windpipe. She coughed, threw her head back again, and gasped.

"Can I get you anything? Water?"

Betty gasped once more, then said, "I wouldn't want anything from you. You're not sure crippling drug dealers is decent."

Maude said, "Let me think about it."

"Can you think?" Betty asked. She stood up and led Maude back down the front stairs to the street level.

Maude felt her thoughts tumble as she walked back to her car. She opened the Mini-Cooper and tried to start the engine. The engine wouldn't start, then did and made grinding noises as though the car chewed its pistons and rods.

Maude went back in the restaurant and called Esther's garage. Turner answered.

"Hi, this is Maude with the Austin Mini-Cooper. It's died."

"When Roach gets back, we can come tow it."

"How long will that be?"

"Maybe four. Where are you?"

"Main Street, across from the courthouse." Maude felt that Betty had done this to mock her.

"If you could leave the keys in the car, we could get it later."

"I need a ride home."

"Isn't Esther working for you? Couldn't she come pick you up? We can get the car later."

Maude thought, *I'm not thinking.* "Sure." She hung up

and called her house. Esther answered. Maude said, "Esther, my car died in Taylorsville. Could you pick me up?"

"Where?"

"Down behind town where they're planning a park. I'm going to see Reverend Springer, if he's in."

"That's not a real good idea, Maude," Esther said.

"Betty has one of his paintings in her basement."

"That's not a good sign, either."

"He never thought I was really crazy."

"If you need to be told that, I could have told you. But, if it's what you want to do, I'll pick you up there. Your grannie's sleeping."

"In about fifteen minutes."

"How'd your car die?"

"Sounds like it was grinding itself."

Esther sighed. Maude wondered if Esther saw the car as Maude's own mechanical double. *Mr. Car, he dead.*

Maybe I can't think. Maybe all my thoughts are jumbles of book quotes, things other people told me, entity insertions. Maude began walking toward the road that cut behind Main Street to the shacks where the day help lived.

When Maude got near, she saw Reverend Springer, wrapped in a coat, rocking on his front porch in a cane rocker. He looked purple and green. His head slowly turned.

"My Aunt Betty has one of your paintings in her basement."

"Stole it. Can't break me."

"Sue killed herself."

"Can't break me."

Maude wondered if paranoid schizophrenics were too rigid in their own dementia for entities to find room to insert thoughts. "You always said I wasn't crazy."

"I understand you better now. I learned what you were hiding from. She couldn't bring me upstairs. My painting would get her. It's a true painting."

"My Aunt Betty told me your painting was very aggressive, but that she'd tame it or break it."

"She won't. I don't believe she will."

"I need to find a place in the other universe."

"Destroy this one. Bring in logic, machines."

"I couldn't find a place in the other universe when I was in Berkeley."

The Reverend Springer stopped rocking and said, "It's not enough not to be a witch."

"What can I do?"

"Stop looking for other people to tell you what to do."

"What if I'm wrong?"

"I'm a certified paranoid schizophrenic with delusions of grandeur. You asking me?"

"You knew I wasn't crazy."

He didn't say anything, but started rocking again. When Esther pulled up at his house to pick Maude up, he nodded at Esther and said, "Can't hold as is forever."

"Whatever happens is God's will," Esther said back.

"Funny thing about the Bible," the Reverend Springer said. "Read it literally and you worship a demon. Read it as metaphor and it tells you being a racist, or deciding people not in your church ought to die, is like being swallowed in isolation as though in the belly of a great cold fish."

Esther said, "The word is the word. God's will is forever, before us and after us."

"You get preserved in grace, hallelujah, but the witches get the rest of the people."

Maude said, "I hope Betty never tames your painting."

"Maybe I'll steal it back from her. Let me know when you need a distraction."

Esther's lips moved; a silent prayer, Maude decided. Then she turned the car motor on and drove Maude back toward Kobold.

"What was that all about?"

"He crazy." Esther's foot pressed down harder on the accelerator.

"It's God's will," Maude said.

"Don't mock me, who's got your grannie's comforts in my hand."

"Sorry. I feel like I've got to do something, but I don't know whether what I do will help or whether I'm being deluded by my desire to feel self-righteous."

"And you thought a crazy picture painter would help you sort it out. Excuse me, Miss Maude."

"That's all right."

Maude wondered if God willed Sue's death. Perhaps the Norsemen were right. The gods included the Norns, Loki the Trickster, and the Fenrus Wolf. Despite all the human suffering and striving, no human could interfere with the final destructions. She thought about what the Reverend Springer had said about the biblical God, as though the Bible was the language version of the paintings that showed gestalts of crone and young woman in the same desposit of paint or ink. *Hold two things in the mind at once.* What else was like that, Maude wondered. Betty saw herself as heroine, the bright and cultured woman fighting centuries of ignorance and spite only to die abandoned by the gods in the end. The gods told her she wouldn't amuse them forever.

"If you went to the magicians, what's the guarantee you'd be a success with that?" Esther asked.

"Can you do more than pray?"

"My question doesn't scare you?"

"I'm too confused to be scared by a question today," Maude said. "You'll have to take me to pick up my car later."

"Same mechanics? They're very good mechanics."

"Do you think Martin's people will try to kill John?"

"Depends on what drives them to it. Some black people into magic, too."

"Whatever happens, will you help me?"

"If I can."

Maude was grateful. "I could be dooming myself," she said.

"Only one Dying Lamb," Esther said.

"Ah, you're speaking figuratively."

Esther shook her head and smiled. "We always been having a figure in the Great Speckled Bird."

"After I help my grannie die and do what I can to put Bracken back in the physicists' reality, after the magic's killed, will I feel like a fool? Will the world seem stripped and simplified?"

"You making it more complicated than it is." Maude was home now. Esther pulled into the driveway and let Maude out.

Doug rose from where he'd been sitting beside Partridge's bed. Partridge was asleep, far inside her clammy skin. Her eyes rolled in REM sleep, her hands twitched. Maude sat down while Doug limped to the bathroom. She touched her grandmother's inner wrist and felt the pulse—fast.

Doug came back and said, "She's been fussing all day. I told her she ought to be a bit more considerate. She said when I'm dying and know it, then I can criticize her. She expects us to be totally involved in her dying."

Maude looked up at Doug. "Be careful."

"I don't know why old people expect younger people to be so concerned about old people's dying. After all, I could die before her. We never know what's coming."

Partridge opened her eyes and said, "That's right. You could die tomorrow. But you wouldn't understand what your death means. Maude might die, too, but she knows why." She reached for the hand Maude left on her wrist and squeezed. Her fingers were weak. Maude squeezed gently back and held on.

Doug turned to Maude and said, "She was trying to tell me I had to work for Follette. You women seem to think I'm something that needs to be hidden away on the back of a pickup. Your Uncle Luke says he might have something for me that would last after the funding's been cut for Follette's projects." He went to the front of the house.

"If they kill him, would I miss him that much?" Maude asked.

"Luke craves him bad. He's more to eat than a redneck druggie. John'll trap his mind in a calabash gourd and make it work against his kind."

"I wish he wouldn't be such a jerk about listening to us."

"You thought you were gonna get rescued by a straight-thinking engineer, now he's all kinky for magic and refuses to realize he can't have it."

"I've told him."

"He doesn't believe you. You're a girl. He's a mental adventurer, and we're the women telling him he's in danger."

"I know. I'm proud of what you're doing. Do you need to talk?"

"Not yet. You'll be here. You don't have a car now."

"They'll have it fixed in a week or two."

"The car is dead."

Maude felt tears welling in her eyes. Crying for a machine made her feel stupid, but didn't stop the tears.

"Not just tears for the car," Partridge said. She squeezed again. "Why did you bring that fool boy anyhow?"

"Sorry."

"Sure is. I've been trying to help you both. Quit pestering me. I've got to get some sleep."

Maude put her hand on her grandmother's brow. Partridge said, "Are you doing that because you really feel for me or because you're watching how noble you look when you put concern on your face?"

Maude felt hurt, but realized she had been watching herself, the noble young woman tending her dying grannie rather than going out and getting laid.

Partridge said, "Keep in mind you weren't doing anything decent when Betty called you out of Berkeley."

"I thought that had been you."

"Only a little."

"You both were fighting over me. You've won."

"You know she tempts you. Don't make my dying a fool thing, Maude."

"Maybe you'll be looking down from heaven."

"Don't kid yourself. When I'm dead, I dissolve."

Maude imagined Partridge's body liquifying and shuddered.

"Go away, you're making me nauseous. To imagine my body doing that."

"You saw my mind. You're still using magic, then."

Partridge pressed her lips together. Her face wrinkled deeper. She squeezed her eyes shut, then opened them. They looked completely untouched by age. "Magic seeps out the cracks. Always a bit left, Maude, no matter how you try to squeeze it out of you or push it away."

Maude bent over her and kissed her on the forehead. Partridge began to cry.

Only one more square to add to the quilt top. Maude decided to put it aside.

16

THE HOUSE'S INMATES

The next morning, sitting in the room with Partridge, Maude looked at the Rand McNally maps of America, found California, and sighed. "I miss California," she said.

"It's Nevernever Land," Partridge said.

Maude thought about the roads heading out of San Francisco going north, the difference of it, the land shifting under foot, wired by phone line through the Sierra winters to the East Coast, attached by the Pacific to Japan and China.

Doug came limping in and saw what Maude was looking at. "So was I an exotic fuck, too?"

Partridge stared at Maude.

Maude almost said *yes,* but didn't answer. Partridge smiled.

Doug pulled at the atlas until he could see it. "I was born there." He pointed to Maryville. "My grandfather lived on a ranch in the Sierras. The Indians hated him."

Maude said, "I'd like to go back."

Doug shrugged.

"You could borrow Esther's car and at least get out of the house," Partridge said.

Maude asked, "Doug, you need to get out?"

"I feel centuries of European life and mysticism piled on my head. And my foot hurts."

Partridge said, "Get him out at least for a day."

"I can't leave the county," Maude said. "And I'd feel a little silly borrowing a car from Esther."

"I wouldn't," Partridge told her.

"I would. Maybe that's the difference in the times."

Doug said, "I'm going to stay here. I lost my job in Berkeley before I came here. When I was in North Carolina, I called a realtor and put the house on the market."

So Doug had crash-landed at her grandmother's house. "Are you going to work for Follette's research institute?"

"Why do you keep harping on that? I've had two other offers. Luke wants John to have one of them. It's only temporary, anyway, rigging a work monitoring system for a small assembly shop."

"Sounds 1984 to me," Partridge said.

"Luke wants to tell me about the other job later."

They heard Esther coming in and sat silently as she came to the back. "If you need some errands run, I can go out for you," Esther said. Meaning, Maude thought, *don't ask to borrow my car and get it eaten up by the folks who want to trap you.*

Doug said, "I'd like to get out of the house some."

"I can take you with me. Maude might want to sit some alone with her grannie."

Partridge said, "You could all go."

Maude closed the atlas on California. "Better if someone was here. Betty might drop by."

"Or Luke," Partridge said. "I'm not one of those fools who trusts Luke."

Doug said, "I'll ignore that. Couldn't we all go and leave Partridge alone for a little bit?"

Esther went to get Partridge's medical record book. She came back, took Partridge's pulse, entered it, stuck a thermometer in Partridge's mouth, then said, "When a person's dying, folks you trust got to watch over. To make sure the soul leaves in peace."

"Okay." Doug got up and tried to stand on both feet. His knee bent over the shot one. "Maude, we need to take a walk, then."

"Can you?"

"I've got to get some exercise."

Maude also thought he wanted to talk to her in private. "Okay."

Doug got his crutches and hobbled out. It was cold. *Winter equinox, Christmas, ceremonies against the dark,* Maude thought. "Were you planning to be here for Christmas all along?" she asked Doug.

He didn't answer right away, then, on the road, said, "Maude, I don't understand what's come between us. I feel like something's not quite right."

"I've told you not to trust the witches."

"Doesn't that mean I couldn't trust you?"

"Why should you trust me? I'm just a country witch you picked up in a Berkeley bar."

"Maude."

"What is this? Did Luke suggest you make up to me?"

"Maude, it's not like that at all."

"Maybe it's just biology. You're bored. I'm female. We're sniffing each other all the time."

"And your grandmother is dying. Do you think I'd be here if I didn't have some feeling for you?"

Maude felt rebuked. She felt uneasy that he could do that. "So?"

"Maude, I wish we could start over again."

"Back in Berkeley. I want to live where there are no poor families to exploit or ignore if they do manage to accomplish something despite their lack of charms. Let's live where you're judged on what you do and what you know, not on who your people are or what entity's behind them. I thought I could get away from that in the North, but who my people were became even worse. My people were Southern. I always thought Yankees went against the South because we were bigots and if I wasn't one, I'd be welcome. But no. Yankees got to be both anti-black and anti-Southern. I didn't play the class card."

"But, Maude, you come from a good local family. Luke and Betty have an original Picasso print, Claes Oldenburg prints. Luke knows French."

"I have my father's people to consider."

"Ignore them. They're just religious fanatics."

"Who told you that?" She could tell by his face that Luke had. She continued, "If people are fighting Luke and his kind, then maybe those people need the kind of religion my father's people have."

"Luke's civilized."

"Maybe you could bring little ugly but nonpolluting factories to scare the tourists and the urbanoids looking for a quaint country getaway with amusing, uneducated locals to patronize. Bring something here to give good jobs to the locals."

"But it's so beautiful here."

"Like a naked woman in a battlefield," Maude said.

Doug looked toward the small mountain across the road. "More naked without the leaves. Maude, you could protect this place."

"Ugly little factories would protect it better."

Doug didn't answer. Maude saw crows mob a redtail hawk and wondered how Belle fared. Doug didn't notice the commotion. They walked on further, then he said, "I'm getting sore."

"Okay, we'll go back now."

"Maybe I shouldn't have been so quick to bed a country witch when I met one. You think I'm too easy."

Maude said, "Doug, I get the impression Luke asked you to court me again."

"Maude, I'd rather you believe it was us being in the same house together than for you to think I'd do that."

"If you don't like the idea of working for Follette, take the job rigging the computerized work station monitors. Don't let John do that."

"It's just temporary."

"So are you. So am I."

"But you don't have to be."

"A long time isn't forever." Maude wondered if he understood yet that he couldn't have magic. She asked, "Do you understand now that magic isn't something you can learn?"

He stopped at the door and set the crutches aside. She swayed slightly as he gathered himself to take her in his arms. Clinging to her, trying to bend her to him, he kissed her. Maude felt cold but compassionate. He pulled back and brushed his hand across her forehead, moving some hairs. She would have leaned into him, but he was too unsteady on his feet. She almost felt sorry for him for the life he'd lost in California. Or maybe what she missed was the life she could have had, had she not been so cynical, lazy, deluded into thinking just abstaining from witchcraft made a life.

"Let's go in now," she said. "We can talk about this later."

"I feel like you've got untapped strengths."

"If I were them, I would get me out of here."

"Them?"

"The people who want Partridge's soul."

"Maybe you're the target, not Partridge," Doug said.

And you, Doug, are the lure, Maude realized, *only I'm like Belle, an unromantic hawk that expects people will feed her, so why hunt.* How far could she push that metaphor—buteos and accipiters returned to the fist when they missed. "Oh, Doug, why did you have to lose your job?"

"The company lost its grant."

Maude wondered if the previously California money found its way to Virginia, to Follette's research institute. "But you could be looking for work back home."

"I can live for a couple of years here on the house sale money. Houses here cost about a third to a half what my Berkeley house is worth."

"Has it sold yet?"

"No."

Money as hypothetical as the life Maude waited for, the future always so boldly promising, its gaudy colors and significant patterns just tricks of perspective if they existed at all. When a piece of the future turned to the present, it came so spaced from what was yet to come that one could never recognize the entire pattern. The future that really happened never had much connection with the imagined future. While its fragments accumulated in the past as jumbled memories, the future stayed bolder and gaudier than ever. Maude thought that an imaginary future had seduced her into a decade's wait.

The past once was the fabulous time, when the ancestors negotiated with the entities, conquered the barbarians, spoke language that called directly to things. Times changed. Now the future was the promised land. Maude hadn't realized until now that the future, too, could seduce humans from the present, where all the real patterns form.

When Maude got to the back room, Esther said, "Roach called and your car is dead."

Maude felt jolted into a present more real than the one she'd been imagining. "So, I'm really stuck in the house."

Doug said, "I can buy a car."

"When your house sells?"

"No, I've got some savings."

Esther said, "I can take him to get to his money and maybe the garage people have a used car to sell."

Maude went to see Partridge. Her grandmother was sleeping. Sweat dampened the fine hair at her temples. Maude stroked it and wondered if the sweat meant anything. "How is she doing?"

"Not well, Maude," Esther said. She held up the quilt top. It was finished. "Now we've got to quilt it, but I can take it to my circle and have it done in no time."

Maude felt an itch between her shoulder blades. "Don't rush. When can you take Doug to look for a car?"

"We ought do it now, so you have a ride if you need to take her to the hospital at night."

"Now?" Maude asked. "Shouldn't you call to see what's available?"

"I can afford a new car," Doug said. "I do have savings. I have enough in my checking account to make a down payment. I ought to arrange to have the rest of my money transferred here."

Maude suddenly didn't want them to leave her alone with Partridge. She realized that she'd enjoyed having Doug's company all these nights, even if they hadn't had sex since Lula died. *Just a male body in the house.* The present had been busy with her despite what she thought. Or perhaps the satisfaction she got from having Doug around, despite their disagreements, was simple biology. "What if she gets worse while you're gone?"

"Maude, you can always call an ambulance," Esther said. "You did it before Doug and I came to help you."

I wish Doug had come to help me, Maude thought, but she said, "I keep waiting for things to happen."

"Doug, let's go get you a car," Esther said. Even though he had to brace himself against a wall, Doug helped Esther put on her coat. Maude realized she'd never before seen a white man help a black woman with a coat. Then Doug put on his coat and said, "Tomorrow, we can take a ride up to Roanoke."

"I don't believe in that tomorrow," Maude said. She wondered what insane witches did with their powers. *Can't take it, go nuts, hitch back to California, get injected with Prolixin for being a meds resister.*

"Maude, you seeing something?" Esther asked.

Maude felt foolish then because she hadn't really seen anything. Thoughts injected themselves into her brain. Just a normal paranoia, perhaps. "Go on. As you say, I can always call the ambulance."

"You sure?"

"I've got to do something someday, I might as well start being responsible today." As she spoke, Maude felt that sounded less like a commitment than a confession of past indecision. *The future is now. It's shaped by tricks of perspective.* "Go on. I can deal with whatever happens."

"Try," Esther said. She went to Partridge and felt her pulse, then looked at Doug and nodded.

Maude sat down by her grandmother and took Partridge's hand. The blue veins shrank as Maude raised the hand, then swelled again as she put it down on the sheets.

Partridge opened gummy eyes and asked, "What happens next?"

"I'm with you. Esther took Doug out to buy a new car so we're not trapped here."

"Until they get back, we're trapped here."

"Grandmom, I can always call an ambulance."

"If the line isn't busy." Partridge closed her eyes.

"We have the right to interrupt a party-line call for an emergency." Maude tried to remember. Hadn't they gotten a private line?

"Betty will know," Partridge said. Her eyes opened again, glittering.

Maude remembered this woman had outlived all her children. "I won't be eaten. I won't let you be eaten, either."

"Oh, Maudie, you think I'd do that to you? When you're dead, it doesn't matter how long you've lived."

But Maude felt her grandmother's will push at hers. "No, Partridge. I'll pray for you, but . . ."

"Can you pray? Do you believe?"

"I believe in a universe of consistent rules. No special deals."

Partridge closed her eyes. "You believe there's nothing to me after I'm dead."

"I'll have them bury you in the family plot, not at the church. With men digging the hole and men filling it, so you aren't trapped in the grave. If you want to haunt me, you can. Do you know why you asked me here?"

"Maudie, you were supposed to give me courage."

"You thought ambivalence took courage?" Maude leaned toward her grandmother. Partridge's breaths rocked her body.

"It hurts, Maude," she said.

"Badly enough that you need to go to the hospital?"

"I don't know. Take my pulse."

Maude took her grandmother's wrist between her fingers. The pulse was faint, rapid. "Where does it hurt?"

"I'm afraid."

"Where does it hurt?"

"I need some bicarbonate. I need to get up."

Maude helped Partridge sit up in bed. Her grandmother's body was sweating under her nightgown. She grabbed Maude's shoulder as though she were drowning. Maude asked, "Where do you want to go?"

"I want to go to the graveyard and talk to my mother."

"The graveyard is too far to walk."

"No, we can make it."

"Please, grandmother."

Partridge's fingers clawed into Maude's neck. "Why do I have to hurt?"

"I don't know." Maude wondered if the pain was nature's way of blocking the path back to life.

"The universe you believe in wants me dead, Maude. It's hurting me."

"Grandmother, did you eat all your children?"

The old lady's fingers dug deeper into Maude's neck. "I'm hurting."

"I can take you to the hospital."

"Don't want Betty here."

Maude heard the old Essex pull in the driveway. "She's already here."

Partridge released Maude's neck. "I need to go to the bathroom."

"How do we get rid of Betty?"

"Take me to the bathroom. She can wait."

Maude helped Partridge into the bathroom and sat her on the toilet. The old woman's ass dangled between her spread legs. Maude expected Betty to break in at any moment, Betty's face to appear in the bathroom window despite the fifteen feet between the glass and the yard below.

Partridge strained, then said, "I need Epsom salts. It hurts." She urinated, then took a washcloth to wipe. Maude pulled toilet paper off the roll and wiped, then threw the washcloth into the sink and ran water over it.

"You waste paper," Partridge said. Maude helped her off the toilet and pulled the nightgown down over her grandmother's grey pubic hair.

Betty was banging on the door now. Maude asked, "You don't want her in?"

"Get rid of her."

Maude went to the door. She almost expected Betty to be transformed into a long-toothed beast, slavering, but when she opened the door, Betty stood in a blue wool suit, lapels bent, not pressed flat, holding out gloved hands. "How is Partridge?"

"Fine."

"I don't think so."

"She's taking a bath. You might come back later."

"I've seen naked old women."

Maude realized she'd have to either let Betty in or block her physically. Betty pushed against Maude's shoulder with one gloved hand and said, "You're being paranoid."

"I suppose so, but you can't come in."

"How are you going to keep me out?"

Maude closed the door, locking herself on the outside with Betty. "I'll see you to your car."

"Give me the key."

Maude shook her head. She felt the key in her hand and crossed her arms over her breasts, the hand with the key tucked in her armpit.

Betty reached for her. Her aunt's hand seemed to take days extending, the joints mechanically unfolding, the tendons and ligaments turning to steel wire under the skin. The nails, dead protein, touched Maude's left wrist.

"Why, Maude, you have some talents, but you're hurting me. And yourself. And Partridge." The fingers squirmed.

"We're all just biological machines."

"Give me the key, Maude."

Maude shoved Betty back with her right arm. Betty became a blur of figures, one Betty falling to the ground, another lurching back but keeping her balance, others wringing their hands. "Could you live with breaking my hip, Maude?"

Maude couldn't tell which was the real Betty. She reached out to see what she could feel. Fingers grabbed her wrist again. She twisted free of them, but dropped the key. The blur of figures cleared. The only real Betty reached for the dropped key. Maude decided the frail body was an illusion and shoved Betty back hard. *Couldn't break her hip for trying.*

Just as Maude grabbed the key, sprawling down on her hands and knees, she heard two cars slowing down to pull in the driveway. *Are they real cars?* She looked up through her hair to see Betty smoothing her gloves and smiling.

Esther came in with Doug. *He has his car, but now I can't leave,* Maude realized. *As long as Partridge is alive, I've got to defend her against Betty.*

Betty said, "Maude's being paranoid again."

"She can't come in. Partridge doesn't want to see her." Maude smoothed back her hair and looked at her muddy knees. "You sure found a car quick."

"We been all day," Esther said. Maude looked up then and noticed that the sun was in the west. All day?

"Maude postpones things. It's her vice," Betty said.

"Maude, you mustn't be doing that," Esther said.

"I'm sorry, but she can't come in," Maude said. She wondered again what happened if a witch went insane.

"Maude, I'll try another day then." Betty looked at the others as if to say, *what a rude girl.* "You seem to have lost your manners. And we've always been so kind to you."

"You polite'ed on me. Manners in the South frequently conceal ruthless rudeness." She looked at Esther, wondering if the black woman would rebuke her for saying such a thing, but Esther moved slightly toward her. Doug, on the other hand, seemed bewildered.

"I've got to go check on Partridge," Maude said, her voice finally as collected as Betty's. "We're really busy right now."

"I understand. I'll be back later."

"Well, we won't see you in, then," Esther told her.

Betty said, "Maude, you're filled with ambivalence. Consider what might happen if you *did* lose your mind."

Neither Maude nor Esther said anything as Betty walked back to the Essex. Doug said, "If I'm in the way, I'll move my car." Maude saw that Doug's new car, an Asian subcompact sedan, sat beside the Essex.

Betty said, "My car can manage."

As Betty pulled out, Esther said, "A mean sucking bitch with a mean sucking car. Check the oil before you drive it again, Douglas."

"What was that all about?" Doug asked. "I don't think she's a bitch at all."

"We got to keep Maude's grandmomma safe from soul suckers."

Maude said, "She was in pain." They went in the house and found Partridge sitting up in bed, her eyes wide open, blinking slowly. Very slowly.

Esther reached for Partridge's wrist and said, "You make things go slow or was that Maude?"

"I hurt," Partridge said. "I hurt. Get me bicarb."

"Now, I don't know if bicarb'd be good for you."

"It hurts."

Maude said, "She tried to pass her bowels . . ." Her mind's eye threw her the image of her grandmother straining at the toilet. "But she couldn't."

"I can give her an enema. Doug, why don't you take Maude for a little drive."

"No, I'll stay here."

Partridge said, "Don't hurt me."

"Call her doctor," Maude decided.

Esther said, "I tangled with that doctor on another case. He lets old people die without fussing over them. But I'll try." She went to the phone in the kitchen and called.

Maude, sitting by her grandmother, heard Esther say, "I don't know if more pain pills is really what she needs." Then Esther came back and reported, "He says he'll phone in a prescription for painkillers."

Maude said, "I wonder if I should talk to him. I've never met him."

"He says the trouble with her is she's dying."

Maude agreed with the doctor, but wasn't as happy with his detachment as she wanted to be. "I could pick up the prescription." She looked at Doug and said, "If you'd drive me."

"Sure."

Esther nodded. Partridge's eyes were glassy and unfocused. Maude asked, "Can you keep Betty away?"

"With the Lord's help," Esther said.

Maude wondered, then she remembered how Betty had gone when Esther came back to the house. She didn't really think an omnipotent entity helped Esther but rather Esther's own strength of mind, formed as it might have been around an illusion. Maude knew she'd never been strong-minded because she saw so many mental strengths founded on illusions. *Perhaps the illusions have nothing to do with the strength?* She backed two steps away from Esther, then turned to walk away with Doug.

Night had come. Maude got in the passenger seat and stared out beyond the headlights.

"You have to tell me where we're going," Doug said.

"I'd have thought you knew the county perfectly by now," Maude said. "I don't even have a car anymore."

"I can help you."

"But you hate weak people."

Doug didn't answer for a mile. Then he said, "I don't like working out ways, technical ways, to empower stupid people. Maude, I'm not responsible for your financial state or your being here, but I have offered to help."

"Sorry. I'm worried about my grandmother. It makes me bitchy." Maude knew she said that to distract him.

"I've decided I'm going to work for Follette's research

institute. The other job sounds like Big Brother wants to
wire the workers so he can get maximum effort out of
them.''

"But is the pay at the assembly plant good?''

"What?''

"If the pay is good, then the good workers want the boss
to know they're working hard.''

"Have you ever been a factory worker?''

"No, but I've talked to them.''

"Maybe they just tell you what they think a middle-class
person wants to hear.''

"I was on welfare at the time.'' Maude remembered she
was now dependent on a dying woman. "I don't want her to
die so quickly.''

"You are worried about your grandmother.''

"Yes. Turn at the hospital. The pharmacy is in the office
complex behind it.''

Doug turned, found the building, and parked. Maude
went in and saw, above the counter, cases of radio parts—
glass tubes, wax-covered resistors, cylinders with thin wires,
speaker cones. She said, "I'm here for Partridge Roar's prescription. What are those?''

"The history of radio in parts.'' The pharmacist looked
through a file, found the prescription, and went to the back
to fill it.

Maude looked at the radio parts and wondered if the
man was celebrating the development of radio or dismem-
bering radios in hostile acts. "Do you like radios?''

The man came out with the prescription. He said, "My
grandfather said the world has never been through such a
change as from the time he was a boy to now.''

"But is it a good change?'' The pharmacist looked as
though he didn't want to offend Maude. She added, "Ideas
spread faster.''

"Sometimes lies spread faster.''

"How much is the prescription?''

"Your grandmother has insurance that covers it.''

And I didn't know that. Maude said, "I'll probably be back."

"We've been serving your people for a long time," the pharmacist said. Maude wondered if he also sold herbs and quicksilver for charms and alchemy. He handed her the pills and she signed the receipt, then left.

When she got back in the car, Maude said, "Everyone knows my people here."

"Shall we go home now?" Doug asked. Maude thought he said it to be polite because as he spoke, he turned the key in the ignition.

Maude stretched her legs out as best she could in the small car. As they pulled back onto the highway, Betty's Essex glided up behind them. Doug's car backfired, then lurched ahead. He fought the steering wheel.

Doug said, "I can't believe all witches are bad, but maybe you're right about her."

The Essex dropped back, then turned off to the left. Maude knew that back roads paralleled the highway. The Essex could beat them to Kobold. Neither she nor Doug spoke until they saw her grandmother's house. The Essex wasn't there. Maude twisted her torso to ease the muscle tension. But as soon as she opened the front door, the wall phone in the kitchen began to ring.

"Hi, Maude, this is Terry. I understand Partridge wants to be buried in the family plot."

And Terry lives on the family farm, beside the family graveyard. "Yes," Maude said.

"We'd like to come over and talk to her."

"Who?"

"Aunt Betty and me."

"She doesn't want to see Aunt Betty."

"Can you put her on the phone?"

"She's sleeping," Maude said, not bothering to check.

"I'd hate to think Betty and Partridge couldn't be reconciled before Partridge dies."

"Perhaps you could come to the hospital," Maude said.

"It seems cruel to take your grandmother to the hospital to die when she could go comfortably at home, surrounded by people she knows. The doctor could prescribe pain pills."

Maude heard Doug and Esther talking in Partridge's room behind the kitchen. She listened for Partridge's voice, but only heard water from the bathroom sink, then that stopped and Esther murmured something. Someone, probably Partridge, swallowed.

"Partridge is taking a pill, isn't she?" Terry said.

"Your phone is awfully acute."

"Please, if I come over by myself, could I talk to Partridge and find out why she doesn't want to see Aunt Betty before she dies?"

"Let me ask her," Maude said. She lay the phone down on the counter and went back to Partridge's room. Partridge lay propped up against pillows, her face looking as though she'd been swimming and was only half dry. "Terry wants to see you."

"I must be dying."

Esther said, "We're with you."

Doug asked, "Is Terry a problem?"

Maude nodded but said, for the sensitive phone and the listeners behind it, "It's the rest of Partridge's life, so whatever she wants."

Partridge shook her head. "I'll see Terry later," she said. She moved her hips and winced.

Maude went back to the kitchen phone and said, "Probably now isn't a good time, Terry."

"Tell Partridge she's being selfish," Terry said. "Maude, you ought to consider the feelings of the people who'll be alive after Partridge passes on."

"Sorry, Terry, but it is the rest of Partridge's life I'm protecting."

Terry hung up. Maude put the phone receiver back in its cradle and wondered why she was so determined to protect Partridge. The woman had been an active witch.

Esther said, "We ought to take her to the hospital."

"Let's wait to see if the painkiller we brought back helps," Maude said. "I don't want to move her at night." *We've been serving your people, the pharmacist had said.* She sat down by the bed and touched her grandmother's head at the hairline, feeling the skull. "What is this all about anyway? Maybe . . ." Maude almost said, *I should give her to Betty,* when Partridge's eyes opened.

"Let me be a ghost to help you," Partridge said.

Esther came over and took Partridge's pulse. She said, "No better, no worse."

"Please keep Betty away," Partridge said.

"Terry, too?"

"Her, too. She doesn't know what she's doing."

"You're going to leave me to them."

"Is that what's tempting you?" Esther said. "Doug and I will be with you."

"Doug's more tempted by them than I am."

Esther asked, "Is that true, Douglas?"

Doug nodded. "I can't believe all magic is bad."

Esther said, "And you an engineer."

"Luke has plans for him."

"I do hate being witness to these witch things."

"Aren't you a witness to warn others?"

"If it comes to that," Esther said.

"Betty wants my soul, too. She's offered to train me."

"If you have good people who love you around, they keep off the witches," Esther said.

"But Betty's still trying to get to see Partridge."

Esther didn't say anything then. She looked away from Maude, looked at Doug, and went to her purse. Out of it, she pulled a small New Testament. She opened it and began moving her lips silently. Maude wondered why she put any trust in a woman who moved her lips while she read. Superstitious, ill-educated, perhaps not even that bright.

"Shame brute power, don't surrender to it," Esther said. "I'll stay with you tonight."

"You're sure you don't have some magic?"

"No, Maude, I don't. And I know white people tend to look down on folks who read moving their lips. But it shapes the word for me."

Maude was embarrassed.

Doug asked, "Does someone have to be awake with her at all times?"

"Yes, you go get a nap now. Maude, you too, if you can sleep from worrying."

"I don't think I can."

"You ought to try. I'll be up with her."

"I'm afraid to lose consciousness."

"Do they get you in your sleep?"

"I'm afraid they will."

Doug said, "Well, I better sleep then. Someone needs to be able to drive in the morning."

Maude found a straight hard chair to sit in and turned on the radio to a PBS station. Doug went to the bathroom, then left them by Partridge's bed.

Esther's lips moved over her New Testament. Maude wondered if Esther was as protected as she thought. She wondered why she was pitting herself against Betty and Luke when they seemed to really want to train her in their ways. She nodded in her hard chair. Esther came over and said, "You might as well sleep lying down as to be jerking your neck in that chair."

Microsleeps. As open as long ones. Maude nodded and got up. She saw the room through sleep green and the graininess of eyes that had almost shut down to the outside. "Wake me if anything happens."

17

MACROSLEEP

I'm paralyzed, Maude thought, *dreaming.*

Betty materialized, first her clothes, then the bones inside the clothes, then the face. Betty said, "If you won't talk to me in the air, we'll talk here."

Is this the Betty I made inside my head or is this really Betty, inserted into my head? Maude remembered that she should look at her dream hands when in a dream that seemed frightening. According to something she'd read in Berkeley, this was supposed to give the dreamer control of the dream. She tried to look at her hands, but was distracted. She and Betty were riding on a Berkeley bus. "I've got to go home," Maude said.

Betty in the dream took Maude's hands in her own. *Oh, there my hands were all along,* Maude thought, *but Betty's looking at both pairs of hands, too.*

"All I'm asking is that you let me say good-bye to Partridge. I'll help you find your way home then," Betty said. "Remember, we're kin."

"She asked me not to," Maude said.

"She can't be sanctified this late in the game. You wonder if she ate your mother and father. Or failed to protect them."

Maude thought Betty should have known for sure. This was her own Betty-side.

Betty said, "Or is it? Do you really think I know everything?"

"If you don't know everything, we can win, then."

"Who? You and Partridge? Or you and me."

Maude got off the bus. She was dressed in a satin mini-skirt, boots, and a low-cut blouse. As she walked, teenaged boys of all races began to follow her. *I've got to get home,* she thought. In the dream, she lived in a rented apartment. *I haven't been there long and I don't remember exactly.*

The boys made her feel naked in her whore gear. Betty had disappeared when the boys showed up, but Maude only realized that dream minutes later. "I'm trying to find my way home," she told a Chinese boy in a black leather trench coat. The city around them looked vaguely like San Francisco, not New York. The blocks of streets were set at angles to each other, interrupted by expressways and business deserts.

"We'll help you," he said. But none of the boys seemed to know where Maude should go.

Maude walked through a campus building that seemed to be the interface between a good neighborhood and a bad one. She vaguely recognized the college. It was rumored to be near where she lived.

The street numbers twisted into new configurations. The teenagers following her seemed slightly less menacing. "Are you lost?" a white boy asked.

"Yes," Maude said, firmly in the dream.

"Don't you have an Aunt Betty who lives around here?"

"No," Maude said. The boys seemed threatening again. She looked up and thought she saw her block ahead, slightly uphill. "She doesn't live here. She lives in Virginia."

"How you know this isn't Virginia?" a black boy said. "Looks like Richmond to me."

Maude found the block where she thought she might be living, but couldn't recognize any of the houses. "How can I be dreaming about Richmond? I've only been there once."

"You could go home with me," the black boy said. Maude wondered if he looked like the boy John killed. Perhaps he was the boy John killed. She tried to look at her hands again, to raise them in front of her eyes. *What do I want to do?*

Maude wanted to find her home. She was lost. The boys seemed less like rapist wannabes and more like kids following someone strange to see what would happen. She pulled out a key from her purse and tried it in a door. It didn't fit. She looked around her and saw another set of buildings that looked familiar and began walking toward them.

Aunt Betty came up and said, "Enough of this. I'm going to take you home. And what were you doing out in the city wearing whore rig?"

Maude remembered men putting folded-up money under a mirror in her apartment, the one she'd never find now. I was a whore, she thought, but she just crossed her arms over her breasts. She looked down at her hand, but couldn't remember why seeing her hand was important.

Betty draped a coat around her. The boys circled them. "You technically weren't a whore, but you were as bad as one, selling your blood to go drinking and looking for men," Betty said. "Your bar men fed you in good restaurants. So now you want to be super good. This is rather hypocritical. It's like Partridge deciding not to be a witch now."

The black boy said, "I want to go home, too." He was the soul John had trapped when he shot the cadaver. Maude wondered if John taught him burglary to begin with.

I've got to get out of here. Maude woke up and stared at the windows, shrub shadows moving over the curtains. *Am I really awake?* She sat up. The covers fell away from her shoulders and she was cold. Awake, then, most likely.

A car that sounded like Betty's Essex came down the road. Maude decided to check on her grandmother and talk to Esther or Doug, whoever was staying awake now. She pulled on a robe and went to the back of the house.

Partridge lay awake. Her eyes seemed luminous. Esther was slumped in the chair, the New Testament dropped to the floor, pages crumpled. Horrified, Maude touched Esther, expecting cold flesh.

"She's asleep," Partridge said.

"I dreamed I couldn't find my apartment." That didn't explain the nightmare sense of the dream. Maude wondered if she should wake Esther. She picked up the New Testament and smoothed down the pages. The book was open to John. Maude knew the writer lied, claimed closer connections to the times and people than was possible. "And Betty said I was as bad as a whore."

"It hurts," Partridge whispered. "Oh, please."

Maude felt stupid and mean. "Where?"

"Stomach."

Maude shook Esther and said, "We've got to get her to a hospital. Even if it still is night."

Esther said, "I was dreaming about my father's funeral. His corpse had a smile. That's because he died sanctified."

"Okay, but I'm going to wake Doug."

Esther looked at Partridge, whose eyes gleamed in the dark. "I'll get Doug."

Doug came out of his bed on his own then. "What is it?"

Partridge groaned. Maude said, "We've got to get her to the hospital."

"Okay, I'll get dressed."

"She won't be able to lie down in your car if we all go. And I want Esther with me."

"We can call an ambulance," Doug said.

"I want to take her myself," Maude said. "We cross a spur of Wart Mountain between the mortuary and the hospital."

Esther told her, "Drive my car. I had it blessed."

Doug said, "I don't understand why she doesn't want to call on magic, at least to kill the pain."

Partridge groaned, "Magic don't . . . never . . . kill . . . pain. Ask Follette."

But Esther's father died with a smile on his face, Maude thought. Probably a misinterpreted rictus or a dead face sagging.

"Okay," Doug said.

"We need you to help get her to the car."

"I've got to get dressed."

Maude felt very anxious. While the women waited for Doug to get dressed, the Essex drove by the house again.

"That one can smell loose souls," Esther said.

"What do you mean by magic never kills the pain?" Maude asked Partridge, not sure her grandmother could answer her.

Partridge opened her eyes even wider and opened her mouth. Maude heard clamoring voices, the dead inside her grandmother. Something inside her own head said, *we haven't been amused.* Maude thought of Follette, betrayed by his entity and his fighting birds. She thought back, *our purpose isn't to entertain you.*

Doug said, "I'm ready to help."

Esther asked, "Can you carry her out while we bring her things?"

"I can help, but I'm not sure I should trust my foot."

"I . . . will . . . walk," Partridge said. "Dress me."

"It's all right, honey," Esther said. "We can carry you out wrapped in a quilt."

"You finished it."

"Not that one. I left it with my church circle to quilt."

"Damn you."

"No, ma'am, I don't think so," Esther said.

"I want to be dressed," Partridge said. "I want shoes on."

Maude said, "You won't be doing any walking after the hospital." Shit, how cruel, she thought.

Doug said, "I think you ought to let her get dressed."

"Well, then you'll want to step out," Maude said.

"No," Partridge said. "He needs to see. Esther, get what I told you."

Maude wondered if Partridge was trying to horrify Doug with an aged female body or if she wanted to display herself naked before a male one last time. Esther brought Partridge her underclothes—a pair of linen drawers washed almost transparent, icy cold to the touch, a matching camisole, a silk shift and hose.

Partridge stripped and stood naked. Then, her body turned young again, a beautiful body with high breasts. Doug gasped. The body faded back to old as Esther helped

Partridge into the linen drawers and the bodice. Maude felt pity and some resentment for Partridge's trick, but she sympathized, too.

Doug said, "You needed me to see that."

Esther shook her head, but Partridge said, "Yes." She stood erect, head up, in her linen underclothes. Maude wondered if the aides who undressed her at the hospital would be surprised to see such linen.

"You were a beautiful woman."

"Yes," Partridge said. "Now, the dress."

Esther brought in a blue worsted dress that buttoned down the bodice. Maude realized her grandmother and the nurse had decided earlier what to wear for this final live dressing. She felt excluded.

Partridge raised herself off the bed so Esther could drop it over her head. The old woman's right arm slid through the sleeve, but Esther had to reach through the sleeve for the left one. Then Partridge put her right hand on Esther's shoulder while Esther buttoned her in. Then, before Esther helped her put on her shoes, she sat down. She said, "Maude, bring my teeth. The dish is by the toilet."

Grandmother is giving quite a show, Maude thought. *I hope her entities are amused.*

But it's not for us, an inhuman thought inserted.

Partridge collapsed as though what held her up had thrown her down. Maude pushed her grandmother's nightgowns and false teeth into an overnight bag. Doug took the bag from her and went out to Esther's car.

"Get hold of her shoulder, Maude," Esther said.

"I want to walk out," Partridge told them. Maude and Esther supported Partridge. She leaned most heavily on Esther. The three of them went sideways through the house doors. Esther sat Partridge down in a porch chair while Maude locked the house, then they continued out into the yard.

Partridge said, "Turn me around to face it."

Maude and Esther, still holding Partridge up, turned so

Partridge could look at her house for the last time. Her eyes moved from the chimneys to the windows to the front door. "Your granddad . . . had to have . . . an electric house," she said to Maude. "It had a Delco battery plant and a gas generator to recharge. You understood . . . electric'ty . . . then."

Maude wished she'd talked more with Partridge about that past unconnected to the witches and the bewitched. "I bet you were proud of having an electric house."

"It half ate me," Partridge said. "Lit up for any fool."

Doug came up. "Need any help?" Partridge looked back over her shoulder at him and then back at the house. Esther tugged very slightly at Partridge. The old woman stiffened, then moaned slightly and relaxed. Maude and Esther eased her back around and helped her the rest of the way to the car. The sun was beginning to come up, but the snow patches crackled underfoot.

Partridge looked in the rear seat of the car and said, "Can't lie down."

"I want to go with you," Doug said.

"Bring Esther in your car. I don't want anyone else with me," Maude said.

Esther asked, "You sure you'll be all right? It has child locks." Doug opened the doors and set the locks so the doors couldn't be unlocked from the inside.

"She needs a quilt," Maude said. She gave Esther the house key and said, "Bring the one off my bed." Esther went and came back. Together, they put Partridge in the back seat and used the quilt to cushion and cover her.

Maude said, "We've got a spur of Wart Mountain to cross."

"You drive your grannie. Doug and I will follow."

Maude wished she could have Esther with her, but she knew Doug couldn't defend himself against the witches and the magic. She knew not to leave him alone in the house. "Okay, let's go."

As she looked out the back, Maude noticed Esther let Doug drive.

As Maude pulled out into the road, Partridge said, "Bury me . . . at the old place."

Maude wondered if Partridge would walk as a ghost or dissolve. Her grandmother, on different occasions, said both. "I'll bury you with your people."

"Confused . . . need to get out."

"Of the car?"

Partridge didn't answer. The Essex passed Esther's car and pulled up on Maude's bumper.

Why am I taking this old lady to die? Maude wondered.

"Ready to die now," Partridge said. "Couldn't collect my nerve and get ready again."

The Essex headlights brightened into a glare in the rear-view mirror. Maude flipped the mirror to the night position. The windshield flared.

Two old men started crossing the road. Maude had almost hit the breaks when she realized she could see through them. *Betty's slipping.* She hit the accelerator.

The sun began to show. Maude flipped down her visors and saw Betty's face in the mirror inset in the right visor.

Betty's mirror face said, "You're both being foolish."

Maude flipped the visor up, but the sun glared at her. *I'll ignore her,* she thought. When she flipped the mirror back down, Betty's face was gone. The radio came on. "You could become as I've become. Just pull the car over."

Partridge said, "No."

"She's too confused to set herself up as a ghost," Betty's voice said.

Maude wondered why it was so important to have her grandmother's spirit dissolve. "I'm doing what she wants."

"That nigger's rotted her with prayer."

Esther's car shuddered. Maude wished Esther rode with her. "It's what Partridge wants."

"If she's going to throw herself away, then I've got the right to her."

"I don't think so."

"You never understood family, Maude."

"I'm half-loser," Maude said, pressing down harder on

the accelerator when she felt air resistance. Spell or wind, the car jumped ahead.

Maude tried to visualize the combustion process—air through the air filter to the carburetor to the pistons where the fuel mixed with it. A spark, contained explosion, and the piston blew down, turning the crankshaft. Then the other pistons firing raised the piston she'd been focusing on. It pressed out the burnt gases. Air and gas entered the cylinder again.

The radio died. Maude wondered if heavy thinking about automotive reality damaged Betty's old Essex. Surely, without magic, age would have damaged the cylinders. The rods and piston heads could be metal fatigued.

Maude's own car started to falter. *What did I think wrong?* Maude wondered. *Could it be?*

"No," Partridge said from the back seat.

Maude visualized shards of metal flaking into the Essex valves. She saw the Essex swerve.

"No," Partridge said.

Maude asked, "Why not?"

"You witch."

Maude realized she'd been attacking the Essex with magic.

The radio said, "Why shouldn't she try to outwitch me? Mechanically, my Essex is in fine shape."

Maude wondered how the Essex could be.

"We've cannibalized many a car for this one," Betty said. The Essex came closer.

Esther's car seemed to be speeding up without Maude's foot pressing harder on the accelerator. The sun was in Maude's eyes. She realized the Essex rode in her car's shadow. Esther's blessed car.

"Do you want to kill us?" Maude said to the radio.

Betty's face materialized in the visor mirror, in the rearview mirror, in the side mirror. The three faces looked around the car. "I'll get what I want if you don't die instantly."

Maude didn't believe in Esther's God, but she knew that

people with strong beliefs could defend against witches even though they could never defeat them. But anyone from those communities who doubted was instant witch food.

Magic, witches, wasn't this all crazy? Maude began to wonder. She tried to remember seeing magic witnessed by others. *Doug?* But then she'd thought Doug was a madman when they met. He wanted magic to exist.

The sex was incredible. The fairystone waved its arms at them. They saw the tiny research institute in the back of Follette's pickup. The gun shot Doug's foot.

What can I believe in? Maude passed the pool hall. Daylight wrecked the building, showed the falling siding and broken windows. *What showed yesterday, last night?* Were charms cheaper than rebuilding, or was the difference only between night imaginings and what real light showed? *I want a universe with constant laws, even laws that tell us nothing can be completely predicted.* She hadn't gotten to the Wart Mountain spur yet, but she realized she'd have to stop at the highway. The hospital, she realized, was at the top of the spur.

Suddenly, Maude imagined telling her social worker in Berkeley about this and giggled. *Oh, no, please, don't make me laugh.* She stopped at the stop sign and wondered if she was truly paranoid, hallucinating old ladies in the car mirrors, voices in the radio.

The Essex didn't do anything, just pulled in behind her. The mirrors reflected only the world parallel to them. A tractor began pulling out up the highway. Maude decided to pull out just before it got there, blocking the Essex. No, that's craziness, she thought, pulling out well before the tractor arrived.

The Essex came behind her. Now the tractor was between the two front cars and Doug's car. Maude wondered if behind her terrible fear of the Essex was a benign reality, an Aunt Betty who was concerned about her kinswomen and happened to be passing through when they took Partridge out to the car. Betty, in this non-witch reality, would have realized they were taking Partridge to the hospital and would have wanted to follow. Maude's insanity twisted the reality into . . .

"No."

"No, what?"

"Not . . . crazy."

Maude wondered what Partridge knew. She remembered her dream and felt lost again. "I can't rely on anyone, not even myself," she said. Could drugs numb witchery?

"If you're . . . crazy . . ." Partridge didn't finish what she was saying. "Hurry."

"I don't know." She slowed the car down to thirty miles per hour, hoping Betty would pass her.

"Hurry," Partridge said.

If I'm insane, Maude realized, *an entire county is, too. I can't afford to doubt.* For the duration, witches and entities were real. She pushed down on the accelerator and felt her sanity rip away.

"No, I don't think so," she said out loud to whatever caused the delusion.

The road vanished. She felt the car tires on the road and decided she just couldn't see the road. Perhaps Betty wanted to crash them and come upon their bodies. If so, Maude floored the accelerator to make sure the bodies would die instantly. She wondered if the accelerator was real.

"Yes," her grandmother said as the car went faster.

The road reappeared, but not in Bracken County. The Essex was still behind them, but around them was a high country of the gods—neglected ones—or a posthuman future.

Glaciers converged at bulldozer pace on a ruined shopping mall on an altiplano in air thinner than that at twelve thousand feet. Along the road itself, rocks shattered from seasons that cycled from heat to subzero in sixty seconds. The land swayed. Continental granite floated like boats on an ocean.

Maude tried to remember the road that led to the hospital. She drove through the shattering rocks, but the pavement was still under the car tires.

The car stopped. No, Maude still heard the pavement under the tires. Various minor gods surrounded the car, pissed at being neglected.

"Go away," Maude said to them.

Then, in front of her, larger than four billboards, completely blocking the road and the rest of the landscape, Maude saw the Minotauromachy. If she broke through, a whole self was gone, the cultivated witch with gloves, tea sets, art, and a thousand minor humans sacrificed to her. Betty wanted to like her. Betty had so much to offer.

Aunt Betty reappeared in the mirrors. "Why are you committing yourself to death?" Betty asked. "I don't want to hurt you."

"Do you remember the Pleistocene?" Maude asked. "Are you as old as the human race?"

"I never lived at the expense of worthy people."

Maude tried to wipe Betty's reflection off the mirrors.

The reflection appeared startled, but stayed. Its lips moved, saying, "Oh, Maude, do you love your grandmother for what she did to your mother?"

I've always hated these people. "My mother died in an accident. You can't have my grandmother." Maude drove the car through the Minotaur. The print blew away in huge tatters. The tires on the left side of the car hit dirt. Maude pulled the wheel sharply to the right. She tried to see the road, struggled to get magic to work for her.

"Now you don't scruple to use it, but I'm stronger."

"You'd just have stopped the car." Maude realized that if they had stopped, then Esther could have caught up to them, and Doug. William Blake's lines came to mind about Newton killing the garden. Maude felt the car crest the hilltop. Time to turn.

"You're just opposed to me because you like being an underdog," Betty's radio voice told Maude. "Being an underdog means you never have to be responsible."

"I am responsible. I'm taking my grandmother to the hospital."

The road reappeared around her. Betty said, "Taking her to the hospital to die. Then to the cemetery to rot."

Maude wondered if Partridge could be buried in the family cemetery after this. Betty's image faded from the mirrors. Suddenly, Maude felt tired, grubby. Her pants were sweaty, perhaps she'd pissed them pulling the car back on the road.

More cars began appearing on the road now, an ordinary workday with a dying woman in the back seat. Maude was beginning to think she'd won when a pickup veered over into her lane. The front bumper was one huge plank, protruding inches from the sides. Maude saw the grain swirling through the wood.

No, I'm not going fast enough. She swerved away from truck, felt as much as heard the bumper grind against her door. Maude didn't know whether Betty had tried to wreck her and failed or what. She looked behind to see that the Essex had dropped back.

A car pulled from nowhere and crushed her right headlight.

"You won't be far from the hospital when you crash," the radio voice said.

"What have I done that you'd do this to me?"

"You refused me. You want to be a loser."

Maude wondered whether she was listening to Betty or the entity behind her. "What if I reconsider?" Lie to liars.

"It doesn't really matter if we don't get Partridge. Let her die and get pickled in formaldehyde, her guts trocared out of her belly, her face plumped out with wax, buried as a half-flesh, half-chemical mock of a real woman."

"It's just her body."

"We'll be generous. We will let you bury her in the family plot."

The magic faded. But as Maude turned into the hospital entrance, she felt magic again. She hit the accelerator at the entrance to the emergency room and passed it. Hook waving, jacked-up Ford rocking, Jake sped out of the hospital parking lot, nearly hitting her. Maude looked behind her and saw that the Essex had stopped. She turned around and came back down to face the Essex in the other lane. She paused to look through the car windows at Aunt Betty. Betty sat weeping. She nodded at Maude. When Maude turned, the Essex turned to follow.

They'd entertained the entities. Maude almost pitied her aunt for not realizing witchery was only the spurs that entities put on her for her fights with other humans.

She remembered Jake's face just seconds before, speeding by her. It was not enough that they took his hand; they would have killed him to get her. Maude realized she couldn't afford to pity her aunt. She pulled the car up to the emergency entrance.

Attendants came out to the car. "Man, what happened?"

The car was crumpled, front headlight out, metal dragging against the right tire. The driver's door was smashed shut. Betty's Essex pulled past them and parked in a lot beyond the emergency entrance.

"My grandmother needed to come here," Maude said. "She's hurting." She slid across the seat and opened the right-hand door, then got out and unlocked Partridge's. The attendants brought out a gurney.

"Why didn't you call an ambulance?" a nurse who'd come out said.

"Thought this would be faster," Maude answered. "She could still walk when we left the house." She wondered where Doug and Esther were. She was sorry about Esther's car.

Partridge sat up and looked at the emergency room attendants. Maude was startled. The nurse looked at Maude as if perhaps this was some kind of hoax. Then Partridge said, "It hurts." She scrabbled at the car door as if trying to pull herself up to stand. The attendants took her by the shoulders and hips and laid her on the gurney.

One pulled his hand away from her dress and said, "She's bleeding. Do you know if it's rectal or vaginal?"

"I don't know," Maude said.

"Who's her doctor?" an aide asked.

"Her doctor's not a surgeon. We need a surgeon," the nurse said. "We'll call Dr. Armitage."

As they wheeled the gurney away into the hospital, Betty came walking up to Maude. She touched the wrecked side of the car, then went around to see the headlight. As Betty rubbed one kid-encased finger around a shard of headlight glass, Maude thought, *she still has her gloves on.* Betty pinched the glass between her thumb and forefinger and wiggled it free from the remains of the headlight mount. She asked Maude, "Are you happy? Or do you feel like a fool?"

"I'm doing what she wants."

"You're weak. You could be stronger."

"I got her here."

"As though letting her die to spite me was a victory."

"As you said, I feel virtuous being a loser." As soon as her tongue dropped and lips closed, Maude felt she'd been stupidly brave to say that. She realized everything this woman told her could have been lies.

"Well," Betty said, "let's go in to see Partridge."

But the medics had Partridge now. The nurse said, "We'll let you know what happens. The surgeon is on his way."

Doug and Esther came in then. Maude said, "I'm sorry about your car."

Esther looked flustered. "How is your grannie?"

"I don't know."

Doug looked from Maude to Betty and back. "Shouldn't you call in a report on hit-and-run? Esther's insurance company might need it."

"I'll pay for the damage," Betty said.

"As you're responsible," Maude said.

"Now, Maude, don't go delusional on us," Betty said. "Esther, we appreciate your loan of the car." She pulled out her purse and began to count out money with her

gloved fingers. "It's $200. That should cover the damages."
Her arm extended toward Esther, the bills drooping off the
fingertips.

Esther took the money, turning each bill over before she
put the money in her purse.

"Don't loan Maude your car again," Betty said. "She's a
terrible driver when she hallucinates."

A nurse overheard Betty and said, "Is she on drugs?"

Maude said, "No."

Betty spiraled her finger near her ear—*no, just touched.*
"We can all wait at my house. It's closer. The number is 666-
6660."

The nurse wrote the number down and smiled. "She's
in good hands. We'll call you."

"I'd like to see her," Betty said.

"No, not now," the nurse told her. "We're trying to
treat her as aggressively as possible."

Betty looked elderly, then, and slightly confused. *The fluorescent lights do it,* Maude thought, *and the computer screens.*

Esther said, "I'll call you, Maude."

"I am sorry about the car."

"Was supposed to be worse. God watched."

"Who's the next of kin?" the nurse said. "We need you
to sign permission for surgery."

Maude said, "I'm her granddaughter. I came home to
take care of her."

Betty put her gloved hands to her face and mumbled, "I
don't want her to suffer. Just sedate her and let me in."

The nurse brought a clipboard to Maude. Maude wondered if surgery wasn't cruel. Sedate Partridge, let her die
without the surgery. Her grandmother now had found the
courage to die. Keep Betty and the other witches out, watch
over Partridge—the simple rites of womenfolk. Wash the
body, wrap it in a shroud, hand it to the men to put in the
coffin. Wail behind the men with the coffin on their shoulders.

"You could have let her die at home, but you brought

her here," the nurse said. "You must know this is best. Dr. Armitage hates to see old people let to die because they're a burden to their families."

Dr. Armitage came out in his greens and said, "This the family?"

"Yes," Maude said.

"You should have brought her in sooner."

Betty said, "She's ready to die. We thought you could deal with the pain and then . . ."

"I'm a surgeon. We don't work that way."

Betty said, "I don't think my cousin wants to live. I want to say good-bye to her."

"Who's next of kin?" Dr. Armitage asked.

"I am," Maude said. She signed the consent form and handed him the clipboard.

Dr. Armitage looked at it and said, "I'm going to scrub. Send in the anesthesia nurse."

"I didn't want her to throw her life away," Betty stated.

Doug said, "Let's go home, Maude."

"Aren't you coming to my house?" Betty asked. "It's closer."

"Perhaps I should," Maude said. She grinned at Betty. She wanted to know where her *soi-disant* aunt was during the surgery.

As they walked out to the cars, Betty said, "Doug, leave your car here. Maude, you beat me."

Maude felt her face flush as though her body was embarrassed to hear this. She couldn't make up her mind as to whether Betty lied to her or not.

"Really, you won. Your grandmother will die there."

"But you will let us bury her in the family plot?" Maude asked.

"Yes, I drop the fight. If Partridge wants to rot in a grave near her kin, then I'm in full agreement. Get in the car, Douglas, in the back." He did. Betty turned to Maude. Under the sodium vapor lights, her face looked like a rotten corpse face, teeth bright flashes of light. "So, you get your way. You're the death of decent lives. Your body knew to be ashamed to hear my confession.''

"I'm not sure I believe you," Maude said. "But, we ought to be decent about this. After all, we're kinswomen." She sounded forced to herself. Betty stood by the driver's door until Maude remembered her manners and opened it. She got in the passenger-side door and looked at Doug in the back seat. He seemed dazed.

"What happened on the way here?" she asked him as Betty started the Essex.

"I don't remember anything peculiar," he said. "I'm so tired. By the way, I forgot to tell you. My Berkeley house sold. I've got no further attachments there."

No real attachments anywhere, Maude thought. Esther's church circle would quilt Partridge's death quilt. The dying would be over soon. "I'm tired, too," Maude said.

"Old women like Partridge and me don't sleep as much as you young ones," Betty said. She smiled.

The Essex picked up power as it moved away from the hospital. Soon, they were at Betty's house in Taylorsville. As Maude opened the car door for Betty, she hoped there would be a truce between them now. They could be two normal women grieving the aging and death of someone they both loved. She was emotionally drained now.

Betty did seem in tears as she unlocked her house door. Doug followed them and said, "Sorry, I hadn't realized we'd arrived."

Maude realized by Betty's standards he'd failed to show proper manners. The man was to open the car doors. He didn't even help Betty with the house door.

Luke was sitting in the dark parlor to the left of the front door. Betty turned on a light and shook her head. Maude felt her heart spasm. Doug said, "I hope we got her to the hospital in time."

Luke snapped on a light and said, "Betty, that fool is painting at us. I feel every brush stroke."

Betty went to the back of the house and parted the

drapes. Maude followed her and looked down. The lights were on at the Reverend Springer's shack down in the hollow behind the highway.

Betty let the drapes fall closed. She looked at Maude and said, "A certain uncontrolled talent."

"Is he a witch, too?"

"Yes, of a different sort," Betty said. "Do you want some tea?" She began to strip off her gloves and walk toward the kitchen. Maude kept following her. Betty laid her gloves on a phone table and filled a kettle from the sink.

Maude took the kettle from Betty and put it on the stove. She wondered what came next.

"What comes next is Partridge comes out of anesthesia into pain," Betty said.

"I did what I felt was right."

"Go to sleep," Betty said. She picked up her tea canister and measured tea into a teapot. Maude watched her carefully. Betty said, "If you think I'm going to drug you, you're being paranoid."

"Does Luke know what the Reverend Springer is painting?"

"Sue killed herself because of what you and that black man did."

"What's he painting?"

"I don't know."

"So, you don't know everything."

Betty poured the tea into cups. "Or I'm lying. You do believe I'm a liar."

"Yes."

"How can you, a woman who is either insane or a welfare cheat, know what's honest or what's real?"

Maude looked at the teacup Betty was holding toward her. "I don't want your tea. I may be wrong but I don't sacrifice other people to my own needs."

"Bullshit." Her aunt's profanity shocked Maude.

"Who have I sacrificed?"

"Both Partridge and Sue, to your self-righteousness."

Maude didn't believe this was quite accurate, but she felt confused. Then she felt something wet and cold go down the center of her mind, as though traveling between the lobes of her physical brain.

Betty must have seen Maude's surprise because she said, "Even your allies aren't pure. He's a witch, too, just very undisciplined."

"You can't keep eating people forever."

Betty drank her tea and didn't answer. When they went back to the parlor, Luke had turned off the lights again and Doug was in bed. Luke, a shadow against the streetlight beyond the house, said, "Go to bed with Doug."

"I don't feel like sleeping."

"Don't you want to let him comfort you?"

"You will get sleepy," Betty said.

"I ought to have gone home."

"It's snowing now. You couldn't walk back to the hospital."

"What was it I saw, driving to the hospital?" Maude asked.

Betty said, "Ice gets us all in the end."

"The allochthon isn't forever, either."

Luke said, "Heat death is forever."

"We'll bury Partridge's corpse in the family plot. Go to sleep now," Betty told her.

"I'm not . . . ," Maude began to say, but she felt her body dropping and hands catching her.

18

HEX VARIATIONS

Maude woke up. She was lying, still dressed, under covers in a bed somewhere near the roof. Light came in slanting at about nine o'clock. *They got to me.* She sat up in the bed, listening. The house seemed empty. Not, perhaps, completely empty.

I tried, Grandmother. Maude found her shoes and her coat and went to the front door. She opened it and saw six inches of snowcover, with tire tracks from the house to the road. The Essex had chains on.

Maude closed the door and called, "Doug? Aunt Betty? Uncle Luke?"

Sue's ghost materialized before her, head half-blown off, holding the image of a frying pan. Maude wondered if Sue blamed her for her suicide. The ghost spoke, words slow and cold as snow in Maude's ears, "I was murdered."

"Do you expect me to help you?"

The ghost didn't answer, wavered toward invisibility, then another ghost, the murderess from 1910, took the first ghost's arm. "Dissolve us."

"Isn't it better to be a ghost than to not exist?"

"No," Sue's ghost said. Both ghosts jumped up, then sank through the floor, disappearing.

Maude wondered if the ghosts came to distract her. But Sue said she was murdered. After Maude put on her shoes, she looked out to see if other cars were moving. Although earlier cars had marked the streets, nothing passed while Maude watched. No cabs would be running. She wondered if she could walk, then decided to call the hospital to see if Luke and Betty were with Partridge, or had been at the death.

The hospital switchboard put her through to Intensive Care. "Your grandmother's still alive," a woman's voice said. "Your aunt and uncle were here earlier, but they didn't feel comfortable going in to see her hooked to the machines."

"Watched by machines of loving grace." Maude didn't know where she'd read that, or heard it, but she felt she comforted Sue's ghost to say that.

The woman continued, "Your grannie's nurse came by earlier yet."

Esther, thank you. Quilt that top fast. Maude hung up the phone and went to the rear window overlooking Reverend Springer's shack. He came out barefooted in the snow and saluted toward her with a big paintbrush. Maude wondered if he could see her, if he was the exception to the rule, a good witch, or just plain crazy. But he could sleep now, having worked his art all night. He'd left the day to Maude and went back inside the house. The chimney smoked harder. Maude realized he'd fired up a wood stove. Then the lights went out.

Crazy, dignified, in a place where when voices cursed you inside your head nobody thought your brain was flawed. Maude wondered what would happen to him if the magic faded. But Reverend Springer was defending her, even if the next reality made him crazy again. She owed him.

Maude went into the kitchen and scrambled eggs in a frying pan that was the real model of the ghost frying pan Sue had been holding.

She was just cleaning up breakfast when the Essex pulled up. The key screeched against the lock plate, then went in. Cylinders turned and the front door banged open. She heard two people come in. "Is it still snowing?" she asked.

The door banged shut. Luke came in and said, "You bitch." He came toward her. Maude raised the frying pan. *He murdered Sue.*

Betty came in and stripped off her gloves, then unpinned her veiled hat. "Maude, your technological world strips people of personality."

"Where's Doug?" Maude put the frying pan back on its hook.

"He's following us, but slowly. He doesn't have snow tires or chains."

Maude looked out the window to see if it was still snowing, but it wasn't. "How was Partridge's surgery?"

"Your allies have no real power," Luke said.

"Can't we be just normal people for a few minutes, even if you have to fake it?" Maude wanted a truce in this battle for Partridge. "I'm losing my grandmother."

Betty smiled. Luke smiled. *That's how they could put me to sleep last night,* Maude realized. She'd tired of hating and had relaxed.

Doug's car pulled into the driveway. Luke smiled deeper, his teeth showing. He turned and went back to the front of the house to let Doug in.

Doug shimmered with glamour, his skin glowing, his eyes as though he'd seen his first naked woman or his body's first sexual erection. Maude knew Luke and Betty laid the glamour on him, but the spell more underlined his own beauty than gave him something unnatural. The sexual vulnerability of the male, balls and beard dangling to be grabbed, Maude thought, memories of statues coming to mind: the Trojan priest and his sons strangled by the god-sent snake, a dying Gaul, bodies twisting in marble.

"So, you dressed him for me," Maude said. His vitality lay close to his skin, in the play of the neck tendons, the movements of his nostrils, the blue veins over his wrist bones. A rip in the wrong artery could cut the vitality out.

"We won't fight you over Partridge's treatment anymore," Betty said. She put her hand on the small of Doug's back as though presenting him to Maude.

"Doug." Her voice spoke his name as though saluting a sacrifice.

"Partridge is in intensive care," Doug said. "She's not speaking to anyone."

"I'd like to go see her," Maude said. "We need to get snow tires for your car."

"You can drive the Essex," Luke said.

"Doug needs to be able to get around," Maude said.

"I'd like to drive the Essex," Doug said.

Maude almost told him to drive by himself. *No, the Essex would eat him.* She felt the Reverend Springer turning in his dreams, exhausted after his night vigil. He'd painted her a place to fight, but she had to do the fighting. The two ghost women hid from the witch couple. Maude felt out for Esther and felt needles against her fingers. Esther's church circle quilted away. Maude wondered if she should let her aunt and uncle take Doug, a trade to give Partridge the death she wants. "I'll get my purse and coat," she said. "We'll see her, then I need to go home."

Outside, Doug said, "Luke thought I ought to call Follette and tell him I'll take his research job."

"Why don't you wait?" The snow was powder underfoot.

Doug opened the passenger-side door. "I might as well get on with my new life here."

"Luke wants John to have the work monitoring job, then."

"That's only a temporary job." Doug turned on the Essex engine and began backing around his own car.

"The research institute could lose its funding when Follette dies."

"Luke said he'd help me."

"They're gonna sacrifice you to help John."

"Maude, maybe you should see a therapist."

"They've laid a glamour over you."

"Maude, you're awfully inhibited for a woman who picked up strangers in Berkeley bars."

"You think you naturally glow like a young god?"

"Maude, don't be ashamed to be sexually aroused while your grandmother's dying. Death sometimes does this to people." He squirmed slightly under the steering wheel, thigh muscles outlined through his wool pants. The pudge around his waist was invisible.

"Victims always get lots of sex," Maude said.

"Losers aren't that sexually attractive."

"We aren't talking about the same thing." Wart Mountain reached for them, but the hospital machines thwarted it. Doug, looking only normally attractive, turned into the visitor's entrance.

At the main desk, a volunteer directed Maude and Doug to the intensive care unit.

Her father's people were sitting with Partridge. One was Elehu, the man who'd brought Esther to her the first day. The other had to be his wife, a woman in a faded cotton dress. Her hair was dark blonde going to grey and her hands were rough, on her lap stroking each other slowly, as though one hand was the other's pet.

Maude wished they'd leave so she could talk to Partridge in private. "Thanks for sitting with her."

"It's a duty," the woman said.

"I appreciate it."

"You know why we're here?" Elehu asked.

"To protect her soul," Maude answered.

"Esther called us," Elehu said. "She said we ought to trust you."

The woman said, "But you can understand why we're not leaving." She looked at Doug as though noticing him for the first time. "He's painfully pretty, ain't he?"

Maude wondered if the witch glamour clung to him despite the machines. She realized she didn't want to see it. "Now Luke wants him to work for Follette."

"I *am* in the room," Doug said.

The woman asked, "Then, how did you get into this?"

"I met Maude in Berkeley. I wanted to learn about magic."

"Even the decent heathen religions condemn magic," Elehu said. "That's enough for us."

Maude went to Partridge. Her left hand had a huge IV needle going into it. Partridge opened her eyes and looked at Maude. "Maude," she mumbled.

"I'm here."

"Maude?"

"Want something?"

"Sorry." Partridge closed her eyes again.

Maude wondered what Partridge was sorry about. Was it Lula? Or that she'd given up keeping herself alive at other people's expense? "It's all right. We're here."

Elehu said, "There're good people at this hospital."

Above Partridge's head was a display that showed a green light line that jerked with Partridge's pulse. Maude stared at the machine until her vision blurred. "I don't know what's best," she said.

"You're half ours," Elehu said.

Maude said, "I thought I could be a strong witch, if I gave into it."

"You know it don't work that way," the woman said.

"At least Betty promised me Partridge gets to die the way she wants."

"And they lie to us," Elehu said.

"I'm not one of you," Maude stated.

"Half us," the woman reminded her.

Maude asked, "Well, Doug, are you sorry you followed a half-witch to Bracken?"

Elehu said, "You don't have to be a witch at all."

"I'm not going to bind myself with Jesus."

Partridge's monitor began running a longer line between blips. A nurse came in and said, "We'll take care of her now."

Maude went to her grandmother and kissed her on the forehead. The flesh was sweaty and cold. She said to her father's people, "If only you had something to offer that was between heaven and hell." She said to Doug, "Let's go home," meaning to the house in Kobold.

As they drove, half the snow on the road melted. Maude
didn't know if the drive took longer than usual or if
Bracken County time slipped out from under the Essex
wheels. She realized Doug went slow because of the chains.
"We ought to get the chains off," Doug said as he pulled
into the driveway. Maude thought that sentence came out
incongruously from his mouth, the glamour wrapping him.
Painfully pretty, the woman had said.

"We ought to go back for your car."

"I thought we'd be staying at Luke's while your grandmother's in the hospital."

"I want to be in my own house. I feel safer," Maude said.

"You need to be with your people."

"Which people?"

"The powerful ones." Doug took her in his arms and
hugged her.

Victims get lots of sex. Maude wondered if he didn't, would
they still kill him? Knowing Betty and Luke, the answer was
yes. Maybe she had to trade Doug for Partridge. "I feel so
lonely," she said.

"Your people will take care of you."

Sleeping with a victim had charm. Maude could be his
last lover. He'd never cheat on her, never grow old. She
moved her left hand up to his neck, feeling the spine embedded in the flesh. She pressed the vertebra that bent out
at the top of his shoulders, cervical vertebra five or six.
Maybe Doug would become a revenant, living death, a
corpse animated by John's will.

"Shall I unlock the door?" Maude asked.

"If you can get your hands off."

"What did they promise you?" She swayed away from
him and went through her purse to find the house key,
found it, and unlocked the door.

"They said they could . . . they'd take care of me. You'd
be more cooperative."

Maude reached into his head for the sentence he hadn't
completed. *They said they could make you love me.*

Maybe she should just give up, be a half-witch helper for

the entities and witches with more power. She'd fall in love with Doug, be the mourning lover at his death. If Luke and Betty wanted, they could give him back to her, a cold corpse animated in just the right organs.

Fuck the dying and the dead. The house door swung open and Maude smelled the growing mold, the decaying mouse urine and shit. Once Partridge left it, the house aged. Maude turned on a light and saw spiderwebs in the corners of the living room.

Doug came in, his clothes a stain on his radiance. Maude felt annoyed that Luke could work on her this way. *I'll take him on Partridge's bed.*

She had a moment's fear that Partridge would die this instant, contaminating it, but the real problem was that Partridge had bled on the sheets.

Some how and when later, they were naked between clean sheets, old fine linen ones washed almost transparent. Maude thought of all the women who'd seen a death coming and had spun for the shroud, linen from the Fates, the Norns. Her throat was making strange noises—*hu, hah, huh*—babbling in prehuman.

For an instant, Doug fumbled, an ordinary human lover, then it was magic again.

But when they were lying spent, Maude looked over at him. He looked dying already, the pulse naked in his throat, the skin chilled by drying sweat.

Then she heard the Colt whispering and realized she'd stopped hearing it lately. *Kill, kill, kill,* it said. *Defend and deafen with me. Grease my barrel with your magic. Your father's people gave me to you.*

"You're not that big a gun," she told it. She got out of bed, leaving Doug sleeping, and opened the desk. The gun wasn't loaded, but the bullets were beside it in a coin purse marked with a cross. Maude opened the purse and looked at the cartridges. They were almost as long as rifle cartridges, she thought.

The gun seemed to sigh when she slid the cartridges

into the cylinder charge holes. Womb of death, Maude thought, closing the cylinder.

Instructions from childhood, from her father's side of the family, floated up from memory. *Don't put your finger in the trigger guard until you're ready to fire. Pull the trigger almost back to the firing point, then aim and pull the rest of the way.*

Maude felt absurd, naked, squatting with a gun in her hands. She laid the gun down and dressed, then put the gun carefully in her purse. *Don't talk now,* she told it.

Doug rolled in his sleep. Maude looked down at him and wondered what he might have had to offer the county if the witches hadn't seduced him. She pried off his glamour and saw him as real for an instant. *I wish he was a sacrifice to someone better than John.* Then he was the dying beloved again, until he woke up. The beard stubble appeared as soon as he said, "Could you make breakfast while I shave?"

When they were eating scrambled eggs and toast, the phone rang. Betty said, "We've traded fair and square." Maude knew Partridge was dying or dead. "Is she dead?"

"Not yet, but you won't see her again alive."

Maude hung up the phone and said, "We've got to get to the hospital."

As they went by the funeral home, a hearse pulled out behind them, tailgating, frustrated with the Essex's speed. Doug said, "I should have taken off the chains."

"It's for Partridge. She's dead."

The hearse driver seemed to recognize them then, or the Essex, and dropped back. But as they turned in the visitor's entrance, Maude saw the hearse turn in the emergency entrance. Beyond the emergency room doors, Maude remembered she'd seen another set of double doors, doors for the dead.

Aunt Betty and Luke were in the general hospital waiting room. "She's gone," Betty said.

"Can we bury her with her people?" Maude asked.

"I've already said you could," Betty answered.

"I wanted to make sure."

"I'll be very surprised if she can make a ghost," Luke said. The doors to the wards opened and Maude's other kin, Elehu and his wife, came out. They looked at Betty and Luke, nodded at Maude, and kept on going.

Maude noticed that Betty and Luke looked frustrated. "You tried to get her up to the last, didn't you?"

Luke said, "You're a weak person and we're trying to help you. You ought to be more grateful."

19

VISITATIONS

Maude went home in Doug's car. "There's so much to do," she told him. She'd discovered the mechanical routine to a funeral—getting the insurance policies, talking to Partridge's lawyer about the will, deciding on the coffin, talking to Terry and John about hiring a digging crew, explaining to a minister that he'd speak his final words over a private and unsanctified grave. Maude realized she didn't have to tell the minister that. She half-thought about calling the Reverend Julian Springer, but, no, she wouldn't challenge the witches at this point.

First, Maude needed to find the burial insurance policy. She found a leather pouch near where the gun had been. The gun, when she thought about it, began muttering in her purse. *Shut up. Not now,* she thought back as she opened the pouch. All the documents she wanted were inside. Maude also found antique photos on metal—daguerreotypes, she realized. One was of Betty, looking about forty or fifty, not half as old as she looked these days. The second was of another woman. Maude recognized a resemblance to her grandmother's grandmother whose photos she'd seen as a child. The third was of a black woman holding a white child.

Betty was born in the nineteenth century. She isn't really that old. Maude realized she'd been hesitating to kill Betty, if she could kill Betty, because she thought, whatever Betty had done to stay alive, the old woman did have centuries worth of memories. *She's not so unique. We've got plenty of testimony from the nineteenth century.*

"I've got a picture here of Betty," she told Doug.

He came over and picked up the photograph. "Antebellum?"

"There's a slave in the third one."

"If it could just double my life."

Maude almost told him, *your life it will halve.* She felt like she'd overgorged on glamour. Doug's beauty and fragility, all the spell that made him so desirable earlier, seemed overdone and obvious now. "What would you do for a doubled life? Kill?"

"If I knew the person I killed was not contributing to society, was going to O.D. or kill someone himself, I'd do it."

Maude wondered if the gun put itself in her purse. "What if someone killed you to double . . ." She didn't want to fix a gendered pronoun to the sentence.

"I don't think you understand your witch kin. They're not that kind of people."

Maude didn't respond, but changed the subject. "All the insurance policies seem to be here, and paid up. I guess we need to call Terry to get the cemetery unlocked for a work crew." She went to the phone and dialed. When Terry answered, she said, "It's Maude. We need to arrange for Partridge's burial."

"Betty's already told me. She's hired the crew. Look, I imagine you're really wasted. Would you and Doug like to come over for dinner?"

"I don't know."

"Ask Doug."

"Doug, Terry's inviting us to dinner." Maude hoped she'd said it flatly enough to discourage him.

"Okay, if John doesn't play with his guns."

"We'd be happy to if John keeps his guns up," Maude told Terry.

"You need to be around family. And we've finally got my stupid hawk to fly at rabbits."

Maude wouldn't have characterized Belle as stupid, just realistic about not wanting to work when she'd still eat mice regardless of what she killed. "I'd like to see that," she said. "What time do you want us?"

"About six," Terry said. "I'm sorry about Partridge but she was in pain, wasn't she?"

"Yes."

"Betty felt it was rather crass of your father's people to take her over the way they did. She hardly got a chance to say good-bye."

Maude wondered if Betty got Partridge despite all the Christian predestinarians. God's will, if the time before Partridge died held such a concept. "I hope Partridge is at peace."

"Well, we'll see you at six then."

Maude told Doug, "I've got to get these papers to the funeral home."

"I'd have thought the womenfolk would have tended the corpse at home."

"We're not that primitive," Maude said. She wondered if the cosmetics and filler clays of the undertaker would trap her grandmother's soul, keep her from making a ghost. What did embalming do? Normally, Maude hated ghosts, their ectoplasmic confusion and babble, but if she saw her grandmother's ghost, she'd know that Betty hadn't won, at least not completely.

Doug drove her to the funeral home, but stayed in the car while she went in. She arranged for visitations at the funeral home, and checked to see if the paper had all the facts right for the obituary. The mortician asked, "Do you want to see your grandmother this evening when we've laid her out?"

"How late will you be open?"

"We've got another visitation this evening, so we should be here until nine or ten."

Maude wondered what she'd get out of it and said, "My cousin and her husband invited me over for dinner. I don't know how late we're staying."

"Your aunt suggested a coffin. I assume what she says goes."

"I want to see it," Maude said.

The undertaker led her back to a display room. Maude ran her hands over the lacquered wood, the real metal coffin handles, the satin interior. "Is it real silk?" she asked.

"Your aunt brought us real silk. My wife will take this out and tack in Betty's fabric."

Maude wanted to tell him to use acetate, polyester, machine fabric, but since she couldn't explain why she didn't want her aunt's silk around her grandmother, she nodded.

"Partridge lived a good life," the man said, as though he knew Partridge could have lived longer at others' expense.

"Is it difficult being a mortician in this county?"

"I guess it's hard to come back to a place like this, just to have your grandmother die." A good Southern conversational swerve.

Maude felt on the verge of tears then and said, "I trust you'll make sure the burial goes well."

"I understand there might be a sacrifice."

"I'm shocked that you'd speak so openly about that," Maude said, hearing tones of her aunt in her voice.

"It's better if you cremate that body."

"Are you a witch, too?"

"I bury all the bodies," he said. "I work with what's the custom here."

"My grandmother wanted to save her soul. Remember that."

"We'll honor her memory," the undertaker said, not promising anything about her soul. "Miss Maude, I'm not the one carrying a revolver."

"You are a witch."

"I looked in your purse," he said, bowing slightly to her. Maude nodded and went out.

Doug's luminosity seemed corny. He smiled at her and started the car again. "Everything's been arranged," she said.

When they got back to Kobold, Maude saw Esther's car parked in the driveway. Esther was on the porch swing, holding the finished quilt.

"Betty gave them some silk to line the coffin with," Maude said.

"She needs to be wrapped in this," Esther told her.

Maude took the quilt. "Come on, Doug, we've got to go back to the funeral home."

Esther said, "I'd come to the visitation, but I'm not sure all your people would approve."

"Nonsense, you've got to come."

Esther didn't say anything, but turned and went to her car. Maude followed her. Esther sat behind the wheel crying. She said, "Some folks think we nurses try to keep their people alive so we get more money, maybe a payoff from the doctors." She dabbed at her eyes. "And if we come to the funeral, they think we're angling for a tip or that we . . ."

"I couldn't take care of dying people for a living."

"I'll do something else for a while, clerk in a store," Esther said. "Then I'll call the agency and get someone new to take care of. You will take the quilt to your grannie, won't you?"

"Yes." Maude decided she'd go in after supper and ask to be alone with her grandmother. Then she'd open the lower half of the coffin and wrap the quilt around Partridge's body.

Esther said, "Drop by sometime and see me."

"I will."

"You've got some good people on your father's side."

Maude didn't like either side, not the embarrassing and intense country Christians or the witches who thought they duped their entities. "Neither God nor the Devil. That's the cynic's motto."

Esther said, "Sounds bad to me." She rolled up her window and drove away. Maude put the quilt in Doug's car and went back to the house.

She fucked him because fucking, in the past, relieved

tension. "Whoa, you're a little rough," he said, pulling away from her teeth.

Maude's teeth ached to bite his cockskin. "Isn't this magical," she said. He tried to pin her down, but she was slippery and he wasn't fully committed to all-out wrestling. "I'm the priestess and you're Adonis."

"I don't think so," Doug said. "Maybe you're the maiden who gets thrown into the volcano."

"Not a virgin," Maude said. Her teeth snagged his nipple and she had to resist biting it off. *What makes me do this?* Did he piss her off because he was such an easy victim?

They rolled off each other and quickly chilled in the sixty-five degree house. "We could turn the thermostat up," Doug said, "or build a wood fire in the dining room and make love in front of the flames. But gently."

"I think we ought to get dressed."

"I don't mind love nips, but I was afraid you'd really bite down. I might have hurt you back. A man's so much stronger than a woman."

"Physically."

As Maude dressed, Doug stayed sprawled on the bed, head back, throat exposed, pulse beating visibly in his neck. His loin muscles bulged slightly above his groin—*thrust muscles,* Maude thought, *rape muscles.* One leg bent outward from the hip, tendons pulled to visibility. Maude hooked on her brassiere, still staring at his body. "I might as well go back to the funeral home with the quilt now," she said. "Can I drive your car for once? I let you drive mine."

"I would rather stay here," he said. "The keys are in my pants."

Maude fished them out and threw the pants over him. "Is your foot healed now?"

He laughed. "Were you working magic on it?"

"No. I just wanted to know."

"It's still a little stiff."

Some entities wouldn't take a scarred sacrifice, but Maude doubted imperfection mattered in Doug's case. "I'm sorry if I bit too hard."

Doug moved his hand to cover his cock. "No, I just wasn't sure."

"Women don't know whether guys will hurt them or not."

"But you weren't trying to give me a sensitivity lesson, were you?"

"No." Maude found her coat and purse with the gun in it and left him draped with his pants.

She drove back to the mortuary with a suspicious lack of problems. What if Betty tricked her, got Partridge's soul despite the Christians. Maude didn't believe in Christians. The mortician was surprised to see her again so soon. "I thought you would come later."

"I want to put this in her coffin," Maude said, clutching the quilt against her breasts. Since she hadn't bathed, she suspected she stunk of cunt and come. Maude watched the mortician's nostrils. He seemed oblivious—perhaps embalming fluid ruined his sense of smell.

"We're tacking in Betty's silk now."

"Put it in over Betty's silk," Maude said. "Please. It's what my grandmother wanted."

For a second, Maude thought the mortician was going to say, *but your grandmother's beyond wanting.* Instead, after a pause, he said, "Follow me."

He led Maude to a workroom. The coffin lid was on one table, the coffin on another. The acetate lining lay in large shreds on the floor. The mortician's wife was fastening down Betty's silk with a small hammer and brass-headed tacks. She looked up and said, "Hello, Maude. Do you want to see your grandmother?"

"No, I've come to put this in her coffin. We worked on it while she was dying."

The mortician and his wife took the quilt from Maude and held it up between them. The quilting stitches made embossed crosses across the pattern squares. Maude said, "Perhaps you ought to wrap it around her down in the coffin."

"We don't want to offend anyone," the mortician's wife said.

"Or fold it and put it under her, between her and Betty's silk."

"Does Betty know how it's quilted? With the crosses?"

"No. Esther, my grandmother's nurse, took it to her church circle."

The mortician's wife took the quilt away. Maude wondered what she'd do with it. The mortician said, "We can't afford to offend anyone, not your grandmother's people, not your father's."

"You just open a third of the coffin, so I'm sure you can arrange it so it's not visible."

"Do you know what you're trying to do?"

"My grandmother wanted to have her soul dissolve."

"Have you considered that hell could be a possibility?"

"I'm trying to protect her from Betty's silk."

The mortician's wife came back in with the quilt and declared, "It didn't blister the body."

The mortician told Maude, "If Betty notices, we'll say we left you alone with the coffin. We don't want to offend anyone."

Maude said, "Neither God nor Devil." She wondered if they really would put the quilt in the coffin. The woman lay the quilt beside the coffin and went back to tacking in Betty's silk.

"Trust us," the mortician said.

Maude didn't want to drive back to Kobold immediately. She wanted to abandon Bracken County, drive to Boulder, drive to New York. Get a typing job, learn computers, forget all this. Let Betty have Doug, her grandmother's soul. Steal this car.

No, Maude didn't want to do those things. She wanted Partridge to be alive and dying for fifty years, Esther to help Maude and Doug, and no witches to bother them.

The mean allochthon seemed to fold up at the corners, trapping her. Standing in the funeral home parking lot, she felt its malice. The sky overhead was another mineral. Perhaps, in this car, she could drive out of the county. Nobody, not even Doug, would be surprised if she turned car thief. They'd bury Partridge after stealing her soul, sacrifice Doug to John's weirdness.

Welfare would tempt her. *My lost life,* Maude thought.

While Maude stalled in her escape dreams, the Reverend Springer walked up to her car. He said, "Can you give me a ride home?"

"What are you doing here?"

"I came for a visitation," he said. "The bodies here get integrated even if the other stuff is a bit backward."

Maude wondered why he didn't ride back with the people who brought him, but decided she wasn't going to escape to New York before the funeral.

"I'm thinking about driving to New York," she said. "Just leaving this mess."

"Maybe you should take me home first."

"Sure." Maude unlocked the car and Reverend Springer got in.

"You were awful irresponsible in Berkeley," he said. "Making a mock of real madness."

"Sorry." Maude suspected she deserved this.

"But you've been good here."

"Paint thinner got your nose?"

"I never considered sex as a hideous sin. Sort of like eating pig. You can always quit or marry the man."

Maude flushed. "I don't know what's going on."

"Oh, yes, you do. We been allied in this struggle." He looked at Betty's house as they passed it. The Essex wasn't in the driveway. "They're preparing the man who killed the Richmond people's boy."

"Doug and I are supposed to go over there for supper."

"You're doomed to conclude this."

Maude said, "Let's park somewhere where people won't know I'm at your house."

"Park behind the house," he said. Maude pulled up on

the grass and pulled behind the shack. She followed him in the back door. He flipped on a bank of lights in the tiny kitchen. Maude saw he'd painted the walls here, too. She saw a painting of herself confronting Betty and Luke, with the two women ghosts behind her and the Reverend Springer shielding her with a translucent paintbrush.

"I felt like a paintbrush went up my brain," she said.

"You can kill the magic. You ought to for keeping Doug alive."

"If I kill the magic, won't that make you crazy again?"

"Lord wanted me. But to paint, not preach. God makes it so his toys go crazy if they don't do his will."

"I don't believe in that, either."

"No, you don't believe in that. But you do believe in magic and the pagan gods. Only you don't like them. Quite rightly."

"But you'll go crazy." *And after the magic's dead, I can't be good by simply abstaining.*

"I'll be okay. People take care of me."

"I don't know what to do."

"You started right with the quilt," he said. "The murdered boy's people want to take care of John. But they're not strong enough."

"When?"

"At the funeral."

"They can't attack him at a funeral."

"He stole their boy."

"It will just make things worse," Maude said. "John will eat them."

"You're right. You're the only one who can stop it all."

Maude knew she could slow time, but would that slow her own mind, too? "All I have is one stupid trick. And I don't want to be a witch."

"Be a witch to kill the witch in you forever. You want some coffee?"

"What?"

"You want some coffee? Sit down with me and pass some time. You don't have to be anywhere soon."

Maude felt slightly dizzy. Coffee was too ordinary for this room with its painted ghosts. "Doug will worry."

"Bet Doug's sleeping."

"I should call him." The Reverend Springer had been insane in Berkeley, drugged to mute his inner demons, had hated her for her mockery of his real condition.

"We've got to take things to a better way," he said. "It'll redeem you from Berkeley."

"I've never . . ." Maude almost said she'd never used her powers, but she had.

"Take the powers out and break them. Would you rather have tea?"

"Do you have any herb teas?"

"Chamomile," he said. "It's a special nerve unwinder, even if it never stopped voices." He went to the sink and filled a battered enameled pot, then set it on a gas burner.

Maude sat down on an armchair covered with a polyester tablecloth. "I hope Doug doesn't worry about the car."

"He knows you been cooped up. He might fuss, but doesn't mean much by it." Reverend Springer took out a square plastic box filled with dried chamomile flowers. "Greeks sell the best chamomile." He rummaged through a drawer and found two tea strainers, the sort that look like miniature flour sifters. "I make it strong."

After he poured the boiling water over the chamomile, they sat quietly while the tea steeped. Reverend Springer took one strainer out and handed that cup to Maude. She took it and looked into the greenish liquid. He took the strainer out of his cup and said, "There's honey if you want it."

Maude sipped the tea. It was hot and bitter, but honey wouldn't be right. Taking tea with Reverend Springer had turned into a ritual, like Japanese Tea, but she didn't want to break the mood by saying so. "No, it's fine as it is." Under the bitterness, Maude tasted other things.

Reverend Springer didn't reply. They sat drinking the tea. His paintings were crude and powerful. His tea was subtle. Maude wished he'd tell her what to do, but she couldn't whine to him.

After they finished the tea, she took his cup and hers to the sink and washed them. He said, "I can't tell you how to work. You know them better than I do."

"Can't you keep the Richmond people from the funeral?"

"It's the killed boy's uncles and brothers now, not the women. They can't see it's a witch hate sucking them in."

"Sue's ghost?"

"Got to lay the magic down for all the ghosts, let them go out."

"Dissolve?"

"Ghost is an insane spirit. God's got to take it home and fix it."

The Reverend Springer was so much saner in this magic space. How could she send him back to a real biochemical madness? "You don't deserve to be like you were in Berkeley."

"In that world, God's mercy is that deserving has nothing to do with how things work. Rain falls on sinners and the righteous. Also, problems with neurotransmitters."

"Maybe there is no God."

"I'll keep my God, thank you."

Maude said, "I don't know what to do, what to think, how to stop them."

"It's the after you're really afraid of," he said. "You ought go now or they'll start working to find you."

Driving back and forth, Maude felt her tire vibrations shaking the allochthon. The land itself seemed opposed to her, waiting. Bracken County hadn't had any earthquakes in centuries. A normal fault had dropped it down from its overthrusting and wedged it tight against the Blue Ridge, but it quivered under Maude.

Doug was gone when she came back to the house in Kobold. Maude knew he was powerfully attractive to women who didn't understand glamour charms for victims. *He's off fucking.* She cursed herself for being such a fool to tell him victims got lots of sex.

He hadn't left a note. Maude went into the bathroom and washed his odor away. She stripped the sheets from her grandmother's bed and ran them and her clothes through the hottest cycle the washer had.

After the washing cycle ran for ten minutes, Maude realized she'd put the bloody sheets in there earlier. She'd cooked in her grandmother's blood on the first set of sheets. "Fuck, fuck, fuck," she said, sliding down to sit, legs sprawled, with her back to the hot machine.

Maude sat there crying for a few minutes as the machine spun the wash water out, then decided she'd better call Terry and John to tell them Doug had gone out and she didn't know if he'd be back in time for supper.

"He called earlier," Terry said. "Follette wanted to talk to him."

Follette, not nubile mortals yearning to fuck a god's surrogate. "I wish he'd left me a note."

"He thought you might have wanted to go driving."

"I drove a little," Maude said.

"Well, you're not married and you're both adults," Terry said. "We'll see you both for supper, then, and go to the funeral home later."

"I didn't think visitation was until tomorrow."

"We're family," Terry said. "See you tonight."

"Wait—" Maude heard the receiver click down. She wondered if Betty and Luke would be there, if the quilt would wrap Partridge's body.

Maude decided to go for a walk until the washing machine finished, then see if she had set the blood on the sheets.

She remembered when her parents had died, when she was twenty. In a car crash, Partridge had told her, on the outskirts of Atlanta. Maybe they'd died of the sort of accident that happens to the just and the unjust, like rain, like the true brain-eating schizophrenia. An indifferent universe was a horrible idea, Maude had decided when she was fourteen, allying with her grandmother against her parents. *I forgot the map when the hormones hit.* Now she wondered if she'd wished them dead, could have protected them more. Her mother should have known how to deal with magic attacks, but her mother and her father both fled Bracken County, her witch kin, his rigid Christian kin, for a universe that wasn't really personally waiting to get them with a drunk and a pickup.

They got got. Maude finally realized she felt guilty that she hadn't magically protected them.

While she dithered between a pocket universe and the big impersonal picture, two undiluted witches had dropped Maude into sleep. *Now I can't manage even the little things,* Maude thought. She went back inside and pulled out the sheets. Partridge's blood had set. Maude began to cry again.

Doug and Follette came in. "Are you okay?" Follette asked.

"I don't know what to do. Partridge's blood . . . set on the sheets."

"You can bleach it out," Doug said. "I guess you loved her."

"I've been thinking about my parents," Maude said.

"How did they die?" Follette asked.

"In a traffic accident. Drunk in a pickup." Maude got up and pulled a paper towel off the roll. She wiped her face with it and said, "They'd moved away from Bracken. Nothing for them here."

"Senator Follette wants to change that," Doug said.

Maude looked at Follette for a moment. *He's like me, trying to use magic to fight magic.*

"It doesn't always work," Follette said, commenting both on bleach and on what she thought. He looked terribly tired.

"The senator would like to come to Partridge's funeral."

"Senator, did you tell him?" Maude asked. She knew Follette knew what role Doug was supposed to play.

"I know you have an invitation to supper with your cousins. Perhaps we could invite them to dinner at a restaurant? It would be rude for me to just join you."

Maude called Terry and asked, "Would you want to meet us for dinner at the Mayo Inn? Senator Follette had some things to discuss with Doug."

"Bring him here," Terry said. "We can feed him."

"Let me check," Maude said. She looked at Follette, who'd surely gotten the gist of the conversation even if he hadn't magicked out Terry's words. Follette looked at the opposite wall for a second, then sighed and nodded. "Okay, we'll be over at six, then."

After Maude hung up, Follette said, "I won't be able to eat much. I'll take my car, too, in case I have to leave early."

For an instant Maude wondered if he couldn't eat enemy food, then she realized he meant the cancer treatment affected his appetite.

The old house glittered with lights when they drove up. Doug parked his car. Senator Follette pulled in beside them and came up to open Maude's door. "Leave your purse in the car," Follette said.

Maude nodded and shoved the purse, heavy with the gun, under the seat.

John and Terry came out to greet them. "Senator Follette, what a surprise," John said.

"Doug's working for me, now," Follette said.

John nodded. "I got the job for the new assembly place setting up employee monitoring."

"I heard that was just a temporary job," Doug said.

"Well, one never knows. I've been thinking about selling guns, too. Oh, shit, I know I'm not supposed to bother you about guns tonight."

Doug didn't say anything. The three of them followed John and Terry into the house.

"Drinks?" John asked. "I've got some local product, if that wouldn't offend you, Senator, and some single malts from Scotland."

"Single malt," Follette requested.

"Local product," Doug said.

Terry smiled. "It's surprisingly smooth."

"Be careful, Doug," Follette warned.

Doug laughed. "I've heard it burns your throat."

"Not this," John said. He opened a cabinet and pulled out a gallon jar with plum slices floating in liquor. Terry handed him a ladle and a glass. John pushed the ladle down and pulled out a few plum slices and a couple tablespoons-ful of liquor. He poured all of it into the glass, the plum slices splashing, and handed it to Doug.

Doug sipped and said, "It's like kirsch or something. Slidoviz?"

"Damson liquor," Terry said.

"Distilled from damson wine?" Doug asked.

Follette said, "No, they put the damson in later. Some-times to conceal off flavors, bad making." Meaning, *be extra careful.*

"I can't tell how strong it is, but it would be diluted by the fruit juices," Doug stated.

"Some," Follette said. John smiled and found a bottle of Scottish whiskey with a Washington, D.C., excise stamp on it.

Maude knew Glennfiddich, but she hadn't heard of this brand, couldn't figure out how to pronounce the tangle of letters, couldn't remember the name without the sound. John held the bottle out toward Follette. Follette nodded and said, "Just a little." John poured the single malt into a small brandy snifter.

Doug, Maude saw, had finished his drink. He looked happy. Follette tasted his whiskey and looked at Doug's glass. John asked, "Maude, what do you want?"

"I'm fine."

"Oh, don't be a party pooper."

"Alcohol's a depressant. Do you have some tea?"

"We have chamomile," John said. He smiled. *We know where you've been, half-witch.*

"A plain tea."

"With stimulants in it?" John mocked her.

"Yes, a teabag tea would be fine." Maude wondered if she ought to check the tag at the end of the string.

Doug said, "This is so smooth."

"Want more?" John asked. "Celts always get drunk at wakes."

"Don't take any more right away," Follette said. "Wait until you see how strong it is."

Doug looked at Follette. Maude saw that his eyes seemed to track slower than his head moved. "Oh, it's okay."

John refilled Doug's glass with liquor, no plum slices, then smiled at Maude and went into the kitchen.

Maude asked, "How much did you tell him?"

"About the funeral games? Doug, are you listening? I don't speak when the mind isn't taking me seriously. They've set up a word-ward. Doug's not going to hear anything about being killed tomorrow."

"He knows about magic."

"He can't imagine people would hurt him," Follette said. He thought at her, *Miss Maude, who are you carrying that revolver for?*

Don't know, she thought back. For herself?

"I wouldn't want to lose Doug," Follette said.

John came back with the tea. Maude saw a teabag soaking in hot water with a staple, no label, at the end of the string. "Thanks," she said.

"Sugar, milk? I know you can take bitter teas," John said.

"Cut the crap, John," Follette said. He looked at Doug as though he wanted to say more about the liquor, but put his hand to his side. Maude knew his cancer hurt him just then. She sipped the tea. As far as she could tell, it was not a potion.

Doug drank his second glass of the damson liquor and declared, "Maude said victims get lots of sex." He tried to stand up but wobbled and sank back into his chair. "That's stronger than it seems. It was so smooth."

"Doug," Follette said.

"I'm really drunk."

"You drank it too fast." Maude shook her head.

Terry brought in a huge boar's head on a platter. She told her guests, "It's rare you can get one of these, but I knew a farmer who was culling his stock."

Doug finally managed to get up and walk toward the table. He sat down heavily and touched the boar's jowl and said, "Food, drink, sex."

John grinned. "Yes. Lots."

Follette said, "I'm not feeling at all well. I'll try to see you all at the funeral tomorrow. Doug, Maude." He didn't speak the others' names, but put on his coat and walked out to his car. Nobody spoke until he'd driven so far the motor noise disappeared.

"Old fart," John said.

Doug asked, "What else are we eating?"

Terry went back into the kitchen and brought out unleavened bread almost like crackers, and a salad of flowers. John began carving the boar's jowls. After being cut, the meat was less startling, like any other roast pork. Then he cut out the eyes and fed them to Doug on the end of a fork. Doug tried to protest, but he was too drunk. John put a plate of jowl meat in front of Doug and broke bread for him. Maude wondered if she could safely eat this food Follette fled from. John pulled four beakers out of a closed cabinet behind them and filled them from a jar already on the table.

"Mead," Terry said. "It's a marvelous future for us. John will be setting up a monitoring system for the high-tech factory. I'm making burial urns for a California crematorium chain."

Doug, his face greased with pig, lifted the beaker with both hands and held it at his face.

"Doug, aren't you drunk enough?" Maude asked.

John said, "He's got a right to blow out every once in a while."

Was the hangover so bad after these feasts that the victim didn't fight dying in the morning?

Doug pulled the beaker away from his face and said, "I feel very intense."

"Very drunk," Maude corrected.

"Don't be a spoilsport, Maude," Terry chided.

"You're going to . . ." Maude couldn't say, *you're going to sacrifice him tomorrow.* The word-ward had gotten stronger after Follette left. "He's got to drive home."

"You're sober enough," John said.

"I'll let you drive," Doug said. "I want to go home with my head against your pussy."

"Doug."

John filled the mead beaker again. Doug looked at it dubiously, then looked at Maude and drank.

Maude wondered if they could get home tonight. Terry said, "You could stay overnight here."

"Aren't we going up to the funeral home?"

Doug said, "You women can go wail. John and I will get drunk like men."

Maude noticed John wasn't drinking. He carved more meat from the pig's head, then sawed open the skull. Terry dipped a spoon down and ate a brain chunk. She went back to the kitchen and brought out a gravy boat.

The brains were good with rice and gravy. Maude remembered eating sheep's head at a gypsy restaurant in San Francisco, $1.50 a head, affordable on a welfare budget supplemented by plasma sales and gentlemen's dinners. *Never touch the escape money.* Perhaps she'd doomed herself by doing precisely that, using the money to come back to Kobold.

Doug looked at her as if he was going to be sick. "You've drunk too much," Maude told him.

"I'm really sorry, but I've got to go lie down."

"We'll play you some music," Terry said. Maude won-

dered if she and John would play flute and drum by Doug's
bed or if the music would be electronic.

"Terry and I are going to the funeral home. Let me get
your car keys," Maude said. He stood swaying while she
fished in his pants pocket for the keys. Then he shambled to
a couch in the living room and collapsed on it.

John said, "I'll stay with him."

At the funeral home, a ring of Christians sat around the coffin. Betty and Luke stood outside the circle. Betty said,
"They've claimed her, Maude, but they never converted
her."

"She wanted to be at peace," Maude said.

"One of your father's people is preaching the sermon,"
Luke told her.

"Does it matter now?" Maude asked.

"We'll have our own ceremonies at the grave," Betty replied.

"I'm going up to see her." Maude walked up to the coffin. Partridge looked like a realistic wax figure of herself. A
tiny edge of the quilt was visible below the corpse hands.
Maude bent over the body and kissed the cold forehead.
She wished Esther were there.

20

PREACHING TO DEAD EARS

When Maude woke up, the clock said 7:30. She remembered she'd left Doug at John and Terry's. He'd been too drunk to fool with.

Maude sat up and felt around for ghosts. No grandmother. No NAACP ghost. She didn't want to do anything this morning, but the funeral was at ten at the mortuary. Then the hearse would take Partridge's body across the highway and over to the family plot. Maude went to her closet and found the closest thing she had to a black dress—a dark tweed suit with a black velveteen collar. She'd found it in a thrift store in Sacramento, probably some ex–New Yorker's officewear too sweaty or too formal for California.

After dressing, Maude looked at herself in a mirror. Except for the long hair, she looked like a businesswoman, not a welfare hippie. *A business witch?* She brushed out her hair and looked through her grandmother's things for hair clips, bobby pins, something to keep the hair out of her eyes.

Two real tortoiseshell combs—bingo. Maude slid them through her hair. In the mirror she looked like her mother. She thought about seeing if she could get her hair cut before ten, but decided not to bother.

Nylons, heels, Maude put on things she never fooled with during her other life. She put a pair of jeans and a sweatshirt into an overnight bag she found under the bed in the center bedroom, the one Doug had slept in.

Does Doug have to die? Do I have to sacrifice Doug? Maude wished she could talk to Follette about what was coming this day. Now she needed to find out how Doug was. She called Terry. "It's Maude. Is Doug awake?"

"He's still sleeping," Terry said. "Why don't you come on over?"

In fifteen minutes, Maude was at John and Terry's. Doug slept until Terry and John played bamboo flute and tabor at him, just as Maude had imagined them playing the night before. He propped himself up on an elbow and listened. The glamour clashed with his hangover.

"What do you take for hangovers?" Maude asked.

"Hair of the dog," John said. He left the bedroom.

"No," Maude said. Doug was naked between the sheets. Maude wondered who undressed him.

"It's country to get drunk at funerals," Terry said.

John brought in the damson liquor jar and a glass. Doug looked at the liquor and said, "Water and coffee with lots of sugar."

"It's going to be an exciting funeral," John said. "We may have to defend ourselves. Maude looks like a woman in the executive protection business herself."

Feeling the gun's weight in her purse, Maude flinched. "You think being hunted is exciting?"

"Of course. His kin versus my kin. It will be beautifully tragic for them."

"Could you hand me my pants?" Doug said. "I'll get my own coffee."

"It would be better if you drank some of this," John said. "Clean your mouth out."

Maude handed Doug his pants and shorts. He pulled the pants under the top sheet and wiggled into them. He said to John, "I had more than enough to drink last night. Maude, why did you leave me here?"

"Last time I looked, you were too drunk to sit up."

"Why didn't you warn me?"

"Follette and I both warned you."

"I thought you were teasing or something."

"Witches kept the words from you."

John grinned. "Damson liquor this morning should make you feel better."

"Take it away, John," Maude said.

"We're going to fly Belle over the graveyard," Terry informed them.

Maude wondered if Belle would turn into a mankiller hawk, swoop down and tear Doug's liver out. "I'm going to get Doug coffee, okay?"

"Well, you know where everything is," Terry said. "John and I will check on the gravediggers." They stood watching, though, not leaving.

Maude thought, *go set up gun emplacements,* but nodded. Doug pulled the sheet aside and sat up, his bare feet on the floor. He held his head in his hands and looked over at the damson jar. "If I don't feel better soon, I'll be tempted."

John said, "It would help." Then he and Terry went outside. Doug followed Maude to the kitchen and sat at the table while she found a teakettle and filled it with water.

"I made a fool of myself last night," Doug said.

"You weren't that bad, just drunk."

"I ended up in bed with both of them, I think. I was so drunk."

You stupid son of a bitch, I should shoot you myself. "Both of them? Could you get it up, drunk as you were?"

"I vaguely . . . Maude, don't look at me like that."

"How?" Maude felt both fascination and disgust, plus anger that he'd gotten so sloppy.

"Like I was a dog who'd gotten chewed up going after a bitch in heat."

"Is that what John meant by cleaning your mouth out?"

"It was the liquor."

"Right, it was the liquor. Do you know how human sacrifices are handled? They get to screw lots of people, they get drunk. . . ."

Doug turned even paler. "I thought this had something to do with magic."

"Damn right. Their magic."

"Why did you leave me here, then?"

Why, indeed. "I've tried to warn you time and again." Last night she couldn't speak directly because of a word-ward. Now, perhaps speaking directly amused the entities. "You've never believed me when I've warned you. You preferred believing lying men to any woman. Luke had you charmed."

"John drew something on my back."

It was a target, red and black, about an inch and a half round, right over his spine between the shoulder blades. Maude went to the sink and wet paper towels, then tried to wash the target off.

"Is Follette coming to the funeral?"

"He said he'd try," Doug said.

"John put a target on you. I can't get it off without soap." The teakettle water was boiling now, so Maude fixed Doug instant coffee with lots of sugar and added some cold water from the tap so he could drink it immediately. She found dishwashing soup and squirted it on another towel.

"Are you feeling any better?"

"No. I'm sorry."

"You don't know what you're up against. The wannabe witches at Karmachila had no powers. You had to want to fuck them to end up in bed with them. That's why I lived there—folks like that repel most real witches. Here, Terry and John have power. They're so used to it they aren't conscious of it."

"Do you have power?"

"I can't even get this damn target off your back."

"Luke will help me."

"Why in God's name do you listen to Luke? Listen to Follette. He's at least been decent to you. Luke and Follette have been rivals since the early nineteenth century."

"Follette, then."

"No, listen to me. Get in your car, get back to California as fast as you can. Drive to an airport and fly back."

John and Terry came back in the house. Doug's face changed. His magic lovers returned. Maude felt mocked.

"Belle flew away," Terry told them.

"Hawks have no gratitude," John said. His eyes on Maude, he moved behind Doug and pressed his finger against the target.

"Doug, are you feeling better now?" Terry asked.

"Not particularly, but I'll live."

John ground his finger into the target. "We should change for the funeral. And we could go early, to see the corpse."

Maude thought, *at least I won the fight over Partridge.* Or they tricked her so thoroughly she'd never know the difference. "I came dressed."

Doug went over to the sink and rinsed his face with cold water. "I need a shower."

Maude asked, "John, why don't you stay inside here if the black kid's family is hunting you?"

Terry said, "We need to stick together."

"I'd like to go early with Doug," Maude said. "You guys can come in time for the funeral later."

"All right, Maude."

Doug went for a shower. Maude crossed her arms over her breasts and sat in the kitchen with Terry and John. None of them spoke until Doug came back dressed for the funeral.

"We'll see you there, then," Terry said.

Maude nodded and went to the car with Doug. She looked up and saw a redtail hawk, perhaps Belle, flying overhead. Her arms were stiff when she unfolded them. Doug said, "I'm sorry about last night."

"You had no defenses against them."

"I should have. I lived in the Bay Area for years."

"They're witches, not just a kinky couple."

"I think you're wrong about them. I think they are just a

kinky couple. I've never seen anything magical in their house.''

"Getting you to bed with John wasn't weird?'' Maude wondered what ink made the target on Doug's spine. Just after he seemed to realize Luke had betrayed him, he began denying what was about to happen.

"Well, yes, but I was drunk.''

"Is Doug inside or am I talking to a flesh puppet?''

The car lurched slightly, but Doug didn't answer. The possessing entity didn't answer either, not in words. *Flesh puppet for real.*

The funeral home director met them at the door. Doug slumped vacant-eyed in the family pew as though he'd been turned off. Maude went up to the coffin and looked at her grandmother's corpse again. She reached into the coffin and felt the quilt. The funeral director nodded, then left her.

Maude leaned on the coffin and began crying. She felt abandoned and trapped. Shouldn't her mother have cheated a little and protected her family with magic? Shouldn't Maude have learned to work her own powers better, well enough to have turned aside drunk pickups?

"You're feeling sorry for yourself,'' Follette said. His face looked lumpy as though the cancer had metastasized overnight.

"I feel trapped.''

"The magicians want you to work with them. The benefits are considerable.''

"Are you tempting me, too?''

"I tried to be a good magician. But magicians don't have as much say with the entities as we'd like to think.''

"I am trapped, then.''

Follette said, "Pity Doug doesn't believe in his own universe.''

"What about me? What about Julian Springer?''

"Springer's trying to stop the black men from throwing themselves against John.''

"I tried to get the boy's soul back. John was stronger."

"Maybe dithering is your strong suit."

"Dithering?"

"It's what you've been doing for a long time, isn't it? Even now."

Maude felt anger jangle her body. "I tried to be good."

"No, you tried to not be a witch."

Maude felt humiliated, and mad at Follette for doing it to her. "So I'm useless."

Follette said, "I won't ever know. I've got to leave now." He looked like he was in considerable pain. A thought inserted, *it's what you get trying to break the deals.*

As Follette walked away, Maude resisted an urge to open her purse and touch the revolver. She turned and watched Follette pause where Doug was sitting. Follette touched him on the shoulder and whispered in his ear, something between men, perhaps.

Maude went to the ladies' restroom, closed herself in a toilet stall, and opened her purse. She held the gun between her two flat hands, barrel pointed at the ceiling, and touched the hammer to her lips. *Technological object. Magic object. Technological object. Magic object.*

Was the God of the Christians something different, Maude wondered, or just another entity looking to be entertained during eternity's long boredom?

Maude noticed she was rocking back and forth, hands and the gun between them raised before her face, thumbs twitching over the hammer. No, this couldn't be just up to her and a schizophrenic religious painter. Up to her, helped by a schizophrenic minister.

"Poor Bracken County," she said out loud. She slid the gun back in her purse, went to the sink and washed her face, then went back to use the toilet and washed her face again.

Back in the chapel, kinsmen from her father's side filled the front pews.

Showtime. Maude joined Doug. He reached over and

touched her hand. *Who's inside now?* She looked at his eyes and saw a human man looking back, no glamour.

Aunt Betty and Uncle Luke came in with Terry and John. John looked excited. As Betty slid into the pew beside Maude, she said, "You can relax, dear. Nothing's going to happen here."

Luke said, "The Christians get to preach over her corpse, then we'll take it back."

The first minister stood. He didn't seem to know whether Partridge might be in heaven or sleeping in the grave until final judgment.

"Theological confusion," Luke said.

Then Elehu, her father's uncle, stood up in ministerial black. He read:

> In the days when the keepers of the house shall tremble, and the strong men shall bow themselves, and the grinders cease because they are few, and those that look out of the windows shall be darkened,
>
> And the doors shall be shut in the streets, when the sound of the grinding is low, and he shall rise up and the voice of the bird, and all the daughters of musick shall be brought low;
>
> Also when they shall be afraid of that which is high, and fears shall be in the way, and the almond tree shall flourish, and the grasshopper shall be a burden, and desire shall fail: because man goeth to his long home, and the mourners go about the streets.

As Elehu explained the text, comparing stilled grinders to teeth rotted out, Maude sensed his terror of death, her fear of aging. Betty whispered, "He's misinterpreting the text. It's about the sack of a city."

Maude said, "I'm relieved they can read the Bible allegorically." She felt Elehu was taking over the funeral service with his own concerns, his craving for recognition. He reminded her of Lower Eastside poets. Both the minor poets and the little preachers connected themselves to big myths to be superior to their day job.

Luke asked, "Doug, you think souls are real or doesn't science cover that?"

Doug answered, "Science had no opinion."

Maude knew souls were real, but doubted anything made could be immortal. She felt betrayed by Elehu, as though she'd been expecting him to preach powerfully enough to convert her. All he'd done was expose his own anxieties. The great male lust to make a mark on the world infected him, too.

"Now they've spoken their little sermons, we can go on to the real funeral," Luke said. But they still had to stand to sing another hymn.

21

FINALITIES BESIDE
THE GRAVE

T he pallbearers were old white men who muttered as they shouldered the coffin. Maude followed them out to see four black horses hitched to a black hearse. The black plumes at the tops of the harness bridles swayed as the horses jerked their heads against the check reins. The hearse body was lacquered black, its metal parts silver. Maude hadn't heard about using a horsedrawn hearse. She wondered if the cars would follow or if the mourners had to walk. The funeral home director opened the back of the hearse so the pallbearers could slide the coffin in.

All the vehicles behind the hearse were horsedrawn. Another team of four, without the black plumes over their heads, pulled an open carriage up to Maude. Doug, Luke, and Betty came up behind her and they all got into the coach.

"Where did you get all the horses?" Maude asked. Behind them were four carriages, drawn by pairs of black horses.

"They belong to the mortuary," Betty said.

"I've never seen a horsedrawn hearse before."

"Funerals like this were quite common when I was a boy," Luke told her.

Betty said, "Maude, I've been fair with you on this. I hope you'll finish this our way."

"Customs from time immemorial," Luke said.

"Or from 1856," Maude said.

Luke held out his hand, "Give me the gun."

"No."

"Who's it for?" Betty asked.

"It just wanted to be with me," Maude said. She looked at Doug but he didn't seem to hear.

"I want the gun now," Luke said.

Maude gripped her purse harder.

"If you shoot Doug," Betty said, "his soul will be wasted."

"I'm not planning to shoot Doug."

"You've thought about it," Luke said. "He's not faithful to you. Killing the unfaithful is an honored custom here."

Maude wondered if they really wanted to have the gun. They could have grabbed her purse and taken it away, probably with the help of those troopers down at the highway stopping traffic for the funeral horses. "The gun wants to be with me. It's too small a caliber to really stop people, isn't it?"

"The cartridges are long for the diameter," Luke said. "Doug should be killed with a stone knife."

"I'm not going to shoot Doug." Maude wondered who she could give the gun to.

"But you have thought about it. After all, he's thrown away advantages you would have killed to have had. Perhaps you could kill to have them," Betty said. "If you ate Doug's soul. You could be a good witch."

"Follette said no one could be a good witch," Maude told her.

Luke scoffed. "Follette has an odd definition of good."

"You wanted someone to bring technology to the county. Doug won't do it. He hates empowering stupid people. You could do it," Betty said. "You'd know what Doug knows after you ate him."

"What, I should eat him to empower stupid people?"

Betty and Luke smiled. The hearse seemed to be moving faster than horses could go. Maude wondered if the horses and hearse was an illusion, the reality the motorized vehicles of the 1970s.

Doug said, "Maude, can't you hear me?"

They were in an Oldsmobile limousine driven by a chauffeur. Maude felt her purse. The gun, or something as heavy, was still in it. "What were you saying?" she asked Doug.

"I wanted to know if Follette said anything about meeting him later today."

"He seemed to be in pain," Maude said. "He had to leave." She wondered if the heavy object that felt like a gun in the purse was still a gun. "Uncle Luke, why don't you like Follette?"

"He always played like he wanted to destroy the old ways but he couldn't quite throw away his powers. Made a mess. Ambivalence does that."

Maude opened her purse and looked in. It still looked like a gun.

"You know that's illegal to carry if you don't have a permit," Luke said. "You ought to give it to me until the graveside service is over."

For some reason, obviously magical, she had to give them the gun willingly. Maude said, "I don't think anyone's going to search my purse unless you tip them off, Uncle."

"It's your problem," Luke said. He smiled.

Maybe it wasn't a gun. If Betty and Luke could bespell her to see horsedrawn funeral vehicles, then they could have bespelled her to give them her gun.

"You're carrying a gun?" Doug asked.

"Yes, the revolver my grandfather's cousin confiscated off a murderer."

"Cousin on her father's side," Luke said to Betty.

"Maude, I wish you'd left that at home," Doug said.

"Why? Because guns empower weak people?"

"You're not trained to use them. You could just get yourself killed pulling it. Anyone who attacked you could take it away. I shot myself, remember."

"Doug doesn't like to think that he might make a pass at a girl and get blown away for a misunderstanding," Luke said. "Give me the gun."

Maude shook her head.

"Well, see if it still works," Luke said. He leaned back against the seat.

The hearse turned down the road to the old homeplace on the lower ridges of Wart Mountain. The limousine Maude rode in followed the hearse.

"You're confused," Luke said. "You can be tricked."

Maude almost told Luke that Follette thought dithering was her strong suit. She folded her arms over her purse and leaned away from him.

"Damn nigger," Luke said, staring out the window.

Maude looked to the right, across Luke's body, and saw the Reverend Julian Springer, with a Bible in his hands, standing in the road's right-of-way, just off the pavement. She said, "I don't think so."

"He's a fool," Betty said.

Luke cast out a search spell so powerful it jolted Maude. "I feel two of them out there anyway."

"Who?" Maude asked.

"Kin of the thief John killed. Coming to die for us."

"Didn't John tempt the boy?" Maude asked.

"John's your cousin."

"Blood kin? Or by marriage?"

"Both," Luke said.

Maude asked, "What are you trying to do, breed a super crazy witch?"

Neither her aunt nor her uncle answered. The Reverend Springer began walking with the procession, falling behind little by little, but still coming on. Maude wondered if he'd disapprove of her gun. She thought, *just a little farther to the grave.*

The horses stopped. No, the hearse stopped rolling forward as the driver calculated how to approach the private cemetery, whether to drive in straight or turn and back in. Behind the wrought iron fence, four gravediggers leaned against their shovels watching. The open grave, surrounded by red clay, looked like an inflamed wound.

As she got out of the limousine, Maude didn't see any of

her father's people in the cars pulling up along the side of the road. The Reverend Springer kept walking toward them.

My only ally is a madman. I don't know if my gun is real. Is saving Doug worth it?

The Reverend Springer came up to her and said, "Work something up under that despair."

"You're not supposed to be here."

"Rare's the chance for a man like me to fight true evil." He kept walking as though he planned to walk all the way to the top of Wart Mountain. Maude wondered what he meant by *a man like me*. A preacher? An insane man?

John and Terry got out of their car, glowing like gods. Doug, ephemeral and glamoured, stood by Luke. They gathered together while the funeral attendants moved the coffin.

"How's your head?" John asked Doug.

"I can hardly feel it," Doug answered. "Luke gave me a special painkiller."

Then the world slipped sideways. A giant black man appeared striding down Wart Mountain, broken chains dangling from wrist manacles, an ex-slave bent on revenge. Maude knew the real man inside the illusion was one of the murdered thief's uncles.

The man kept coming, acre-long strides. *Listen to the Reverend Springer,* she thought at the giant black man. The fury of the arrogant dumb possessed the giant, all the people who wanted to be more than they were, who didn't realize they'd been happier in the days before education tempted them into media star dreams, threatening civil life with their brutal numbers. *That's how Luke sees him.* She tried to see the man as he really was. The giant stopped for a moment. He shrank into a hurt man who'd seen a white man make a thief of his sister's son.

John fired at the giant. Maude grabbed John's gun hand and asked, "What are you seeing?"

"A nigger with a gun."

"Two niggers," Luke said. "We shouldn't have let those people escape the Great Chain of Being. Creation put them low."

Maude turned and saw the Reverend Springer holding the black man's arm in a mirror image of her hand on John's arm. Doug started walking toward the two black men. He was walking very slowly.

Betty said, "Maude, you can't delay forever."

Maude felt time passing, snow circling in a wind. She felt for her grandmother and found the body empty. "What, no ghost?" She felt alone by the grave. The people around her weren't human.

Doug was walking faster toward the black man. *This could be how he dies, trying to stop revenge. But we deserve revenge.* "Doug, what are you doing?"

Doug turned, framed by Wart Mountain. "I've got to talk to him."

The Reverend Springer said, "Let me talk to him."

"Doug, stay out of it, please go away."

Betty came up and touched Maude's arm. "Now, dear, this is between the men."

Make it stop.

Betty spoke, very slowly, the words vibrations in Maude's bones, not movements in air, "Yo . . .u ca . . . n't st . . . o . . . p ti . . . me com . . . plete . . . . ly."

Maude flinched and time jumped forward with a bullet in the air.

Slowly the bullet crawled through space. Maude saw that it would miss Doug, let go, and watched as it crashed into the blackberry brambles lining the road.

They were all in a pit, surrounded by mountains. Doug was ducking a sling-propelled stone, a bullet, an arrow. Then the black man turned into the revenge-mad giant again, but Springer hit him with the Bible, hard, one whack to his right shoulder, one to his left, then one directly against his face. Maude wondered if this happened in the real world or the magic one. Springer must have been a giant in those instants, but now both men were life-sized, mortal-sized, and the black kinsman of the dead thief was lying down in the road.

Springer yelled, "He's stopped. You don't have any excuses to kill him now."

Luke said, "We don't need excuses. Come back, Doug."

Doug turned around. Maude wondered if he was worth saving, if doubting his worth was her own thought or a spell inserted into her mind. The black man Springer had knocked down got up slowly. Springer spoke to him, opened the Bible, and read the passage where Jesus said the rich can no more go to heaven than a camel can go through the eye of a needle.

Luke said, "That's slave talking."

Doug reached Luke and John and turned around to face Springer. He said, "I hate what empowers the weak."

That's it. I don't really care what happens to him. Maude went back to the graveside—they'd drifted away from it—and said, "Grandmother, I hope you're at rest now." The coffin, on a low platform, didn't answer.

The sun moved on. The weather had a promise of spring in it, the late winter thaw that led to February snowdrops and daffodils at these latitudes. Maude's mother hadn't saved herself and her husband. Maude couldn't fight to save a voluntary sacrifice. The other witches waited for her. She said, "Okay, Doug, we'll get on with it."

Luke and John lead Doug back. Betty came up and embraced Maude. The men bent Doug over Partridge's casket, forming a flesh and coffin cross.

"Come hold him, Maude," Luke said. "I'll make the sacrifice."

Doug began sweating. Perhaps, Maude thought, whatever drug Luke had given him was beginning to wear off. She put her purse strap around her head, slung the purse across her body, then took Doug's shoulders. He looked up at her and said, "Aren't they going to teach me magic?"

"The hard way, Doug." Maude moved her hands as

John peeled away Doug's jacket and shirt. Doug began to shiver.

"They really are going to kill me."

"Remember, you volunteered for this."

"For what?"

John said, "Don't talk to him."

"For what?" Doug asked again.

Luke came up with a stone knife. Terry and Betty grabbed Doug's hands. "God, he's slippery," Terry said. Maude wondered how she could deny magic existed now. Perhaps Terry wouldn't remember.

Betty moved in beside Maude and pulled Doug's arms back. She said, "You'll hold him firmer if you slump down. Women can't press down as hard as a man can thrash up."

Maude stayed on her feet.

As Luke raised the knife, Doug begged, "Maude, please stop this."

The knife slowed as it rose. Maude said, "But you don't like things that empower the weak." Luke brought the knife the rest of the way up. Maude wondered if they could hang on to Doug while that stone blade cut.

"That will hurt too much. I'll do it," Maude said.

Luke looked down at her. She pulled out her ancestor's Colt, totally committed to shooting Doug, no other thought at the surface of her mind. Jail would save her from these people.

Dithering is your strong suit. Luke caught that thought from her and raised the knife again, speeding time. The gun, almost with a will of its own, exploded with noise. Luke flinched, but didn't fall. Maude fired twice more, but he didn't go down.

Doug twisted against the other hands still holding him. Maude fired two bullets into Betty's witch eyes. Luke was still standing. He pressed the knife against Doug's left nipple. Maude noticed that the nipple, a miniature of a woman's nipple, was puckered.

One more bullet. Maude didn't know whether to shoot Luke again, or John, or Terry.

A redtail hawk came floating over the hills. Terry looked up at it and said, "Belle."

Behind Belle came schools of the rusty-sided suckers, Bracken's endemic fish, floating out of their creeks in breeding colors despite the season. Out of the water, they still swam toward them, rolling slightly, so huge they seemed life-sized at three hundred yards. Maude wondered who controlled them.

The floating fish didn't get larger as they approached. They seemed life-sized no matter the distance.

Terry said, "Belle, attack."

Belle negotiated her way between the fish and circled the graveyard. She turned and landed on a phone pole.

"Don't waste your time on that fool hawk," Luke said. "Like Maude, uncooperative bitch." He coughed and opened his lips to show a bullet between his teeth. He reached up and took the bullet in his fingers. "Maude, this bullet was completely natural." He closed his eyes as if needing darkness to feel in his body for the other two bullets. His belly squirmed visibly under his bloody clothes.

Maude put a spell in the last bullet and shoved the gun barrel against his left eye, then fired both magic and lead.

The fish attacked.

Doug rolled off the coffin.

Maude crouched on the ground, empty gun pressed against her belly, wondering how she could ever explain killing her aunt and uncle. "Get help, Doug," she said to him.

Doug looked at the fish swarming around Terry and John. "They were going to kill me." His chest and arms were covered with goosebumps. "You helped hold me down."

"How do I explain killing them? Who's going to believe me? I'm fucked. Get away."

"What should I do?"

"Leave." Maude looked up and saw that the gravediggers had disappeared. "I'll bury Partridge myself."

The fish left two mangled bodies and swam back to their

creeks. Belle flew up from the phone pole, circled the grave-yard, and began rising on a thermal.

"I'll help you with the coffin," Doug said.

"Just the coffin." But they couldn't budge it until the Reverend Springer and the other black man came back. The four of them slid the coffin on boards extending over the grave hole. Then, rougher than Maude would have wanted, they lowered the coffin with straps the mortuary crew left behind.

"Natural world was disgusted with them witches," the black man said. "Fish rising like that."

"Go get the law," she told Doug. After Doug put his shirt and jacket back on, the Reverend Springer led him away. The other black man stopped and looked at the bodies. Maude noticed the flesh was gone on both Luke's and Betty's bones. John and Terry had disappeared. Maude wondered if they were still in the world, or had been eaten completely by the fish, or if they'd been so much Luke's and Betty's creatures that they disappeared without their patrons.

Slowly, ever so slowly, Maude filled the grave. The sky turned opaque. *What's going to happen when I'm finished?* The law could wait, she decided. She took off her jacket when it grew warm, put it back on when she was cold. Her stockings shredded, but she didn't notice.

I don't know what to do next, what happens to me next.

Maude buried her grandmother for five years.

22

POSTSCRIPT

Maude put the last shovelful of dirt on her grandmother's grave. The mound sank, covered with snow. Maude turned and walked toward the old homeplace. It looked abandoned. The grass had been cut regularly, but one of the upstairs windows had been broken out.

Do they want me for murder? Maude went up to the porch and sat down. Her arms were tired. Nothing to eat here, she realized, noticing her hunger, her thirst. Maybe she should just lie down herself and die.

Doug drove up in a new car. "Your friend the Reverend Springer said you'd be coming out today. Been here long?"

"I just finished burying Partridge."

"Just?"

"Coming out today?"

"You were in a slow time bubble."

"Oh." Maude remembered being worried about what she'd do after she buried her grandmother, but the worry seemed years old. "I'm thirsty. Hungry. What happened to Partridge's house?"

"It's yours, now. I've got my own place."

"My car?"

"You can drive my old car until you get settled back. Partridge left some land and some stocks. And you've been getting bank statements from Blacksburg."

"How long was I gone? By your time."

"Five years."

Maude stood up and said, "If it had been seven, I guess I'd be legally dead by now."

"Come on now," Doug opened the passenger-side door for her.

Maude got in the car. Doug handed her a canteen. She drank, then asked, "Who sent the fish? I doubted that nature would have waited this long to rise up against Luke."

"Follette, I think. He died about that time."

"So, what do they think happened to Luke? What happened to the bodies?"

"Luke and Betty were shot by renegades, so people remember now, just after the Civil War."

"And Terry and John?"

"They seem to have been more insubstantial. They moved here, then moved away without telling anyone anything. Disappeared after you . . ."

"So, nothing happens to me."

"I'm married."

"Oh." Maude felt numb again.

"You almost let them kill me."

"You betrayed your calling. You're supposed to empower weak people, make things out of rules that work the same for everyone."

"I know that now. Follette's institute finally got adequate funding. Once John was gone, I set up a work evaluation system for the assembly company, then another for a window film company, then went to work for the institute. We're working with the local schools. That's how I met my wife."

"She's a teacher?"

"A principal."

"The school board didn't used to appoint women principals. Things have changed, then," Maude said. Doug drove her to Kobold. At the house, a woman in her thirties came out.

"Reverend Springer was right then," the woman said. "We haven't cleaned the house for nothing."

"Who are you?"

"Doug's wife. I was Lucinda Crofter, married to a Tate for a while."

"Thank you for cleaning the house."

"Perhaps we can see more of each other," Lucinda said, meaning, Maude understood, *perhaps not.*

"Don't leave me here alone."

Doug and Lucinda looked at each other, then Lucinda said, "We can take you out to dinner if you like."

Maude opened her purse and pulled out the gun. Lucinda moved toward her as if to take it away, but Doug shook his head. "What, am I a child?" Maude asked. She opened the cylinder and saw that the barrel and charge holes were corroded, the brasses greenish.

"I have two sets of memories, thanks to you," Lucinda said. "One of a county where I came home with a graduate degree and got stupid. Another where renegades killed the couple in 1866 who mocked my ambitions in 1967 when I graduated from high school. I guess I owe you something if that fight was more than another struggle between witches."

"Doug?" Maude didn't know what she wanted after she spoke his name.

"Let's go eat," Doug said. "Maude, you'll want to change."

Maude looked down and saw that her wool clothes were stained with clay and mildew—blue mildew, black mildew, white mildew. She asked, "Is anything clean?"

Lucinda said, "I washed some jeans and your sweaters. There's a blazer. I didn't know if it was yours or your grandmother's but it's been cleaned."

Maude knew this woman had also washed her underclothes, but wouldn't mention that even in front of her husband, Maude's former lover. Doug said, "I'll wait in the living room."

Lucinda waited until he was out of the room, then told Maude, "I like a man who's been through some pain, who's been hurt by another woman. I trust Doug not to take advantage, even though he does have me wrapped around his cock."

"He . . ." Maude almost told Lucinda that Doug hadn't been faithful to her.

"Oh, but he has been faithful to me," Lucinda said. "And will be." Maude tried to reach out to see if this woman was a witch, too, but Maude's powers seemed to extend only to the jacket Lucinda was holding out to her, Partridge's blazer, cut to fit a dowager's hump. Maude put on the blazer and it wrinkled around her. "Oh, well, you can buy new things," Lucinda said. "Doug's been very good for this county."

"He wanted to be a magician."

"When I was a little girl, I wanted to be a witch, but the witches would have mocked me. Better that I left Bracken."

"My family."

"Not that I care that much for Fundamentalists, either," Lucinda said. "Elehu tried to tell me you were damned for what you did."

"I didn't know Doug liked brittle, bossy women," Maude said.

"Oh, come on. What do you think you are?"

Partridge's jacket, despite its awkward fit, seemed to shush her just as Partridge had done when Maude was a fretful child. "I'll leave you alone," Maude said. "I won't tempt him."

"You can't tempt him. You almost let them kill him."

"So not everyone remembers that Luke and Betty were killed by renegades after the Civil War."

"No, some of us remember a worse life from time to time."

"But I did save him."

"I'm grateful. But he didn't appreciate being played with."

Perhaps Lucinda didn't appreciate Maude's treatment of Doug, didn't believe that a witch kin of the master witches couldn't have warned him off before he was bent across a coffin. Doug had come to find her.

"So you're a principal here now," Maude said.

"Yes, a grade school principal. Both the school superintendant and school board are still pretty sexist."

Doug called out, "Isn't she dressed yet?"

"We're coming," Maude said. She touched Lucinda, trying with what little witch powers she had left to see what the woman was. The woman was tough to the bone, a witch hater, a brother lost to witches.

Maude got in the backseat. Doug kissed Lucinda on the cheek and squeezed her arm, then they drove for pizza. Five years ago, the only pizza in Bracken County had been frozen.

Lucinda said, "You must see Reverend Springer's triptych."

Maude drove by the modern building built where Luke and Betty's house had been to the Reverend Julian Springer's house on the road behind the highway. The little shack was gone, but on the lot was a brick ranch house with an almost incongruous wooden front porch across the whole front of the house.

No welfare crazy could afford such a place. But the architecture was just slightly odd enough to make her stop to look at it. It wasn't quite a brick ranch house. The corners were beveled. After looking a few moments more, Maude thought she saw designs in the textures and colors of the brick facing. The Reverend Springer came out on the porch. He was dressed in canvas pants, various colors of paint staining them, and a clean plaid shirt.

Maude said, "I always remembered you in a suit."

"Makes a mess to paint in a suit, just like it ruins a suit to wear to fill a grave," Springer said. "I heard you came out. Come in."

Another man, a mid-thirties black man in jeans and an expensive sweater, came out behind Springer. Maude wondered who he was. The man said, "Julian, do you know this woman?"

"Been knowing Maude for many a year," Springer said. "She knew me when I was a street preacher in Berkeley."

The other man stiffened. "I'm Dr. Peterson." The accent was Mid-Atlantic, touch of New England.

"Dr. Peterson?"

"I help Julian."

God, a live-in shrink. Maude looked at Springer and said, "How are you doing these days?"

"Fine now that I recognized the Lord wanted me to be a painter, not a word preacher. Get the words tangled sometimes. Dr. Peterson here keeps track of my medicine better than Berkeley."

"So you met Julian in Berkeley," Dr. Peterson said.

"In Berkeley. He followed me here," Maude explained, thinking the black psychiatrist, psychologist, whatever, could make of that what he would.

"From Berkeley." Dr. Peterson looked at Julian.

"She was cheating welfare," Springer said. "Pretending to be crazy. I broke her of it."

"You're in the triptych," Dr. Peterson said.

"Yes, I came to see it, if it's still here."

"Couldn't sell it until you saw it," Springer said. He went in the house.

Instead of following him, Dr. Peterson grasped Maude's elbow and held her back just long enough for the door to close. "He's stabilized nicely now. We don't need him to be stressed."

"His paintings must be selling," Maude said.

"Enough for a middle-class living. He's not rich. I hope you're not going to try to leech off him."

"He can support a live-in shrink, I take it." Maude opened the door. Dr. Peterson fumbled to hold the door for her even though she'd had to open it herself.

"Back here," Springer called.

On the left, Maude saw herself, a worried-looking

woman with pouches under the eyes, long nose bent down at the tip, holding a gun between her hands, gun as prayer beads, rosary. The center panel showed a glacier churning up skeletons, a terminal moraine of skulls, impossibly articulated hand bones, and rib cages. The right-hand panel showed Luke and Betty with shadows around their heads instead of halos.

Maude had been expecting something gaudy, more primitive rococo—her shooting the witches, Doug sprawled on the coffin, the fish swimming through the air. "What happened to the ghosts?" she asked Springer.

"All the souls God wanted he took up to heaven," Springer said. "Others the computers ate."

Dr. Peterson said, "We don't believe in ghosts."

Maude said, "I like the central panel best."

"Oh, it does end in ice," Springer said. "But not for a long, long time."

Maude thanked him for showing her the triptych and drove back to the building on top of the hill. It was a new library. She went in and saw the building was huge, light and airy. Computer terminals sat in various places, green lights glowing alphanumerics. Maude saw three women behind the desk, heard them talking in Standard English, not country, about a new regional library headed by a woman from Indiana. Maude came over and said, "What happened to the old library?"

"It was obsolete," the youngest woman said. "No computers. All the libraries in Bracken County are linked now. We even can get interlibrary loans from any participating library in the country."

Maude sat down to one of the patron terminals and called up all the books listed under automotive engineering, then engineering in general. Maude on the net—in the magic time, that metaphor turned real would make her an electronic spider stepping out on the circuits to eat us trapped in computer tangles. But now, she felt the computer eat away the last of her magic, making her just an-

other person in a world of dying generations. A last fragment of wishing to be more special than the general run of
humanity tugged at her. "We've switched to the universe of
rules that work the same for everyone," Maude said. She
pushed that last fragment of special power into the computer.